Are you prepared?
—Danielle McD

THE
PREPARATIONS

DANIELLE N. MCDONOUGH

HIGH BRIDGE BOOKS
HOUSTON

The Preparations
by Danielle N. McDonough

Copyright © 2017 by Danielle McDonough
All rights reserved.

Printed in the United States of America
ISBN (Paperback): 978-1-946615-95-4
ISBN (eBook): 978-1-946615-11-4

All rights reserved. Except in the case of brief quotations embodied in critical articles and reviews, no portion of this book may be reproduced, stored in a retrieval system, or transmitted in any form or by any means—electronic, mechanical, photocopy, recording, scanning, or other—without the prior written permission from the author.

High Bridge Books titles may be purchased in bulk for educational, business, fundraising, or sales promotional use. For information please contact High Bridge Books via www.HighBridgeBooks.com/contact.

Published in Houston, Texas by High Bridge Books

*Thank you to all the friends who encouraged me,
especially Anna, Katie and Kenna.*

Thank you to my parents and brother for all your support.

*And, especially, thank you to my sister, Becky,
without whom I would never have been able to publish.*

CONTENTS

Prologue: Stains — 1

1. Enemy — 5
2. Midwinter — 15
3. History — 27
4. Firelight — 39
5. First Day — 51
6. Rasby — 67
7. Ambition — 79
8. Astra — 91
9. The Northern Road — 107
10. Into the Valley — 119
11. Seeking — 131
12. Mark — 141
13. Certain Truths — 155
14. Empathy — 165
15. Mystery — 175
16. Terrors of the Night — 191
17. Valley of Death — 207
18. The Thaw — 227
19. Justice — 235
20. Life Mate — 255

21. Before	267
22. The Choosing	277
23. Teammates	287
24. Skill Level	297
25. Team Work	307
26. Internal Dispute	315
27. The Cliffs	327
28. A Team	337
29. Missing	345
30. Finding	355
31. The Cave	365
32. Last Ride	373
33. Training's End	383
34. The Qualifier	391
35. Myna	397
36. Beginning	405
About the Author	415

Prologue

STAINS

In a windowless room stood a woman and a man facing each other. Close by, dying embers lay smoldering on the hearth of a stone fireplace. The glow did little to illuminate the small space, whose walls of hard-packed earth absorbed most of the light and warmth.

The man was ancient, with shoulders so hunched that it was a constant strain for him to keep his head up. Thin strands of white hair grew from his head in patches. The garb he wore was simple: a plain, white robe tied with a black sash. The man leaned heavily upon a wooden staff, which was almost as twisted and gnarled as he was.

The woman was his opposite. She was far younger, with long, black hair and ramrod straight posture. Her clothing was the same color as the man's and included a matching cloak, lined with white rabbit fur. However, she required nothing with which to support herself.

"What did you do in the mountain?" The old man's voice was solemn, as though he knew and dreaded the answer.

"Why do you ask me this?" snarled the woman.

"Tell me." Was his only reply.

Even though the words were meek, anger flashed in the dark depths of the woman's eyes. "I have done only what was necessary. Not for us, but for our people and for their descendants."

THE PREPARATIONS

"I feared as much," the old man whispered. He turned away slightly, a haunted look in his blue eyes. "I will take no part in this any longer."

"We have a mission," she told him furiously. "We have been entrusted with thousands of lives and the very future of mankind. Are you really prepared to turn your back on everything we've worked for?"

"I am sorry," the old man replied gently.

"How can you do this? You promised me your help."

"I know I did, but I find now that I cannot. We were wrong. The path we have followed has always been wrong. I was blind not to see, and I will walk it no more."

"This is Adel's doing," the woman hissed.

"She merely opened my eyes to the truth," the man said sadly. "I wish—I wish she was still here to do the same for you." A flicker of some unknown emotion crossed the woman's face for a single instant.

The old man hobbled a few steps toward the woman. She did not recoil from him as he reached out to embrace her. "This is all my fault," he whispered. "I have failed you in every way, and I am sorry. So, so sorry."

The man closed his weary eyes and held the woman in his arms as if she were still the small child he had known all those years ago.

After a moment of stiffness, the woman returned the man's embrace, bringing her arms up around his back. Something in her hand glinted as the glow of the firelight touched it.

The old man's face relaxed as he rested his weary head on the woman's shoulder. His eyes remained closed, almost as though he were dreaming. The two stood like that until the woman broke the silence. Her words were soft, whispered directly into the man's ear. "No, you have only failed me this once, and I am the one who is sorry, Father. I am so very sorry."

The old man gasped as the woman plunged a dagger into his back. His face contorted in agony, and a second later he was on the floor, convulsing, while a pool of crimson liquid flowed from his body.

It didn't take long before death claimed him. Even once the blood had stopped flowing and the eyes had grown dull, the woman still remained motionless, looking down at the man who had been her father. There was no emotion on her face when she finally turned away.

Her feet carried her to the room's only door. It was set several feet high in the wall and had stairs leading up to it. The woman produced a key and unlocked the door. She pulled it open but did not leave the room. Two men entered immediately, as if they had been waiting. Both took in the body on the ground with astonishment.

"Change of plans," the woman said. "Take care of that," she added, nodding at the corpse.

Without offering another word of explanation, she walked past them through the door. Only once did she glance back to the place of bloodshed. The foundations had already been laid there for a great building. It was to be erected over the hidden room she had just left. The woman turned away a moment later, wrapping her cloak tightly around her body against the winter chill. It was now stained maroon with blood.

Chapter 1

ENEMY

I had always wondered how I would die and what it would feel like. Death is the last mystery; nothing can prepare you. It only happens once, but you will die.

I was sixteen the year that the trials were announced.

It was the middle of winter, and my feet crunched softly in the freshly fallen snow. My breaths made little clouds in front of me as I moved steadily forward. The sun was about to set, leaving the horizon tinted pink with her pending departure.

The winter was worse than usual. Normally, between two and three feet of snow accumulated during the year's cold, dark months. However, before long, spring would always come upon the land, and the patches of white would vanish. But that year had been different. The storms had come early, and the drifts had piled up until there were some over five feet deep.

It was those very drifts that I was using to hide from the enemy. I couldn't see them, but I sensed their presence lurking close at hand.

My friend, Rasby, and I were bent double as we crossed the frozen land, traveling east. It was hard going since there was no road or path to follow. At least we were kept warm by the exertion and the long, maroon cloaks we wore.

I paused briefly for Rasby. She had fallen slightly behind.

THE PREPARATIONS

"It'll be dark soon," I whispered, almost to myself, as she caught up with me. She was gasping for breath and didn't give any answer other than a nod. "We'll be too late then," I added, just as softly.

It would have been better to wait and let Rasby catch her breath, but the sunlight was vanishing from the sky quickly. We had to press on, there simply wasn't enough time left.

"Do you see anything, Myra?" Rasby whispered too loudly.

"Quiet," I hissed, pulling her to the ground and scanning the landscape for movement. After a few seconds, I relaxed a little; it didn't appear that she had given away our position. I motioned for Rasby to remain silent as we continued forward into the most exposed part of the terrain. I was practically crawling on my hands and knees as we crossed the open patch of land.

After traveling another fifty yards, I could hear Rasby behind me, wheezing even louder than before. Internally, I wished she hadn't insisted on coming. She was going to get us both caught. She was only a year younger than me, but she wasn't ready for this kind of challenge. Rasby was my friend, but sometimes she seemed more like the annoying little sister I'd never had.

I glanced back and saw that her pudgy face was bright red. Several clumps of brown, frizzy hair were sticking out of her customary pigtail braids. If the situation hadn't called for silence, I would have laughed. At least there was a, somewhat, determined gleam in her light brown eyes.

The going was much easier when we reached the next snowdrift. It provided a barrier from hidden watchers in the south. I still had to bend over slightly to keep my head and shoulders from being seen. Rasby was nearly short enough that she could have walked upright. I glanced back to make sure she hadn't carelessly decided to risk it.

An abrupt noise made me drop to the ground again. Rasby followed my example. I closed my eyes to listen. There was the sound of crunching snow; someone was approaching our position from due south, where The Paramount lay. The Paramount was the village where I had lived the entire sixteen years of my life. It was the most important location in The Land of the Clan.

The footsteps drew nearer and nearer. On the edge of my vision, I saw Rasby's eyes dart around rapidly. I readied myself to run, hoping she was doing the same; although, she had little chance of escaping a pursuer. I might be forced to leave her behind.

Suddenly, a form came vaulting over the top of the snowdrift we were crouched behind. Rasby squeaked with fright. Before I could even get to my feet, the young man had seized my shoulder.

"Got you," he announced, with a mischievous gleam in his blue eyes.

"Cole!" I gasped, somewhere between anger and relief. "What are you doing?"

Cole laughed softly and shook his head to free it of loose snowflakes. Then he reached up to brush the hair off of his forehead. There were a few unusual golden highlights that streaked his black locks. The moment he removed his hand, the hair he had pushed back fell forward again.

I glared at him, hoping he could see the anger in my gray eyes. But when he finally met my gaze, he just laughed again. "Come on, Myra. That was pretty funny."

"This is serious," I insisted. "We have a job to do."

"Alright, alright," Cole said. "Let's be serious." I could tell from the wry smile Cole flashed me that he wasn't being serious at all.

I sighed and turned away, suppressing a smile of my own. It was impossible for me to stay angry with Cole. He was two years older than me, but he still had a childish joy about everything. It was frustrating and endearing all at once.

Rasby had recovered herself. "Is anyone else out there?" she wondered, nodding toward The Paramount.

THE PREPARATIONS

"I didn't see anyone," Cole told her.

"Hopefully, they didn't see you either," I couldn't help adding.

Cole shrugged. "If they had, there's no way we'd still be sitting here discussing it."

"Fine," I consented. "But we should keep moving."

Cole nodded, and the three of us set out toward the east. It didn't take long before Rasby was lagging behind again. Since the sun was touching the horizon, I didn't slacken my pace to compensate for her.

"There it is," Cole whispered to me a moment later. He pointed to our destination, which lay sixty yards ahead of us.

A five-foot long stave had been erected in the snow. A long piece of maroon cloth was tied around the top, blowing freely in the wind. It didn't look like much to the casual observer, but to me, it was a most welcomed sight.

I glanced over my shoulder. We had fifteen, maybe twenty, minutes left.

"Let's go." Cole started moving forward, but I grabbed his arm.

"Wait," I said.

"No one's there," Cole argued.

"No one you can see," I corrected him.

"Then we'll just go really quickly."

I shook my head. "Wait," I told him again.

Cole sighed, but yielded to my will and plopped down in the snow. I sat beside him; Rasby joined us a moment later.

At first, the landscape remained deserted. After what felt like an eternity, but was probably less than five minutes, I saw movement.

"It's Bala," I hissed. She was a small girl about my age, with short, black hair. If she saw us, everything would be over.

"What should we do?" Rasby asked in a trembling voice. She was biting her lower lip in a way that she only did when she was afraid.

Cole shrugged. "Maybe she'll go away."

I checked the sun; we were all running out of time. "We need a distraction," I whispered. "If one of us can lead her away, the other two have a chance of making it." Cole nodded his agreement, but Rasby looked uncertain. "Rasby, you'll be the distraction," I told her.

"She'll catch me!" Rasby cried. I was surprised that her teeth didn't go through her lip with this exclamation, as they chopped down on it fretfully.

"Possibly," I admitted. "Hopefully, you can get far enough away that she'll turn back. By that time Cole and I will have—"

Rasby cut me off with a high-pitched whimper. "I can't; I'm scared."

"I know," I said, gritting my teeth and trying to be gentle. "But sometimes, sacrifices need to be made."

There was indecision on Rasby's face. I wished she would just suck it up and accept the role assigned to her.

Why did she follow me all this way if she's just going to sit behind a snowdrift and wait for the sun to set? I thought angrily.

"I can go instead," Cole offered.

The tension went out of Rasby's body. "Thanks, Cole," she said, smiling weakly at him.

"We'd have a better chance the other way around," I muttered, but didn't try to argue. The sun would disappear any minute.

Cole stole away from us, back the way we had come. Soon after, I saw him about twenty yards to my left. He was pretending to creep towards Bala and the stave, moving along stealthily, but being just clumsy enough to catch Bala's attention.

It worked. She saw him and started forward to investigate. A moment later, she was running towards him. I didn't wait to see if Cole would escape. Instead, I sprinted toward the scrap of maroon cloth. Rasby was somewhere behind me, trying to keep up on her short, thick legs.

Out of nowhere, a figure lunged at me from behind a snow bank. I twisted away reflexively and locked eyes with the enormous young man who had tried to grab me. He was turning and preparing to give chase.

The blood roared in my ears as I pelted back the way I had come, desperate to escape his huge, outstretched hands. I passed Rasby, and she turned to follow me, her eyes wide with panic.

I could hear our pursuer closing the distance between himself and us with gigantic strides.

"Go left!" I yelled back to Rasby who was about four feet behind me.

It took her a moment to process my words, and then she swerved to the left, and I swerved to the right. Fortunately, the brute behind us went after Rasby since she was closer to him. I peeled away from them and twisted around, heading back toward the stave at full speed.

The sun was almost completely below the horizon. It was too late to be cautious; I threw myself forward, heedless of danger.

Out of the corner of my eye, I saw a maroon-clad figure racing toward me from the opposite direction. I couldn't tell if it was Bala, Cole, or someone completely different.

Putting on another burst of speed, I made it to the stave and reached up to seize the piece of cloth. It came loose in my hand.

I held it up in the air above my head and cried out, "Victory!"

The figure who had been charging—it was Bala—pulled up just in front of me. "No fair," she muttered, spitting contemptuously into the snow.

I ignored her complaint and called in a loud voice, "The game is over; I have secured the token! Everyone can come out!"

There was a moment of utter stillness where Bala and I seemed to be the only living beings in the world, and then I saw Cole heading toward me. From the other direction, Rasby and the guy chasing her, Jase, came walking over. Rasby's face had gone paler than the snow.

Several more figures emerged from nearby snowdrifts, walking our way.

Counting them in my head, I turned to Bala. "Where are Larna and Flant?"

She scowled. "They went home almost an hour ago."

"Again?" I asked with disgust. "Why do they keep ditching?"

Bala just shook her head. She had a small face with a funny, little, turned-up nose. It twitched whenever she said something indirectly mean. Her nose twitched a lot. She was clever and could look anyone straight in the eye and tell them a bald-faced lie without batting so much as an eyelash, even though it was against the rules of our people.

Cole reached us first. "You almost had me, Bala," he said, giving her an encouraging smile. "If you hadn't turned back when you did, I'm sure you would have."

Bala shrugged. "Wouldn't have mattered much since Myra got past Jase." Bala turned to glare at Jase. "Why didn't you catch Myra?" she snapped at him.

He had to think for a minute. "I was closer to Rasby."

Bala rolled her eyes at his simple answer.

Jase was completely unremarkable in every way, save for his size. He was almost two feet taller than me, long-limbed, and covered in muscle. However, everyone knew Jase's incredible strength came at the expense of his brain. There was a rumor that he had been planning to request a transfer to a new village when he turned twenty the following year and was considered an adult. Since the numbers and time management skills which ran The Paramount had never come easily to Jase, I wouldn't have been surprised if it were true.

I could see him going straight to The Barracks. The Barracks was the closest of the other villages to The Paramount. It was where our soldiers lived.

THE PREPARATIONS

We called them soldiers, and they did train for combat, but there had never once been so much as a real skirmish in The Land of the Clan. Mostly, they were responsible for transporting all the goods—food, clothing, wood, etc.—from village to village as the items were needed. Loading and unloading the crates and boxes all day kept them in good physical shape, as did all the time they spent traveling between the different villages in The Land of the Clan. It sounded menial and unimportant to me, but I figured Jase would be perfect for the position.

"I told you Myra would be one of the greatest threats," Bala growled.

Jase wrinkled his forehead. "Oh, yeah. I'm sor—"

Bala cut him off. "Why is it so hard for you to figure this stuff out? You should have caught Myra and then caught Rasby, provided she hadn't run off crying."

It was rather amusing to see Jase being scolded by a girl half his height. Bala could be a tiny terror when the mood took her.

"I'm sor—" Jase started again.

This time it was Cole who interrupted.

"Bala, lay off will you." Jase was Cole's best friend, and Cole hated when people picked on him. Cole turned to Jase. "Next time, just remember to keep an eye on that one." He pointed at me, and I gave them a coy smile. "You really did a great job," he assured Jase.

"You *would* say that, since he's your team's best player," Bala announced. Her nose twitched.

A second later, two more figures joined us. It was Tiera and Tirea, a pair of sisters slightly younger than Rasby. They could almost have passed for twins. Their eyes, mouths, and even the shapes of their bodies were identical. Everything except their noses. Between the two of them, they had exactly the right amount of nose for each, but it was poorly divided. The older one, Tiera, had a bulbous nose, too large for her face. The other, Tirea, had hardly any nose at all.

"Where have you two been?" I demanded. The pair were supposed to have rendezvoused with Rasby and myself half an hour ago.

"We got caught," Tiera started.

"By Jase and Flant," Tirea finished.

I wondered if the two realized how annoying it was when they spoke in that way.

"I got caught too," Rasby announced. "It was scary!"

"More like—"

"Boring," the sisters told her.

"We've been sitting—"

"In the snow for an hour."

"Waiting until someone—"

"Got the token."

"Or—"

"The sun set."

I turned away from the sisters and Rasby. I could only take so much of their finishing-each-other's-sentences thing.

Several more maroon-clad figures joined us as the sun vanished from sight.

"We should meet up with the others, and then head home," Cole said.

Everyone else nodded their agreement, but I cringed internally.

"You may have won today," Bala announced, giving Cole and me a malicious smile, "but tomorrow, it's our turn to attack."

Chapter 2

MIDWINTER

Since there was no school the following morning, we were free to begin our game of Attack and Defend early in the day. It was just as well, because it was also Midwinter, and there would be a Telling once the sun went down.

Bala and Jase's team was attacking, so they left The Paramount from the south, while Cole and I led our teammates in the opposite direction. Once we reached the place where the stave was still stabbed into the ice, I replaced the maroon cloth I had taken the previous day. After finishing, I turned to the others and began reviewing our strategy.

It was more challenging to win when playing the defense. If any member of the opposition made it through our ranks and got a hold of the cloth, we would lose. Our only hope for victory was to catch every member of the other team. Once we tagged them, they would be immediately removed from the game. After the allotted amount of time had elapsed, if the token hadn't been secured or the attacking team hadn't all been captured, the game would end in a draw. I hated draws; it was just as bad as losing.

"Maybe we should all stay here and ambush them!" Rasby suggested.

"Won't work," I countered, shaking my head. "Bala's smart. She doesn't want to lose. I bet she'll have a few players hang back. That way, even if she doesn't win, we won't either."

Cole nodded. "Bala has used that ploy in the past."

Technically, Jase was just as much of a team leader as Bala, but most of the time, I thought of it as solely Bala's team. Jase

THE PREPARATIONS

might have been older and more experienced, but everyone knew who was really the brains of the outfit.

"We'll need at least two groups to go and hunt for them," Cole continued.

"Tiera and Tirea?" I suggested, hoping to get the annoying pair as far from me as possible.

"If you don't mind," Cole added, glancing at the sisters.

The pair exchanged a long look, as though speaking without words. Both girls were good at moving along without being seen. They weren't particularly fast, but they worked well as a pair and could use that to ensnare the enemy.

In unison, the girls turned to us and nodded. A young, lanky boy, who had joined our team only a few days ago, volunteered to go with them. We sent three more of our teammates in the other direction. After circling The Paramount, the two groups would eventually meet up on the far side of the village.

The rest of us spread out and hid ourselves among the mountainous drifts of white powder. The very worst part of being the defenders was the waiting. Even sitting in the sun, wrapped in my cloak, I could still feel the chill of the snow all around me. The game was supposed to end at sun high, giving Bala's team two hours to pick a strategy and recover the cloth.

They took their sweet time. It wasn't until after the first hour had completely elapsed that I finally saw some movement. Three maroon-clad figures were coming our way from the west. Judging by height, the one in the middle had to have been Jase. The identities of the other two I couldn't make out.

Instantly, I suspected a trap. If those three were approaching from the west, then there had to have been others coming from the east or south. I slipped over to where Cole was concealed.

"We've got incoming," I reported, pointing to my right.

"Want me and a few others to go check it out?" he asked.

"Alright," I said, "but don't take too many. They're probably meant to be a distraction."

— 16 —

Cole called Motik, a tall boy of fifteen, and Ashlo, a girl several months younger than I was, to join him. They were two of our most athletic players. Stealthily, the three began creeping toward the approaching figures. I gathered the rest of our team, Rasby and two others. We moved to the southeast side of the stave and took cover behind a low snow bank. It was a dangerous way to play, leaving the cloth so unprotected, but luring the enemy in was our only chance at true victory.

Nothing moved in front of us. I pricked up my ears, but there was not a sound to be heard, save the baited breath of my teammates. Suddenly, a cry from Cole's direction rent the air. Without hesitation, I broke cover and raced toward the stave, calling for the others to follow. We arrived just in time. It looked like Bala's entire team was bearing down on us.

Bala was inches from the maroon cloth, her hand stretched forward, reaching for victory. I leapt toward her and would have caught her before she could free the cloth from its tether, but she shoved one of the younger members of her team into my outstretched arms and fled.

"No fair," he whined, twisting free of my grasp. With a pouting demeanor, he went to sit in the snow a little way off, the first of his team to be captured.

"Don't get too far from the token!" I instructed my teammates. "They'll try to tempt you away. Don't let them!"

Even while I was giving instruction, Bala had rallied her team, and they charged us again. We were hard-pressed to keep them at bay. We wouldn't have been able to hold out very long just the four of us, but a minute later, Cole, Motik, and Ashlo returned.

The wave of reinforcements caused a great deal of confusion in the enemy ranks, and three more of Bala's team were caught.

Now that the numbers weren't so uneven, it was easy to keep them away from the token, but my instinct was to try to catch them. We had less than an hour left, and if we didn't begin picking them off soon, we would give up our chance of victory.

THE PREPARATIONS

Our team had formed a tight ring, encircling the stave, while the opposition huddled around their leaders, probably preparing for a third assault.

Cole came to stand beside me, eyes never leaving the enemy. "You were right," he told me. "It was a diversion. As soon as we got close to that group, the rest of them popped up between us and the stave. It was all we could do to yell before they were on top of it."

"Nicely played, Bala," I muttered. She had almost won with the sudden charge.

"Guess we'll have to chase them down one by one," Cole sighed.

I nodded; it was never much fun when everyone was out in the open. Plus, the likelihood of either team winning was all but non-existent.

Even so, we dedicated almost forty minutes to trying to catch all the members of the other team. Rasby was useless when it came to running, and one of the other girls was too young to do much good. However, the rest of us took turns charging the opposing team.

By the time midday rolled around, we had only managed to catch about half of them. Most disparagingly, the game ended in a draw.

"We'll have to play again tomorrow after school," Bala said, as we headed back to the village together. I nodded in agreement.

"Should we mix the teams up a little?" Cole asked.

"Jase and I could be interested. Make us an offer we can't refuse." Bala's eyes turned toward Motik and Ashlo.

"I don't think that's going to happen," I interposed quickly. Knowing Cole, he would trade away half our team just to give Bala and Jase a chance to win.

The teams had been formed a long time ago. Traditionally, the two oldest players were co-captains. The teams took turns adding to their ranks when new kids were old enough to join.

Trades could be made either for a short amount of time or permanently. In the past, the teams had sometimes turned out lopsided, with one team far better than the other, but, for the most part, our teams were evenly matched.

After parting ways with the others, I reached my empty dwelling. The only person I lived with was my mother, Myna, for whom I was named, and she was not there. I assumed she was with the council, making plans for the Telling that night. Even when we were both inside the dwelling, it still felt empty. The place had not been a home to me since my father, Rilk, had died eleven years ago.

Most days, I didn't even think of his absence, but every once in a while, the sharp pain of his passing would flare up again. Somehow, I knew it would never completely fade away. Some wounds couldn't be healed, and some things had to be carried forever.

I couldn't actually recall his face completely, and each year I lost a little more of the fragmented image. All I had left was an impression of his warm eyes and joyful smile.

The things I remembered most about his character—the love and gentleness he had always shown me—were a far cry from Myna's frigid demeanor. One day, three years after my father's death, when I was eight, I had fallen out of a tree and broken my arm. The tree had grown on the outskirts of The Paramount, where the buildings ceased and open fields began.

Several other children had been climbing the tree too, but I had made it the highest. I had kept going even when the branches had grown thin and weak. I had wanted to show them that I was the best. To that end, I had climbed so high that none of them had dared to follow. I could still remember the horror of feeling the branch snap beneath me and the terror of plunging to the ground.

The fear, more than the pain, was what had brought tears to my eyes. I had known something was wrong because, when I had finally caught the breath the fall had knocked out of me, I hadn't been able to move my left hand. I had started screaming, and Cole had run back to The Paramount for help. It had felt like forever that I had sat there under the tree, my broken arm cradled to my chest, with a small group of children huddled around me, unsure of what to do.

When Myna had arrived, instead of coming to my side and holding me in her arms like I had wanted, she had just stood there, examining me with her cold, gray eyes. I remembered reaching my good hand out to her, but even then, she had not taken a single step forward. Instead, she had turned to Cole and had sent him to find a healer.

I had continued to scream and sob until the healer, Gretch, had arrived. He had glanced at Myna, as if he hadn't been able to understand why she hadn't approached me. The moment she had finished explaining the situation, she had left, deserting me to the care of a stranger.

That was the day I had stopped turning to others for help. If my own mother didn't care enough to aid me, why should anyone else? I decided then that I would survive by myself or not at all. I never asked her for anything after that, and I refused to even think the word 'mother' of her in my mind. I began calling her Myna, and she did not appear to notice the change.

She was the Second Clan Leader, the second most powerful person on the council. From the outside, I'm sure people only saw her as one of the great leaders of The Clan. For nearly fifty years Myna had held the same position. There were few who could remember a time before her appointment.

The obligations of leading The Clan kept her busy, and I had my friends and school, so there was little chance of interaction between us. It was for the better; when we were together, it just made her rejection of me that much harder to bear.

Until the Telling began, there was little enough for me to do. I busied myself cleaning the main room of the dwelling. Every day, rations of wood and food were delivered to each family.

Since neither Myna nor myself were around much, we used very little of the supplies, and they tended to pile up.

I restocked our scant, indoor woodpile. The firewood ration from the past couple of days had begun to pile up outside, threatening to block the door. I lit some kindling to try to warm the room. The previous night's fire had died, and it was practically warmer outside than in. The fire was made in our stove, a big, black box with a pipe attached to one of the dwelling's exterior walls. It served as both a place to cook our meals and a heater for the entire dwelling.

The two wooden shelves, where our food rations were meant to be stored, had been completely full for months. The extras had overflowed onto the table, still sitting in their crates.

From the stench, I knew some of the supplies were rotten. I picked through and separated the putrid-smelling perishables into an empty crate. Once full, I hauled it outside, where it would be collected and disposed of when the new food rations arrived in the morning.

It took most of the afternoon, but, eventually, the dwelling was spick and span, aside from the table filled with extra ration crates. As evening fell, I cooked myself some dinner. Generally, I just ate whatever happened to be lying around. But that day I hadn't had lunch, so I took the time to bake a little bread, roast some meat, and even boil a potato for myself.

After devouring the little feast, I cleaned everything up and set out for the Telling. It was almost completely dark, and the temperature had dropped drastically. Thankful for my fur-lined winter boots, I trudged through the deep drifts, wrapping my cloak tighter around my shoulders. Soon, I made it to a path that had been packed down by many feet, all going in the same direction.

I saw others along the road, each bundled in a cloak similar to my own. Our destination was the same: the amphitheater. It lay just outside of The Paramount. As I drew nearer to my destination, the crowd around me thickened, until I could no longer

THE PREPARATIONS

see the hard-packed snow of the path before me. My view was limited to the multicolored splash of different cloaks ahead of me. Some were the same maroon red as mine, but most were different colors, representing all nine of the different villages.

The Paramount was located in the very center of The Land of the Clan. It was where the council members, the scribes, and the clerks lived with their families. Out of all the villages, ours was the smallest, but we carried the greatest responsibility.

Night had fallen by the time I reached the amphitheater. The twenty thousand members of The Clan were almost entirely assembled. The normally short trek had taken twice as long because of the great press of people.

When following the northern road out of The Paramount, the path was level and straight, but the land at the southern end dropped away into a small hill once you left the village.

The amphitheater rested on the eastern ridge of the rise. Spectators sat on the slope, facing away from The Paramount, and looking down toward the wide field beyond. The seats were long slabs of rock forming huge semi-circles, each tier with fewer stones than the one before it as they proceeded down the hill. The last semicircle, the smallest, rested on flat ground. A wooden, rectangular structure, a few feet taller than me, made the stage. The black night behind the platform was a perfect backdrop of darkness. There were four vacant chairs set up in the center of the stage and several dozen more lined up along the back.

A huge bonfire blazed in the giant fire circle between the seats and the wooden stage. It illuminated the entire space with dancing, crimson flames. The fire's heat reached almost to the top rows of the amphitheater, but still, the families seated in the back huddled close together.

In all my sixteen years of life, I couldn't remember any night as cold as that one, and I had no family to give me warmth. Myna would be on the stage with the other council members. As usual in that kind of situation, I searched the crowd for a familiar face, looking for someone I knew well enough that I would be comfortable grafting myself into his or her family for the evening. I didn't really have many options.

The first person that I recognized was Rasby. I enjoyed her company in general. Most of the time, she was relaxing and easy to be around. With Rasby, it really didn't matter what I did. Even if she left crying one day because of something I'd said, she would still come back the next, ready to make up.

However, I would have preferred to sit with Cole. His father was the First Clan Leader, the only person more important than Myna. Because of our parents' positions, we had been thrown in together a lot. It was good for us to be seen together; it showed the unity of our families and of The Clan.

I descended several rows, scanning the crowd in the dim firelight for maroon forms that might be either Cole or a member of his family. Rasby turned suddenly and saw me. She waved, and our eyes met. I sighed resignedly, knowing I couldn't pretend I hadn't seen her. Shoving my way through the assembly, almost to the very front row, I dropped onto the icy stone beside her.

Rasby smiled brightly at me. Her blotchy complexion was redder than usual from the excitement, and her frizzy hair had been freed from the braids.

Our appearances couldn't have been more different. I had straight brown hair, which I almost always tied back in a ponytail. My eyes were a clear gray, instead of a muddy brown. I had skin that was tan and flawless. People often said that I looked fierce. No one would ever say that about Rasby.

On the seat beside her, I was close enough to the bonfire to feel the heat from the flames. I enjoyed the sensation and closed my eyes for a moment, pretending that it was summer and the sun was shining down on me. I loved the summer. Winter always felt dark and depressing. It was nice, even for just a fleeting moment, to bask in the warmth of a pretend sun.

THE PREPARATIONS

My revelry was interrupted by Rasby. "It's so cold, Myra!" she squealed, leaning closer to her father, who was sitting on her other side. "I hope they cancel. Do you think they will?" she asked.

"No," I said. "They never cancel. It's Midwinter, and we can't break tradition. They have to tell us the history of our people, no matter how cold it gets."

Rasby pouted slightly. She was the youngest of four and the only girl. It tended to make her rather spoiled. She didn't like to be uncomfortable and was used to letting other people, including me, handle problems for her. Most of the time, I didn't mind too much, but it was frustrating that she couldn't seem to do so many simple things herself.

I glanced at the stage. What Rasby had said was true; it was bitter cold. From the number of people crowded into the amphitheater, it appeared that even those from the most outlying villages had arrived; soon the Telling would begin. Privately, I was hoping to hear something other than the history of The Clan that night, which was told twice a year, at Midwinter and Midsummer.

Rasby and I did not speak again. She was clearly unable to think of anything beyond the chilly wind that buffeted us, and I was lost in my own thoughts. Mostly, I was caught up in the hope that the trials would be announced that evening. The thought had been growing on my mind every year since I had turned twelve. The trials only took place once every fifty years, but I knew they were due again in the next decade. I just hoped they wouldn't come too late.

After several more minutes, the amphitheater was completely packed, with hardly enough room to fit everyone. The entirety of The Clan had assembled. There were some soft murmurs from among the seated people, but the majority were silent, like me. The fire crackled, the wind whispered, and we waited. I was focused forward, watching the flames lick the logs; the ruby patterns on the wood were mesmerizing.

Finally, the time came. It could have been minutes or hours later for all I remembered, but at last, Core, Cole's father, stepped onto the empty stage and waited for silence to fall before he addressed us.

The crowd hushed almost immediately. Core, who was approaching seventy, was a hunched man with shoulder-length, white hair. He wore thick pants, such a dark red that they almost looked black from where I was sitting. On top of that, he had a bulky, maroon coat several shades darker than mine, trimmed with white fur. Despite his age, his voice still rang out loud and clear as he spoke.

"Greetings to The Clan," he called, not in the common tongue, but in the high langue, a second language that we were all taught but rarely used in day-to-day life. It was reserved for special occasions.

We called ourselves 'The Clan' because we were a perfectly structured society. There were long lists of laws that dictated how best to live our lives in perfection and peace. I didn't like all of the rules, but I always understood that their design was to keep everyone safe and all things well-ordered.

"Greetings," we replied to Core in the high language. It was incredible to hear twenty thousand voices speak one word at exactly the same moment. Core smiled. He must have felt our unity; even from a distance I saw his eyes all but disappear into the wrinkles of his face.

Unlike Myna, Core was a warm and joyful person. He often left the council meetings early and rarely traveled to the other villages of The Clan. Instead, he preferred to spend the time with his family. I'd often wished that he had been my parent instead of Myna. But that would have meant giving up the little bit of memory I still had of my father. I wasn't sure it would have been worth it.

Other than Cole, who was eighteen, all of Core's children were much older than I was, most living in other villages with families of their own. Cole must have been a surprise to his parents since he'd come fifteen years after his last brother.

Normally, on Midwinter, Core would launch excitedly into the history of our people after greeting us, but not that night. That night, his words were even and rehearsed. However, I sensed that under his façade, great emotion churned.

"It is time for the six months of preparation to begin," he said, speaking in the common tongue. There was dead silence. I closed my eyes and smiled as Core continued. "The trials will be held this coming year!"

Chapter 3

HISTORY

"Everyone between the ages of twelve and nineteen is now a potential," Core explained.

"On the morrow, you will begin preparing yourselves for the challenge ahead. In five months, all of the potentials will assemble, and the contenders will be chosen from among them. There will be one hundred and twenty-five teams each consisting of six contenders. Every contender will be assigned a rank within the team to establish the order of leadership.

"Prior to Midsummer, each of the teams' members will face an individual proficiency test. If at least four members pass, the whole team will qualify to compete in the trials. Six months from now, on Midsummer's day, the trials will begin and will continue until one team returns victorious."

At the conclusion of his speech, there was a moment of utter stillness as the meaning of Core's words sunk in. The beat of my heart accelerated, filling my body with tense and eager excitement. Each passing year had brought me closer to missing the opportunity of being a contender in the trials. However, at sixteen, I was the perfect age.

Deep within, anticipation continued to grow in my chest until I wasn't sure how I could possibly contain it all. I desperately wanted to be chosen. If I wasn't, I didn't think I could bear it.

On the stone seat beside me I felt Rasby shudder, from the cold or from the proclamation I didn't know, but I could easily guess. She wasn't like me. There was no passion or drive in her.

THE PREPARATIONS

If placed on a team, she would give up before they even passed through The Valley of the North Wind.

Rasby was already a burden to those around her, but things were different in The Land of the Clan. The games we played weren't really dangerous, and the victories we won didn't really mean anything; what did it matter if I had to pull her weight as well as my own?

However, once the trials began, I wouldn't be able to carry her anymore, even if we were on the same team. Never once in her life had she pushed herself or been willing to do anything uncomfortable. The skills and discipline necessary to survive were something Rasby would never have. She was not meant to be a contender in the trials, nor was she meant to be a Clan Leader.

My eyes traveled to Myna. She was standing in the shadows, just off stage. Unlike Core, who was clearly hiding what he felt, her face and posture left one to believe that she had never felt an emotion of any kind. I struggled to gain composure, trying to mimic her cool calmness. If I was going to be in the trials, I would need it.

"It has been my pleasure serving you all these years," Core said, breaking the silence. "But it is time for myself, Myna, Falow, and Joel," he gestured to Myna and the two other men he had named, "to see a new beginning in The Clan's history." The other three Clan Leaders quickly mounted the stairs and joined him on the stage.

He paused and looked at each of the other three in turn. There was an unspeakable depth of emotion in his eyes. The four had spent the majority of their lives leading The Clan together, ever since their team had won the last trials.

As with all teams, theirs had started with six members, but only those four had survived. Three were all that was necessary to claim victory, so up to half of a team might die, and the strongest could still continue on to become the winners. An experience filled with such hardship and danger would bind a team together as nothing else could. The members were forced to trust each other with their very lives.

On the stage, Myna took Core's hand. The two faced us and bowed. They had been First and Second Clan Leaders since before many of us had been born.

I tried to capture the moment in my mind. Someday, I planned to be the one bowing before The Clan after a lifetime spent serving them.

Silently, the oldest of The Clan's members among us rose. They were the ones who remembered the last time the trials had been announced and the ceremony required for such an event. Around them, like ripples in a puddle, others began to rise, until everyone was standing.

Rasby reached for my hand. At first, I did not want to give it to her. I detested when she was clingy. However, a moment later, I saw that the entirety of The Clan was joining hands, so I allowed her to take mine.

I also reached for the hand of the woman on the other side of me. She was young, but not young enough to be a potential. Her hand felt worn and calloused, and I noticed a few bits of sawdust on the dark green clothes she wore. The sawdust alone would have indicated to me that she was from Treescape, even if I hadn't seen her garb.

Realization of what was about to happen washed over me. Everything was going to change; nothing would ever be the same again. In six months, the trials would begin, and I would do whatever it took to be among those chosen.

In all of our history, no winning team had ever returned with all six members. I would change that. Not only would I lead my team to victory, but I would do it without a single casualty, and The Clan would remember my name forever.

A moment after we had joined hands, we bowed to our leaders on the stage. Similar to when we had all risen to our feet, the elderly—the ones who had witnessed it all before—started the motion, and the rest of us followed their lead. Then, slowly, we took our seats, eager to hear the rest of what Core had to say.

"Once the winning team returns, we will spend a year with them, guiding them and making sure that they are well-prepared to lead you."

He paused, and when he spoke again, his voice was different, much of the tension had gone out of it. "Now, I will tell you the history of our people as far back as we know."

Core glanced at the other Clan Leaders and waited as they repositioned themselves to three of the four empty chairs in the center of the stage. Some years, one or more of them would do part of the Telling, but it seemed that Core would be the only speaker that evening. The elders and village leaders joined them on stage as well, silently taking the seats along the back.

Each village had five village leaders assigned to it. Those officials were appointed by the council from among the most prestigious members of The Paramount. Three out of the five lived full-time in their designated village, ensuring that the required quota of goods was produced each day and that the village's needs were met. The last two village leaders acted as representatives to the council. They traveled back and forth between the village where they were assigned and The Paramount. If ever a problem arose, they addressed the council on behalf of their village.

The best and wisest village leaders were asked to return to The Paramount and join the council as elders. The Clan Leaders, elders, and representatives made up the council. However, the representatives were only included when the discussion involved the village they spoke for.

There were plenty of disagreements, but matters almost never came to a vote. Generally, topics were discussed until everyone present agreed on a course of action. Since that could take a considerable amount of time, the council meetings tended to be quite lengthy, sometimes lasting as long as ten hours a day.

HISTORY

Very few of the members attended the meetings every single day, but Myna did. I wondered if she intentionally came up with things to discuss just so she wouldn't have to come back to our dwelling until after I was asleep.

I turned my thoughts back to Core, standing on the stage in front of The Clan. After clearing his throat, he began to recite the history of our people. He had a deep, rich voice, and as the words poured forth, they twisted into the account of our ancestors. I had heard it many times, but I loved listening to the history. It spoke of an age long before The Clan had existed, when danger and chaos had confronted our people.

"A very long time ago," he began, "the world was different from how it is now. Our ancestors lived outside The Land of the Clan in a beautiful, golden city called Axella. It was a place of perfect happiness. Great knowledge was gathered there in the form of books. People devoted their lives to the study of medicine, astronomy, botany, and hundreds of other scientific pursuits. The culture thrived and flourished beneath an upright and principled leadership. But it was not to last.

"A dark enemy was lurking nearby, a plague that watched the people of Axella with malice and hatred. The people of Axella were oblivious to what was taking place outside their glorious city.

"If they had any fault at all, perhaps it was that blindness: the inability to see what lay beyond the safety of their walls. They did not realize their own vulnerability or the growing threat just outside their gate.

"The darkness came upon the great city late one night. It settled over the rooftops, blotting out the moon and the stars. The inhabitants of Axella woke in terror to find their home being torn to pieces.

"They were left with no choice, save to flee. Some made it out, but many more were trapped inside and devoured by the darkness. Those who had escaped, scattered, seeking refuge anywhere they could find it. The darkness pursued them.

Hundreds and hundreds were killed. The earth was washed in blood, filled with horror, and shadowed by misery. Children cried in the night for parents that would never come to save them.

"After a year, the darkness tired of the chase. Instead, it intertwined itself with the earth, so as to persecute our ancestors anew. The ground grew black and hard, and it didn't matter what you planted in it, nothing would grow. People could no longer eat the sweet yields of the field, so they turned to eating meat. They stripped the land of its game, trying to find enough to feed themselves and their families. Parents were forced to watch their children starve.

"Still, the darkness was not satisfied. Growing impatient, it stretched up through the earth, releasing a disease from deep within. The sickness caused men to become blind and deaf; their skin burned and rotted on their bones. Soon, so few were left that the darkness was certain man wouldn't survive. Three years after Axella was razed, the darkness faded from the world, having burned itself up in the extermination of our ancestors. Even once gone, it left behind a legacy of blackened land, disease-afflicted creatures, and dark shadows filled with death. The remnants of our once proud race were left to die in the ashes of their forsaken city.

"But our ancestors did not die. They crawled from hiding and searched and searched for a place of safety and peace. Finally, they found the only land the darkness had left untouched; the same place where we have dwelt ever since the days of the darkness. It was the only sanctuary that still existed on the earth. The last place where the ground was still fertile, the water still flowing, and the air still clean.

"They began to work the fields and found that this place was good for producing food. They built dwellings and a village. The community began to grow. It looked like our race might be saved. The man who had led them was named Peter;

HISTORY

he is the father of The Clan. He united the fragments of our people and brought them back from the brink of extinction.

"In those days, all men did not speak the same language. When they couldn't communicate with each other, distance grew. Peter had studied and learned all the languages of the earth at Axella. He used his gift to teach others the common language and the high language, both of which we still speak today. This was the last piece to uniting mankind: a common tongue. And so, for a decade, it appeared as if our ancestors' troubles were finally at an end.

"But Peter was very old when this land was found. After only eleven years of leading The Clan, he passed away peacefully in his sleep, and what remained of our race almost died with him.

"There were two men who rose to vie for his position. No one realized they had been infected with the darkness, body and mind. The two began to manipulate the people, and with the help of their life mates and a few close friends, they sought to gain support. They began spreading lies about each other, both determined to make themselves king of The Clan, no matter the cost.

"With the people divided and a lingering remnant of the darkness remaining among them, blood would have been shed and the final hope of our race dashed to pieces, if Jessica, Peter's only child, hadn't intervened. She saw the darkness in the hearts of the two men and exposed their brokenness to the people of The Clan. She told them that if the peace couldn't be kept, then mankind would be erased forever.

"The Clan heeded her words and drove away the two men and all those who had aided them. Never again were they permitted entry to the beautiful land that was a home to the rest of mankind. They were forced to return to where the earth was black and the sky gray instead of blue. It was there, in a land without hope, that the evil men and their followers met their end. They are an example to us that outside our land, death is waiting. It is only our peacefulness and compliance to the rules that keeps us safe.

"The rest of The Clan wanted to make Jessica ruler in place of her father, but she wouldn't allow it. Jessica declared instead that The Clan would never have a single king or lord again. She formed the first council from the wisest of the elders. They elected her to join them as the First Clan Leader.

"While Jessica served with the council, she and the others created the trials. They knew that leaders had to be strong, wise, and cunning. But most importantly, they needed to be certain that the leaders could work together and that they would be willing to do whatever was necessary to make sure The Clan survived. The trials were designed to ensure that only those worthy of the position would ever lead The Clan. There would no longer be power struggles; never again would The Clan tear itself apart over such things. The first trials were held eleven years after the council was formed.

"The rules were then as they are now. Teams of six contenders train, qualify, and then embark on the trials with a sole objective delivered from the Clan Leaders.

"Each team is handpicked and designed to have the best possible chance at success. To that end, the members are to be chosen from at least three different villages, but no individual is to be without someone they know and have trained with. Siblings are never to be placed on the same team, since this can confuse the loyalties of the team members.

"The first team to return having completed the task set before them with at least three members still living, is to be named victorious, and its surviving members are to be the new Clan Leaders. Together with the council, they are responsible for guiding The Clan for a span of fifty years.

"The first Clan Leaders and council were the ones who set up our society so that we, and our descendants, could be completely self-sufficient. They divided The Clan into the nine villages, with The Paramount in the middle and the others spread out around it like the spokes of a wheel. They gave each village its own purpose to ensure that we would always have everything we needed. Through their care and stewardship, the land has grown plentiful.

"To this day, we must still remember and thank our ancestors for the legacy they have left us. Though we will never regain the knowledge stored in the library of Axella, now lost for all time, they have left us everything we need for a peaceful and quiet life."

Core paused for a moment. He had come to the end of the history. Next, he would lead us in the adage of The Clan. "We are The Clan. We were created to be order when all else was chaos. We have lived in peace as our fathers have taught us. We show justice to all without hesitation. We will continue as we have been: the only perfect society."

As soon as he finished the recitation, the entirety of The Clan took up the words, in the high language this time, and repeated what he had said as one.

Core nodded approvingly at us. "Now, the time has come to ready ourselves. On the morrow, we will begin the preparations for the eleventh trials of The Clan."

Core's final words were met with cheers.

I was carefully watching Myna. I'm sure her face was still a mask to most, but I, who had lived with her so long, saw something new there. Was it sorrow? No, it wasn't sharp enough for sorrow. Regret maybe. But what could she regret? She had won after all.

As the cheers died away, I thought I saw a tear run down Core's cheek, but it might have been a trick of the firelight.

All around the amphitheater emotions were running high. Parents hugged their smaller children, fearing for what was to come. Some of the children—potentials now—looked enthusiastic; others were frightened, like Rasby. A few held themselves composed as I did, whether for excitement or fear I didn't know.

THE PREPARATIONS

At that moment, I caught Bala's eye. She was off to my right, a few rows back. She gave me a small smile, sly and happy. She was every bit as pleased with the evening's outcome as I was. She would be fighting hard to make sure she became a contender.

Bala would certainly be an interesting teammate to have. She was a middle child in a large family that never took the time to notice her. Just like their daughter, Bala's parents always seemed to be unimportant. Neither held a prominent position; her mother was a clerk and her father a distributer, someone responsible for delivering the food and wood rations that came to The Paramount each day.

Bala wasn't exactly what I would call a friend. We'd been opponents during Attack and Defend so many times I wasn't sure we'd ever be able to work together. Although, I had learned a lot of strategy from being pitted against her. She could make a good ally, if I could deal with her personality. She had a mean streak a mile wide and always seemed to be slinking around in the shadows, trying to learn things she wasn't supposed to know. On occasion, I'd seen her pinch her baby brother until he screamed, for no other reason than to vex her own mother.

Core stepped back, taking his seat. Myna replaced him on center stage. She was short compared to Core, and her dark brown hair didn't even reach to her shoulders. Her face had few wrinkles, except around her mouth where the skin was oddly taught. Two eyes, the same gray color as mine, were set deep in her face. The dark maroon dress she wore was covered by a cloak even darker than the dress itself. The crowd quieted for her instantly. One day, I would command that kind of respect.

"Tomorrow, the preparations will begin. Early in the morning, all potentials must assemble at the town center of their respective villages. A council member will give them directions." She glanced back at Core for a moment before continuing. "Potentials, we will begin watching you from this

HISTORY

moment forward. Do not disappoint The Clan. You are our future."

Chapter 4

FIRELIGHT

When the Telling ended, Rasby turned to me. "What's going to happen tomorrow?" she asked fretfully.

I shook my head; it was the only answer I had for her. Slowly, I rose to my feet. The stone beneath me was nearly as cold as when I had sat down.

"How are we supposed to prepare ourselves?" Rasby panicked. I shrugged, turning toward the fire. It wasn't as large as it had been when Core had begun speaking, but the remaining flames still appeared warm and inviting.

"Everything will be alright, Rasby," her father, Cliv, promised.

Without glancing in their direction, I pushed forward through the crowd. My seat had not been on the front row, and I had to descend several tiers before I was standing on level ground. With measured steps, I approached the bonfire, only stopping when the heat became too much for me to bear.

My eyes were locked on the flames, studying their rapid movement. The noise of The Clan behind me faded away as I focused solely on the crimson tongues of fire.

The crowd dispersed quickly; it was too cold for them to linger long on such a wintery evening. The Paramount was close by, but those from the outlying villages would have to travel a considerable distance before reaching their dwellings.

Half an hour later, all was quiet. I glanced backward to make sure I was really alone.

I wasn't.

THE PREPARATIONS

A figure was standing on the crest of the hill, looking down on the amphitheater. I wished whoever it was would go away. My desire was to be alone with my thoughts, as I considered the future.

Everyone between the ages of twelve and nineteen was a potential. There were probably at least fifteen hundred eligible children. One hundred and twenty-five teams would be assembled, which meant that only seven hundred and fifty of us would become contenders. Half. With those kinds of numbers, how could I not be chosen?

I looked at the figure again. A thick cloud obscured the moon, and the firelight didn't reach high enough for me to decipher anything more than a silhouette. All I could distinguish was a long cloak of some dark color, wrapping the figure in shadow.

"What are you still doing here?" someone asked to my right.

I managed not to jump, but whipped around and came face to face with Cole.

"Do not do that to me," I hissed. Cole laughed. He wasn't a particularly stealthy person. Even still, he'd somehow managed to sneak up on me twice in as many days.

"But it's so much fun!" he protested, round face split by a huge grin.

Quickly, I glanced back over my left shoulder to the top of the amphitheater while Cole finished laughing. The dark figure had vanished into the night.

"Seriously though, shouldn't you be headed to bed?" he wondered.

"You think I'll be able to sleep tonight after what your father said?" I asked.

"Good point," Cole conceded. "But what else is there to do?"

"Strategize," I told him.

He laughed again, but it wasn't as merry as before. "I should have figured. Do you have your team picked out already?"

"Yes and no," I replied. "The Clan Leaders will ultimately choose the teams, but maybe we can help them."

Cole perked up at the serious tone in my voice. "What do you mean?"

I sighed; hadn't he paid any attention?

"The teams will be constructed from those who work well together," I reminded him. "So…"

I paused, seeing if he would pick up on what I was getting at. He didn't. He just continued to look at me expectantly.

"So, I think, if you spend a considerable amount of time training with someone, you're more likely to end up on a team with that person," I finished.

Cole cocked his head to one side. "I hadn't thought about that."

Obviously, I sighed mentally.

"Do you want to be on my team?" Cole blurted out.

I hesitated. Cole wasn't as passionate or clever as I was, but he was good at making friends and could certainly help me build a strong team with his charisma. Plus, I had known him my entire life and felt comfortable around him, something I couldn't say regarding very many people.

"I guess. You wouldn't be my last choice," I told him grudgingly.

"You're so mean," Cole complained, a twinkle of amusement in his blue eyes.

"Only to you," I teased.

He shook his head. "But really," he persisted, "do you want to be my teammate?"

I considered playing with him a bit longer, but it really wasn't the night for it.

"Yes," I told him. "I would like that very much."

Cole's face lit with a brilliant smile; it was easy to make him happy.

I had known Cole for so long that I couldn't even remember when we had first met. However, it wasn't until about seven years ago that I had actually begun considering him to be a friend.

It had been a dreary winter night. Both he and I had been waiting outside the council building, which was a large, circular structure with only one entrance, opening into the courtyard of the town center. People often met there for important occasions, but that night, it had just been Cole and myself. Children were almost never permitted inside the council building, unless they were in a lot of trouble.

My dwelling had been close by, but, back then, I had dreaded being there alone at night in the dark.

Cole's own dwelling, warm and well-lit, had been less than two hundred yards away, so I had been unable to comprehend why he'd chosen to wait in the cold. However, I had been grateful to not be alone.

Finally, the door to the council building had opened, but only Core had emerged. He had been shaking his head and muttering to himself.

"They would be in session every hour of every day if they could!" He'd noticed me then and had spoken more softly. "I'm sorry, Myra. I think your mother is going to be a bit longer.

"They are trying to determine if it would be more efficient to repair the road to The Farm or build a new road using the pieces of the old one," he had explained. "I told them that repairing the road would be much easier than building a new one and would save everyone a lot of effort. But they keep talking about saving more time in the future by making the new route more direct. That way, it will save everyone who walks on it three and a quarter minutes.

"Supposedly, in the generations to come, we will end up gaining more time than that which will be spent paving the new road now."

Core had laughed as he had spoken in mockery of the meeting still in session behind him. "It's all about numbers to them. In my opinion, they should get out for a bit instead of arguing all night."

My heart had sunken at the phrase 'all night'. It was a term I'd come to understand only too well.

"They know what I think," Core had continued, "and honestly, they can do whatever they want. I have given them more than enough of *my time* for tonight."

He'd turned to Cole, and the pair had headed off toward their dwelling. I'd remained frozen, trying to decide whether or not to linger there any longer.

Cole had followed a few steps after his father and then paused. He'd glanced back at me: a small, lonely figure, waiting dejectedly for a parent to appear.

"Father," Cole had said, causing Core to stop and look at him. "Can Myra come home with us? Her mother could be a long time, and it's getting cold."

Core had looked at me with friendly eyes. He had seemed to be able tell how desperately I had not wanted to return to my dwelling alone. "Alright," he'd agreed. "If she would like, she is welcome to join us."

Technically, his offer wasn't allowed according to the rules of our people. Unless special permission was obtained, everyone was supposed to eat from his or her own food allowance and sleep in the dwelling assigned to their own family. That way, wood and food could be properly rationed. However, on that evening, no one had even mentioned that we were breaking a few rules.

Cole's dwelling had a cheery fire on the hearth, and Cole's mother, Wren, had just finished heating a savory pot of stew.

THE PREPARATIONS

The food had been delicious, but it had been even better to pretend, just for one moment, that I actually had a family and people who wanted to take care of me.

Cole and I had been allowed to stay up late, in case Myna had come to fetch me. Core had left a note explaining the situation on the door of our dwelling.

As the embers on the hearth had turned to ash, my eyes had started to droop. I'd fallen asleep with my head resting on Cole's shoulder and hadn't even remembered when someone had draped a blanket over us.

In the morning, when I had returned to my dwelling to prepare for school, the note had still been in its place, and no one had been there. I'd realized then why my own life seemed so empty.

To everyone else, Myna and I appeared to be a normal mother and daughter. Only the two of us knew the truth of our distant relationship. After that night, things had only gotten worse between us. I told myself I didn't mind being the only one in the dwelling, and I spent no more nights waiting in the town center.

Cole had shared his home and family with me. There wasn't anything more precious he could have given. I'd never told him, or anyone else, how much that gift had meant. The last thing I would have ever wanted to do was let Cole know what the situation really was. That was the reason I didn't tell him why I had chosen to linger by the fire.

"How do you think we can get them to put us on the same team?" Cole asked.

"I suppose we should train together as often as possible," I replied.

"Sounds good."

"But we can't be too exclusive," I added. "We want them to see that we can work with other people." Cole nodded as I continued. "However, whatever group we end up with each day, you and I should always be the leaders. We need to be ready to step up and meet any challenge given us head-on."

Cole smiled. "You're so smart, Myra. It hasn't even been an hour, and you've already got everything figured out."

"Well, you know how much I love strategy," I reminded him.

The smile slowly faded from Cole's face. "You're going to win," he said softly.

"What?" I asked.

"It won't matter what team you're put on, or what rank you're given, or what the task is. You're going to win."

"I plan to," I told him.

There was a moment of silence. "We really should head back," Cole finally said.

Overhead, the clouds had thinned, revealing the sliver of moon which hung in the black sky. The stars seemed dim, as though slightly shrouded by a misty veil.

The fire was nearly dead, and on the horizon, a dark cloudbank promised more snow. In my dwelling, there was a bed calling me to rest for at least a few hours before it was time to rise and begin training. I didn't have any other reason to hurry back to my dwelling. Even if Myna was there, she would shut the door to her room, and I would be as alone as if she had never existed.

I nodded my consent and fell into step beside him as we began ascending the hill to The Paramount. The path was easier now, after so many feet had crushed the snow flat.

"Who else do you want on your team?" Cole asked me, when we were halfway to the top.

Not Rasby, I thought hastily, but didn't speak the name aloud. Instead, I said, "I wouldn't mind Jase."

"Definitely," Cole agreed easily. "He nearly missed his chance, since he'll be twenty in a few months."

"But think of the advantage he'll have over all the younger contenders once the trials actually start," I pointed out. Yes, Jase would make a powerful teammate, but he'd have to be ranked below me. I couldn't imagine how a team under his command would function.

"Then there's Motik and Ashlo. They're so athletic; I'm sure either of them would be a great asset," Cole stated.

I shrugged. They were both quiet, but good at taking orders. I would have to keep a close eye on them during the preparations to see if they had any potential. It was remarkable how many unintelligent and boring people lived just next door.

"We need to broaden our perspective. There's a good chance each team will only have one or two members from the same village," I reminded Cole.

He scowled. "I don't really know anyone outside of The Paramount."

"I know a few," I told him. "And so do you. What about Golla?"

Cole puckered his forehead. "Who?"

"Golla of The Golden Fields," I told him.

Most of The Clan's food was grown at The Golden Fields. It was the largest of the villages, surrounded by fields and orchards. It sat in the richest part of our land, to the southeast, and was close enough to the river to have a steady supply of water for the crops.

"The name sounds familiar," he answered after a minute. "Her mother is their representative, isn't she?"

I nodded. "Yes, she took that position about eight years ago. Before that, she was the scribe responsible for keeping the genealogy of The Clan."

"That's right," Cole recalled, and then shook his head. "I still can't picture her. Isn't she too old for the trials now?"

I had to think for a second. Golla was a bit older than me, blonde, blue-eyed, and beautiful. The two of us had a lot in common since both our fathers had died when we were little, and our mothers' time was mostly occupied elsewhere.

Golla was full of strange notions and bizarre ideas, most of which could have gotten her in a lot of trouble. One of her favorite topics was what had happened to her father. He had died of an illness, but that wasn't the part she questioned. What she had always wondered was where he was now. It wasn't really considered polite to discuss death in the villages, so she had never discussed her questions with anyone but me.

I had to admit that before meeting her, I had never thought about where my own father was. I had always assumed that death was the end, but Golla didn't believe so. She couldn't say what happened, but she was sure there was more. I hoped she was right and death wasn't the end, but what if what came after was bad?

Neither Myna nor Golla's mother would have ever spoken about something like that, but the two of us enjoyed discussing it. When her mother had been reassigned and Golla had moved to The Golden Fields, I had lost my only friend.

It had been a very lonely time for me, until I had found a new confidant in Cole. However, since his father was alive and well, I couldn't talk to him about things like I could with Golla.

We had reached the brink of the hill, and I paused for a moment, in the same place I had seen the figure earlier, to glance eastward. In the distance, I could just barely make out the twinkling lights of The Barracks. They weren't the lights from the dwellings, but those of torches. The streets of the Barracks wouldn't be empty and quiet like The Paramount's. Soldiers were alert and active at all hours.

"I guess we should focus on trying to match up with potentials from other villages," Cole said.

"It's not a bad idea," I told him. "However, I'm more interested in focusing on my own training. It matters less to me who is on my team and more to me what rank I'm given."

"I see." Cole's voice carried an unusually deflated note.

"I mean, as long as we're together," I amended quickly.

THE PREPARATIONS

Cole smiled, but it wasn't his usual smile, and I feared that I'd hurt his feelings. We had reached the town center, the place where our paths split. I couldn't let it end like that, so I stopped walking.

A dim glow of firelight emitted from the evenly-spaced, circular windows set high in the council building's walls. We were standing in exactly the same place we had stood all those years ago when our friendship had begun.

I waited to speak until Cole had turned to look back at me. "We will uphold our parents' legacies," I promised him. "We'll do it together."

Cole let out a quiet laugh, and his face relaxed. "I don't think I could possibly doubt you."

I smiled too. Being with Cole was so natural. We spent a lot of time together, and, over the last few years, I had begun to wonder whether Cole thought of me in that special way boys sometimes thought of girls. He was already eighteen and would be an adult in less than two years. We'd never spoken of the subject—it would have been inappropriate if we had—but for some reason, whenever I pictured my future life mate, it was Cole's face I saw. With the trials about to start, the future was all the more clear.

Just like our parents, we would win the trials. I could see it, our lives laid out in front of me. We would be made Clan Leaders and have everything we had ever wanted. Cole and I would become life mates, drawn together by our experiences. We would have a beautiful son with Cole's dark hair and my gray eyes. We would name him Covil after his father.

Then we would have a daughter, and she would have my gray eyes too. We would name her Myla or Myka or something after me. We would be a family, and I would finally have someone to walk through life with.

It's a nice thought, I told myself, *but too far away to think about now. Better to focus on winning the trials than on what may come after.*

If the trials were about to start, it was quite likely that a lot of the participants wouldn't make it back. I couldn't say what the percentage was exactly, but I did know that a large number of contenders never returned.

It wouldn't be my fate. For the past eleven years, I had taken everything life had thrown at me. What could have prepared me better for the trials than that? I was able to adapt, I was determined to survive, and I would see things through to the end. My only concern was winning. I had to win. To do that, I would need a strong team. Which brought me back to Cole.

"We will win," I reiterated.

"I hope you're right," Cole replied. "But that starts with a good night's rest, which neither of us is going to have at this point."

"Goodnight then," I told him.

"Goodnight, Myra," he said, as we went our separate ways.

I hastened to my dwelling, trying to calm my thoughts. What I needed to focus on was getting some rest. I dreaded the thought of my cold bed, but there was no help for it. I was sure the fire had died ages ago. In the winter, I was always cold. There was no warm place for me to return to. No family members waiting to snuggle together against the chill.

The winter was like being dead.

Spring would come soon; the sun would shine and warm my body. Maybe then, once I could feel the warm blood flowing hot through my veins, I would know for sure that I was alive again.

In the entirety of the village, my dwelling was the only one that was dark. All the others had smoke drifting up from the chimneys, and glinting sparks of firelight shone through cracks in the shutters.

I sighed. My breath billowed out and was caught by the wind. Tiny snowflakes started to fall from the wispy clouds overhead.

THE PREPARATIONS

I opened the door to my dwelling. It felt colder inside than outside, or maybe it was my imagination. Outside, the wind was talking and the lights of other dwellings gave away the presence of living beings, but not within. It was silent as the grave, and the whole place felt as if it had been abandoned long ago. I quickly stirred up the embers of the fire, adding half a dozen logs.

The door to Myna's room was cracked. That never happened when she was inside.

I entered my room and kicked off my boots. Finding my way by touch rather than lighting a lamp, I crawled into bed. The coverings were a soft, rabbit-skin rug topped by a thick blanket knit from the fleece of the sheep that lived at The Farm.

Even as cozy as I was, it took me a long time to get warm enough to fall asleep. During my walk back from the amphitheater with Cole, I hadn't felt the frigid air once. However, as soon as I was alone, the cold had seeped into my core. Every joint and bone felt full of winter.

I tried not to think about anything. Surely, I had thought enough for one day. Instead, I stared into the dark void above me and concentrated on breathing.

And, even though every night I swore I wouldn't, I listened for the sound of Myna coming in the door and heading to bed. As usual, I fell asleep without hearing her arrival.

Chapter 5

FIRST DAY

Darkness still lay heavily over the village when The Paramount's bell started tolling. It was located in the town center, just outside the council building. Each morning it was sounded to wake the village and signal that work and school would begin in one hour.

Groggily, I opened my eyes. It felt far too early for the day to be dawning. I couldn't have slept more than five hours. For a moment, I remained in bed, snugly wrapped in the warm blankets. Sleep had nearly reclaimed me when, suddenly, the memory of the night before swept it away.

It was the first day of the preparations.

I leapt out of bed, shedding blankets and pillows everywhere. The room was freezing and so dark I couldn't even see my hand in front of my face. Normally, I put things where they belonged, but the previous night I'd been too excited to bother. As a result, I had to grope around to find where I had discarded my boots by the foot of the bed. I laced them up as best I could with quivering fingers. Whether they trembled from the cold or from my great excitement, I didn't know.

I'd slept in the long pants and thick tunic I'd worn to the Telling the night before. They weren't too rumpled, so I didn't bother changing them out for fresh ones. After draping myself in my maroon cloak, I was finally able to stop shivering.

I entered the main room of the dwelling and stirred up the embers of the fire. The stove was so full of ashes that the small

THE PREPARATIONS

flames were nearly smothered. I cleaned them away before stocking the metal box with a fresh supply of wood.

Once the task was finished, I stole a glance toward Myna's room. Clearly, she hadn't come back to the dwelling, or she had already left again. The door was open a crack, and through the slit I could see that everything looked exactly the same as it had the day before.

All of the dwellings in The Paramount had one large room with multiple, smaller ones coming off it. The main room was spacious and was where most of our possessions were stored.

My dwelling only had two extra rooms. Myna's and mine. They were just large enough for a bed and a wooden chest to hold clothing.

I extended my cold hands over the stove. The warmth it emitted made little difference in the icy room. I hoped that by the time I returned in the afternoon, the place might be thawed a bit.

Quickly, I bolted down a few scraps of dried meat. Our grain ration was useless, because I didn't have time to make bread. Instead, I selected a dried apple and a few more strips of meat to eat later, and then headed out into the chill of the morning.

The clouds of the night before had vanished, leaving only a fine dusting of new snow. A few stars still lingered in the sky, even though dawn was approaching. The narrow streets of The Paramount looked much as they always did at that time of morning. Lamps had been lit in most of the stone dwellings, and the families within were enjoying their morning meals. Through the wooden shudders, all closed against winter's frosty touch, a few beams of golden light escaped.

I lived on the outskirts of the village, but it was less than a five-minute walk to the town center. Most of the villages in The Clan were spread out and had grassy spaces between the buildings, but not The Paramount. Everything in my village was built close together, so no one had to waste time walking from location to location.

A few potentials were already gathered in the town center when I arrived. There were only about twenty-five children eligible for the trials in the entirety of The Paramount. I couldn't imagine the chaos taking place in the other villages, some with hundreds of potentials. In The Paramount, however, everything was calm and sedate.

Deep shadow lay on the village, though I knew it was awake instead of asleep as it had been the previous evening. The town center looked nearly identical to how it had been the night before, with only the addition of a few figures. Even the light emanating from the council building had not been altered by the past five hours. A steady glow could be seen coming from the door and the circular windows close to the roof.

Rasby had not arrived yet, but Cole was there. I nodded to him, and he smiled as I came to stand by his side. There was an edge of anticipation about him.

"Nervous or excited?" he asked.

"Excited, of course," I replied. "You?"

He shrugged. "A little of both, I guess. And cold, don't forget cold."

Larna of The Paramount approached us a moment later. She was blonde and blue-eyed, but not pretty. Her face was thin, and she had two creases encircling her mouth even though she was only seventeen. She was taller than me but awkwardly built. Her legs and arms were thin, but her stomach was round and full.

She smiled at Cole with crooked teeth. "Isn't this exciting?" she asked; her voice was like the drone of a mosquito. "We're going to be part of The Clan's history! One of us might come back as leader of our people!" She blinked at Cole a couple of times, and then glanced at me. Her smile got wider but not any happier. "Wouldn't it be great if some of us were on the same team?"

I didn't think so. I really just wanted to slap her. Didn't she understand that it was possible she might not be chosen? I'd never pick her. Besides, if her team happened to win, who would want to watch her tell the history of our people each year, with her mosquito voice spewing words over her crooked teeth?

A horrible thought struck me. If she ended up on my team, I might be doomed to be a Clan Leader with her. Forever.

Larna had tried to befriend me once about four or five years ago. She had been annoying and tiresome the two times I had allowed her to play with me, so I'd started avoiding her. I'd run away every time I'd seen her coming and had ignored her when she'd said 'hi' while walking by.

It had taken her nearly a year, but she'd finally gotten the hint and now usually left me alone. In the excitement of the morning, she must have forgotten that we were not friends.

Cole smiled at her kindly. "That would be great!"

I hoped he was lying. Surly, he had more sense than that.

Jase arrived a moment later and asked Cole if we would be having school at some point. Turns out, he hadn't studied for a test we had been told we would be taking that day. I rolled my eyes; school was easy. Who needed to study? I could have taken the test blindfolded and still gotten a better score than Jase. He had come to The Paramount when he was nine and had never really adjusted. In school, he was one of the worst students; most of the teachers had completely given up on him.

More potentials began to trickle into the town center. The older children, those fifteen and above, nearly all arrived first. The younger ones, quite a few with a parent in tow, didn't turn up until it was nearly time to begin.

Rasby was later than most. Her nose and cheeks were bright red and her eyes bloodshot and puffy. There were also still faint traces of tear stains on her face. At least she hadn't made one of her parents bring her.

She didn't say anything, just stood there miserably in the snow by my side. I turned away from her. If she kept acting in that manner, there was no way she would be chosen as a contender. And if I was seen with her, they might not choose me either.

To my surprise, Bala was almost late. The sun had just begun rising when she finally appeared, two of her younger siblings and her mother following close behind. Bala was scowling, and she stomped her feet as she led the small procession.

The younger of Bala's siblings, a little girl name Bacet, was clinging tightly to their mother. In contrast, Bala's younger brother, Inead, raced forward toward a group of his friends. As he passed Bala, she shot out her foot and tripped him. The little boy fell flat on his face. He got up moist-eyed, but managed not to cry, apparently used to such hard knocks.

Bala's mother wasted no time in laying into her for her nasty trick. Bala just rolled her eyes and swore it was an accident.

I turned away from the spectacle and back to Cole. "Was your father out all night?" I asked.

He nodded. "They had to finalize the list of the potentials. I'm not sure when he made it home, but it was quite late."

At least he came home, I thought.

As Bala's mother finished the scolding she had been giving, Myna stepped out of the council building, drawing the attention of the waiting children.

In her small, white hand she carried a long paper rolled into a scroll. The coat covering her shoulders was different than the one she had been wearing the night before, so maybe she had gone back to the dwelling after all. The color was the same dark crimson as most of her other clothing.

"Welcome," she greeted us, not even glancing in my direction.

"Welcome," everyone but me parroted back to her. Cole glanced my way when I remained silent, sympathy in his eyes. I lifted my head arrogantly; I didn't want his pity, or anyone else's.

THE PREPARATIONS

"Today begins the six months of preparation," Myna continued. "One month before Midsummer we will announce the teams, and on Midsummer itself the trials will begin.

"For the next five months, you will be given the first two days out of four in order to prepare yourselves however you see fit. All nine villages will hold training sessions each day to pass on the knowledge of that village.

"After teams have been assigned, it is the team leader's decision where and when the members will train."

Most of what she was saying Core had already told us the night before. The preparations were simple. We trained, got assigned to teams, trained some more, and then had to qualify as a team for the trials themselves.

Some of the other details had been repeated from past preparations years ago and had been passed around from village to village, even though we weren't supposed to discuss them. Regardless, I'd latched onto every piece of information that had come my way, but what I was really interested in learning about was the trials themselves.

I'd never heard a single word spoken concerning what happened once the teams left The Land of the Clan. The preparations may have been a discouraged topic of conversation, but speaking of the trials was completely forbidden. Several times, I'd attempted to count back the years, trying to determine when the trials would begin again. However, I didn't dare ask too many questions. Anyone caught discussing them would get a mark.

"Each morning you must all assemble here before choosing which of the nine villages to visit for your training session," Myna instructed us. "Anyone who is absent without cause will be answerable to the council. On the third day, you will attend school as usual and the fourth you will have off."

Normally, school was held three days out of every four. The first day would be schoolhouse classes, where things such as reading, writing, mathematics, and so on were taught. Day two

FIRST DAY

was an application day. We would be given some task like aiding the scribes in ordering the record rooms or binding new schoolbooks to send to the other villages. In that way, we were useful to society and learned how The Paramount was run. The final day of the three could be either a general information class or an application day, depending on the need of society.

At The Paramount, there didn't tend to be a lot of third-day application days. In some of the other villages, more application days were necessary during different seasons. For example, during the fall harvest, the children of The Golden Fields would have a lot of application days, in order to help bring in the crops. On the flip side, during the winter when there was little work to be done in the fields, the third day would always be schoolhouse classes.

The fourth day was a free day for all the children of The Clan. We could do whatever we wanted, as long as it wasn't prohibited. Mostly, I spent those days with Cole and the rest of my team, trying to defeat Bala and Jase's team or playing other strategy games.

Lost in my own thoughts, I hadn't heard what Myna had said next. I silently reproached myself. It was very important to pay attention. She could have been saying something that would give me an advantage in the trials. But most of what I had missed seemed to be a speech on using time wisely. Living in The Paramount, we had all been subjected to the same lecture nearly every day of our lives.

Finally, she finished, and we were free to decide which villages' training session we wanted to attend. A few of the other potentials hovered around, talking with each other. The air buzzed with excited chatter. I could see a few council members observing us already. They must have been noting which of us had taken the 'no wasting time' speech to heart.

As I tried to determine what useful skills I might learn at each different village, I quickly ran through them in my head. The Paramount first, of course; the very heart of The Clan. I was certain potentials would be taught organization and time management at The Paramount, neither of which I was lacking in.

Treescape next, where there was a large forest and a mill. They focused primarily on woodcutting and carpentry. The wood ration delivered to my dwelling each day came from that northern village. South of Treescape was The Quarry, which was where stonework and mining took place. Even farther south was The Farm. That was where animals were raised for wool, milk, and meat.

Due south of The Paramount itself was Riverside, a small village built right on the lakeshore. They used boats to fish the lake, but had to be careful not to go past the gentler waters into the strong currents of The Great River.

In the southeast, The Golden Fields could be found, surrounded by miles of orchards and fields. Excluding meat, that was the village where all of our food came from. It was easily the largest of the villages and actually had nine village leaders, instead of the customary five. The Barracks, which could be seen to the east of The Paramount, was full of soldiers and would be certain to provide some form of combat training.

North of The Barracks could be found The Making. It always gave the impression of being a peaceful place, filled with buildings of long halls where crafting, sewing, and weaving were done. Many of the common items found in each dwelling were produced there, everything from blankets to spoons. Lastly, due north of The Paramount and everything else, was The North Wind. It was the second smallest of The Clan's villages and a miserable place to live. Those who dwelt there were tasked with raising and training the horses that our society used. The village was located just west of The Valley of the North Wind. Besides crossing the raging river, which surrounded our large peninsula, The Valley of the North Wind was the only way into or out of The Land of the Clan.

Each village would undoubtedly teach something very different. The choice of where to train was being given to us for a reason; it had to be a test of the council. I needed to consider the choices before me carefully. The question was, what would I need most once the trials began? The answer was easy: food.

To that end, I had almost decided to go to The Golden Fields and begin learning about edible plants, when it suddenly struck me that it was the middle of winter, and the trials would take place in the summer. Even if there were any edible plants to be found in winter, that information would be useless. I would have to wait to study plants until the weather had turned warmer and the summer crops began to grow.

The council members were still watching us. In a flash, I decided I wanted to learn how to fight. If nothing else, the physical activity would help me build strength and endurance, both of which I was sure to need.

I caught Cole's eye, he'd been listening to Jase prattle on about something unimportant. I gave a little jerk of my head to the east and set off. If we left together, everyone would want to come with us and that wouldn't do. So, I headed off on my own, assuming he'd follow my lead.

The Barracks was only a mile and a half away, mostly east, but also a little south. Even in the dead of winter it wasn't a very difficult trip. The snow had been well-trodden on the path between the two villages and was easy to traverse.

I didn't mind the journey; in fact, I rather enjoyed it. When I had been younger and not yet old enough for Myna to leave behind, I had accompanied her on numerous trips to the other villages. Traveling and seeing the lands beyond The Paramount had always been an adventure. Plus, I had enjoyed feeling special, since so few people were allowed to spend the night in other villages.

However, as soon as I had been old enough to remain with another family, she had stopped taking me places with her. As a result, my visits to other villages had nearly completely subsided. Most of the villages were at least four or five miles away, and

THE PREPARATIONS

I'd always been too focused on school and leading my team to victory to make those kinds of excursions.

The Barracks turned out to be a popular destination. I observed dozens of other children traveling between the villages. Just like the night before, there were many colors of clothing all mixed together. It was unusual, but I supposed I would grow accustomed to seeing such a variance of shades over the course of the next six months.

The sun had just finished rising as I reached the outskirts of the village. I followed the stream of potentials to the town center where the arena, the largest structure in The Barracks, stood. It was circular and nearly identical to the council building of The Paramount, but it was at least ten times as large. Almost five hundred potentials had shown up, and we all fit inside.

The floor was loose dirt surrounded by walls that were several stories tall. Close to the roof, there were large, circular windows letting in light and cold air; however, with all the children packed in so tightly, I could barely feel the chill.

Kullin, one of the five village leaders of The Barracks, stood alone in the center of the room. Out of all of them, he was the oldest and most well-known. I had heard that the council had asked him to join them as an elder, but he had refused. There were a few other instructors scattered around the arena, ushering the potentials away from the door to make room for everyone.

I took a place close to the center, where I could see and where I would be sure not to miss anything. Most of the other children, however, moved away from Kullin, trying to stand in the back. The elderly village leader must have been nearly seventy, but he was covered in brawny muscles. His white hair was unkempt, and there was a slightly crazed look in the tawny eyes, which were set a hair too far apart. Despite the cold, he was wearing a short-sleeved tunic. It was a dark, burnt gold color, which was a few shades darker than his leathery skin.

As soon as the potentials had stopped filing in and were positioned in a loose circle around the arena, he uncrossed his arms and smiled at us in an almost threatening sort of way.

"My name is Kullin of The Barracks," he said. "I'm so glad you have come; we're going to have some fun now."

Just then, another child walked through the open doorway.

She was more of a woman than a child. The way she carried herself was mature, elegant even. Her hair, which flowed loosely over her shoulders and back, was a rich coppery-brown. She was muscularly built and at least three inches taller than me. A light dusting of freckles covered the high cheekbones of the girl's face, which was pretty enough, I supposed. The eyes were what stood out the most. They were slightly slanted and the brightest shade of green I had ever seen.

What really caught my attention was that the long cloak she wore was black. There was no village that had black as its color.

It wasn't a rule that you had to wear the color designated to your village, but most of us did. The Making, where cloth was woven and sewn into clothing, dyed each piece according to which village it was going to. It would be challenging to obtain a garment of a different color.

I couldn't think of why they would ever dye any clothing black. However, in addition to the cloak, the girl was wearing thick, black pants and black boots that came over her knees. She was probably also wearing a black shirt. I couldn't be certain, because from the waist up she was covered completely by the cloak. It was held together in the front with a silver button, and the ends of it fell just past her ankles. It was similar to my own, only longer, fuller and, of course, blacker.

Kullin turned on the girl like lightning and jabbed a crooked finger in her direction.

"You're late!" he growled. "You must not be from The Paramount." Laughter filled the room, and Kullin slapped his leg with mirth at his own statement.

The girl dipped her head, looking Kullin full in the face.

"No," the girl answered coolly. "I am not from The Paramount."

Kullin's laughter slowly died out. "Where are you from then?" he asked.

"I am Astra of The North Wind," the girl said. "I apologize for my untimely arrival, but I have had a long walk."

The North Wind, I mused internally. *How unusual.*

The North Wind had lots of stables and fields, but not many people and even fewer children.

Most parents were unwilling to raise their children in such a place. The hours were long, the work grueling, and injuries occurred frequently. I had also been told that the children who were there only went to school half the time. As a result, I supposed they were exceedingly ignorant.

Once, I'd overheard Rasby's father discussing the transfer list to The North Wind with a young scribe. He'd explained to her that they only got a handful every year, all of which were approved, because they never had enough workers to meet the numbers required by the village.

He'd gone on to say that most of the transfers were from young adults who had fictitious notations about how things would be. The majority would request to be relocated again after a few years.

Personally, I thought there were a lot of reasons not to want to live in The North Wind. They were a wayward bunch, only following the rules when it suited them. The order that had helped our people survive so long was lost on their simple minds.

Besides, it was always cold there. The village sat close to the mouth of The Valley of the North Wind. No matter where you were, you could always hear the howling of the wind as the icy current of air flowed out of the mountain pass. I couldn't abide the thought of the cold or the constant noise. It was the last place in The Land of the Clan any sensible person would want to live.

FIRST DAY

That girl, Astra, was exactly what I would have expected from someone of The North Wind. Her body was slender, but strong, used to hours of hard labor. Clearly, she didn't respect our traditions; otherwise, she would be wearing the gray clothes that belonged to The North Wind instead of the strange black attire. Plus, there was a touch of secrecy surrounding her, as there was around all who came from the cold northland.

Quickly, I decided we would never be friends. By the way she looked down her nose at the other potentials, I could tell she thought she was better than us. It was laughable really; she was the one who came from the least important of the villages. She might have a pretty face and be the best The North Wind had to offer, but that wouldn't get her very far in the trials.

"Well, Astra," Kullin said. "Since you are here now, why don't you help me with my first demonstration?"

He looked hard at Astra, daring her to say no, but she just nodded. Kullin turned back to the rest of us and started outlining a few basic attack moves. Astra stood next to him, not appearing at all uncomfortable at having been singled out in front of everyone.

She has guts, I grudgingly admitted to myself. Maybe we would get along better than I thought.

After describing a series of attacks—a quick knee jab to the stomach, a kick to the inner thigh, and a round of blows to the head—he turned to Astra and walked through the motions at half speed. Then he had Astra try them on him, so he could demonstrate the best way to block each move.

Astra glided through the series almost perfectly. Kullin only had to stop her once to correct the angle of her fists. After she was done, we were told to split into pairs and practice. Kullin and the other instructors would watch everyone and critique us as needed.

Glancing around, I noticed Cole for the first time. In my excitement, I'd forgotten I'd been waiting for him to show up. He must have slipped in just before Astra, with the last large group to arrive. Jase and Motik were with him. I pushed my way though the other potentials to reach Cole.

"There you are," I exclaimed. "I didn't see you come in. Want to be my partner?"

"Sure," Cole told me, glancing my way for only a moment.

"Great!" I said, but his attention had already turned back to the center of the arena, where Kullin still stood. "You go first," I told him.

"Right," he murmured, forcing himself to look at me. I shifted into a fighting stance ready to imitate what I had seen.

Cole was surprisingly fast for someone as tall and well-built as he was. In a real fight, he would be a powerful opponent. In practice, however, his strikes were so gentle it wasn't at all hard to fend them off. I blocked each one just as Kullin had shown us.

When it was my turn, I didn't go easy on him. However, since he was a foot taller and had at least fifty pounds on me, I wasn't worried about hurting him. Cole managed to stop all of my blows without difficulty.

Most of the other potentials were still trying to get the basic movements down, so Cole and I each went through the whole series of attacks and blocks again. The second time we were faster, smoother, and more confident. We were well-matched partners.

Off to our left, Jase and Motik were just finishing their second run-through as well. I noted that both boys seemed to have picked up the moves almost as quickly as Cole and myself.

Once we'd gone through the motions about five times, I was breathing rapidly. I glanced at Cole. He was panting too, and there was a slight sheen of sweat on his face. He gave me a bright smile, and I couldn't help but smile back. Internally, I felt the strong beat of my heart and the warmth of the blood flowing through my veins. I was alive.

"Very nice," Kullin said from somewhere behind me. I turned and gave him a nod of thanks. "You two are quick learners," he continued. "Next month, after things calm down a bit, we are going to be having an advanced training group that'll meet here in the evenings. I think you would both be good candidates to join."

I grinned. It was all going so perfectly. I hoped some of the elders observing the training session had witnessed our success. They had slipped in unnoticed by most while Kullin had been showing us the attacks.

"Thank you," I said. "We would be honored to learn more." Kullin nodded to us, and then headed toward a pair of younger potentials. They were no longer doing the moves we had been shown, but instead, were wrestling on the ground.

"That's going to be so great!" I said, turning to Cole.

He nodded his agreement, but his eyes weren't on me. Instead, he was looking at something, or someone rather, on the opposite side of the arena.

Astra.

The girl from The North Wind was paired with a blond guy, wearing the brown color of The Farm, who towered over her. He wasn't particularly muscular, but his stature made him intimidating all the same. I couldn't remember ever having seen him before, and, if I had, I was sure I wouldn't have forgotten.

Astra must have told him not to go easy on her, because he certainly wasn't. I could see the tremors running through her body as she attempted to block each blow. She missed one, and her partner kicked the inside of her leg, causing her to go down. The boy from The Farm froze, looking worried.

I wondered if she was going to cry, but she just bounced back to her feet and brushed the sand from her black clothing. She smiled and said something to her partner. I couldn't hear the words, but it appeared to make him relax, and the two continued sparring. A moment later, Kullin approached the pair and, I assumed, told them about the advanced fighting sessions.

Maybe Astra would be a good person to team up with after all. She seemed to have mastered all the moves and clearly wasn't too whiney when she got hit.

I glanced at Cole, who was still staring at her, and wondered if he was thinking the same thing. I wasn't sure I liked that.

Chapter 6

RASBY

The following morning, the bell again summoned us from our beds. I was the first to arrive in the town center. The pressing feeling that time was running out drove me from my dwelling early, even though I knew there would be nearly an hour of waiting.

The other potentials began slowly assembling, but after twenty minutes, only eight others had arrived. I wanted them to hurry up and take role so I could get on with training.

I nodded to Motik as he entered the town center. He bobbed his dirty-blond head in response but looked unsure of whether to approach me or not. In the end, he awkwardly took a place on the edge of the group, keeping his eyes on the ground and not speaking to anyone. I suppressed a sigh; he would make a fine contender if not for his debilitating shyness.

The air wasn't as bitter as it had been the day before, but it was still cold enough that I shivered inside my coat. The hem of my cloak had become sodden during my travels the previous day, so I'd left it to dry by the stove. The coat wasn't as warm, but I would have to make do.

I was actually looking forward to walking to The Barracks. It would give me a chance to get my blood flowing and fend off the chill.

I wish everyone else was here, so we could get a move on, I thought. Although, I was certain it wouldn't matter and roll would not be called early for any reason. We were in The Paramount after all.

THE PREPARATIONS

In contrast to Motik, Cole approached me immediately upon his arrival.

"I'm thinking we should go back to The Barracks for more combat training today," he told me. "What do you think?"

"I agree," I replied, without telling him that The Barracks had already been my intended destination.

Leaning closer to him, I quietly whispered, "The more the council sees us together, the more likely it is that they will put us on the same team. We should be sparring partners again today."

He nodded, a smile lighting his face. A great deal of the anxiety I'd been feeling abated. Most of my fears centered on the idea that I might end up on a team alone. I knew but a handful of children who were eligible as contenders. The day before, I had seen a great number of the potentials—hundreds of them—and that had not even been half of the total.

In the long run, I supposed it didn't matter. I would still work harder than anyone else to ensure my team's victory. However, the path would be incredibly smoother with Cole by my side.

I heard the sound of shuffling steps and turned to find Rasby approaching us. I hadn't seen her at all since leaving for The Barracks the previous day. She gave Cole a shy smile but spoke directly to me. "Where are you going today?"

"The Barracks," I told her.

Rasby nodded, but didn't look pleased. "Is that where you were yesterday?" She glanced between Cole and me.

Cole had moved away, heading toward Jase, who'd just arrived. For some reason, he was attempting to climb one of the two tall, wooden posts that held the village bell suspended between them. Cole said something to him, and an instant later he dropped back to the earth, but he didn't land properly and ended up on his butt in the snow.

I sighed; nothing new there. Jase was constantly making an idiot out of himself. At least he was always good for a laugh.

"Yes, I was at The Barracks yesterday," I said, returning my focus to Rasby. There was a moment of silence. "What about you?" I wondered curiously.

Rasby's gaze fell to the ground. "I—I stayed here," she stammered.

Typical Rasby.

"I didn't know where you had gone, and I didn't want to walk a long way in the snow." Her voice was so soft I had to strain to catch it, even in the quiet morning air.

I made no response; I just gave her a contemptuous look. We had spent most of our lives at The Paramount. I wouldn't deny that there was a lot of importance in what was done there. However, the primary purpose of The Paramount was to maintain an already formulated society. Little, if any, of what was done in my village related to surviving in a world where food and wood weren't delivered to your door every day.

Rasby wouldn't meet my eyes, but I was sure she could feel my disapproval, even without seeing it.

It took Rasby a moment to gather what little courage she actually possessed and find her voice. "Can I—can I come with you today?" she begged.

I sighed. Why was she having such a hard time understanding? If it was anyone else behaving this way, I would have told them 'no' on the spot. However, Rasby and I had been friends for a very long time, and it felt wrong to abandon her completely.

"Yes, you can come," I grudgingly agreed. An expression of joy crossed her face. "But Cole was my sparring partner yesterday, and we are going to be partners again today. So, you'll have to pair up with someone else." The hope that had gathered in Rasby's eyes when I'd said 'yes', vanished.

"We'll be sparring? Like fighting?" Her voice was thin and weak.

"Naturally," I replied flatly.

I was spared further conversation by the appearance of Falow, the Third Clan Leader. He had the list of names and quickly took roll. Only one child was absent, a girl named Chast. She had been coughing the previous day, and I imagined she was most likely worse. Her body was thin and weakly built; it would probably be for the best that she stayed indoors. Clearly, she was too weak to cope with the elements.

As soon as Falow had finished calling roll, we dispersed. I fell into step with Cole and tried to ignore Rasby, trailing behind me like a stray lamb. Jase joined us too, walking on the opposite side of Cole. There was still a fair amount of snow caked to his coat from his earlier mishap.

I noticed Bala heading west with Ashlo, a member of my Attack and Defend team. A few others were with them. Larna, the ugly girl, was heading northeast with her friend Flant and the two sisters, Teira and Tirea.

The walk to The Barracks was much more enjoyable with companions. While Jase was foolish, he wasn't annoying. I actually found him quite humorous. Not, of course, that he said things either witty or clever, but his stupidity was quite laughable. He didn't seem to mind making himself the butt of the joke, often laughing longer and louder than either Cole or myself.

Rasby didn't laugh once. She spent the whole of our journey struggling not to fall even farther behind. Occasionally, I would hear her whining that we were going too fast. Cole was the only one who bothered slackening the pace to accommodate her.

Long before we reached The Barracks, I was a hundred percent certain that I did not want Rasby on my team. She was so pathetic.

Just before entering the arena, I glanced back at her, still fifty yards behind us, shuffling forward at an uneven gait. I didn't bother waiting since the lesson was going to be starting at any moment.

Once I was inside with the boys, I stood as close to Cole as I could, ready to be his partner again. I knew he planned to pair up with me, but I feared he was too kind-hearted to say no if someone else asked him.

Turning in a slow circle, Cole scanned the faces of the other potentials. I tried to pretend he was just sizing up those who might be his teammates or his competition, but I knew that wasn't the case. Deep down, I could easily guess who he was looking for.

I didn't understand why she had left such an impression on him, but, apparently, she had. Astra had left a strange impression on me too, and I was more than a little relieved to see that she was not in attendance. Although, she had been late the previous morning and might appear without warning, since those of The North Wind cared nothing for timeliness.

Cole's eyes turned toward the door as another potential entered, but it was just Rasby.

She looked awful. There was a strangled, wheezing noise coming from her as she gasped for breath. Her face was blotchy and covered in tears. I wasn't sure if she had been crying or if the cold had simply caused her eyes to water. Even when she came to stand beside me, I tried not to notice.

Looking at her out of the corner of my eye, I wasn't sure why we had ever been friends. How had I put up with her all those years? Well, we were done now. She had nothing to offer me, and I wasn't interested in carrying her weight during the trials.

She probably wouldn't survive anyway.

That thought brought me up short. I felt a slight twinge in my heart, but I was sure I wouldn't be able to complete the trials with Rasby in tow. Sometimes sacrifices had to be made, no matter how painful, in order to achieve our goals. My mother had shown me that.

I comforted myself with the thought that Rasby would probably never become a contender—definitely not, if the council was watching her now. I hoped they were. Rasby was meant to stay in The Land of the Clan. She didn't want to leave, and she would never be able to survive beyond the borders of our land. Plus, there was no way she would ever win, so what was the point? It would be better for everyone involved if she could just remain behind.

With such reasoning, I could nearly assure myself that while the trials were going on, Rasby would be safe and sound in The Paramount. My only concern should be making certain I wasn't seen with her, so they wouldn't choose to make me remain behind as well. It would be an unbearable fate.

I took another step closer to Cole, away from Rasby, and didn't so much as glance in her direction.

The rest of the morning, as I sparred with Cole, I could feel Rasby watching me miserably. I ignored her. She didn't want to participate in the trials; I did. We couldn't be together. I would not risk my chances of being chosen for her. I think she knew it too, because at the end of the day she headed back to The Paramount alone. I stayed a little longer with Cole, to receive some extra instructions from Kullin. I took careful note of the fact that Jase chose not to join us.

Cole and I walked back to The Paramount together as the sun began to set into a bank of dark clouds. The days were so short. It felt like we had only been training for a couple of hours, not the whole morning and half of the afternoon.

It was just the two of us walking back, and the only sound was our footsteps crunching in the snow.

"What should we plan to do next time?" I asked, breaking the silence.

"Well, tomorrow we have our normal studies," Cole said. "Although, I can't imagine being able to concentrate on them." There was laughter in the way Cole spoke, but beneath it, I sensed a great intensity. "After that, we have our day off."

I nodded. "But on our next training day?" I pressed, curious to see what strategy he would formulate.

"I feel like we're getting pretty good at the basic combat tactics." I nodded in agreement to his words. "And I'm sure there is other stuff that will be just as important to learn. So, maybe we should try a different village next time," he concluded.

"I think you're right," I told him. "It's just hard to know what would be best to focus on. Combat seems the most important to me. It'll make our bodies strong and prepare us for just about any situation." My voice dropped to a whisper. "Especially since there's always the chance that we might run into a Broken."

Cole scowled. "As long as I live, I hope I never meet a Broken."

I couldn't have agreed more with that statement.

The Broken were *the others*, a handful of people who lived outside The Land of the Clan. They were rule-breakers and exiles, infected by the same darkness that had attacked our ancestors. They would do horrible things to anyone from The Clan they found beyond our borders. Something was wrong with them; they were evil, malicious, and violent. Truly broken inside.

Cole was silent for a moment. "I wonder what Astra did today," he said, completely changing the subject.

I froze dead in my tracks. "What?"

Cole, who had continued on a step or two, turned back to me. "Astra, that girl who came in late the first day," he explained, as though I might have forgotten.

I briskly took a step forward, and we resumed walking. "I remember who she is, but why do you care what she did today?"

I watched his face intently, trying to read his thoughts, but there wasn't much for me to pick up on. He shrugged. "She seemed pretty sharp. I wonder if she knows what other skills we'll need out there and where to learn them."

Cole had never even spoken to her, so how could he presume to know her intelligence? I narrowed my eyes, trying to recall a single action that might lead one to believe she was 'pretty sharp'. Nothing came to mind. If anything, I judged her haughty façade to be covering for her own insecurities.

"Maybe Astra was sick today," I suggested, trying not to sound too hopefully. "It's a long walk from here to The North Wind. It was probably dark by the time she got back; I can't imagine she was feeling very well this morning."

Cole nodded. "You might be right. Does seem a little unfair."

That was the end of the conversation and of our talking for the rest of the trip back to The Paramount.

The instant Cole headed towards his family's dwelling, Rasby appeared. She must have been waiting for me for some time, knowing I would walk back with Cole and leave him where our paths split.

She looked better than she had earlier in the day. Her face was washed and her hair was combed. She wasn't crying now, but was biting her lip and had a look on her face that warned she might break down at any moment.

I stopped several feet away from her. We faced each other in silence. She wanted to say something, but I could see she was trying to work up the nerve to get it out. It didn't matter; I could be patient.

Finally, Rasby spoke, and what she said was the very last thing I had expected.

"Myra," she began, faltering a little but getting more confident as she persisted, "I want to be like you. I'm tired of being the weak one, the crybaby. Please help me be strong. I want to do well in the trials. I want to make my family proud. Will you help me and teach me?"

I actually considered her offer for about ten seconds, but I knew better than to agree. How could I? There were only five months until the teams were announced. If I spent all that time with Rasby, trying to help her, it would mean we would end up on the same team for sure. And I did not want her on my team.

"No," I told her, noticing that her eyes started to water. She managed to hold back the tears, maybe for the first time in her life.

"Please, Myra," she whispered. "My brothers are too old for the trials, and you're my best friend. Why won't you help me? I can't do this alone!"

"Rasby, I need to focus on my own training right now. It's your responsibility to worry about yourself."

There was a moment of silence, and then I continued. "You want to be strong? You have to do it alone."

The shock that crossed her face at my harsh words almost made me cringe. I knew I was causing her a lot of pain, but I would not relent.

"They were right." Her words were practically a whisper.

"Who was right?" I asked impatiently.

"Tiera and Tirea," she answered.

I curled my lip in disgust. Rasby had always liked Tiera and Tirea. They were the only other girls willing to put up with her.

The pair was intolerable, and I had made it clear that I wouldn't have anything to do with them when I could avoid it. For the most part, Rasby had appeared to cut ties with them, probably hoping to gain my approval. However, it seemed that she hadn't been completely honest about her relationship with them, if they were the ones she'd turned to for advice.

I rolled my eyes, not even certain why I was bothering to continue the pointless conversation.

"They normally aren't, but what about this time?" I asked, the words I spoke dripping with derision.

"That you were never really my friend," Rasby answered. There was a mountain of pain in her voice, and, I had to admit, the statement did cut me to the core.

"It's unfair to say something like that," I told her. "We've had many good times together, but our lives are taking us separate directions now. It's better if we do it this way. You don't really want to be in the trials, but I do. If we are always together, one of us won't get what we want."

"I wouldn't mind the trials at all, if I could be with you," Rasby desperately pleaded. "Really, if you were there, it would be fun!"

"What you mean is, if you were on my team for the trials, you know I would handle everything and you could just enjoy the ride while I did all the work."

"No," Rasby promised. "I would work hard and learn to be strong and brave, just like you."

"I don't believe you," I told her. "You'll never be anything like me."

Hurt, real hurt, crossed Rasby's face, and her gaze dropped to the ground.

When she spoke, her voice was so small I had to strain to hear each word she said. "You don't want me with you, then? I mean, you don't want me on your team?"

I wanted to ask her what use she thought she'd be to me in the world beyond The Land of the Clan. I already knew the answer. None.

"That's why we need to go our separate ways. We don't belong together anymore," I explained, hoping to make her understand the situation. I should have taken that approach to begin with, tried to make her see that I only wanted to protect her. I hadn't meant the words to come out like they had, but it was too late now.

Rasby's face slowly lifted until she was looking me in the eyes again, head shaking slightly. "You were never really my friend at all." She hesitated. "Do you even like me?"

I swallowed. Deep inside, I was sorry—very, very sorry. Not that the things I had said to Rasby weren't true, but I wished I had been able to persuade her more to my way of thinking. Why couldn't she understand that everything had changed in the last forty-eight hours, and there was no going back now?

"Of course. It was always nice having you around." I regretted the words the moment I spoke them, wishing, yet again, that I had taken a completely different strategy. I should have played on her desire to stay safe inside The Land of the Clan. I should have told her that we would never have gotten on the same team and that I would have spent the whole time we were apart sick with worry. Maybe I could have even convinced her that we would be secret friends until the trials were over. That way, she wouldn't have to leave, but I still could.

Rasby was so stupid; I could have made her believe almost anything.

No, I told myself. *The truth is better. She'll be nothing but an obligation as a real friend or a secret friend. It's better that this ends now.*

Besides, it was too late to worry about that. Maybe later, once she had cooled off, I could talk to her. Explain that I wanted everyone to think we weren't friends anymore, but that I didn't really mean it.

My last words seemed to have hit a hidden trigger in Rasby. The sad, scared look in her muddy brown eyes evaporated and was replaced by anger.

"Is that it?" she shouted. "Nine years I've considered you my best friend, and I was 'nice to have around'? I wasn't your friend! I was just your follower! Someone you needed to make you feel like you had a friend! Well, it might have been fake for you, but the whole thing was real for me! I loved you and looked up to you! You're stupid and fake and—" Rasby's yelling was cut off by a sudden choking sob. I had never seen Rasby angry in my life. She turned from me and fled, probably to cry to her mother or whoever else she could find willing to listen.

She had done the exact same thing many times since I had known her, but that time it felt more final, like she was never coming back. I told myself I didn't care, but as my feet carried me towards my dwelling, I was already missing Rasby, just a little.

I wrestled with my own thoughts for a while before I could reconcile everything in my head. Rasby had said she wanted to be strong. Well, Myna's coldness and absence had made me strong.

Rasby doesn't matter, I told myself over and over. *There is only one thing that matters, and anything that stands in its way has to go.*

Even while repeating those words to myself, I was fighting back tears. I arrived at my dwelling and flung the door open, desperate for a place to hide.

Chapter 7

AMBITION

As soon as the door shut behind me, the main room of the dwelling was plunged into complete darkness. I struck a match and lit a candle. By its light, I hurried to my own room. It was freezing inside the dwelling. The fire had gone out completely while I'd been at training. With shaking hands, I grabbed a blanket from my bed to drape over the coat I still wore, trying to insulate my body against the frigid air.

I returned to the main room and balanced on the edge of the table to kick off my boots. They were damp from tramping around in the snow. Only years of habit made me pick them up from the floor and place them in the shoe niche, which was carved into the wall by the front door. My summer shoes were already inside, and there was still room for at least four other pairs, but mine were normally the only ones occupying the space.

The designers must have expected us to have company from time to time, so there was a matching hollow on the opposite side of the door. The thought was wasted on my dwelling. For as long as I could remember, not a single pair of shoes had been placed in the second niche. No one ever came here except Myna and myself, and neither of us lingered long. I had never asked anyone to come in, choosing instead to visit them at a neutral location.

Looking at the unfilled hole in the wall, I could no longer press down my feelings. The harsh words I'd exchanged with Rasby had rattled me far more than I cared to admit. A few tears

THE PREPARATIONS

were ready to fall from my eyes, when, suddenly, I heard a sound from Myna's room, and I realized I wasn't alone.

I was so shocked that the incident with Rasby went straight out of my head. It had been ages since the last time I had returned to find her in our dwelling while there was still light in the sky.

Something inside me stirred, something I had thought was buried too deep to ever emerge. I had the sudden impulse to knock on Myna's door and tell her all that had transpired. Still standing by the front door, I half raised my hand, imagining my knock.

An instant later, I dismissed the notion and lowered my hand as I turned to go to my own room. It was one thing to experience a private moment of regret, but I could never let anyone, especially Myna, see that weakness.

Just as I reached for my doorknob, Myna emerged behind me. I didn't mean to, but I couldn't help glancing back to look at her.

She was dressed in traveling clothes. They were all the maroon color of The Paramount, a darker and richer shade than most of my own. In her hand she held a pack, which was stuffed with papers. Clearly, she was preparing for a journey.

Seeing her about to leave reminded me of the times, many years ago, when I had traveled with her. On those journeys, Myna had been forced to spend several hours alone with me on the road. She'd almost never responded to any of my attempts at conversation, but we had still been together and that had meant something to me.

Not anymore. I didn't crave her attention as I once had. I despised the part of myself that still longed for those days. But no matter how much I swore I didn't care if I ever saw Myna again, I caught myself wishing I could go with her.

The conflict inside kept me from saying anything as she gathered some food from the table. Wordlessly, I turned to head into my room until she was gone. Her voice behind me came as a shock—we hadn't spoken in days.

"Myra, I have to leave The Paramount for the night. There are some things that must be dealt with in one of the other villages. I expect to return by tomorrow afternoon at the latest." She wasn't looking at me. Her eyes were focused on her bag, which she was repacking to make sure none of the papers were crumpled.

"Since it's forbidden for one person to remain alone in a dwelling, you'll be staying with your friend, Rasby, and her family tonight."

I bit back a scream of frustration at the terrible timing of her announcement. The rule was actually that one person couldn't use a wood ration when no one else shared their dwelling. During the summer when Myna traveled, no one cared if I was alone for a day or two. Unfortunately, warmer nights were several months away.

The fight between Rasby and myself less than twenty minutes ago, came to my mind. I flinched at the idea of being close to her.

I was sure she had already tattle-tailed the details of our falling out to her parents, not that they would have gotten the truth. Rasby was far too emotional to present my side of the argument as a sound, logical perspective to a complicated and unsolvable problem. I was certain she'd make me out to be a cold-hearted backstabber in any recount she gave.

"I do not wish to stay with Rasby's family," I said in the coolest voice I could muster. Half of me hoped that the abrupt statement would shock Myna into wondering if something was wrong. If she would only ask, I might be willing to confess the things I had said to Rasby. However, I was spared from the regret of that divulgence.

"I am afraid that's too bad," Myna told me, without even looking up. She finished rearranging her bag and began tightening the straps to hold it shut. "I arranged everything with her father this morning."

As soon as the bag was tied properly, she shouldered it and headed for the door.

"No." I said the rebellious word sharply.

She didn't stop, didn't even pause; her hand was already on the handle. Instead, the words she spoke were thrown over her shoulder without any emotion in them whatsoever. "You know the rules, please abide by them." With that, she was gone, and the room warmed ten degrees.

Tears blurred my vision, and I again nearly lost the battle with my emotions. After several deep breaths, I managed to blink the liquid from my eyes. Crying was unacceptable. It was a vulnerable and violent form of emotion; it always left me feeling weak and uncontrolled.

Instead, I tried to clear my mind and forget. Even once I was no longer in danger of shedding tears, it took longer than I'd like to admit to compose myself. I spent nearly half an hour sitting on the floor, doing nothing but watching my breath create little, wispy clouds. The candle was my only source of warmth, since I was forbidden to build a fire. In my present calm, I did not feel hungry or tired. I didn't feel anything. It was better that way.

I had no desire to move until morning. My coat was still in place, with the blanket over it. The room would only get colder, but I would have rather faced a long night of icy temperatures, than whatever I would encounter at Rasby's.

The need to follow the rules was beginning to weigh on my mind. Soon it was a presence I could no longer ignore. Just as Myna had said, I was required by the laws of my people to be somewhere else. The candle had nearly burned itself out by the time I finally rose. Slowly, I pulled my damp boots back on, extinguished the small flame, and departed.

Outside, the sun had set and there was only the faintest trace of its light on the horizon. My feet began walking, but they did not take me to where I was supposed to spend the night. Instead, I ended up outside of Cole's dwelling.

Specks of light had found their way out through cracks in the mortar of the stone walls. Something was cooking on the hearth. Even from outside, I could smell the delicious aroma of roasting meat.

I wondered what Cole would say if I told him what had happened that afternoon. It would confuse him unless I also explained other things as well. Things that nobody knew, like how Myna and I hardly spoke, and why I always felt it was better to be alone.

If I did tell him everything, would he even like me anymore? Would he still want me to be on his team? Or would I lose another friend?

I wasn't a good person. Sometimes I pretended to be, so people would think I was sweet and kind and compassionate and caring. But I knew the truth; I wasn't any of those things. Not that anyone really was from my experience. There was always an ulterior motive to the nice things people did.

Cole was the exception to the rule. He'd never seemed to want anything from me in exchange for my friendship. If there was such a thing as a perfect human being, he was it. That was why I couldn't knock on his door and pour out all my pain to him. If he ever saw me for what I really was, he would be repulsed.

I didn't knock. I never knocked. Haltingly, I turned away. It wouldn't do for someone to see me lingering there.

The snowdrifts were still piled high along the edge of the village. I tramped through them until I arrived at Rasby's dwelling. Cliv, Rasby's father, was gathering an armload of wood from a small pile by the door. He was a small man, only half an inch taller than I was. His dark hair was sprinkled with gray. His eyes, the same mud color as Rasby's, were usually friendly to all.

THE PREPARATIONS

I dreaded how he would look at me, but he didn't seem displeased at all by my arrival. Perhaps, Rasby had not yet explained the situation to him.

"Hello Myra," Cliv called cheerfully. He pulled the front door wide with his free arm, allowing me entry. He followed me in and began restocking the woodpile by the hearth.

I'd expected the atmosphere to be hostile, but everything was relaxed. The dwelling wasn't spick and span, but felt lived in, with stray cobwebs in the ceiling corners and old ashes swept lazily beneath the stove. There was a warm glow coming from the fire, and three oil lamps brightly illuminated the entire space.

Rasby was sitting on a cushion at the low table in the middle of the room, eyes fixed on the floor. Her mother, Rasky, was just bringing a plate of roast beef over from the hearth. She set it on the round center of the table, which was a thin, circular piece of stone overlaying the wood. All tables were designed that way so you would have a place to put hot pots and pans without damaging the wood. The stone plaque on my table was covered in a quarter inch of dust.

Rasby's older brother, Clin, was sitting at the table opposite his sister on another cushion. Their mother set a tray of boiled vegetables beside the beef, before taking her place on a third cushion.

Cliv motioned for me to sit as well. I knew I was expected to take the extra place beside Rasby. She still wasn't looking at me, but I kicked off my boots and dropped into the spot next to her without hesitation.

The first thing I did was to make my apologies for being late and express my gratitude for being allowed to stay the night with them while Myna was absent. After that formality was completed, I tucked into the food. Rasky wasn't an amazing cook, but her food was much better than anything I could make. After a couple bites of the juicy meat, I felt my appetite return in full force.

The family's conversation quickly turned to Rasby's oldest brother, Clev, who had recently transferred to Riverside. He was apparently becoming a wonderful swimmer and was enjoying learning how to handle boats on the small lake.

It made me glad to hear that he was fitting in so well and that he had discovered what he wanted to do with his life. Both of Rasby's brothers were a good five years older than I was. Even though I had been in school with the pair for several years, the age distance had kept us from spending much time together. However, I had been well-informed of their activities by Rasby. She loved to boast about their skills and accomplishments as if they were her own. That evening though, not a word passed her lips, save to ask for a second helping of every dish on the table.

It was surprising that no one addressed Rasby's lack of conversation. She was the loud one in her family, and her mother usually had to warn her repeatedly not to talk with her mouth full.

After the meal was over and the dishes cleaned and carefully put away, Rasby headed for bed immediately. I dreaded sharing her room, even for one night, but it was my duty.

As I turned to follow her, Cliv spoke. "Myra, I'd like to speak to you for a moment. If it's not too cold for you, would you step outside with me?"

Too cold? For me? There would never be anywhere colder than where I had lived the past eleven years. I grabbed my coat, stepped into my boots, and followed Rasby's father through the front door.

"It'll probably be at least two more months before the first thaw," Cliv announced, as he paused just outside the dwelling. His eyes were on the dark horizon. A heavy overlay of clouds had choked out all the starlight. Not even the more lustrous silver beams of the moon could pierce the thick shroud.

I didn't answer directly, but nodded when he turned his gaze my way. Rasby and I had been friends a long time, and I was no stranger to her family. Cliv had spent enough time with

THE PREPARATIONS

me to understand that small talk wasn't really going to get him anywhere or make me feel more comfortable.

He let out a sigh, and I could tell he was about to try the direct approach. "Look, Myra, the trials are a very hard time for everyone."

I opened my mouth to protest, but he raised his hand to stop my words. "I know, you're probably excited—a lot of potentials are—but that doesn't mean that it still isn't hard for you. So much has changed in a very short time. All your priorities have shifted. You've begun looking towards a new and different future, and, well, you can start behaving differently."

He was silent for a moment, but I knew he had more to say. My instinct was to be defensive, but that would imply I felt I had done something wrong, so I resolved to hear him out before speaking.

"I know Rasby hasn't taken any of this very well, and you don't want that to reflect poorly on you. It's understandable." He licked his lips quickly, and then hurried on, as if he had been planning his speech all the way through dinner.

"She's not like you, Myra. You are the most intense person I have ever met. It will serve you well in life. You will always be the best—or close to it—but it won't necessarily make you happy in the end."

He shook his head. "Sometimes, I think of you, with no one really to talk to, and I wonder how you keep all that passion bottled up inside. You've used it to excel in school and everything else you've ever done. Now, you think you see a chance to make all your dreams come true, and you've latched onto it, desperate to prove your true ability.

"I know I'm not your father, and you don't have to listen to me. But I understand, I really do. I was young and ambitious once..." he trailed off for a moment.

Our eyes met. *It's not true,* I thought. *You might think you know me, but you don't. No one does.* My gray eyes must have given some hint of my thoughts.

Cliv looked away, out to the west. "I'd like to tell you something. Something that I've never told another person before, but it has to be just between us." He glanced at me, and I nodded, giving him my word.

"I was born and raised Cliv of The Quarry, a young man with all the skills to be a great mason or stonecutter or anything I wanted to be.

"The work in The Quarry was enjoyable, but I always felt called to something higher, like there was a need for me to be better than anyone expected.

"When I was old enough to put in for a transfer, I did. I wanted to come to The Paramount and do great things for The Clan. My transfer request was rejected. It's very hard to get a transfer to The Paramount.

"I was required to wait a year before I could apply a second time. Again, I was denied, but I had made up my mind and was willing to wait another year and try once more. A few months later, I met her.

"Feela was her name, and I—I fell for her hard. She liked me too, and pretty soon we had an image in our heads of a perfect little home for the two of us.

"There was only one problem, she didn't want to leave The Quarry. All of her family lived there, and she was content.

"But I wasn't." Cliv's voice dropped to a whisper. "We argued about it fiercely many times. She tried her best to persuade me to give up on my impossible desire, but I would not relent. Finally, Feela acquiesced. I'll never forget the night she told me, with tears in her blue eyes, that she'd follow me anywhere."

Cliv's voice was breathless. He seemed to have been drawn into that time, many years ago, when the events he spoke of had transpired. Back when he had been a very different person, with different goals and different dreams. It took a moment before he found the words to continue.

"Another year passed." Cliv's voice was softer, filled with churning emotions. "I applied again for a transfer to The Para-

THE PREPARATIONS

mount and, for a third time, was denied. It was so infuriating. I had been a model member of The Clan my entire life and, without any explanation, I was being refused once more.

For two weeks, I contented myself with the plan of continuing to be patient. However, the passion inside of me would not give me any peace in The Quarry. I woke up in the middle of the night a few days later and walked to The Paramount. Once dawn arrived, I demanded to see the council, determined to discover what their reason was for rejecting me.

"Of course, I was not admitted to see them. It's doubtful that they were even informed of my presence. My only option was to turn around and go home. I was defeated; I didn't have any hope left.

"On my way out of the village, I saw Rasky for the first time, and a new plan came into my mind." Cliv, who had turned his attention to the west again, suddenly looked at me very hard. "I am ashamed now of what I did then, so very ashamed. I spent the next three months traveling to The Paramount to spend time with Rasky. As soon as I felt she might accept me, I asked her to be my life mate."

Cliv paused, letting his words sink in. It was a new concept to me, the idea that someone might choose a life mate for the sole purpose of being admitted to a new village. It was hard to get a transfer to The Paramount, sure, but the idea was beyond anything even I could have schemed up.

"Feela was heartbroken, of course," Cliv went on. "I was too, but couldn't show it. Even now, the words I said to her hurt me to think of. I told her that she had never meant anything to me. That she had just been something to keep myself occupied with until I could arrange my transfer. She didn't believe a word of it. She knew the truth—what I had done and why. But she still loved me, and she still cared about me just enough to let me get away with it."

Cliv raised his hand to rub his forehead slowly. A cold wind began blowing from the north. It tugged at the hem of my coat, and I could feel more than see the small flurry of snowflakes it brought with it.

"I've nearly achieved my ambition; I'm here in The Paramount. Maybe one day soon they'll ask me to be a village leader, but then again, they might not." Cliv let out a long sigh.

"It doesn't matter so much anymore," he told me. "I do love Rasky, very much, but she will never be the perfect life mate Feela could have been.

"The years have changed the way I see my life. Everything I used to think I wanted seems superficial. I've done well enough for my ambition to be content.

"However, I'll never know what I gave up. What the path I didn't take might have been. Or what my life with Feela could have looked like."

Even the wind was silent as Cliv concluded his narrative. "I'm sorry," he apologized. "I didn't mean to drop all of this on you, but I think you can understand what I'm saying. Ambition is powerful. It might be the only thing that can lead you to your goal, but once you get there, you'll have to look back and see all the other opportunities you missed. I just want you to be careful. Life is a hard road, but you don't have to walk it alone."

He was wrong. I had always been alone. I would always be alone. The pretense of walking with others was something I had given up long ago.

I was the only one I could depend on, the only one I could trust. My entire life had taught me to keep people out, and that wasn't going to change just because one man, who wasn't my father, told me that I might not be happy when I got to the end of my road. He was wrong. I knew what I wanted, and I would get it, no matter the cost.

"I hope you find happiness on whatever path you take," Cliv said. He smiled gently and pulled me into a quick embrace. It came so unexpectedly that I didn't respond at all. A moment later, he released me, and we headed back inside.

THE PREPARATIONS

When I entered Rasby's room, she was pretending to be asleep. She'd left enough space on her bed for me to join her there, but I just grabbed an extra blanket and lay down on the floor. I had much to think about, but I wouldn't change my mind. Until the trials were completed, I couldn't be Rasby's friend.

It would have felt nice to cry myself to sleep that night, like letting all the stress of the day that had built upon my shoulders drain from my body. But even though I was finally in the dark, where no one would see, I couldn't seem to bring forth the flood of tears I had held in twice that day already. So, I just lay awake a long time, staring into the blackness above my head.

Chapter 8

ASTRA

Rasby's snoring woke me before the village bell was even rung. My body was stiff and cramped from sleeping on the floor all night. The past two mornings I had risen full of vigor and excitement, but not that morning. There was no training to be excited for, only school.

Still, I didn't linger in my slumber, but rose and gathered together my things. I hadn't brought much with me, so I was ready to face the day in a matter of minutes. Rasby hadn't even stirred from her bed.

I left her to her sleep and headed to the main room. Rasky was there; she greeted me with a sunny smile and a warm piece of bread, fresh from the oven. It was slathered with gravy from the drippings of the previous night's roast beef.

Rasky looked very much like an older version of Rasby, with the same wild, frizzy hair, heavy build, and ruddy complexion. She had a kind face, but she was constantly squinting due to ailing vision.

I sat down to eat my breakfast at the table and wondered how early she must have risen to make sure the rest of us would have a hot breakfast. My hope was to escape the dwelling before Rasby got up. I didn't want to have to walk to school with her.

As I swallowed the last crumbs of my breakfast and leapt to my feet, Rasby emerged from her room. A red mark across her cheek showed where she had been sleeping. Her tangled hair was tied back out of her face, revealing a pair of sullen eyes.

THE PREPARATIONS

Wordlessly, she declined the piece of bread her mother tried to give her and walked to the door.

I followed, quite shocked. I had never seen Rasby turn down food before. Cliv was outside, just returning to the dwelling with a fresh bucket of water.

He smiled warmly when the two of us emerged. I hoped he wasn't getting any kind of false hope that Rasby and I had patched up our relationship.

"Good morning, girls," Cliv greeted us.

"Morning," I replied.

"Morning, Dad," Rasby echoed distantly.

"Your mother should be back tonight, Myra," he told me. "But if she's not, you're more than welcome to stay with us again." Rasby didn't appear any more thrilled by that idea than I felt.

"Do you know which village she went to?" I asked, wondering for the first time what business had called her away so late the previous evening.

"She went to The North Wind," Cliv answered over his shoulder, as he vanished into the dwelling.

I expected that Rasby would wait for him to reappear, since the records building where he worked was on the way to the schoolhouse. Rasky would also be heading out soon; her position was a simple one. After Rasby had turned six and begun attending school, Rasky had been assigned to paper making. While the product they produced was important, the job seemed menial to me.

Instead of waiting for either of her parents, Rasby trailed me as I headed for the school building. I had no idea how I would keep my mind on the lessons. With the trials going on and Myna vanishing so suddenly—to The North Wind of all places—it seemed school would be the least interesting thing I would be presented with that day.

Last time Myna had been gone overnight, she'd been at Treescape. I had never heard all of the particulars, but the rumor was that one of the woodcutters had been stealing wood and using it wastefully.

After the investigation, the man had been declared insane. He had even gone so far as to take pieces of his house apart and then use the scavenged bits to try to fasten the wood together. No one knew what his intent had been, but everyone knew that what he had been doing was wasteful and dangerous.

If something was necessary, it was created where they had the proper tools and designs. Anyone stealing materials that belonged to the community for their own personal use was considered a disgrace. The man was deemed extremely dangerous and unpredictable. He was sentenced to exile, the strictest punishment our people had, which was reserved only for the worst offenders of our laws.

The schoolroom was mostly empty when I reached it. Even the teachers hadn't arrived. I took my seat, thankful that Rasby had to sit two rows in front of me, so I wouldn't have to feel her watching me all day.

A few minutes before class began, Cole arrived, and I gave him the best smile I could manage. He waved at me, and then headed to his seat, off to my left.

In some of the villages, where there were lots of children, the students were divided by age. Not in The Paramount; there were too few of us, usually only about forty in all.

We sat on rows of benches with long tables in front of us. The building was designed like the amphitheater. Each row was a step above the one before it, so those in the back would be able to see. The room could have easily sat three times as many. There were six empty tiers behind me, which had never been filled.

My assigned seat was positioned on the far-right aisle, so I had only one neighbor, a thirteen-year-old boy named Hinn. He was small and quiet, never asking me for help or trying to cheat off my work, so we got along fine.

There must have been something wrong with his nose though, because sometimes he got attacked by violent sneezing fits. Oddly, they never came on during the winter, when most people were sick, but during the spring, when it started to warm up. A couple times last year, the teachers had sent Hinn to rest in his dwelling because he had been unable to stop sneezing. The village healer had taken a look at him and had said nothing was wrong, but that some people were just prone to sneezing.

Hinn was not there as I took my seat. I tried to prepare myself for the coming lecture, but it turned out that my earlier assumption had been correct. I was unable to focus on anything being taught. We finally took the test Jase had been dreading. I hadn't thought about it or studied for it in the past two days, but I still got a perfect score.

Our teachers were mostly elderly people, who weren't strong enough physically or mentally to work a full day as a clerk or scribe. They were often grumpy, and that morning was no exception.

Everyone else seemed to be having the same concentration problems as I, which did nothing to improve the teachers' temperaments. Normally, I enjoyed school, but with the preparations going on, it seemed so pointless.

After failing the test, Jase spent the entire time staring through a crack in one of the shutters. He didn't get a single answer right when called on, but that was pretty normal for him. Rasby pretended to be paying attention, but I observed her doodling all over her paper. Normally, she would have been reprimanded for wasting resources, but neither of the teachers noticed. She pretended to be taking notes whenever they looked her way.

Larna, a row in front of me and a few seats to the left, kept whispering to her neighbor, Flant. He was about as ugly as a person could be and still live. His body was flabby, he already appeared to be going bald, and his face was mushy. They made the perfect couple.

The pair usually only whispered to each other if we had instructors who were hard of hearing. The teachers that day clearly were not and kept chiding them for talking, giving each several demerit marks, which made me smile. I had never received more than one demerit mark any day in my entire life. The two would end up having to do all the school chores themselves; at least it would give the hideous pair more time to bond.

Tiera and Tirea were also whispering constantly, but they were smart enough not to get caught. Maybe I had underestimated those two. They were certainly more intelligent than Rasby and much cleverer than Larna and Flant.

Across the room from me, Cole's gaze was front and center; however, there was a distant look in his eyes, and I sensed that in his mind he was far away.

Afterwards, I couldn't remember one thing the teachers had said, except when they had given marks to Larna and Flant, both of whom did end up having to do all the school chores, which suited me perfectly.

As soon as we were dismissed, there was a mad dash for the door. Everyone had kept their energy bottled up all day, and it seemed to explode as we poured out of the school.

I caught up with Cole a short way from the building. He saw me heading his direction and stopped to wait.

"That was the longest day of my life," he announced.

"Mine too. I didn't think it would ever end. Where are you off to?" I asked.

"I'm going to the council building," he replied. "I'm supposed to meet up with my father. He's been so busy lately, but he promised to leave the meeting early today, so we could spend some time together. I'm going to show him the sparring moves we've been learning."

Cole was so enthusiastic that I didn't point out the fact that Core had probably gone through the same training as we had during the preparations for the last trials.

THE PREPARATIONS

I wished I could ask Core, or even Myna, what the trials were like and how best to prepare, but it was forbidden. We were told about them twice a year when the history was recited to all The Clan, but other than that, they were never to be mentioned. That was the main reason why no one under the age of sixty had known when the next trials would take place.

Once, long ago, I'd tried to ask Myna about them. Her reaction had been violent; it was the one time I had received her ire instead of her ice. Sometimes, I thought about asking again, just to see if I could elicit another such response, but I feared the laws of our people too much for that.

Few would risk breaking that particular rule, as it was punishable by banishment. However, with the trials still six months away, I didn't see how I could possibly wait so long to learn the truth.

"What about you?" Cole's voice cut into my thoughts.

"Huh?" I wasn't sure what we had been discussing.

"Where are you heading?"

"I'm going to the council building as well," I decided aloud. "I want to see if Myna—my mother has returned from The North Wind."

"What did she go there for?" Cole wondered.

I shrugged as if I didn't care. "Trouble of one sort or another I guess. She doesn't like to discuss the council's business with me."

Cole nodded. "Yeah, but who visits The North Wind during this kind of winter? There's nothing but mountains of snow between here and there." It was easy to forget about the icy fields and puddles of slush that started not even a hundred yards away, when all the snow inside The Paramount was packed down and easy to traverse.

"She's very determined," I said with grudging admiration. Time and again I had witnessed that there was nothing Myna wouldn't or couldn't do once she had set her mind to it. Her determination was something I had inherited.

Together, Cole and I trudged to the town center in the middle of the village. We couldn't go inside the council building, so we would have to wait, as we had waited so many times before.

Only once had I been taken inside the forbidden building. It had been the day my father had died. I didn't remember anything about the interior, or even about most of that day, except the wracking grief that still tainted my memories. I never knew the reason I had been summoned to stand before the council.

All I had done was cry while someone had asked me numerous questions. I'd only managed to reply to a few of them before putting my head in my hands, closing my eyes, and blocking out the world.

The town center was empty as Cole and I approached it. Sometimes, when an important issue was being discussed, people would gather outside the council building to garner information from anyone going in or coming out.

"What are you planning to do tomorrow on our day off?" Cole asked, when several minutes had elapsed.

I shrugged. Normally, we would have been planning a strategy for Attack and Defend with our team, but the time when we had enjoyed the simple game felt like it had been years ago.

"I've been thinking about a few things," Cole began, chewing his lip.

"What do you mean?" I pressed.

"To be honest," his voice dropped to a whisper, "I was thinking of going to The North Wind."

I couldn't keep the horror and shock from my voice. "Why?" I asked.

Cole looked taken aback by my reaction, and I quickly pushed down my feelings, trying to erase the surprise from my face.

"Well," he said very quietly, "when the trials begin, we'll be leaving from there, through The Valley of the North Wind. It

THE PREPARATIONS

might be nice to see the lay of the land. You know, become familiar with at least the first part of our journey."

What Cole said made sense, except everything would be covered in sheets of white; it would look very different when spring came around. The venture would be nothing but a tedious, miserable trip through the snow. Plus, there was a huge risk of being caught and getting into serious trouble. We could visit The North Wind if we wanted to, but entering the valley was against the rules. We would be in twice as much trouble if we got caught there now, since the trials had already been announced.

"Weren't you the one just asking who would visit The North Wind in this weather? Something about large drifts of snow?" I recalled.

Cole smiled sheepishly. "Yes, I did say that. But your mother is older and less agile than we are. If she can make it to The North Wind and back, why can't we? I was thinking of inviting Jase to go with us, but I wanted to talk to you first. What do you think?" Cole asked.

I was a little put off by the thought of having Jase along, but how could I say no? Cole was trying to think strategically, and he wasn't wrong about the knowledge giving us a huge advantage.

"Sounds like an adventure," I said. "I'm always up for an adventure." The last part of my statement wasn't quite true, but I was willing to let Cole think I was braver than I really was.

"Great!" Cole said. He sounded so genuinely happy that I actually started looking forward to the trip. *It might even be fun*, I told myself. "I'll ask Jase tonight; his dwelling is next to mine. Meet us before sunrise?"

I nodded. "I'll be there." No one would even notice I was gone.

"Remember the last time we were at The North Wind?" Cole asked. "What was it, three years ago?"

"I think that's right," I said. The day Cole was talking about was hard to forget. One late summer morning, completely out of the blue, our teachers had announced that we would be going on a trip instead of doing class work. It happened from time to time and was a nice change of pace. However, trips to The North Wind were never as much fun as those to other places, like Riverside or The Making, since they put us to work instead of just showing us how things were run.

Cole smiled fondly at the memory. "Remember that old nag Jase tried to catch?"

I laughed softly at the recollection.

After we'd marched all the way to The North Wind, poor, softheaded Jase had been sent to bring an old mare in from a small pen to put her in a stall. However, he'd forgotten to close the gate when he had entered the paddock. That might have turned out all right—the mare really was ancient and not very spirited—except that in his haste, Jase had charged straight for her.

I may not have known anything about horses, but it was common sense not to run full tilt toward any animal's head, especially if you are the size of Jase. The nag had been spooked, naturally, and had spun away from him. She'd spied the open gate and had escaped into the yard. Once she had been a good distance from Jase, she'd begun cropping the grass.

Again, it wouldn't have been much of a problem if Jase hadn't charged her a second time. He had ended up spending two hours trying to run down the poor animal. By the time one of the supervisors had realized what had been going on, both had been blowing and covered in sweat.

That had been the last time they'd let Jase near the horses. The rest of that day, he'd been put to work moving hay bales and bags of grain. I was pretty sure it'd been a relief to him. He just couldn't handle facing anything bigger or stronger than he was.

"We'll have to keep Jase away from Buttercup, or whatever her name was," I said to Cole.

"I think that's probably a good idea," Cole laughed.

Just then, Core came out of the council building. He looked oddly somber as he greeted us.

"Everything alright?" Cole asked, taking in his father's troubled expression.

Core just shook his head. "Sometimes, I—" he cut off and smiled, but it was a fake smile. "Just business as usual."

Cole nodded.

"Is my mother back?" I asked quickly, before the two could leave.

"Yes," Core told me. "She's inside right now. I don't know that you should wait for her. It might be a long night." He gave me a sympathetic glance before walking away with Cole.

I wanted to tell him that I couldn't have cared less. My only reason for asking was to know if I was allowed to sleep in my own dwelling that night. Since it appeared that I was, I headed there and built a nice fire in our stove to chase out the frosty chill that still lingered from the night before.

After the fire was burning well, I started preparing some of our unused flour ration. If I was going to be trekking all over The Land of the Clan the following day, I was going to need to take more than just a few strips of meat with me.

I baked a couple loaves of bread and packed some dried apples and preserved meat into my backpack. I hadn't even put a dent in our food rations from the previous four days, not to mention the two months prior to that.

While the bread was cooking, I couldn't stop thinking about the look on Core's face. Something had upset him. Normally, I wouldn't really have bothered about it, but with my food prepared and nothing really to do but fret about the following day's venture, I decided to divert my attention. Half an hour later, I found myself headed back to the council building. Maybe someone there could give me more insight into the situation.

No one was around when I re-entered the town center. The sun had nearly set, and all was quiet.

Two minutes later, there was movement from the council building. A woman I didn't recall ever having seen before stepped out. She was wearing a thick jacket the smoky gray color of The North Wind, a pair of stained leather boots, and a furious expression. Her hair was streaked with white, and she wore it in a long, simple braid.

The elderly woman was muttering under her breath as she emerged. Even though I had been intending to find out what was going on, I hastily decided not to speak to her. A moment later, Myna exited the council building as well, closely followed by the girl I'd observed the first day of training, Astra. My mouth dropped open when I saw her. What could she have possibly been doing in the council building?

Astra was still wearing all black, looking exactly the same as when I had seen her at The Barracks. Her long hair was loose and fluttering slightly in the wind. She dipped her head respectfully to Myna and hurried after the older woman.

Before she had caught up, the woman spun around and yelled angrily at Myna, "I don't know how you can be so shortsighted! I understand the child's foolish desire, but you are supposed to be one of the wisest in The Clan, and for you not to see—" The woman's words came to an abrupt halt. She trembled with fury and couldn't even continue speaking.

Quite a crowd was gathering to see what the commotion was about. Arguments and raised voices inside the council building was one thing, it happened occasionally and no one paid it any mind, but to be yelling outside was inappropriate. I wondered if the woman would be chastised, but Myna was as impassive as ever. "I am sorry, but the council has spoken. Please respect our wisdom even if you do not understand it."

The woman's face contorted, and I could see that she was about to start screaming again, but Astra intervened. Her demeanor was as cool and calm as Myna's.

"Litis, please calm down. There is nothing more to be done here. The verdict has been given." Astra took Litis's hand and began leading her away toward the northern road.

Good, I thought. *Go back to where you belong.*

Even as they walked away I could hear Litis protesting to Astra, "But it was the wrong choice! You don't know what you're doing; you're only a child!"

I barely caught Astra's reply before they were out of my hearing range. "It's my decision," she said firmly. "Even if it is a mistake, I won't change my mind. I have to do this."

Myna turned her stern gaze on those who had gathered to stare at the spectacle. The crowd began to break up almost immediately; most, I'm sure, were headed to their dwellings for dinner. I expected to see Myna disappearing back inside the council building, but she was still looking after the pair from The North Wind.

Then, to my eternal surprise, Myna looked at me. "Come, let's go home, Myra."

Without waiting to see if I would obey, she headed through the village to our dwelling. I followed, trailing her like a duckling, unsure what had happened to elicit such a response from her.

There was something in the slope of her shoulders that spoke of an unseen burden. Maybe it was simply weariness, but I doubted it. Between her actions and Core's discontent, something had to have been terribly wrong.

Once we were inside our dwelling, I stopped to observed her. She walked to the center of the room and stood with her fists clenched, facing away from me. I waited. After twenty seconds, her body relaxed, and she sank onto one of the rarely-used pillows beside the table.

She still did not speak or move. Finally, I could bear the silence no longer. "What was Astra doing before the council?" I asked.

Myna turned and looked at me, really looked at me, with great interest. "You know her?"

"Yes, sort of. She was at The Barracks the first day of training."

Myna nodded, and there was another long silence. Again, I was the one to break it. "Why was she here? What did that woman—Litis—want?"

I didn't think Myna would answer; she had turned her eyes away from me and seemed to be staring at nothing at all.

I couldn't comprehend the tone she used when she finally answered me. It was more than weariness, more than sadness, something closer to utter despair touched her words. "She requested that Astra not be allowed to participate in the trials."

My eyes widened. Wasn't every eligible child a potential? Surely, they could make no exceptions. Even children with physical and mental deformities participated. Never, not once in our history, had I ever heard of anyone being exempt.

"Last night, I traveled to The North Wind so as to explain to Litis and the others that their request was not even going to be considered. Of course, everyone there was in an uproar. The disorder of that place..." Myna trailed off in contempt.

"In the end, Litis marched herself and Astra all the way here, insisting to be permitted to address the council. Of course, they denied her request, just as I told her they would before she made the journey."

"Why would she ask such a thing?" I wondered. "Is Litis Astra's mother?" Most parents hoped their children would do well and win honor and respect from their peers during the trials.

"No, she is not Astra's mother. Astra's parents are dead. She is an orphan, a ward of The North Wind. Litis asked it because she claims they are short-staffed, and, according to her, Astra is a hard worker and one of the best handlers they've got.

"She doesn't see how they can do without Astra for the preparations, not to mention the trials. I told her that if they needed more help, they should ask, and we here at The Paramount would do everything we could to investigate the situation and ensure that they had the required manpower."

"What did she say to that?"

"Litis said that it wasn't about manpower, that it was horse people they really needed, and there are precious few of them left among The Clan anymore. She told me they don't just want whoever we have lying around. They need passionate people, who have a way with the animals." Even though Myna's voice was monotone once more, I could tell she thought the entire conversation was ridiculous.

"Did Astra want to be exempt?" I asked. I didn't really care, but Myna so rarely divulged things to me, I did not want her to stop.

"No," Myna answered. "She said that it was her duty and her privilege to participate and become part of the legacy of our people."

I nodded. I should have known that answer. You could see in the arrogant tilt of her head that Astra would never have asked for a pardon. I wanted to know more and find out why the situation was bothering Myna so much. However, I wasn't certain what approach to take. The entire thing seemed very simple to me. It had been easily dealt with and was at an end. So, why had it drained Myna so much?

I supposed it could all have been on account of her long journey. Traversing the forsaken road to The North Wind and back was certain to be a hardship. Besides, if it was freezing in The Paramount, I couldn't imagine what the temperature must have been like there, with the wind from the valley breaking frigidly over the small village.

Myna rose to her feet. "I'm going to bed," she announced. "I feel slightly under the weather." She took ten steps and was in her room. The door closed behind her, shutting me out once more.

I sat up later than usual, my mind unable to calm itself with sleep. The woman, Litis, was clearly lazy and not happy about having to take on extra work. There was no help for it, the preparations had begun, and soon the trials would start as well.

What really perplexed me was that there were at least two dozen other children from The North Wind who were potentials as well. No one was making a fuss about them being exempt. Why was Astra so special?

Chapter 9

THE NORTHERN ROAD

Something woke me in the middle of the night. I heard the strange sound of someone weeping. I knew it wasn't a dream; I never dreamed. After listening for a few minutes, I decided it was just the wind crying in the night beyond my shutters. Sleep took me again, and I remembered nothing more until morning.

When the bell rang on the fourth day, it was only to summon the adults to work. Normally, I would have rolled over and gone back to sleep for a few more hours.

Not that morning. I practically sprang out of bed at the first toll of the metal bell. I'd laid out my warmest clothing the night before in preparation for the journey. I quickly dressed by feel, not bothering to light a candle or lamp. Unfortunately, in my haste, I kicked my pack under the bed while stepping into my pants.

After pulling on my cloak, I dropped to my knees and thrust an arm as far beneath my bed as it would go. The pack was not where I judged it should have ended up. Without being able to see anything, my fingers blindly searched the space that I had always thought of as being so tiny.

That was when I touched something small and hard. Its shape was unfamiliar, and, in the dark, I couldn't see well enough to have any clue of what I was holding. The object felt like a long, cylindrical piece of metal, thick on one end and tapered at the other. I pushed it back under the bed to investigate further when I had time to get a light.

THE PREPARATIONS

I reached under the bed again, and my fingers found my pack. I yanked it free and was out of my room in a few moments.

As I pulled my boots from the shoe niche, something brought me up short. Myna's boots were there, next to where mine had rested in the hollow. It had been years since the last time I'd risen with the bell and not been the only one in the dwelling.

The adults in the community worked seven days and had the eighth day free. Their schedules were alternated so that on every fourth day, half the adults worked and the other half rested.

But Myna had never taken a day off. Ever.

It wasn't in her nature, especially considering everything that was going on. With the impending trials, the council would be busier than ever before. All the data that had been gathered during the first two days of training would have to be analyzed. Every potential would have to be carefully assessed as the council tried to determine who should become a contender and who should not.

Yet, Myna was still asleep in her bed as I stole from the dark dwelling. Everything was turning upside down in more ways than one.

The village was shrouded in twilight. Its streets all but deserted. Each time I passed another figure in the gray light before dawn, I felt my heart lurch. Bundled up as I was, I hoped they'd mistake me for an adult.

I knew it was silly to be so anxious; I hadn't done anything wrong yet, and there was still a chance I wouldn't have to at all. If only I could persuade Cole to be satisfied with just looking at the valley from a distance and not actually trying to enter it.

The day before, I had been far too distracted to fully comprehend what we had been planning to do, but now, fear of breaking the rules weighed heavily on my shoulders. I told myself to stop being so worried. Once we reached The North Wind,

Cole would probably feel the same anxious guilt I was feeling, a consequence of being raised in The Paramount. Perhaps, he would be able to content himself with just poking around the village.

I found Cole standing outside his dwelling. The place was dark and would have looked deserted if not for the thin tendril of smoke curling lazily out of the chimney.

There was no sign of Jase, which pleased me greatly. I'd been more than half hoping he wouldn't show at all. Without Jase, it would be far easier to talk Cole out of doing anything stupid. If Jase came, he would be sure to agree with whatever Cole said, and I would be outvoted.

"Morning," I murmured softly, my breath white as it hit the chilly air.

"Morning," he returned, giving me a bright smile before dashing my hopes. "There's Jase now."

I turned as Cole's blue eyes locked onto a point behind me. There, indeed, was Jase, huge and hulking as always. No one would mistake him for anyone but himself.

There was no point in standing around, so before Jase had even come to a halt, Cole began leading us away from the village, towards the north.

We did not speak as we passed through the dark dwellings. I walked alongside Cole, leaving Jase to bring up the rear. Fortunately, there were only a few people between us and the edge of the village, none of whom seemed to have any interest in asking questions. Still, the three of us together were fairly recognizable. My nerves started going crazy, and I regretted that we had not arranged to meet outside the village. In contrast to me, Cole clearly didn't seem to care if anyone saw us.

Maybe he'd changed his mind and wasn't planning on breaking any rules after all. Cole wasn't exactly the rebellious type. Like me, he almost never received marks in school.

However, from time to time, I'd observed his father bend the laws, like when I'd been allowed to stay the night with his family. Perhaps, Cole thought it would be ok to do the same whenever need arose. Core was a good leader, but if everyone acted as he did, our society would no longer be built on order but on feeling. A society like that would falter and fall.

Myna was different. To her, the rules were as inflexible as stone. If events had played out the other way around on that night, Cole would never have been permitted to sleep in our dwelling without the proper authorities notified, the event meticulously recorded, and the appropriate amount of additional rations procured. Myna believed in the letter of the law, and I had grown up feeling much the same. Even though sometimes they seemed stupid, there were good reasons for the rules to be obeyed. They were the only thing between us and chaos.

As we neared the edge of the village, Cole slowed to a halt. I quickly scanned the area to find the reason why. A figure was approaching us. There was enough light for me to see who it was.

"Come on, it's just Larna," I whispered to Cole, impatient to complete our escape. "She's got no right to question us." Hopefully, he could hear the urgency in my voice.

"I know," Cole nodded. "I was just wondering if we should ask her to join us." My mind recoiled at the thought. Compared to Larna, Jase was as welcome as a morning of springtime.

I bit my tongue, so as not to express my real opinion of the loathsome girl to Cole. Quickly, I searched for a better way to put an end to his dreadful idea.

"There are already three of us," I hissed. "If we let her come, we'll have to bring Flant too, and then half The Paramount will want to join."

Cole considered for a moment. "I suppose you're right; if we decide to go into The Valley of the North Wind, it'll be easier to spot four than three."

His words did not give me much comfort. Personally, I thought we would have been much harder to spot without Jase. I didn't mention that, though. Whatever it took to keep Cole

THE NORTHERN ROAD

from inviting Larna to join us was fine by me. I doubted she could have even made it to The North Wind and back. Her body was not particularly athletic.

Cole nodded to Larna as we walked by. To my great relief, he didn't stop to exchange words of greeting. Knowing Cole, he probably wouldn't have been able to keep from telling her where we were going, and he never would have been able to say no if she'd asked to come along.

As Larna paused to watch us pass, it was all I could do not to give her a smug smile. Instead, I ignored her and walked straight ahead. From my peripheral vision, I saw a disconcerted look on her face as we left her behind. I relished the idea of her standing there alone; Cole and I had obviously chosen each other—and Jase too I guess. That should help throw the words from two mornings ago back in her face. Clearly, no one wanted her on their team.

I was just glad we hadn't met Bala. She might have followed us, just to see where we were going. Bala had a way of figuring things out. Generally, it was better to include her from the start, otherwise she would purposely ruin everyone's plans out of spite. Still, there was no way I would have ever invited her to join us. Years of competing against her had shown me her true nature. She was a liar and a cheat; I did not trust her, and I did not want her on my team.

Larna was the last person we saw before reaching the northern road. The snow on the way to The North Wind was as thick as I had imagined. However, the two-hour journey wasn't all that miserable. Once we were a safe distance from the village, there was no one to hear us, so we talked and laughed freely. The sun had risen after the first half hour, revealing the land spread out before us.

Up ahead, The Mountains of the North Wind stood tall and imposing. As long as it wasn't too cloudy, they could easily be seen from The Paramount and just about everywhere else in The Land of the Clan. Even in summer, they were capped with snow.

THE PREPARATIONS

The view from their summit must have been truly breathtaking, not that anyone had ever climbed them. The mountain range was strictly off-limits.

The day continued to grow brighter, but little warmer. My eyes ached from the sharp glare of the rising sun on the snow. Glancing upward, I saw a few hazy clouds drifting languidly in the sky above. Hopefully, they would expand and cover the sun before the light became unbearable.

As we walked toward the mountains, which never seemed to get any closer, Jase began relating what had happened the day his little sister had been born. He'd only been seven at the time, and the concepts of pregnancy and birth had been confusing to him.

"I kept asking my parents where she'd come from," Jase explained to us. "Finally, my dad lost his patience and told me that she had grown from the earth like a flower." As he spoke, Jase began to laugh, making some of his words hard to understand. "So naturally, I figured my mother had picked her and brought her home!"

Cole was laughing too, probably more because he was trying to encourage Jase than because he found anything amusing in Jase's retelling of the event.

"And they let me believe that for two years!" Jase bellowed. "Eventually, they explained to me that she was just like all the other babies."

I snorted, finally amused by his ignorance.

"He still calls her 'flower' sometimes, just to tease her," Cole told me.

"Better than what your sister and brothers called you," Jase muttered.

I gave Cole a questioning look. If his cheeks hadn't already been red with cold, I was pretty sure he might have blushed.

"Do tell," I commanded.

Cole shook his head, so I turned to Jase.

"When he was little, Cole's Mom told him—" Jase began.

"Wait," Cole interrupted. "You're not doing it right. I'll tell her." I glanced at Cole expectantly. "It started when I was five. All of my siblings were older and too busy to have time to play with me. I spent two years begging my parents to have another child, but they just kept saying no. Finally, my Mother got so sick of my nagging that she told me that I was their last child because I was so perfect.

"Obviously, it wasn't the truth, and she had only said it to stop my asking, but I told everyone else that night when they came over for a family dinner. They thought it was quite funny and all pretended to be offended, plaguing our mother for weeks by calling me the 'perfect, pristine one'.

"After that," Cole went on. "If I ever got into trouble and my mother was going to scold me, one of them would turn up and ask her how she could scold her poor perfect, pristine one. It actually worked in my favor, because most of her scolding would then be turned on them instead of me."

Cole laughed at the memory. "They were really much nicer to me than I deserved. I was a brat of a little brother. I missed them all so much when they moved to different villages," he sighed.

We fell silent for about a quarter of an hour. I was lost in thought, trying to recall a happy time in my childhood that I could share, when Cole turned to me and asked a question. "Do you wish you had siblings?"

"No," I replied quickly, but then reconsidered. "Well, I guess maybe I do."

I hadn't ever really thought about it before. If I had had an older sibling, I wouldn't have been as independent as I had become. A younger sibling might have been better. Rasby was the closest thing I could imagine to a little sister, and I had enjoyed our relationship—until recently that is. With a real sister, though, I wouldn't have had the same worries about the trials, since they said siblings were never put on the same team. But that would have meant saying goodbye. I still remembered the pain of my father's passing. I never wanted to feel that again.

"I guess I'm glad not to have a sibling," I decided aloud. "Look at Tiera and Tirea; they are nothing without each other. Like halves of a whole. I want to be something on my own. I want to choose my own path, not have to talk it over with someone else."

Cole silently thought about my answer. I hoped he wouldn't read into it too much. A life mate would be different.

"I mean, at least not when it's someone you aren't going to be with forever. Tiera and Tirea will have to separate sooner or later, and it will be hard for them." I added lamely.

Cole was nodding, so at least he probably grasped my meaning. I doubted Jase had been able to keep up, but he was used to that and had learned to hold his tongue instead of showing his ignorance. A wise choice that some people far more intelligent than he could have benefited from.

After another half hour, we could see the village of The North Wind in the distance. The sun was clear of the horizon, and its watery light was cutting coldly through the thickening cloud cover. I'd known that The North Wind would be colder, but the first couple blasts of icy wind took my breath away. The long walk had warmed up my muscles, but the cold of the wind cut like the blade of a knife.

"Time to play with the pretty ponies," Jase announced. Cole and I laughed, remembering Jase and Buttercup.

"How are we going to do this?" I asked, bringing the boys to a halt.

Jase shrugged, but I hadn't really been talking to him anyway. I moved closer to Cole, using him to break the wind while we formed a plan.

"I guess we shouldn't march straight through the village," Cole considered. "Let's veer to the right and come around that way."

I nodded, agreeing with his suggestion. Maybe he was slightly more worried about getting caught now that we had reached The North Wind and weren't in The Paramount anymore.

Up until then, we had been following the road. Although, 'road' was a generous description. The path had been covered in snow and ice and hadn't even been visible in most places. However, it had been worn smooth by people traveling to and from the village, so the surface was harder and flatter than the surrounding fields of white.

Once we were off the road, it didn't take long before I began to miss it. Traveling through the soft snowdrifts was much more difficult and tiresome. We had all slipped and skidded on the icy road, but without it, the snow was a living thing. It sucked down on your legs and gave out unexpectedly under your feet.

Soon, we began encountering fences surrounding the outlying pastures. They were made out of wood and easy to scramble over. Cole and I managed them without difficulty, but Jase got tripped up a few times and once even fell head first into the snow.

When the land thawed, the pastures would be filled with long grass for grazing. Until then, all of the horses would be tucked up cozily in their stalls. Part of me was jealous of them. We had been traveling for over two hours. I was exhausted and worn out, but I knew, no matter what happened, we still had at least as far to go to get back.

We floundered in the snow for another half hour while making a wide circle around the east side of the village. The entire time I was painfully aware that our maroon clothing showed up only too well against the pure white of the snowy fields. Thankfully, all was still, and we saw no one.

It had become a gray, cloudy day, and everything about The North Wind felt forlorn and unimportant. Who would ever want to live there, forgotten in a desolate waste? If that had been my situation, I would have nagged my parents until they had agreed to request a transfer to any other village.

After The North Wind was finally behind us, there was nothing ahead but the mountains themselves. The dark gray walls of stone towered high above our heads. I had to crane my neck to look up at the misty peaks.

"There." Cole pointed ahead of us, to a place where The Mountains of the North Wind opened to reveal a small path leading into The Valley of the North Wind. It was widely known to be the only way in or out of our peninsula.

The narrow passageway would have been easy to miss if not for two towering poles of wood set on either side. The poles were marked with all the colors of our villages. Maroon on the top for The Paramount, followed by deep purple, the color of The Making, then gold for The Barracks, light green for The Golden Fields, tan for Riverside, brown for The Farm, royal blue for The Quarry, dark green for Treescape and finally, at the bottom, dark gray for The North Wind.

I glanced back and saw something move in the village behind us.

"Get down!" I hissed, pushing Jase and Cole forward. The three of us dropped behind a snow-covered outcropping of rock, the mountains to our right and the valley opening a dozen yards in front of us. If we were caught in that location, there would be awkward questions, even though no rules had been broken yet.

Looking towards the village, I saw a lone figure.

Astra.

I was sure it was her, even though all I could make out was the black color of the clothing. She was walking out of The North Wind, heading in our direction. I doubted she had seen us since the village was about half a mile southwest of our position.

Beside Astra was a long-legged, brown horse. A leather saddle was strapped to the beast's back. The large head was raised as the creature turned its eyes in every direction to take in its surroundings.

Once they'd cleared the outskirts of the village, Astra turned her attention to the animal. Her movements were slow and precise as she ran a hand along the creature's neck.

Slowly, she pulled herself into the saddle. The horse remained still while she mounted and adjusted her legs. A moment later, she started the beast in our direction, and the pair began galloping straight toward us.

I looked at Cole and saw my own terror reflected in his eyes. We hunkered down as far as possible behind the outcropping. Again, I thought of how brightly our clothing stood out against the gray of the rocks and the white of the snow. I didn't dare watch the horse's approach, but I could soon hear hoofbeats pounding the frozen ground far too close for comfort.

The three of us could do nothing but remain completely still as Astra and the horse raced toward our position. A moment before she was on top of us, the hoofbeats turned sharply to the left and headed off into The Valley of the North Wind.

We listened to the horse's footfalls grow fainter and fainter. When we could no longer hear them at all, we dared to move again. I carefully checked for other riders emerging from the village, but the landscape was deserted once more.

I can't do this, I thought, fighting down panic.

If I was to express my concerns aloud, would the boys think me a coward? Or even leave me behind? My feelings of apprehension had grown stronger with the terror of almost getting caught. No matter what I did, I couldn't shake the knowledge that we were not supposed to be there.

Cole and Jase moved carefully out from behind the rocks that had shielded us. They didn't seem as confident as before, but they still advanced towards the narrow opening. I bit my lip, battling with the turmoil inside.

Finally, I had to say something. "Wait! We shouldn't do this. It's against the rules. If we get caught, they'll give us all marks, or worse."

Cole responded coolly, as if he'd known all along that he would need to persuade me. "Look, Myra, we came all the way here; it would be stupid to stop now. The trials aren't going to be easy, and we need to be as ready as possible."

"But—" I started to protest.

"Astra went in, didn't she?" Cole reminded me. "So, why shouldn't we?"

I hadn't thought about that. She was doing exactly what we were: scouting the land. Only, she hadn't hesitated for a moment. She'd even taken a horse from her village to assist her.

If she can do it, I can do it, I thought, gritting my teeth.

"You can't follow every single rule your whole life; it'll make you crazy," Cole told me, confirming my suspicions of the night before.

Despite my doubts, he could see my resolution wavier. "Let's go," he said, reaching out his hand to me. I took it reluctantly and allowed him to lead me into the valley.

Chapter 10

INTO THE VALLEY

I was surprised to find that inside the valley there was hardly any snow at all. For a moment, I even dared to hope the air might be warmer as well. In that, I was disappointed. The tall, narrow walls served as a channel for the icy wind, directing it straight into our faces.

About twenty yards beyond the entrance, the track widened a little, providing enough space for the three of us to easily walk abreast. The walls slanted away from each other as they climbed into the sky. At their pinnacle, a hundred yards above my head, they were far enough apart for half The Paramount to walk side-by-side.

I stared up in awe at the rocky heights. On any given day, I could have looked toward the north and seen the same mountains, but they appeared far more impressive looking up from beneath. My whole life, I had seen the same land and the same places over and over again. In the valley, there was something new, something different, and it was only a three-hour walk from my dwelling.

A sudden curiosity overtook me and a great longing to see the land beyond the valley welled up. How did those not chosen for the trials stand never seeing it? For a moment, I felt the urge to leave the peninsula and never return. I checked the thought instantly. Yes, it was exciting to see new places, but I belonged in The Land of the Clan. That was where I wanted to live my life, grow old, and someday, far in the future, die.

THE PREPARATIONS

Beside me, Cole's head was tilted back as he took in the view with the same wonder I felt. The impact of seeing some place new was lost on Jase. He didn't seem to comprehend that for the first time in our lives, we were beyond the borders of our land.

Without the obstacle of the snow, our progress was rapid. We weren't able to speak much, because the wind stole the words from our mouths and flung them back the way we had come. Jase tried yelling once, which was a terrible idea. His voice echoed off the stone walls twice as loudly as the moaning wind. The only way to communicate was to put our mouths close to each other's ears.

After about a mile and a half, the road split. To the left, the passage appeared to grow narrow. Jase was more than twice my size, and Cole's shoulders were far broader than mine. No matter how cramped the trail got, both of them would have to stop long before I would.

In contrast to the left route, the path to the right widened. Cole and I exchanged a glance, and then, without discussion, took the road to the right.

A short time later, we came to a second split. Both paths were unremarkable.

"We can't go on like this," I said, speaking into Cole's ear. "We're going to get lost."

Cole nodded, but didn't seem to have any inspiration. I glanced around, and something caught my eye. There was a thin piece of wood laying a little way down the righthand trail. I couldn't imagine how the stick could have gotten there since there wasn't a plant to be found.

I figured it must have come off of a tree concealed from our sight, growing on the high slopes of the mountains above. Snatching the stick up, I broke off a small piece of the end. The wood was reddish-brown and stood out quite well against the gray stones surrounding us. Placing the small piece carefully on top of a large rock, I marked the trail we had just left.

"When we come back," I informed the boys, "all we have to do is follow the pieces of stick."

"Genius," Cole complimented me.

The trail wound on and on, gradually sloping upward. There were dozens of turn-offs and splits. Since we didn't have time to check them all in a methodical order, we tried to select the ones that looked the most promising.

However, every road we took brought us to nothing except dead ends. At one point, Jase clumsily tripped over a large, round stone, sending it flying into a nearby wall. The resulting crash caused about a dozen large boulders to come free of the rocks above and plummet earthward at a frightening velocity.

Jase was the only one to be struck by the falling debris. A small rock clipped his left shoulder. He cried out in pain; the sound brought down even more stones. Cole pulled him against the nearest wall, where I was already sheltered. After everything was still, we silently made our escape, not even daring to speak until we were far away.

"Is it bleeding?" Cole asked.

"I don't think so," Jase answered. He pulled his shirt to the side, stretching the neck hole wide in order to check. "Nope, no blood," he reported.

Cole nodded sympathetically. "Well, that's good, but I'm sure there'll be a terrific bruise. We have to be more careful."

That wasn't our only close call. Several times, the sound of our footsteps or the howling of the wind seemed to be enough to cause a small landslide. We learned to step lightly and move with great caution.

Finally, we picked a trail that appeared to be different than all the others. It led up and curved around one of the smaller mountains. Just when I was certain we'd discovered the way to the other side of the valley, the path was cut short by a gaping abyss. The drop below was terrifying; I hadn't realized we'd climbed so high.

THE PREPARATIONS

At this new failure, frustration coursed through me. It was midday, and we knew nothing more than we had five hours ago when we'd left The Paramount. There was no other option but to turn back and try another path. The only good thing was that the wind appeared to have blown itself out, and we could talk to each other again.

"At least we're learning all the trails not to take," Cole announced. He sounded almost amused. I gave him a seething look, which I was sure conveyed all of my feelings of frustration. Apparently, he found my expression humorous, because I saw him trying to suppress a smile. His cheerfulness did actually make me feel a bit better, until we arrived at yet another dead end.

I was ready to scream. The valley was a complete maze. With no outlet, I was starting to feel trapped. The low hanging clouds choking out the sun only helped to enhance the illusion.

I looked up, studying the sky for a moment. Something about the clouds directly above us didn't appear quite normal. They seemed to be rising from the far side of the ridge, off to our right. Their color was darker than those higher up in the sky. My distracted gaze led me to trip over a rocky outcrop, and I decided my time would be better spent watching my feet.

The three of us fell into a pattern, which continued on for another hour. We would choose a fresh trail, traverse it for a short period of time, and then find that it ended in a cliff or precipice. I lost track of the number of times we repeated the process.

At one point, I thought I saw a human skull among the rocks. There was a full skeleton on display at the schoolhouse in The Paramount so we could learn about how our bodies worked. I'd never before stopped to wonder whose bones they had been.

Seeing the skull made me shudder. No one came into the valley, so where could it have come from? I glanced at the white object again and realized that it was really just a rock. The eerie place was having a strange effect on my imagination.

Once we were a safe distance away, I suggested we take a break. The boys agreed readily, plopping down on the nearby stones to rest.

I pulled out the food I had brought and shared it around. It would have been hard for either Jase or Cole to bring much with them since their parents would have noticed if the family rations had gone missing.

They'd each brought a little but were more than happy to take my additions.

"This is really delicious," Cole told me, his mouth full of bread. I knew it wasn't true since I wasn't very good at baking. However, it was nice of him to say, and I'm sure he was hungry enough to half believe it.

We set off again after eating and found nothing but more dead ends. At one of them, it looked like there might have been a way to scale the pile of rocks cutting off the trail. I wouldn't have minded investigating further, but at that moment, the wind picked up sharply, and a couple of fist-sized stones clattered to the ground. Instead of poking around, we left in a hurry.

"Let's go back to the first divide and try the left path," Cole suggested a short time later. "Might as well see what that side of the valley looks like before it gets too late."

I didn't have enough energy to say anything, so all I did was nod my agreement.

Getting back to that split took longer than I thought it would. More than once, when I felt it should have been just ahead and wasn't, I had to fight down my growing panic. The little pieces of wood we had left to mark our trail worked quite well, and we did, eventually, find our way back.

At first, I didn't think the left-hand trail was going to lead anywhere and expected it to simply taper off. The path was a bit narrower than the right-hand road, but never so much so that Jase and Cole couldn't walk shoulder to shoulder. After a quarter mile, it widened considerably.

I counted a few turn-offs, but there was definitely a main passage, which we followed.

The path split only three times. Twice we had to turn back, but soon we came to a long stretch with no side trails at all. It led up and up, until we could look back and see The Land of the Clan laid out behind us. I wished there was time to pause and simply admire the view, but I feared that if I stopped, I would never be able to get my aching feet started again.

Soon, we came to more splits, and we constantly had to backtrack due to dead ends. Finally, we crested the top of the slope we'd been climbing, and the land opened in front of us.

Everything seemed to freeze for just one second as I realized that, for the first time, I was seeing beyond The Mountains of the North Wind. The revelation brought questions flooding into my mind. How big was the world? What was out there? Nothing but death, according to our history.

The expanse before us was just as frozen and snow-clad as The Land of the Clan, but it was winter now. In summer, would the land still appear dead and forlorn? Hopefully, I'd find the answers in six months when the trials began.

From what I could tell, the path we were on leveled out for a hundred yards, and then started climbing again, all the way to the summit of The Mountains of the North Wind. Toward the top of the peaks, the path twisted around to meet up with the land beyond the mountains. Part of the path was hidden, but we could easily see the rest of it on the far side of the peaks.

We had found it: the passage through The Valley of the North Wind. I didn't really think there was any point in traveling all the way to the top. The thought of taking one more step up was exhausting. Especially considering how far we still had to go before the end of the day. In addition, if we didn't turn back soon, we'd never reach The Paramount before nightfall.

Cole had gone slightly farther than Jase and I. "What's that?" he called softly, pointing down the slope to where the walls of the mountains ended and the terrain beyond spread out.

I craned my neck and saw what appeared to be four figures far in the distance, close to the valley's exit. All I could make out about them was that they were garbed in the golden color of The Barracks. Although, the clothes were so stained they appeared closer to brown.

"Do you think they're doing what we're doing?" Jase asked. "Finding the way through the valley for the trials?"

My mouth was hanging open in surprise. I quickly shut it and shook my head. "Those are adults, and look, they have a fire."

"I think I see a tent or something too," Cole added. I looked again and saw that he was correct. At least two structures had been erected to serve as a shelter against the elements.

"Why?" Jase wondered.

"They must be stationed there," Cole said reasonably.

"I've never heard about anything like this before," I commented.

Cole shrugged. "I guess that's because it doesn't have to do with The Paramount. Let's just be glad they're guarding the far end of the valley, instead of the close one. Otherwise, they would have caught us."

"What if there are guards at our end? They might have stepped away for a moment when we arrived," I choked out. "If so, we'll be trapped!"

Cole shook his head calmly. "I doubt that. I've been to The North Wind before and never seen anyone guarding the valley." Even as he spoke the words, I could see a small flicker of doubt in his eyes.

"We've seen what we came to see," I replied. "On the day the trials begin, we'll know the right path to take. I vote we go back now, before any of those soldiers come this way."

"I agree," Cole replied. "We've learned all we can for now."

Jase offered no argument.

THE PREPARATIONS

The going was easier downhill, but I spent the entire time listening with dread for the sound of anyone behind or before us.

We were only about a mile from the entrance to the valley when I heard the pounding of hoofbeats behind us on the road. We were in a terrible place; the walls were smooth as far we could see, and I didn't remember any turn-offs nearby.

"Run!" Cole said, and we did. The sound of hoofbeats must have carried farther than I thought, because we were not instantly overtaken. We turned a corner, and I saw a large boulder that had the possibility of offering a hiding place.

"Quick," I called. The thunder of hooves was louder now. It sounded like a whole herd of horses was right on our heels. Jase was the fastest. He threw himself forward and tried to get out of sight, but he was far too large to squeeze into any of the clefts around the boulder.

Cole and I reached it a moment later, but we were forced to wait as Jase attempted to wriggle into a hiding spot. I wanted to scream that it was too late for him, he was already caught and should get out of the way so I could hide. We didn't all need to get in trouble.

However, even if I had told him to move, it would have been pointless; Jase was stuck. Cole grabbed one of his arms to try to pull him loose. I caught the other, and we tugged. The instant he was free was the instant that the source of the noise appeared, charging toward us.

It was just one horse, and Astra was sitting on its back. The beast pulled up sharply as it came around the corner and saw us. Its nostrils widened, and it reared, front legs flailing in the air five feet above our heads.

A moment later, the horse was on all fours, breathing heavily. Astra had managed to stay on and was fighting the beast for control of the reins. She won, and the animals stood stock still, gray flanks twitching.

"What are you doing here?" she asked us in a surprised, but very superior tone.

It was Cole who responded. "Taking a look around, same as you," he told her in an even voice.

"If you tell on us, you'll incriminate yourself," I couldn't help but point out.

Astra appeared confused by our statements. "I'm not 'taking a look around'. I already know this place as well as I know the rest of The Land of the Clan."

"You mean you come here often?" Cole asked in disbelief.

Astra nodded. "There's a meadow at the top of the mountain that never gets much snowfall. We use it for training because it's kind of hard to exercise a green horse when the pastures are covered in ice." Her tone made it perfectly obvious that she doubted our intelligence.

Maybe that was where the upward path led, before descending down to the end of the valley. I certainly hadn't seen anything resembling a meadow in the parts we had explored. If we had continued on, we might have found it ourselves.

"That doesn't matter, you aren't supposed to be here," I put in.

Astra turned her attention to me fully for the first time. "Well, let's just say that at The North Wind, we don't always follow the rules that don't make sense.

"I use this place all the time for training, not just in the winter, but in the summer too. I've ridden hundreds of horses here," Astra continued nonchalantly.

I was speechless. What would Myna say? To hear that Astra had broken one of our most sacred rules hundreds of times, and that she was supported by an entire village? All that would stop when I became one of the Clan Leaders.

Cole looked surprised too but not as upset as I was. "What about the soldiers?" he asked.

THE PREPARATIONS

Astra finally looked uncomfortable. "You saw them, then," she said. We were all silent for a moment. Astra's green eyes studied each of us in turn. She opened her mouth.

Whatever she was going to say got cut off as the horse beneath her stirred. I had once heard that animals, horses in particular, could sense when someone was nervous or upset. Was the animal reacting to her emotions?

Astra took a few seconds to calm the beast. "Look," she said to us, "his muscles will tighten up if he stands here much longer. I'm not going to tell anyone I saw you, so don't worry about that. But you really need to get out of here. They'll change the guard in a couple hours, and you'll be in real trouble if they catch you."

With a gentle nudge, Astra moved the horse past us.

"Wait," Cole called after her. "What are the soldiers doing here?"

"I'll tell you some other time," she threw back over her shoulder. "I have to go." With that, she pushed the horse into a trot, and they disappeared around the next bend.

"I'm confused," Jase admitted.

"Yeah, this whole thing is pretty strange," Cole told him. "I'll have to catch up with her later and find out about the soldiers."

I didn't like that suggestion or the way he stared after that—that horse girl.

"No," Jase responded, "about the horse. She said it was green, but it actually looked gray to me."

I nearly laughed. If the encounter with Astra hadn't put me so out of sorts, I would have.

"Green just means inexperienced," replied Cole. "You see."

I missed the rest of Cole's explanation.

This isn't right, I thought. There was a nagging suspicion in the back of my mind that I had missed something important. Perhaps it would come to me later. I hurried to keep up with the boys, who had picked up a faster gait than before.

"If you want to know about the soldiers, you could always ask your father," I pointed out to Cole.

"Oh yes, I'll go right up to him and say, 'Hey dad, today I went to the most forbidden place in The Land of the Clan. By the way, I have a quick question about it, if you don't mind.'"

"That wasn't what I meant," I protested. "Be subtle. Ask if there is anywhere soldiers are posted regularly."

Cole sighed. "I could try it, but I think it'll be easier to just ask Astra."

I frowned. Maybe if I found her first, I could get the information and relay it to Cole. That way, there would be no reason for them to speak to each other at all.

Chapter 11

SEEKING

"I'll go first," I told Cole and Jase, as we neared the beginning of The Valley of the North Wind. They paused in order to let me take the lead. Pressing myself close to the rock wall, I peered cautiously out of the valley. The monochrome landscape was void of life as I searched the surrounding fields for signs of danger.

Hastily, I motioned for the boys to join me. When the three of us had finally crossed the threshold of the valley back into The Land of the Clan, a warm feeling of relief washed over me. We were safe.

I glanced once more in the direction of the village. It appeared nearly exactly as it had that morning, except there was no Astra riding toward us on a brown horse.

A brown horse.

She had been riding a brown one that morning, hadn't she? But when we had seen her that afternoon, the horse had undoubtedly been gray.

Either I was imagining things or something else was going on. I would have asked Cole if he could remember, but I didn't want him to think the fatigue was affecting my mind.

Cutting across the fields was twice as difficult on the return journey. I had already lost most of the feeling in my extremities hours ago. Each leg seemed to weigh a hundred pounds and just lifting them made me short of breath.

THE PREPARATIONS

At one point, I slipped while scrambling over a fence and fell back into the snow. Cole offered me his hand and pulled me to my feet.

When we reached the road, the tension, which had been building inside of me all day, vanished. It didn't matter who saw us now; no one would suspect where we had been.

I was beyond exhausted. it was all I could do to put one foot in front of the other. With each step, my body ached more. The miles seemed to stretch on forever. The boys were just as worn out as I was. None of us had enough energy to speak, so the only sound was our feet crunching on the frozen road.

For over an hour, we trudged along in the fading light and then stumbled along blindly once it disappeared completely. Clouds were thickly covering the sky, and there wasn't even a hint of moonlight.

I couldn't remember ever being so fatigued in my life as I trailed along behind Cole and Jase. My breath was coming in ragged gasps, and the icy air burned my lungs.

By the time we made it back to The Paramount, it was completely dark. All I wanted was to collapse into my bed and sleep until the following free day. Jase stopped to re-strap one of his boots. I passed him and managed to catch up with Cole.

"What's the matter?" I asked. His brow was furrowed, and he appeared concerned.

"I didn't think it was going to take us this long to get there and back," He admitted. "I'm sure to have been missed."

My first impulse was to help him come up with some account to explain his absence. Telling lies was one of the worst rules to break; then again, so was what we had been doing all day.

I'd been banking on the fact that Myna wouldn't realize I'd been gone. Even if she'd noticed, I doubted she would care enough to ask where I'd been. On my days off, I didn't hang around the dwelling much. There was nothing to hold me there; it was simply a place to eat and sleep. Because of that, I hadn't really thought about what Cole's and Jase's families would think.

We were almost to his dwelling, so there wasn't much time to come up with a good explanation.

"Where have you two been?" Both of us jumped as Core appeared behind us. I had never seen Core look angry before, but he was definitely not pleased with us.

"We went to The North Wind," Cole said quickly.

"Really?" Core didn't sound like he believed us. "Just the two of you?"

Cole and I shook our heads. "Jase came too," Cole reported.

Core's eyes narrowed, but just then Jase come around the corner. "I think my strap's broken; all that walking must have..." Jase cut off as he suddenly caught sight of Core.

To my relief, the fire in Core's eyes died when he saw Jase, validating our statement. "Why did you go all that way in this weather?" Core asked, sounding more curious than hostile, for which I was very thankful.

"We saw Astra," Cole said quickly.

Core didn't respond for a long moment, and then wrinkled his forehead. "Astra? A friend of yours?"

It was funny to me how Core asked almost the same question Myna had the night before.

"Yes," Cole said. "She's been training with us."

There was just enough truth in Cole's words to make them believable. We had seen Astra, but only for five minutes in the middle of The Valley of the North Wind.

By omitting certain truths, Cole was able to keep from telling that we had broken the rules without actually saying anything untrue. It was still lying; Cole was misleading his father with his words.

However, I didn't want to get in trouble any more than Cole did. So, even though I knew it was wrong, I held my tongue. Funny, how once we'd broken one rule, we instantly had to break more to keep out of trouble.

THE PREPARATIONS

"That's a long way to go to visit a friend, but I guess it's good that the preparations are helping to build relationships throughout the villages." Core seemed genuinely pleased with us, which made lying to him so much worse.

"Next time, tell someone where you're going, and try to be back before dark," Core chided his son.

Cole nodded and turned to Jase and me. "Goodnight, see you two in the morning."

"Night," I said, departing for my own dwelling.

There was no light coming from within, and the place felt dank and cold. After building a large, glorious fire, I stripped off the outermost layer of my garments. They were soaking wet from the long journey, so I hung them close to the stove to dry.

Once I had stopped shivering and the feeling had returned to my fingers and toes, I left the fire in favor of my room. I fell into bed, not caring that I was still mostly dressed. I hardly remembered my head hitting the pillow before unconsciousness claimed me.

My sleep was deep, and when the bell rang the following morning, I leapt from my bed only half awake. A moment later, I sank back down with a groan. I felt awful. My calves and thighs were on fire, and the lower part of my back ached in ways it never had before.

Perched on the edge of my bed, I carefully tested every muscle in my body. It seemed no part of me was free from stiffness or soreness.

The previous day's expedition had strained me more than I'd ever been strained before. Moving very slowly, I left my room and proceeded to put on my boots and cloak, which were mostly dry at that point. I was very thankful that I hadn't bothered to undress the night before. It took me nearly five minutes to get my boots on, and my blistered feet were screaming in protest by the time the last strap was in place.

I left the dwelling and walked very slowly to the town center. Despite my encumbrance, I was still among the first to arrive. That fact made it hard for me to ignore Rasby, standing with her new friends, Tiera and Tirea. I purposefully turned my back on the three and went over to Bala.

"You ok?" I asked, taking in the sour expression she wore.

"Just fine," Bala snapped.

I nodded, ready to let the conversation drop, but she apparently wasn't.

"Unless you ask my parents," she muttered. "In which case, I'm the most selfish person in the entirety of The Clan."

"What happened?" I wondered. Having often heard similar statements from Bala, I knew there was more to it.

"Apparently, I'm not good enough to go on walks with my father. He only wants to take my sister, Bacet."

"Maybe he just wanted to spend some one on one time with her," I suggested.

"He never gives me any one on one time," she hissed under her breath.

"Did you follow them?" I asked.

"No, but as they were leaving, I opened the window in my and Bacet's room so I could watch them walk away. I should have been allowed that much at least.

"Then my mom called me to help make dinner—no one else has to help make dinner—and I forgot to close the window. When Bacet was sent to bed, there was a pile of snow on top of her blankets.

"Of course," Bala continued, "my parents thought I did it on purpose. They said I have to do everyone's chores until our next free day. It's so unfair!"

"That's rough," was all I said, knowing Bala wasn't as innocent as she claimed, especially since it hadn't snowed at all the day before.

Ashlo had joined us halfway through Bala's lament, so Bala started re-telling it. Even though the second version was slightly more dramatic, I didn't pay much attention. Most of my energy was focused on ignoring Rasby and keeping a lookout for Cole.

I caught his eye as soon as he arrived in the town center. From the way he moved as he approached me, I gathered that the trip had left him sore too.

"We need to find Astra," he whispered into my ear. Chast, the girl who had been ill the previous day, had joined the two girls on my left. Whatever ailment had kept her in the day before, seemed to have vanished. I causally moved a few steps away from the group as Bala launched into her third recount of the previous day's events.

"Why?" I hissed back to Cole. "So, there are a few guards. What does it matter?" I was sure it was no big deal, and I would have been content to completely forget that we had even bumped into Astra in the valley at all.

"It just really felt like there was something she was going to tell us, and I want to know what it was," he said.

I sighed, not wanting to argue, but it was hard when he was being so stupid. "How do you recommend we find her?" I asked.

"I don't know, but let's split up," he suggested.

I really didn't like that idea. However, if anyone was going to talk to Astra alone, it was going to be me. That meant I needed to figure out where she would be.

For a moment, I imagined I was Astra, in a world full of musty stables, wild horses, and the mournful cry of the wind.

On the first day she had come to training at The Barracks but not since.

Why?

Was there a logical reason for Astra to have not returned on the second day? Had she found the lesson boring? Could it be that she thought she wouldn't need the skills The Barracks had to teach? Or was she overconfident in her abilities?

I furrowed my brow. If that was the case, then why had she been there the first day? It was obvious that they were going to focus on physical combat, so no one should have been surprised.

SEEKING

Suddenly, I understood. None of us knew what skills would be taught at each of the villages. I had surmised most of them easily enough, but a few were still a mystery.

Astra must have decided to investigate each village before deciding what to focus on. Her approach made so much sense, I wasn't sure why I hadn't thought of going about things in the same way.

Now that I had guessed what her strategy might be, how could I use that to find her? There were nine villages. Astra had already been to two, but I only knew one of them. I had a one in eight chance of being right. At least I knew one village that she would not be going to: The Barracks.

"Any ideas on where she'll go?" Cole interrupted my thoughts.

"Not The Barracks," I answered. He nodded without asking me why, and I decided not to explain my conclusion to him for the sake of time. Jase appeared a moment later, and Cole motioned him over to join us.

"We're going to split up today and see if one of us can find Astra," Cole said.

Jase looked confused, but nodded. If he were the one to find her, he wouldn't have a clue what questions to ask or what the significance of her answers would be.

A sudden idea struck me. "Wait here," I told the boys.

I approached a group of two little boys and a little girl, the youngest potentials in our village. "Did any of you happen to go to The Making or The Golden Fields last training day?" I asked the trio.

All three of the kids shook their heads. "We stayed here last time," the little girl said.

"Did a girl wearing black clothes join you? She would have been older, about my age."

Again, the children shook their heads 'no'. I was about to walk off, when the smallest of the three, a little boy with light

THE PREPARATIONS

hair and blue eyes, spoke up. "My big brother, Flant, went to The Golden Fields."

"Thanks," I called over my shoulder. Quickly, I scanned the group of potentials until I saw Flant's familiar, plump shape.

He was standing by himself, glancing around as though looking for someone—Larna, I assumed. She was yet to appear, although almost everyone else was already present.

"Hi," I said to Flant, smiling at him.

"Hey," he responded, a little uncertainly.

"So, what village did you go to last time?" I asked, trying to be casual. It was hard, because normally he wasn't the kind of person I would have had anything to do with.

"I went to The Golden Fields. Finding food will be important when we're on our own," Flant chuckled, as if what he had said was actually witty.

"Yes," I agreed, trying—and failing—to join in his laughter. "You didn't happen to see a girl there named Astra, did you?"

Flant shook his head, making his pudgy neck wobble. "I'm not sure. There were a lot of potentials, and I didn't catch many names. What does she look like?"

"She has reddish-brown hair and wears black clothes," I told him.

Flant thought for a moment. "You know, I did see a girl there wearing all black. I thought it was really odd, but I heard she was from The North Wind, and honestly," he said, leaning closer to me as if he was going to tell me his deepest secret, "they're all a little strange up there."

I laughed softly, and it was almost legitimate, because he was most definitely correct.

Time to get away.

"Thanks, that's what I needed to know." Quickly, I left Flant and returned to the boys.

"Did you find something out?" Cole pressed, looking at me expectantly.

"I have a couple of guesses," I admitted.

What I didn't say was that I was pretty sure I knew exactly which village Astra would choose. Cole would want to be the one to go there, and I was reserving that privilege for myself.

"Jase, you go to The Farm," I instructed. Jase nodded. He didn't appear sore at all from the previous day, which was why I gave him the farthest destination.

"Cole, you take The Making." Cole nodded too. There was a slight chance Astra would turn up there, but I was pretty sure she was visiting the villages in progression. Just in case she switched the order, Cole might as well get to talk to her, just so we could put all of the questions behind us and start focusing on what was important.

"I'll take Riverside," I announced.

Just as I finished speaking, a member of the council appeared. She called roll in a high, nasally voice, before sending us on our way.

Larna was the only one missing; I wished her loads of punishment.

Chapter 12

MARK

I appreciated the peaceful morning air and still silence of the landscape as I walked to Riverside. The wind was nothing more than a gentle whisper, too light even to lift a feather from the ground. Glittering piles of snow refracted the early morning sunlight, casting multicolored rays of their own. Everything about the southern road was more welcoming than the northern road I had traveled the day before.

After ten minutes, my muscles loosened up. Even though I still felt sore, it was pleasant to stretch my aching limbs. The only place I continued to experience discomfort was my feet. Moving across level ground wasn't so bad, since the boots I wore were soft and supple, but every time I had to take a step up or down, I winced in pain as the leather pinched one of my many blisters.

None of the other potentials from The Paramount had chosen Riverside as their destination for the day. In fact, from the empty road, it appeared that almost no one was heading there. I began regretting my choice.

Riverside was the southernmost of The Clan's villages. It was medium-sized, positioned right on the edge of land and water. Because of the danger of flooding, no other village was built within half a mile of The Great River. However, since everything in Riverside was centered around the water, I supposed it was more efficient to fix possible flood damage than to hike half a mile to work each day.

THE PREPARATIONS

Dwellings made of gray, weathered boards were clustered tightly around the town center, which lay on the northern edge of the village. The layout was the exact opposite of The Paramount, where the dwellings were placed on the outskirts. I'm sure the design was to keep the inhabitants of Riverside as far from the river as possible. Although, in the southern part of our territory, there wasn't a river so much as a lake. The land formed a natural bay, causing a great expanse of water to stretch out around the village.

Throughout the winter and early spring, the lake remained frozen, rendering boats useless. Far in the distance, I could hear the sound of the river, flowing as steadily as if the cold didn't exist. The inhabitants of Riverside would have at least another month's rest before the waters of the lake were free once more. During the winter, their time was spent repairing boats and mending nets.

When I entered the village, the first thing I noticed was the smell. It was far less pungent than during the summer, but even still, the odor of dead fish hung in the air.

About a dozen potentials were waiting in the town center when I arrived. My eyes ran over their clothing quickly. Most of it was dark blue, brown, or green but no black. One of the boys wore tan and had an ankle wrapped in linen cloth. I assumed he had twisted or sprained it somehow and that was why he'd chosen not to leave Riverside.

I ended up hearing the account of how the injury had taken place while we waited for the training to begin. One of the older boys from The Quarry asked him what had happened.

"I was at The Farm yesterday," the boy began. "Just as we were leaving for the day, a cat came walking across one of the fields toward one of the barns. They have lots of cats living in the haylofts who hunt the mice. I'm not sure if this one was out exploring or what not, but she looked exhausted.

"Just as she was getting close to us, a badger came leaping out at her and grabbed her with its claws. I ran toward them screaming. The badger saw me coming and tried to run off with the cat, but I threw a chunk of ice and hit him, so he dropped her."

"Was the cat ok?" a girl from The Barracks inquired.

"A little shaken up, but otherwise fine," the boy nodded. "She was really happy when I picked her up and took her to a warm nest in the hayloft."

"But what happened to your foot?" the boy from The Quarry wanted to know.

"When I threw the ice at the badger, I slipped into a hole under the snow. It wasn't so bad yesterday, but when I woke up this morning, it was hot and really painful. Hopefully, it will be better in a few days."

As the boy finished speaking, an old woman joined us. Her name was Hapa, and she was to be our instructor for the day. Her hair was white, and she had a hump on her back that caused her to be bent almost double. The skin of her face was brown and weathered from constant exposure to the elements.

We waited another quarter hour, during which time a dozen more potentials joined us. Then, just as Hapa seemed ready to start the lesson, Astra appeared.

So, I had been correct all along. I usually was.

I gave her a smug smile when she looked my way. The surprised expression on her face when our eyes met was delightful. She hadn't expected me to find her quite so easily. Honestly, it hadn't been very hard.

Hapa offered Astra a warm greeting, even though she was late. It wasn't quite fair that no one seemed to care when Astra showed up. However, I supposed that those not from The Paramount couldn't be expected to understand the immense importance of timeliness.

Also, it was hard to begrudge Astra, when I knew from the previous day's venture exactly how far she had to travel every morning. Still, excuses didn't make the clock go 'round, and I

THE PREPARATIONS

assumed Astra rode at least part of the way to her destination each day.

The training session began, and I put Astra out of my mind—or at least tried to. It was an impossible feat. Several times, I sensed her watching me, but I tried not to so much as glance in her direction.

Hapa spent the morning showing us how to make fish hooks out of bits of old bones, shells, and pretty much whatever else was laying around. We also learned to make bobbers and line. The old woman was a genius. She seemed to be able to turn anything into an instrument for fishing.

"Why don't you make fishing hooks out of metal?" Astra wondered two hours into the session. She had just finished sharpening the end of a well-shaped hook.

"We do sometimes, but they can only be used by those who fish from the shore," Hapa told us. "Metal is too heavy and sinks too fast. Any boat that goes out on the lake with so much as a scrap of metal in it, will go down and never come back up again."

"That doesn't make sense," Astra said. "Why—"

"It is against the rules," Hapa replied, cutting Astra off. "For good reason too. When I was your age, I witnessed several young men take a boat out for an afternoon fishing excursion. One of them had a metal fishhook with him. It pulled the boat straight to the bottom, and they were all drowned."

Astra appeared skeptical, but didn't say anything.

All morning I paid close attention to what Hapa showed us. The skills I had picked up at The Barracks interested me more, but there was no denying the importance of the information to be gleaned at Riverside as well.

Even while focusing on the lesson, I unconsciously kept one eye on Astra, following her every move. Hapa praised her several times for being 'very clever with her hands'. Astra returned Hapa's compliments with a small smile and a nod. I had the sense that she knew I was watching her and that she was watching me too whenever my back was turned.

In the afternoon, Hapa demonstrated how to assemble all the parts we had made into a fishing pole. Once everyone had crafted a passable specimen—it took some of the potentials three or four tries—we moved on and began learning how to use them.

Hapa lined us up along the lakeshore so we could practice casting out onto the frozen water. After my first couple of casts, I had some trouble with a tangle in my line. When Hapa noticed, she came over to assist, but I'd already worked it out. The old woman remained for a moment and watched me cast my line again.

"Here, hold it like this," she instructed, stepping forward and repositioning my hands on the pole. "Now, cast nice and strong."

"Much better," she said after watching me send the bone hook several dozen yards out onto the ice.

"Hapa, why isn't the river frozen?" the little boy beside me asked. He pointed a pudgy hand beyond the icy lake to where the river raced by, as if the two were unconnected.

Several of the nearby potentials followed the boy's finger, and then looked to Hapa for an explanation. "The river flows too quickly for the water to freeze," Hapa told us.

"Then, how come there aren't any boats out fishing on the river?" the same boy asked. He was from The Quarry and looked far too young to be a potential.

Hapa shook her head. "The Great River is treacherous. It's full of rocks and strong currents. No boat that ventures near it will ever return. We have to be very careful not to leave the safety of the lake."

"Has it ever frozen?" a girl from The Making asked. She was about my age, with straight, blonde hair and big, brown eyes.

Hapa shook her head. "No, if it ever did, the entirety of The Clan would be vulnerable. Anything, even the great darkness itself, would be able to cross the frozen surface and walk among us."

The group of children laughed at the fake menace in her voice.

It was a chilling thought, although, completely ridiculous, as if darkness was a tangible thing that could be warded off by flowing water.

"So, no one has *ever* swum across?" asked another boy. He wore the light green color of The Golden Fields, the closest village to Riverside from the east.

Hapa laughed at his question. "Of course not. Haven't you been paying attention? The river has a strong undertow. It is an impenetrable barrier that protects us from the darkness in the rest of the world."

"I'm going to swim across one day," the boy with the bandaged foot announced. "When I'm bigger and strong enough, I'll be the first person to ever make it across."

"No, you won't, Joss," Hapa chided him. "You'll do no such thing. It is against the rules to even try."

I glanced at the boy, Joss. He was rather short and scrawny for his age. It would probably be a long time before he was ready to attempt such a feat.

When the afternoon began to wane, the training session came to a close. Hapa told us that the following day's session would focus on how to scale and clean fish. She added that the following month, they would be teaching us to make rope and nets. I made a mental note to return soon. Items such as those would be invaluable during the trials.

When Hapa released us, we all thanked her for the lesson. She beamed at our gratitude and bid us all to take care while returning to our villages.

The other potentials were standing around in little clusters talking and laughing. Astra headed out immediately, walking at a good pace to the north. I hurried to catch up with her.

"Wait," I called, half running after the darkly-clad girl. She had already reached the road. Astra wasn't that much taller than I—only a few inches, really—but her legs seemed so much longer than mine.

"Wait," I yelled again. Astra glanced back. I could almost see her weighing the decision between waiting for me and not. Even though her expression was far from pleased, she did stop.

"Why are you following me?" she asked as soon I was within ten paces.

"I think you know," I replied, stopping just in front of her.

Astra studied me intently for a moment. "Where's your boyfriend?" she asked. 'Boyfriend' was a very improper word to use. It degraded the search of a life mate to something shallow and short-lived.

I gritted my teeth against her rudeness. She knew I wasn't at the appropriate age to even start considering a life mate. Her words were meant only to antagonize me.

"Cole is at The Making," I replied.

Astra furrowed her brow. "No, not the First Clan Leader's son. I meant the big guy."

Frustration nearly overwhelmed me. If striking someone had not been such a serious offense, I would have punched the sarcasm out of her mouth. If her first comment had offended me, the last one had made me ready to kill her. On top of it all, she was smiling, like she knew exactly how much her words had annoyed me.

Be like Myna, a voice whispered.

I took a quick breath, and when I spoke, I knew my words betrayed little, if any, emotion. "Jase and Cole are both just friends. As is proper, I will not start seeking anything more until after I am an adult."

THE PREPARATIONS

Astra nodded, seeming slightly disappointed that I hadn't risen to her remarks. "So, what do you want?" she asked.

"I have questions."

"You mean about The Valley of the North Wind?"

"Well, yes, but also—" I paused. *What exactly did Cole want to know?*

Maybe it would be better if we could talk to her together. Then, Cole could get his answers and see what a nuisance Astra was.

"Come back with me so we can all talk together," I said.

Astra shook her head. "I'm not interested in talking about anything in The Paramount."

"Why?" I asked. "What's wrong with The Paramount?"

Astra glanced around, even though there was absolutely no one in sight but the two of us. Slowly, she leaned in close to me. "There are too many ears listening." She pulled back. "There are ears everywhere, but I fear the ones in The Paramount far more than those outside it."

I had to push down my annoyance again. The Paramount was a great place. No one there was a spy or a snoop. "I'm not walking all the way to The North Wind," I growled.

Astra considered for a moment. "Here's the deal. The Paramount is on the way home for me. Let's go there, pick up Cole and the big guy, and then we can leave the village and talk on the road. As long as it's just us."

"Fine," I agreed, desperately wanting to get the business over with.

Things being settled as such, we struck out for The Paramount. At first, we traveled in silence, and I was determined not to be the one to break it.

The first half of the trip passed quietly. Finally, after forty-five minutes of walking, when we were half way to our destination, Astra turned to me.

"I'm curious, how did you know where to find me?" she asked. There was no hostility in her voice.

"I figured out your strategy," I responded.

Astra raised an eyebrow at me questioningly.

"You're visiting each of the villages to find out what they teach," I explained. "You went to The Barracks the first day and The Golden Fields the second, so it made sense that you would be at Riverside today."

"That's pretty good," Astra replied. "But if you knew I'd be here, why didn't you bring along your boyfriends?"

The casual way in which she used the unseemly word made me start to wonder if its use wasn't quite so scandalous in The North Wind.

"I mean, if they all wanted to talk to me so badly, why didn't they come here?"

"Because I like to hedge my bets," I answered. "If I hadn't chosen correctly, we stood a better chance of finding you by spreading out."

"Smart," Astra commented. It sounded like there was a bit of respect in her voice.

She turned to examine me once more. Not so much scanning my outward appearance, but she seemed instead to be staring through my flesh with her green gaze. "I believe there is more to you than meets the eye, Myra."

So glad you approve, I thought sullenly.

Even though I'd never told her my name, somehow, she knew it. Then again, she hadn't told me hers either. Was it possible that Astra was as hyperaware of me as I was of her?

That was the end of our conversation. Astra didn't seem to have anything else to say, and I wasn't keen on giving her more insight into my mind or life.

As we reached the outskirts of The Paramount, I could tell something wasn't right. There was a loud murmuring of voices—voices that should have been working. Dozens of people were hurrying along towards the already crowded town center.

Suddenly, the bell rang. Normally, the bell was only rung to indicate the beginning and ending of each day. The only other reason for it to be rung was to call the inhabitants of the village together when something important occurred.

I exchanged a quick glance with Astra, and we both took off running. We arrived just in time to see what was going on.

The entire council, including Myna and Core, were assembled in the middle of the town center. At least three quarters of The Paramount's population had gathered around them.

Pushing through the crowd, I tried to imagine what could possibly be going on. It was a complete mystery until I caught sight of Larna, who was standing close beside Core. Tears were running freely down the girl's face. I suddenly recalled that she had been absent when they had taken roll that morning.

"Has someone died?" Astra whispered to me. "Was anyone sick?"

I shook my head. Nothing of that sort had been mentioned recently. Usually, it was common knowledge when someone was ill. People generally tried to avoid those who were contaminated, thereby stopping the spread of disease. The only ones who would go near the sick person were their own family members and the village healers.

Even though the position of healer was highly respected, it was not something I had ever wanted. I knew that they were serving their community by saving one life at a time, but that was not how I wanted to serve mine. Their lives were unpredictable because they weren't bound to any certain place and could be transferred whenever and wherever the council deemed necessary.

The position wasn't something you could apply for; you had to be chosen. They normally selected gentle, soft-hearted children around the age of ten, but I had heard of them approaching people as old as twenty. Those chosen would train with a healer in their respective villages every third day out of four until they were granted full healer status.

When someone died unexpectedly, a village meeting would be called, and a healer would usually explain the cause of death. That afternoon, there were no healers present that I could see.

Once nearly everyone in the village had gathered, Core stepped forward. "People of The Paramount and guests from the other villages of The Clan, thank you for your presence here today," he greeted us. The crowd was leaning forward, eager to find out why they had been called.

"Most days, I find it a pleasure to serve you as Clan Leader. Today, however, I must perform the most unpleasant of my duties: punishment."

Core did look grieved. His serious tone was met with complete silence.

I glanced at Myna, standing to his left. If she had spoken the exact same words, I couldn't imagine anyone believing her. She didn't appear to care one way or the other.

I turned my attention back to Core as he continued speaking. "Today, Larna of The Paramount will receive her first mark." There was a stir among the crowd. It was unusual for one so young to receive a mark.

Marks were used to note bad behavior, just like in school. However, the marks in school weren't very serious and were wiped away at the end of the day. A mark from the council remained forever. They were only given out for the most serious of crimes. If a person received three marks, they would be banished from The Clan, an unimaginable fate.

"The reason for this punishment is to be noted as follows," Core continued, nodding to a pair of scribes close at hand. One of them would be recording the First Clan Leader's every word in a daily log book.

The second held a large scroll. Whenever there was a birth in The Paramount, the child's name was added to the scroll. Each village had its own list. The space beside Larna's name, which had always been empty, would have a dark mark beside it for the rest of her life.

Core cleared his throat, and then recited the charges against Larna. "Attempting to gain information about the trials and asking inappropriate questions with the intent of gaining information regarding the trials from an unstable adult." As Core made the pronouncement, I saw the pens of the scribes move. One in a series of rapid movements; the other in only a single long stroke.

"You have all witnessed the justice of today and will bear testament to it in the future," Core addressed those gathered in the town center.

A small sob escaped Larna's lips, drawing my eyes to her. A moment later, she buried her face in her hands.

I recalled that she had a grandmother who lived in Treescape with her oldest child's family. Age had made her forgetful and soft in the head.

Perhaps, Larna had tried to get her to talk about the trials. That might have even been where she had been going when we had seen her the previous morning. At least she had been caught and not us. Otherwise, it would have been me standing there, in front of the whole village, marked forever, and one step closer to banishment. In the future, I would have to be more careful.

It was obvious that Larna was being made into an example for the rest of the potentials; otherwise, her offense might have been overlooked. Seeking knowledge about the trials was highly forbidden, but giving out a mark was serious too. Now, no one else would dare ask questions or even bring the topic up.

Core gave Larna a sad look and spoke a few words, too low for me to hear. Knowing him, he was probably trying to pass on some wisdom to the sobbing girl, generously encouraging her to learn to live with her mark and not incur a second or, even worse, a third.

A moment later, he turned back to us.

"We are The Clan," Core began, voice ringing with conviction as he recited the familiar words. "We were created to be order when all else was chaos. We have lived in peace as our fathers have taught us. We show justice to all without hesitation. We will continue as we have been: the only perfect society."

At the conclusion of the adage, the crowd began to disperse. Core, Myna, and the others slowly filed back into the council building. Larna was left standing in the town center completely alone. No one approached her, not even her own family or Flant.

There was a slight twinge of pity in my stomach, but I pushed it down. Larna wouldn't be an outcast forever. It would take a while before anyone would see her and think about anything other than her mark, but the trials were starting soon. All else would be forgotten as Midsummer approached.

I glanced at Astra, suddenly worried that the incident would make her no longer willing to talk to Cole and me. She did look upset, but not afraid or even apprehensive so much as angry.

Without looking at me, Astra spun on her heel and marched out of the town center. I followed as she headed straight for the northern road, nearly having to run to keep up with her long strides.

We didn't speak until the village was a quarter of a mile behind us. Only then did she turn on me, folding her arms across her chest.

"Alright," she said. "What do you want to know?"

Chapter 13

CERTAIN TRUTHS

Although the passion with which Astra had stormed out of The Paramount did not dissipate, she agreed to wait for Cole along the road to The Making. I hadn't seen him in the town center and assumed he was probably still at training.

Before long, a group of potentials approached from the north. Some wore maroon and others the assorted colors of the southern villages of The Clan.

I picked Cole out of the group but didn't want to wave or draw the attention of the rest of the children. He turned his head, and our eyes locked. A moment later, he quickened his pace and headed in my direction.

Once Cole reached us, and the other potentials were out of sight, Astra wordlessly led us away from The Paramount, toward the icy fields that spanned the north.

It felt like we were a quarter of the way to The North Wind before she came to a halt. The land was flat there, the snow on the sides of the road undisturbed. It was a clear day, and I could see The Mountains of the North Wind cutting boldly through the blue sky in the distance.

Once satisfied that there was no one around to hear us, Astra turned to me. Cole jumped in before I could say anything. "Why are you allowed in The Valley of the North Wind?" he asked.

"I told you yesterday, I go there to train horses," Astra replied. "Not everyone does it, but those of us who have

THE PREPARATIONS

demonstrated enough skill to be considered trainers are permitted to enter the valley."

Cole narrowed his eyes. "But no one else is allowed to go there?"

"Correct."

"That doesn't seem right," Cole announced.

Astra shrugged. "Why not? Only people from Riverside are allowed to go out on the lake in boats."

"That's different," Cole countered. "They only go out for work, not recreation."

"You think I was enjoying recreation yesterday?" Astra asked. That brought Cole up short.

"It was our day off," I pointed out, taking Cole's lack of response as an opportunity to join the conversation. "You couldn't have been working, so what were you really doing in the valley?"

Astra shook her head helplessly. "I've already told you, but you won't believe me," she sighed. "You were both raised in The Paramount, so I don't expect you to understand."

I was taken aback by her dismissive words. It was the second time she had scorned The Paramount. Never before had I met anyone that had not envied me my birth into the most important and exclusive of The Clan's villages.

"What do you mean?" asked Cole. Even he couldn't keep the defensiveness out of his voice.

"In The Paramount, everything is about numbers and how they look in the books. There's a formula for everything that's done, and it always adds up in the end."

"But just because we're supposed to have a day off, that doesn't mean the horses will feed themselves." She gave a little half laugh. "I suppose if you had horses in The Paramount, you'd probably just teach them to look after themselves."

"We probably would," I replied smugly.

"I'll believe it when I see it," Astra muttered.

Cole's forehead furrowed. "Why do you dislike The Paramount so much?" he asked.

"Because of what we just saw." Astra gestured back toward the village behind us.

"Larna got a mark for trying to ask her grandmother about the last trials," I said, quickly filling Cole in.

His eyes widened in surprise, and he opened his mouth to speak, but no words came out.

Astra shook her head; her voice was soft. "Too many rules."

"But the rules protect us," I argued. "They are extensive, but they all have a purpose. Would it be better to live without them?"

"What rules do you think will protect us out there?" wondered Astra, nodding towards the distant mountains and the valley. We were all silent for a moment; I had never thought of that.

"I've got to go," Astra said, turning away from us.

"Wait," Cole cried, taking a step toward her. "We want to hear the rest of it. What's really going on in the valley?"

Silently, Astra's gaze slid over us. Her face was unreadable, but I imagined she was trying to decide whether to tell us anything or not.

Finally, she decided. "You want me to tell you about the soldiers? Alright, this is what I know. They're always there, sixteen at a time. Eight of them stay in The North Wind, and the other eight stand guard at the far end of the valley where you saw them. They change places every two days. Every eight days, more come from The Barracks to replace them. They ignore me, and I ignore them."

"But what are they doing?" Cole asked. "If they want to keep us from entering the valley, they should be at the other end."

Astra looked at Cole like he was missing the point. "They aren't there to keep us in, they're there to keep others out."

THE PREPARATIONS

"Who?" I asked breathlessly. We'd all heard of the Broken, but as far as I knew, one hadn't been seen in decades. They were nothing more than a handful of starved people, crazy in the head, and hardly adept enough to navigate The Valley of the North Wind.

Astra glanced around, and her voice dropped to just above a whisper. "When people get banished, they don't always want to leave The Land of the Clan. Sometimes, they try to get back in."

The words sent a shock through my body. I'd never considered what I would do if I was suddenly ripped from my place of protection and thrown into the death that lay outside The Land of the Clan.

"What are you saying?" I demanded, half afraid to hear the answer.

Astra was silent for a moment. "The soldiers tell them to leave, to walk away and never come back. If they don't go, the demand gets more physical. And if they still won't listen, the soldiers kill them."

My jaw dropped open. Among The Clan, murder was the worst offense that could be committed. I forced my mouth closed as I processed what Astra was saying.

If those people had been removed from The Clan, then they had no right to expect to be treated as if they were one of us. Whatever happened to them, happened. Exiles were no better than the Broken. Killing them was merciful in a way. They could at least die quickly, close to the land they had known. It might have been better that way. Otherwise, they could end up dying painfully, far from everything they had ever known.

Cole looked far more horrified than I was. "How many people are banished every year?"

"Twenty or so, normally. Some have reached three marks for infractions of the rules. The rest have done something that calls for immediate removal."

I nodded; the figure seemed right. What were twenty people a year against the greater good of so many others?

"How do you know all this?" I challenged Astra.

"They always come through The North Wind," she told us. "Sometimes, if it's late, they spend the night. It's easy to get turned around in the valley after dark, and the soldiers don't want to risk an exile escaping or someone getting killed in a landslide."

"It's not that hard to get through the valley," I blurted out.

Grim-faced, Astra replied, "The main path is mostly safe, but there are a few tricky sections. However, a lot of the smaller passes are unstable. There are at least a dozen fatalities in the valley every year."

"Perhaps, The North Wind shouldn't allow the people from your village to go there then," I couldn't help pointing out.

Astra shook her head. "It's not us."

"If it's not you and the soldiers are so careful, then who dies there?" I asked. I thought back to the white rock I'd seen in the valley, and wondered if it hadn't perhaps been a skull after all.

There was a long pause. It was easy to see that Astra was deciding exactly how much of the truth she was going to tell us. When she did speak, her words came slowly, and she chose them with great care.

"There's a rumor about certain places in the valley. Places where the dead still speak."

Astra glanced at us, taking in our blank expressions.

"The valley is full of whispers, and they say it contains the souls of the dead. Not just those of The Clan who have died, but others, from *before* too. If you have lost someone you love, you can seek out one of the special places and talk to them again."

My father.

Was it true? Could it possibly be true? Talking about the dead was rude, but why had I never heard about the rumor before?

THE PREPARATIONS

"Do you know where any of these places are? Have you talked to your parents?" I blurted out the words and instantly regretted them.

Astra shut down. I could see it immediately. She had told us more than she probably did most people, but I had broached the wrong subject.

"Your parents are..." Cole started, but never finished. I realized he hadn't known that Astra's parents were dead until just that moment.

I didn't expect an answer from Astra, but I heard her quietly say, "No, I haven't."

Part of me wanted to pour out how I had lost my father and would do anything to hear his voice again, but I didn't. I never talked about him, just as I assumed Astra didn't talk about her parents.

We were all silent for a moment.

"I need to go," Astra said. "I've got plenty to do back home."

Cole reached forward quickly and caught her arm. "Thank you for talking with us. We won't tell anyone what you've said, so don't worry about that."

"I won't," Astra replied confidently. "Besides, I've got way worse stuff on you." Her words were very serious, but she winked at Cole as he released her arm.

Cole and I turned back to The Paramount, and Astra began the long walk north.

I had much to think about. In just five days, my world had changed considerably. Before the trials had been announced, everything had made sense. Suddenly, it felt like I'd only brushed the surface of what was really going on in The Clan.

"Are we going to tell Jase?" Cole asked, as we approached the outskirts of The Paramount.

"Tell Jase what?" I wondered. "That there are guards in The Valley of the North Wind? He knows that already. If he transfers to The Barracks at some point, he'll probably find out the reason anyway."

"I still think we should tell Jase," Cole muttered.

"Whatever," I said. It was rather rude to use the word in that way, but the soldiers didn't interest me anymore.

"We haven't really learned anything. Except that The North Wind doesn't seem to think it should have to follow the rules the rest of us live by." I didn't mean to sound angry or bitter, but I knew I did.

"You're not going to say something to your mother, are you?" Cole asked with concern.

Of course not.

"Of course not," I said aloud. Me, tell Myna something? Didn't he pay any attention?

Cole still seemed worried. "I'm not a tattletale," I insisted. "Besides, Astra was right; she's got worse stuff on us."

She had the power to get each of us a mark, or worse. I hated the idea of her—or anyone else—having any sort of advantage over me.

Once the trials began, it wouldn't matter anyway. After I won, she could tell everyone how she had seen me in The Valley of the North Wind, but no one would believe her. They would just think she was acting out of petty jealousy.

We were in the village now, and I gladly changed the subject. "What did they teach at The Making?"

I spent the remainder of the walk listening to Cole explain how to make baskets for collecting food, and even how to seal them to hold water. His words were background noise for my real thoughts, although I nodded and laughed at the appropriate places.

Could there be something special about The Valley of the North Wind? Was it possible that I might be able to speak to my father again? If I could talk to him, it would mean so much. I would have someone to confide in, someone who understood me, someone who loved me unconditionally.

THE PREPARATIONS

Plans flooded into my mind as I considered risking another trip to the valley, despite what Astra had said about it being dangerous. However, when we passed the town center, I let the idea slip away. I would not risk receiving a mark of my own.

Maybe, once I returned from the trials—as a new Clan Leader, of course—I would be able to go and see if the rumor was true. But how could I do that? The entirety of The Clan would be watching.

I bid Cole farewell and had almost reached my dwelling when another thought occurred to me. If I came back from the trials and hadn't won—a painful, yet possible reality—I could always request a transfer to The North Wind. If Astra had become a trainer, I was sure I could as well.

Then, I wouldn't need anyone's permission to go to The Valley of the North Wind. Something about the thought of living without the same restrictions that had confined me my whole life was appealing.

A moment later, I laughed at myself for even considering it. I hated The North Wind. It was cold, and they were completely undisciplined. Plus, it was almost certain that I would never be admitted back into The Paramount.

That was where I belonged, where the world made sense. It wasn't until I had stepped into The Valley of the North Wind that I had started to questions things I had always accepted. Being back where I belonged, it was easier to push those thoughts aside. Everything about The Paramount was perfect.

I went to bed early, still exhausted from the day before, but my sleep was restless. All night, I kept trying to remember if I had heard anything in the valley that could have been my father's voice. Surely, if what Astra had said was true, he would be longing to speak to me just as much as I wanted to talk to him. It was to no avail; I couldn't remember anything.

When we met with Jase in the morning, neither Cole nor I mentioned the things Astra had told us. I was glad to let them pass. What we had learned was nothing but distractions, and our focus needed to be on our training.

"Where do you want to go today?" Cole asked.

"The Barracks," Jase said automatically. "I don't want to go anywhere near animals."

I smiled, remembering that I had sent Jase to The Farm the day before. Given his history, that might not have been the kindest move.

Cole didn't look convinced. "It's great that we're getting good at fighting," he said. "But it's important to branch out a little and learn other skills too."

"But I'm not good at the other stuff," Jase protested.

"We do have six months," I added. "There's no rush." Although, I was starting to wonder if the villages would be teaching the same things each month. Everything was so uncertain; it felt like I couldn't get ahead.

"Still," Cole said, "let's try somewhere new today."

"Sure," I replied, too tired from my restless night to care. "Did you have someplace in mind?"

"How about Treescape?" he suggested. "None of us have been there yet."

I agreed readily enough, and so did Jase, after a little persuading. He was just glad he didn't have to go back to The Farm. But that was something that I would never have allowed to happened, because I knew that it would be Astra's destination. I had no interest in seeing her again.

The northern villages were more spread out than the southern ones. So, we had a five-mile walk, but it was worth it. Treescape was one of the most beautiful villages of The Clan. It was set in a dense forest of pine trees. Many other kinds of trees grew farther north and west, spreading out to the brink of the river.

The buildings of the village were constructed from long, pine tree logs, which were notched on the ends so that they fit together. By using the logs in that manner, they were able to create square and rectangular buildings with slanted roofs.

I wished the dwellings in The Paramount could have been built with pine logs; they smelled amazing. Instead, we used stones cut from The Quarry because they were the best barrier against moister, and all our records had to be kept dry.

As we reached the town center of the village, I could see that it was a popular destination. There were almost as many potentials as had been at The Barracks the first two days.

We spent the session building makeshift lean-to's, which could be used as protection from the elements when a natural shelter, like a cave, couldn't be found.

I actually learned a lot, and what was more impressive was that Jase seemed to learn a lot too. The whole way back to The Paramount that afternoon, he couldn't stop going on about how much he loved building things.

"Do you think maybe you'll transfer to Treescape instead of The Barracks?" Cole asked when Jase finally stopped talking to a breath. Since his lungs were so large, he'd been speaking nonstop for quite a while.

Jase pulled up short, wordless at the idea. "After the trials, of course," Cole added.

"I don't know," Jase said. His forehead was puckered as he thought over the possibilities. "All my life everyone has told me how I would be perfect for The Barracks. I like both places, I really do. I'll have to think about it."

Cole's question worked wonders; Jase was silent for the rest of the walk. Cole and I didn't say anything either, but I could guess what he was thinking about. Even though I tried not to, I'd been thinking about the same thing all day: our conversation with Astra.

I sighed. It was better to let some things go, and what we'd heard the day before was definitely something that should be forgotten.

Chapter 14

EMPATHY

The rest of the month passed in no time. Each day I learned new things I would never have discovered if I'd spent my entire life studying in only one village.

The experiences were eye-opening. Never before had I considered relocating to a different village, but The Paramount was starting to seem small and closed-in.

I had traveled to other villages with Myna and for school, but those visits had mostly consisted of being left alone in strange dwellings or sitting through boring lectures on subjects that interested no one.

Now, I was able to learn for myself. I could touch everything and see everything. I studied simple and complex solutions to problems I hadn't even known existed.

For instance, one day at Treescape, the instructors demonstrated how to move a fallen log by creating a lever out of a rock and a long stick.

Knowledge is power, and I gained a lot of knowledge. It made me proud to return to The Paramount every night, thinking of how much I knew and how easy it would be for me to survive once I left The Land of the Clan.

If I didn't win the trials—didn't become a Clan Leader—could I content myself working as a scribe for the rest of my life? If I was appointed a village leader and managed to make it to the council, would I be happy spending the rest of my days sitting in meetings? Thoughts like those had started keeping me awake at night, or they would have, if I hadn't been so exhausted after training each day.

I saw almost nothing of Myna over the course of that month. I was pretty sure I didn't speak even one word to her. In the mornings, it was never a surprise to see that she was gone. When I returned at night, I didn't even bother to wonder if she would arrive before I fell asleep. Only twice did I hear her enter the dwelling after I'd already gone to bed.

Her absence no longer bothered me. I realized that I had spent far too much time in the past brooding over her actions. Finally, I was able to let all the pain and resentment rest in the face of something more important. It was all still there, but I didn't continually fret on it like I once had.

Cole, Jase, and I trained together nearly every day. Bala, Ashlo, and Motik joined us on a regular basis. The only time Jase left our side was when we were going somewhere like The Making. He didn't take much to crafting because he wasn't cleverhanded and lacked the patience to carve so much as a fishhook. Instead of trying to learn, he focused only on what he was good at and what he was interested in.

Whether that was wisdom on his part or not, I wasn't sure. By the end of the preparations, there would not be many who could best him physically. On the flip side, it was doubtful that he would even be able to feed himself. However, wouldn't it be fair for others to feed him if he could do the fighting and physical labor for them?

Regardless of how the team dynamics panned out, I wanted to know how to do everything I could. Cole thought along the same lines. We spent every day together, trying to round out our skills.

Before the trials had been announced, Cole and I had been friends. In the days following, we had become something more. I didn't exactly need him, but everything was easier when he was with me. I had never trusted anyone before. Not that I trusted Cole completely.

I believed that he was intelligent and, for the present, had both of our best interests in mind. Together, we would have a far greater chance of survival in the trials. The years we'd already spent leading our team in Attack and Defend had been the perfect practice.

Every once in a while, I had to fight off the momentary doubt that we could end up on separate teams. It was easily chased away. We were partners no matter where we went, and we excelled together, no matter what we did. Surely the council had taken notice of our excellent partnership.

Of course, I made it a point to spend time with other potentials as well, but it wasn't the same. Cole and I were the ones who decided where we were going; the others chose if they wanted to come along. It was like we were already the team leaders of our small group.

In the midst of training, school days became harder and harder to bear. The teachers seemed to feel that they had to compensate for all the interesting things we had been learning on training days by teaching us the most boring and pointless subjects ever to exist.

I couldn't help but wonder if classes had always been so boring, and I had just never realized it. School used to be something I had loved, but it had quickly turned into the drudgery of my life.

Another thing to dislike about school days was that I had to see Rasby with Tiera and Tirea. The three were inseparable. They did all their training together, their schooling together, and, I suspected, even spent their days off together.

It was true that I trained with Cole, Jase, Bala, and the others regularly; however, we weren't a trio of little, giggling girls. We were serious potentials, showing that we worked better together than alone.

When teams were chosen, Tiera and Tirea would inevitably be separated, and it would destroy them.

THE PREPARATIONS

Even if I was placed on a team without Cole or Jase or anyone that I knew, it would not change my resolve or my iron will. I hoped to be with them, but I would find a way to survive on my own if I had to. It was very foolish of Tiera and Tirea to think that they might be exempt from the sibling rule. Teams needed to be able to follow a distinct chain of command; sibling emotions ran far too deep to allow any group to function properly.

As it was, I pitied them. Their identities were too wrapped up in each other. They would never be able to stand on their own.

Another drawback of school was that I had to face Larna. For the first two weeks after she received her mark, no one talked to her except Cole. I didn't understand why he bothered making the effort. Not that it mattered in the end. Larna just walked past him like he wasn't there. Pretty soon, he gave up trying. Most likely, her rude behavior was due to her humiliation and the fact that Cole's father had been the one to sentence her.

***

I slept late on the following free day. When I finally did get up, I tried looking over some of the material we'd reviewed in class the day before. However, it didn't hold my attention, and I gave up in a matter of minutes.

I decided to get some fresh air to clear my head. My walks usually led me to the eastern edge of our land. The Great River was calmer there, at least above the water's surface. It was a long way to the nearest village, and the most peaceful place I knew.

On my way back, I usually chose to pass through the amphitheater. It was a very important place, even though it stood empty all but two nights out of the year. I liked to take advantage of its vacant seats and convenient location. It was a good spot to go and think when I just couldn't bear my solitary dwelling anymore.

Also, it held special memories of my father. I remembered coming to the amphitheater with him many times to look at the night sky. My father had loved the stars. He had used to tease me by saying they were brilliant stones hanging just out of reach.

As I passed the wooden stage and looked up the hill toward The Paramount, I saw a maroon-clad figure. Curious to see who had intruded into my normally-abandoned sanctuary, I walked forward. With her hood pulled up and her face buried in her hands crying, I didn't realize it was Larna until I was almost on top of her.

She wasn't sitting on one of the stone benches; instead, she had her knees on the ground with her elbows resting on the gray, stone seat. I considered hurrying away before she noticed I was there. However, no matter how disgusting Larna was, hearing her sob so bitterly bothered me. I couldn't help but recall the many nights I had lain awake weeping after my father's death.

No one had ever come to comfort me.

I still wasn't sure how I had found the strength to get out of bed every morning after crying all night. Those years had been the darkest time of my life. I had felt loneliness and sorrow more strongly than I had felt the will to live.

That was why, as much I wanted to walk away from Larna, I couldn't.

I didn't say anything; I just sat down and waited. It took her a good five minutes to notice someone was there. She raised her head suddenly, saw it was me, and instantly began wiping her face. After another minute or two she had managed to compose herself a bit.

"What are you doing here?" she asked sullenly.

I shrugged, keeping my eyes on the distance and not her tear-stained face. "I don't know," I said softly. It was true. I didn't know how to help, or even if I really wanted to, but I just couldn't leave. We sat there for a long time, neither of us speaking.

THE PREPARATIONS

I was fairly certain Larna started crying again, not sobbing, but I thought I saw a few silent tears course down the two creases in her chin. Since her messy blonde hair concealed half of her face, I couldn't tell for sure.

Finally, as the sun began to set, Larna started to talk. "I didn't mean to do anything wrong," she said honestly. "I just…"

She trailed off.

"You didn't think anyone would notice or mind," I finished for her.

Larna nodded, face contorting like she was going to start crying all over again. "How long do you think everyone will hold it against me?" she gasped, trying to hold the tears in and failing.

I sighed softly; such weakness.

"My own family doesn't even want me around. If they were permitted, I think they would have made me leave our dwelling."

In that moment, I could have opened up to her. I could have told her that Myna had treated me that way my whole life, even explained that I knew exactly the kind of isolation she was feeling.

But I didn't. My pain was my own; I would not trust the truth to anyone.

"The trials will start soon," I told her instead. "Once they begin, no one will even remember."

Larna wiped a tear from her cheek with the sleeve of her coat. "What if I'm not chosen? It'll be because of the mark, and then no one will ever let me forget."

"They'll chose you, if you show them that you're worthy of it," I said. "The mark will make no difference."

My words seemed to comfort her some. We sat in silence a bit longer. When the sun had finished setting, and the sky was beginning to turn from orange to pink, she rose. "I'd better go or they'll miss me at dinner."

She began mounting the slope back to the village. I looked after her, imagining how nice it would feel to be missed at dinner. For all Larna's recent pain and degradation, she was still far better off than I was.

Larna glanced back at me after she'd gone ten paces. "Thanks, Myra," she said, and then turned and departed.

I nodded my acknowledgement at her words, continuing to sit where I was on the stone bench. Eventually, I shifted onto my back, so I could look straight up. Night fell, and I watched the sky darken to blue, and then black.

It was so unfair. Why did I have to be the loneliest person in the entirety of The Clan?

Peacefully, I watched the stars begin to appear one by one. If my father was up there somewhere, a shining star looking down on me, what would he think of the person I had become?

I was nothing like him. He had been loving and gentle, the sort of person who would help anyone no matter who they were. However, he had not been the kind of person who would ever win the trials.

I knew I was more like Myna. She followed her head, not her heart, obeyed every rule without question, and gained the respect of all she met. Her abilities had led her to victory in the trials, and she had become a great guide to our people. However, even for all her cunning and determination, she was lacking.

Myna would never have spent the afternoon with Larna. So, maybe we weren't quite as similar as I feared.

I have to be her, I thought. *I can't be my father, not if I want to win.*

Couldn't you be both? a voice asked in my head.

Maybe someday, but not yet, was my reply.

Until the trials were over, I couldn't afford to let any of my father's personality through. I needed Myna's strength and wisdom to make it back alive. My father's gentleness would only get me killed.

Once I came back, however, maybe I could let my guard down sometimes. Those on my team would become my friends. We would understand each other and be bound together by the hardships and struggles we had faced. The rest of our lives would be spent together, working in unison as a team. More than anything else, that was why I really wanted to win the trials.

I hadn't intended to fall asleep, but sometime later I jerked awake. The nearly full moon was shining down from high above me now. Springing to my feet, I looked around in confusion, not remembering where I was, how I had gotten there, or why it was so cold.

As soon as my brain began working somewhat properly, the evening before came rushing back to me. I finished climbing the slope on which the amphitheater was built and headed into the village, careful not to make a sound. There was no official curfew, but it was generally frowned upon to be wandering around late at night without reason. People started wondering what you had been up to, and then came the prying questions.

I wished the moon hadn't been quite so bright. Had the sky been shrouded with clouds, I would have been nothing but a shadow, slipping along through the snowdrifts on the edge of the village. However, the silver light pouring out of the clear sky made me almost as visible as if it were high noon.

No one else seemed to be awake, and I managed to make it to my dwelling without causing a stir. Softly, I opened the door and stepped inside, heaving a sigh of relief. I nearly choked on it a moment later, when I realized I was not alone.

Myna and Core were standing before the dying fire, talking in low voices. Core froze when I appeared so suddenly. He stopping speaking mid-sentence. Unless I was mistaken, the last word out of his mouth had been 'Astra'.

Myna was the first to speak. "Myra, where have you been? This is no hour to be up."

Then why are you awake? I thought belligerently, but didn't allow the words to pass my lips.

I might have been able to get away with being surly and rude to Myna when it was just the two of us, but in front of others, especially the First Clan Leader, I didn't dare try it.

"I was with a friend," I explained. "I fell asleep and didn't wake up until a moment ago." It was true enough, but I dreaded the next question.

"Which friend?" Myna asked.

"Larna," I told her softly.

I could sense Myna's dissatisfaction with my answer, but, surprisingly, Core spoke up. "That's good," he said. "It's always a shame when someone so young feels the pain of a mark. Nothing will encourage her loyalty more than people being willing to overlook her first offense. I am sure your friendship and influence will help ensure that she takes greater care to abide by our laws."

I nodded. Myna still didn't look pleased, but she let it slide because of Core's enthusiasm.

"Myna, we can finish this discussion in the morning." Core nodded deeply to her, and I moved aside so he could get out.

"I don't want you associating with Larna," Myna commanded, once we were alone. "Whatever Core says, she is a rule-breaker and not to be trusted."

Normally, I would have spoken out against Myna telling me what to do, but that would have involved defending Larna. So, I let the resentment go and just said, "It was a one-time thing. I won't do it again."

Myna nodded. "Go to bed," she told me, and, for once, I didn't mind obeying her.

My greatest worry was that Larna might suddenly start thinking we were friends. I had no desire to inflict any more pain on her, but I did want her to leave me alone.

Fortunately, whether because I was standing with Cole when she arrived for roll call in the morning or because she knew me well enough to know I would never really be her friend, she didn't so much as glance my way.

I was perfectly happy for neither of us to ever speak of what had occurred in the amphitheater. It had been a moment of weakness on my part, and I regretted telling Core and Myna the truth. I did not want to end up on a team with Larna because they believed me to be sympathetic to her plight. I was not.

Chapter 15

MYSTERY

"We still haven't attended a training session at The North Wind," Cole pointed out to Jase, Bala, and myself one morning.

If it had been up to me, I would never have chosen to return to The North Wind while the snow was still on the ground. Winter was a long way from being over, and I was already so worn out from training I couldn't imagine making the exhausting trip.

"That's because there isn't going to be anything useful to learn in The North Wind," I argued.

The day promised to be warmer than any I could remember since before the Telling. Maybe that was why Cole seemed to have forgotten exactly how much snow and ice stood between us and The North Wind.

We were waiting in the town center for roll call. The sun was just beginning to peak over the horizon, and the air was laced with a hint of spring.

"Maybe they can tell us the secret to complete ignorance," Bala scoffed. "Or how to be completely useless."

I couldn't help grinning at Bala's sarcasm.

"Still, I think it's worth giving it a try at least once," Cole persisted. "It's one of the few villages we haven't been to yet."

"I don't want to go there," Jase announced. "I vote for The Barracks."

Cole sighed. "We trained there yesterday."

"What about Riverside?" I asked. "It's been awhile since we went there."

THE PREPARATIONS

Jase nodded eagerly, while Cole wore a discontented expression. He probably would have continued to argue with me, except Jase gave him a pleading look.

"Alright, Riverside it is," Cole consented at last.

I smiled as Jase let out an excited whoop.

The day at Riverside was spent making rope. In the afternoon, the four of us worked together to weave a net. The finished product would have been far better if Jase hadn't tried to help so much. As it was, our net had one corner with holes big enough for me to step through. Before the instructor came to check our work, I quickly added a few more lengths of rope. The last thing in the world I wanted was for Jase's carelessness to reflect poorly on my abilities.

***

Three days later, I found Cole waiting for me when I arrived at the town center. "I'm going to The North Wind today," he announced the minute I appeared.

There was something stubborn in the tone of his voice and the set of his jaw. It was easy to see he wasn't going to give up.

"Fine, let's do it," I sighed, not bothering to argue.

"You'll come with me?" he asked, sounding surprised that he had won so easily.

I gave a reluctant nod. "Someone has to be there to save you in case a horse attacks." We both laughed, knowing I wouldn't be of any use in said situation.

Motik was out sick for the day, but when the others arrived, we invited them to join us. As I suspected, Jase did not want to go. He elected instead to head to Treescape, his new favorite village. Bala decided that she would go with him.

At first, Ashlo said she would come with Cole and me, but she changed her mind after roll call and went with Larna to The Making instead.

MYSTERY

No one else from The Paramount chose to brave the northern road, so it was just the two of us. I didn't mind in the least. What I did mind, was that it was warmer again that morning, softening the snow and creating large, mushy patches all along the path.

"Spring's coming soon," Cole observed.

"It's already here," I growled, pulling my foot out of an ankle-deep puddle of slush.

"We're bound to have at least another three weeks of freezing temperatures," Cole commented. The only response I gave was a nod as I tried to pick my way along the driest part of the road.

Over the course of the trip, I began to dislike The North Wind and its lonely existence on the fringe of The Clan more and more. Because of the weather, traveling to any of the other villages would probably have been much the same. However, I wasn't in a generous mood, and it was easier to have something to blame.

"Has you mother been…different?" Cole asked me. "You know, since the trials started?"

"Not really," I answered without thinking. I'd hardly seen her. "Why do you ask?"

Cole shrugged. "My father seems—I'm not sure how to describe it actually."

I furrowed my brow. "What do you mean?"

"Well, normally, he's thrilled whenever my siblings come to see us, but lately, he's been asking them to join us for family dinners every couple of days."

"That must be nice," I sighed wistfully.

Cole was too intent on his own thoughts to discern the regret in my voice. "I mean, we all have a wonderful time when we're together, but suddenly, it seems like my father wants everyone there all the time."

"And you don't?" I asked.

"Of course I want them around," Cole told me, meeting my gaze. "It's just hard to focus on training and school with a full house."

"I can imagine," I replied, although I wasn't sure I could.

By the time we arrived at the village, the sun was well into the sky. I was mortified; I had never been late in my life. I hoped there were no elders present that day.

I saw them at almost every training session, lurking around to see who was focusing and who was goofing off. They watched us silently, writing notes on the long pieces of paper they carried with them.

As we neared what passed for The North Wind's town center, I was sure we would come walking into the lesson halfway through. Everyone would look at us with contempt, as I had looked at Astra and all other latecomers.

However, my fears were ungrounded. When we arrived, the place was quiet. Almost no one was there. A small group of potentials was huddled outside the largest of the barns. The structure ran parallel to The Mountains of the North Wind, which were about a mile farther ahead. I tried not to look to the northeast, where I knew the entrance to The Valley of The North Wind lay, hidden from view.

There were numerous smaller stables spread throughout the village, but the central one was at least twice the size of any of the others.

Cole and I joined the assembled children, there were about fifteen in all. It was still another few minutes before the instructor joined us. The woman looked tired and had heavy bags under her eyes as if she had been awake for days on end.

She was middle-aged, and her long, brown hair was tinged on the edges with silver. The features of her face were blunt and bulbous. Deep wrinkles had begun emanating from the corners of her mouth, stretching across her cheeks.

I doubted she had a life mate. Unattractive people like her often came to the secluded village to be alone. When she introduced herself as Babbs of The North Wind, I noticed that her voice was deep and had a calming nature to it. I could appreciate her no-nonsense attitude as we jumped right into training; although, it was a little unsettling how quickly I found myself on the back of a horse.

Even with my somewhat frequent trips to The North Wind, I had never ridden before. From what I had seen, horses could be quite unpredictable, but that didn't stop Babbs from thrusting me onto the back of a tall, brown mare.

At first, I felt like I was going to topple off with every step the animal took. Once I got over the strange sensation of not having my feet on the ground, it wasn't too bad. I was able to steer with minimal difficulty and even managed to get the horse into a rough, jolting trot, which was more than some potentials accomplished.

We proceeded to ride in circles for hours. From the center of the oval corral, where each potential sat on their own horse, Babbs gave instructions. 'Now walk.' 'Now stop.' 'Pick up a trot.' 'Circle to the left.'

In less than half an hour, I lost what little interest I'd had. Judging by Cole's face, he was disappointed as well.

When lunch was called, I was ready to head back to The Paramount, but that wasn't an option. I dreaded the thought of getting back onto a horse. However, even though I hadn't seen any, I was certain the council members were somewhere close by, keeping an eye on us.

Lunch was a cheerless event. The wind hadn't let up since we'd arrived. It was driving me insane, constantly blowing my hair one direction, and then the next. I was glad it was tied back; otherwise, I would never have been able to keep it out of my face.

Cole and I sat together, but didn't say much. The other children, mostly from Treescape and The Making, the two closest villages, didn't really talk either.

THE PREPARATIONS

The sun was hidden by clouds, making the day seem bleak, even though the air continued to grow warmer. I dreaded the sodden path Cole and I would have to take back to The Paramount at the conclusion of the day's lesson.

As soon as lunch was over, we filed back toward the riding ring where we had spent the morning. Cole and I were the very last in line. As we passed the gaping doors of the huge stable, something black moved inside. I only caught it out of the corner of my eye. I turned and saw for just a moment someone in black vanish around the corner.

"Astra," I hissed under my breath.

"What?" Cole asked, turning toward me.

"Nothing," I told him. "I'll be right back."

Cole looked confused, but he didn't try to stop me when I darted away from him into the stable. If Astra was there, that meant she'd skipped training, and I wanted to know the reason why.

She was the only one who knew that Cole, Jase, and I had broken the rules. If I had a little dirt on her, it would help ensure she kept that matter to herself.

The stable was snug and toasty inside. I assumed the number of large bodies helped keep the temperature up. Most of the exterior doors and windows were closed, keeping in the warmth but also cutting off the light. It would have been very dim, except that a number of metal lanterns were carefully hung to provide light to the interior.

About half of the stalls were empty. I didn't trust the animals not to kick or bite me, so I tried to stay away from the ones containing horses.

I stole around a corner and saw the fringe of a black cloak, but again it was just for an instant as the figure entered a stall.

Creeping forward, I heard the person murmuring softly to the horse within. I glanced through the wooden slats and saw that it was not Astra. The person I had mistook for her was an old woman — an ancient woman really — with a long, white braid coiled into a high bun.

Wrinkles creased every inch of her face. She was thin and almost small enough to walk right under the belly of the giant horse in the stall with her. He was a massive brute, at least half a foot taller than the horse I'd been riding all morning. His coat was a patchy gray, which darkened to black around his face and on his legs. There was a white linen bandage on the upper part of his shoulder.

The ancient woman gently undid the cloth to reveal a long cut. It looked deep and nasty. She pursed her lips, not looking pleased; the horse even less so. He was blowing and stamping, tail twitching like crazy even though flies hadn't been around in months.

It would have been my own personal nightmare to be in an enclosed space with an animal in such a state: injured and aggravated. But the woman continued speaking gently to him. Her words were in the high language, although they were spoken too softly for me to make out. They did, however, seem to calm the huge beast a little.

Slowly, the woman took out a rag, dabbed some green, pulpy goo onto it, and then started wiping the horse's cut. I knew I shouldn't have stayed any longer, but I was incredibly curious. I had never seen a horse healer before. I moved to the left, trying to get a better view of what the gnarled hands were doing.

Suddenly, the horse sensed my presence and jerked its head up. Hoping the old woman would assume she'd caused the animal's reaction, I bolted away, out of the stable and back to the training session. Cole was the only one who had noticed my absence. He gave me a long look but didn't say anything. I had a feeling he would wait and ask me where I had been during our return to The Paramount. There would be plenty of time.

Thankfully, we did not have to get on the horses again. Instead, we spent the afternoon being shown how to mend broken

THE PREPARATIONS

buckles and leather tack. We also learned some quick-release knots that I thought would be much more useful than any amount of horseback riding.

The day's lesson seemed to drag on forever. I was certain all of the other training sessions had been over for at least half an hour before we were finally released.

As the small group of potentials began heading for their villages, The North Wind, which had been fairly quiet all day, sprung to life. The stable doors were thrown open, horses came pouring into the village from all directions, and gray-clad forms were everywhere.

Cole and I gratefully escaped to the southern road. A cold wind hit our backs as the sun began to set, and I had a feeling the warm weather was over. If there was a freeze that night, all the puddles we had trudged through during the day would turn to ice, but for now, everything was still watery.

As we picked our way carefully along, Cole glanced up sharply. I followed his gaze and saw a solitary figure on a brown horse, riding past us about fifty yards to our right. The animal wasn't on any path but was cutting straight toward The North Wind from the direction of The Quarry.

"Is that…" Cole started, but cut off mid-sentence.

The rider was a young man with ash blond hair. He appeared to be in his early twenties, just old enough to have missed the trials by a few years.

Every scrap of his clothing was black. Cole stared after him until he was out of sight behind us.

"For a moment, I thought that was Astra," he told me.

"Because of the black clothes?" I asked.

Cole nodded. "I wonder where they get them?" he mused. "And why they don't wear the color of The North Wind?"

"I don't know," I answered. "But the reason I left you after lunch was because I saw someone wearing black inside the stable."

Cole's eyes widened. "I was meaning to ask you where you went. Was it Astra or that rider?" Cole nodded back to where the man and horse had disappeared behind a stable.

I shook my head. "Neither. It was an old woman. She was treating a wound on a horse's leg."

"What could those three have in common?" wondered Cole. "There's something strange about The North Wind. A mystery I can't figure out." Cole sounded completely perplexed. "Do you want to come back tomorrow?"

I groaned. "Really? What for? There's no way we're going to have horses in the trials, so learning to ride is a complete waste of time."

"Maybe," Cole said. "But they teach other stuff too."

I didn't say anything; however, I was sure the look I gave him displayed my true loathing of the place.

"I'm surprised at you, Myra," Cole said. "I thought you would be dying to go back to The North Wind, especially to the valley."

"Why?" I asked defensively.

"Because of what Astra said. Surely you remember?"

I set my jaw to keep from speaking. I remembered everything Astra had said.

Cole interrupted my silence, interpreting it as forgetfulness. "You know, about being able to talk to people who have died?"

The taste of blood filled my mouth, and I realized I was biting my cheek. Slowly, I unclenched my jaw and managed to get out a sentence that was only slightly hostile, instead of furious. "And you believed her?"

Cole glanced at me in confusion. "I don't know. You have to go somewhere once you're dead, right? Maybe the valley—"

"No," was all I could choke out, interrupting Cole's words.

He sighed. "You're not even a little curious?"

I shook my head, doubting I would be able to use my voice. My hands were clenched into trembling fists; every muscle inside my body was rigid and taut.

THE PREPARATIONS

"It's been almost twelve years since your father died. Why are you so worked up?" Cole pressed.

It was so easy for him to ask that from where he sat. Both of his parents were alive. They took care of him and doted on him. Plus, his three older siblings were always there when he needed them. Cole had never felt alone in his life.

After my father had died, I'd had no one, save a distant mother. How was I not supposed to still be upset about my father, the one and only person in my entire life who had loved me unconditionally?

I was angry enough to punch Cole, but the thought of Myna stopped me. I didn't care about her implementing punishment, not that Cole would ever have told, but the thought of her shielded demeanor brought me up short. When people made her upset, she controlled herself so well that they didn't know she was feeling anything. I needed to learn to do the same.

Instead of answering, I marched straight past Cole, who had turned back to look at me. I headed for The Paramount, which lay out of sight four or five miles ahead.

From my reaction, Cole must have judged that he'd crossed some sort of line.

He followed me at a distance for almost a mile and a half.

Finally, he caught up, probably figuring that I had cooled off a bit. The opposite was true. My emotions had swelled to the point where I couldn't press them down any more. I was terrified they might explode at any moment.

"Please wait," Cole called, but I didn't stop. His hand fell on my shoulder, forcing me to halt.

"Myra," he began, but it was too late. Tears were already filling my eyes and running down my cheeks. Cole's expression changed when he took in my face. A second later, he wrapped his arms around me, my damp cheek pressed to his chest.

"I'm so sorry," I heard him say softly. "That was stupid and nasty and rude, and I am very, very sorry."

I had to admit, it was hard to stay angry with Cole. He didn't make excuses or say I was too sensitive; he just apologized. There was also something comforting about being held like that. His arms were warm, and, for the first time in a long time, I felt safe.

Once the tears had left my eyes, I looked up at him. I had always liked Cole. He was my best friend, the brother I'd never had. However, at that moment, when my gray eyes locked with his clear blue ones, I felt something more, something deeper. A spark seemed to catch inside of me, making it hard to draw breath, and a feeling I had repressed for years sprang to life.

A blush spread hotly across my cheeks, but I couldn't feel embarrassed because I was too elated. Besides, between the cold and the exertion of the walk, it probably didn't show.

The emotion that took hold of me was something entirely different from anything I'd felt before. The moment seemed to last forever and not nearly long enough.

Cole gently released me. "Are you alright?" he asked.

I nodded, not trusting my voice. The new feelings still lingered, but the overpowering sense of them was slowly fading away, along with the rest of my anger.

After two deep breaths, I felt more like myself. "I—I am curious," I admitted. "About the black clothing and the—the valley. But I don't want to go back."

Cole nodded slowly. I could tell he was making plans. I suddenly feared that he would return on his own, without telling me. The thought of him being injured or killed was unbearable.

"But if you think it's important, we can come back tomorrow," I amended.

Cole smiled. "Great! We'll figure this out in no time at all."

***

THE PREPARATIONS

I woke up the following morning with my legs and lower back on fire. The instructor from the previous day had warned that we might experience some discomfort from riding so much, but I had not really expected it since I was in good physical shape.

Getting out of bed was agony. Every time I bent my legs or back, spasms of pain coursed through my body. It was even worse than the day after our first excursion to The North Wind.

I was almost late to the town center. I literally arrived just moments before they started calling names. My muscles were beginning to loosen up, but I really didn't want to try to walk to any of the other villages, let alone The North Wind. One look at Cole, who was standing on the opposite side of the town center, told me that he felt the same.

After the roll had been taken, the other potentials began to disperse. I slowly crossed to Cole. "I think, perhaps, we should stay here today," I told him.

He nodded. The Paramount training session was the only one we hadn't visited yet. It seemed like a good time to find out what they were teaching.

Bala and Jase headed off to The Quarry when we told them we weren't planning to leave The Paramount. I saw Rasby heading south with her group, but I never found out which of the southern villages they went to.

Only two other potentials remained. One of them was a girl with a sprained ankle. The other was a small boy named Hayden. For his sake, I hoped he would not be chosen as a contender. He was small, and his chances for survival were not good. More than anything else, I hoped he was not placed on my team. From the look of his large, fretful eyes, he would be the first one to get homesick.

It took nearly an hour before other potentials began to arrive. They came in waves. The first couple groups were from the closer villages, while the later ones were from those farther away.

The training session was pretty much what I expected. We were ushered into the school building, and then given a lesson on being organized and planning ahead. The mental aspect was actually rather refreshing after so many lessons involving only physical forms of training.

Once the first lecture had concluded, a female council member stepped forward. In her hand she held a series of scrolls from the records building. She spoke to us about proper nutrition and how much food each person should consume each day.

We also spent some time on basic math problems. They were simple enough that I could do them in my head, but a lot of the other potentials struggled even when given a pen and paper.

The instructors ended the day by taking us outside and demonstrating how to tell the date and time using the position of the sun.

The feat was accomplished by measuring off an area of ground and pressing a number of carefully sized sticks into the dirt—snow in our case—at even intervals. The shadows caused by the sun and the sticks could be used to decipher the time and date. It was fascinating, but probably useless. Although, there was no telling what skills might come in handy, so I converted the measurements to memory, just in case.

The following day, we had regular school classes. Instead of introducing new material, the teachers began a review of all the words in our language. Each of us used a huge book filled with words and definitions to follow along.

I had memorized the book from front to back long ago, so I didn't even pretend to be interested. The teachers must have felt the same way, because they let us go a bit early.

As I left the school room, someone touched my shoulder. I turned to find Cole standing there. He jerked his head to the right, motioning for me to follow. My heart skipped a beat as I hurried after him.

THE PREPARATIONS

He led me to the village woodpile. Every afternoon, firewood was delivered there, and the following morning it was divided among the dwellings. The pile had just been restocked, so it was unlikely that we would be interrupted.

Cole sat down with his back against the stacked wood. It always amazed me how boys could sit on anything and be comfortable, even an icy mound of snow. I grabbed a loose log from nearby and used it as a seat, instead of the frozen ground.

"Do you want to go to The Valley of the North Wind tomorrow?" Cole asked quietly.

I hesitated. "No...and yes," I whispered. "We really shouldn't."

Cole's piercing blue eyes held my gaze. "Why? I thought you wanted to know."

"I do, but I don't want to get into trouble. Maybe some other time, after the trials, when things have settled down."

Cole shook his head. "There's no guarantee we're going to come back from the trials."

I almost laughed at that idea and his serious tone. I was going to survive. My lips twisted into a smile. "In that case, I'll come to the valley and talk to you afterwards."

Cole laughed. "Fair point, but—"

"Alright," I said, "we can go, but if anyone is around, we are not going in."

"We need to find Astra first thing."

My mind recoiled at the thought of her. "Why?" I all but hissed.

"Because she can tell us where the special places are."

I hadn't thought of that, but Astra had intimated that you couldn't just pop into the valley and try to talk to the dead anywhere.

"What makes you think she'll tell?" I asked.

"She'll help us," Cole replied confidently. "She did the last time."

"That was different; she wasn't taking any chances last time. All she did was keep her mouth shut. Why would she knowingly help smuggle us into the most forbidden of places? We could all get marks!"

Cole shrugged. "Maybe. We could at least ask her why there are people at The North Wind who wear black all the time."

"Because Astra is so likely to be forthcoming with everything that she and The North Wind do," I muttered.

Cole chuckled. "At least we know she kept the secret about us and the valley," he countered.

"True," I grudgingly admitted. "But if we keep bothering her, she might not be so trustworthy. She feels like The Valley of the North Wind is her territory, and if she thinks we are going to invade, I don't see her having a problem getting rid of us."

"Going into The Valley of the North Wind?" a female voice said from the other side of the woodpile. Cole and I both jumped, and then exchanged a horrified glance as the speaker came into our line of sight.

Chapter 16

TERRORS OF THE NIGHT

When the young woman who had spoken to us stepped into view, I almost let out a cry of relief.

It was Golla, my old friend from The Golden Fields. I hadn't seen her in many years, but she was easy to recognize. Her bright blue eyes and loose blonde curls were exactly as I had remembered. She'd grown a bit stout, but was as lovely as ever.

A sweet smile enveloped her face as our eyes met. "Myra, you aren't thinking of getting into trouble, are you?" There was laughter in her voice, like the first rays of spring sunshine.

I rose to greet her. "Golla!" I cried. "It's so good to see you!" I put my hand out and shook hers most warmly. Cole had risen and was standing behind me, silent and uncertain.

I turned to him. "You remember Golla, don't you?" I asked. "She used to live here."

Tentatively, the two shook hands, and Cole introduced himself. "I'm Cole."

Golla nodded. "I haven't forgotten you," she said with a wink.

Vaguely, I recalled that when we were children, Golla had thought Cole was cute. She'd constantly tried to force him to talk to her, usually by creating awkward situations in which he had been unable to avoid her. From the look on his face, I was pretty sure Cole was starting to remember those encounters. The twinkle in Golla's eye said that she certainly did.

"What brings you here?" I asked Golla, hoping to ease the uncomfortable silence.

"My mother had some documents for the council, but she hurt her foot and the healer who treated her said that she shouldn't do any walking for a while. Since it's winter and there's not much work to do in The Golden Fields, I offered to come drop them off.

"Now, what's all this about The Valley of the North Wind?" She gave us a mock scowl.

She's not a potential, I realized suddenly. *If she were, she would be training instead of working.*

Golla, an adult. It was strange to think about, but she was two years older than Cole. To have missed the trials by only a few months was the worst thing I could have imagined. However, Golla seemed to be handling it pretty well.

I glanced at Cole. The look on his face was guarded. "It's ok," I told him. "Golla is a friend; we can trust her."

Cole sighed. "I just wish the whole of The Clan wasn't finding out all of our affairs." A pleasant shiver ran down my spine when Cole said 'our affairs'. He and I sank back onto our seats as Golla chose a log of her own.

"I'll do the talking," Cole whispered to me as she got settled.

"Sure," I nodded.

Turning to Golla, Cole began to explain the situation. "Someone told us that in The Valley of the North Wind it is possible to speak to the dead." Cole paused to see how Golla would react.

Her face had lost its joking manner.

"How does he know?" Golla asked.

"She—" I started, but Cole spoke up quickly.

"Our friend claims a rumor to that effect is widespread in The North Wind," he said, completely ignoring the fact that he had interrupted me.

Cole's cleverness sometimes was impressive. Clearly, he was trying to tell Golla as little as possible. He'd omitted the fact that we'd already been to The Valley of the North Wind, and he was calling Astra 'our friend' to keep Golla from learning about our venture directly from her.

"So, you're going to try it?" Golla asked excitedly.

Cole hesitated. As much as he desired to investigate the source of the rumor, and had pushed me to join him, he was loathed to admit our intentions to an outsider.

"We could talk to our fathers," Golla said softly, looking at me when Cole gave her no answer. I could hear all the pain and longing, just as raw in her voice as it was in my heart.

"I don't think it's true," I told Golla, even though I wasn't sure what I believed anymore.

"We should try anyway," Golla insisted.

Cole scowled. "No offense, but we were going to try on our own. If it works—or doesn't—I'll make sure Myra lets you kn—"

"I'm going with you! Do you think you can just leave me behind?" Golla cut Cole off.

"Shhhhhh," I whispered to them both. Their voices had grown uncomfortably loud. Quickly, I glanced around to be sure no one was near enough to overhear us.

What Astra had said about there being too many ears in The Paramount suddenly popped into my head. I repressed the thought. No one was spying on us; we were quite safe.

"You can't keep me away," Golla challenged Cole. She had a defiant look in her eyes, which she turned on me. "When are you going?" she asked.

Now I was caught right in the middle. Cole's eyes hardened as I looked between their faces. He didn't want me to tell her anything.

THE PREPARATIONS

My mind raced as I tried to find a way out of the sticky situation. Maybe, if I could appease Golla for the present, I might have some time to talk Cole into letting her join. I knew it would be much better if we could all go together.

"We haven't gotten that far yet," I told Golla. Out of the corner of my eye, I saw Cole relax. He really needed to get better control of himself; he was completely transparent. "We just found out about the rumor and were talking it over."

Golla narrowed her eyes, but didn't say anything. I wondered how much of our earlier conversation she had overheard.

"Well, let me know when you decide to go," Golla ordered, still looking at me and ignoring Cole. "I have a right to be there."

I remembered all the times we had talked about death when we had been children. Golla was the most curious person I knew, and the look in her eyes told me that she wasn't going to forget what she had heard.

"Of course you do," I said. "Now, tell me about your mother. Nothing is permanently wrong with her foot, is it?"

I listened politely while Golla shared the facts about her mother's condition. After about a quarter of an hour, she switched topics and began telling us about a young man she was interested in making her life mate. Much as I prodded her, she wouldn't name him. As soon as that part of the conversation began, Cole excused himself.

Golla really did lack a sense of propriety. Life mates and death were two of the few subjects that it was frowned upon to discuss—aside from the trials, obviously. It was one thing to confide in me, who had been her friend for many years, but she barely knew Cole.

As soon as he had retreated, Golla's voice dropped the sappy sweet ring that had emerged when she had spoken of the man she was courting.

"I thought he was never going to leave," Golla sighed, still peering after Cole's retreating figure.

I stifled a laugh. It was so like Golla to be completely inappropriate just to chase poor Cole away.

"So, let's go," she said, giving me a nudge.

"What?" Golla had always been impulsive, but she had to be joking. "We can't!" I exclaimed.

"Sure we can," Golla urged. "Your friend is never going to let me tag along, but what right does he have to go? He's never lost anyone." She was completely serious. "Just think, what if dead doesn't mean gone? What if we really could talk to them?"

I shook my head. "Golla, we can't break the rules! Plus, I really couldn't go without Cole. Let me talk to him. If we decide it's a good idea to go, I'll make sure you know."

Golla didn't look pleased, but I quickly redirected the conversation, and we chatted for another half an hour. Finally, she told me she had to head out.

As I watched her walk away, I had the sinking feeling that she would be determined to find out if the rumor was true. Besides being the most inquisitive person I knew, Golla was also the most stubborn.

Suddenly, I was very glad Cole had been so guarded. I dreaded the thought of Golla speaking to Astra. If only it had been spring. Then the fields would have been ready to plant. As it was, with the ground still frozen under foot, I feared that there would be far too many long hours for Golla to mull over The Valley of the North Wind. Just like me, she would never be able to forget what she had heard.

Cole was waiting for me outside my dwelling. "Is she finally gone?" he asked as I approached.

My heart sank. Why couldn't my friends get along? They were both great people. It wasn't like I would let just any loser be my friend.

"Yeah, she's gone," I replied.

"Good," he said, with a sense of finality that assured me Golla was going to be welcome on our trip to the valley.

"Golla's not so bad," I said. "She's actually really intelligent and curious."

"And rude and prying," Cole added. "I bet if she finds out we went without her, she'll tell."

"No," I insisted. "Golla's not like that. Her father died a few months after mine; that's why she wants to come with us. You have no idea what it feels like to lose someone close to you. Maybe one day you will, and then you'll understand." I glanced at Cole, hoping that I hadn't offended him.

He just nodded.

"Did she believe everything you told her?" Cole asked. "I figured she'd try to pry the details out of you after I left."

"I didn't tell her anything," I sighed. "But I hate lying."

"It certainly makes things easier, though," he pointed out.

"I just hope it doesn't end up making things worse."

"How could things get any worse?" Cole asked.

I shook my head. "I don't know, but when you start lying, you have to keep lying. Eventually, it comes back to bite you."

"I suppose," Cole mused. "Have you ever lied to me about something like that?"

"No," I answered quickly.

"Are you lying?" Cole asked.

I felt my face flush. How could he think I would do that to him? I was about to protest, when I saw the amused twinkle in his eyes.

"You—" I started.

"Sorry, I was just kidding." Cole burst out laughing.

I smiled too, some of the weight on my chest lifted. Everything I had told Golla had been the truth. I had just kept some of the more inconvenient facts to myself. Even when I had promised to tell her if we went into the valley, I'd said, 'if we think it's a good idea', and I would never think going into the valley was a good idea.

Cole grew suddenly serious. "I trust you, Myra. I don't trust a lot of people, but I trust you."

I hoped Cole wouldn't notice the flush of my cheeks, but there was no way for me not to blush at his words. I supposed in the area of boys I wasn't much like Myna at all. But then again, I hadn't known her when she and my father had met. Maybe he had made her blush and smile, even laugh.

"Tomorrow then?" Cole asked.

I nodded, knowing that I would never be able to say no to him.

***

We did not go to The North Wind the following day.

I awoke long before dawn, in the earliest hours of the morning. The sound of many voices echoed among the dwellings outside. Not once in my life could I ever remember being woken up like that.

Something was happening.

In the dark, I fumbled for my clothes and boots. Adrenalin was pumping through my body as I left my room, ready to find out what was happening. The fire in the stove had died to embers. I didn't bother stirring them to life as I headed for the door.

The first thing I did outside was stub my toe on a stray log from the woodpile. Thick, patchy clouds blotted out the stars and moon, leaving the village almost entirely in darkness.

Everywhere, people were rushing around frantically, parents clutching their children tight. I headed toward the town center. Surely, an elder would be there, waiting to calm the people and send them back to their beds. As I fought my way through the crowd, I realized a great number of those gathered were from The Barracks. The gold clothing they wore was hard to tell from the maroon of The Paramount in the almost pitch black, but once I noticed it, I was shocked to see how many soldiers were present.

I arrived at the center of the village just as one of the gold-clad figures reached up and rang the bell. *Finally, something nor-*

mal. We would gather, and they would tell us what was wrong and what to do.

It took a quarter of an hour before the town center was filled and everyone was calm enough to listen. To my surprise, Myna, the other Clan Leaders, and the elders emerged from the council building. Core was the only one missing.

I hoped fervently that he hadn't died, but between all the midnight excitement and his absence, that was the first thought that popped into my head.

I had to find Cole. Was he ok? Had there been an accident at his dwelling?

I started pushing my way back through the crowd, determined to find Cole, when Myna's voice rang out. I paused as she addressed our people with the cool composure of a true leader.

"People of The Clan, hear me. I am Myna, Second Clan Leader." I froze and turned back to listen. Surely, if Core had been dead, Myna would not have called herself the Second Clan Leader.

"Something has happened tonight," Myna continued, "which has happened many times in the past. We will deal with it now as we did then, and all will be well."

I could feel some of the tension leave the crowd. If Myna told them everything was alright then it was. They trusted her beyond a shadow of a doubt.

"A Broken was spotted on our border." The crowd gasped in horror. I curled my lip is disgust. The Broken were the vilest of creatures. Why couldn't they just leave us alone?

"It was seen on the far side of the river attempting to cross. We do not believe it could have survived, but our soldiers have mobilized and are doing a complete search of The Land of the Clan. If anything is amiss, they will find it. Please return to your dwellings and remain there until dawn. The soldiers will be checking every dwelling, so expect their visit. Soldiers will remain in each village until the entirety of The Land of the Clan has been secured."

Myna glanced back at the council. "Go now and do as instructed. It is in times of crisis that we must remain ordered. That is our gift. It is what separates us from the beasts of the field and the Broken."

The town center began to empty. I saw Myna head back into the council building. A few of the elders followed her, while some set out from The Paramount, each at the head of a group of soldiers. I assumed they would be going to the other villages to deliver similar messages.

I returned to my dwelling. As I passed the woodpile, I was more careful about where I put my feet.

Taking up two of the largest logs, I headed inside. I couldn't go back to sleep; there was no telling when the soldiers would come to search the dwelling.

The fire had died completely in the short amount of time since I'd left. I added some kindling, hoping it wasn't too far gone. When nothing happened, I took up a flint lying close to the hearth and struck it on the edge of the open stove.

The sparks caught quickly in the dry pine needles and bark. Soon, I was feeding the flames twigs and small sticks. Before long, I added one of the large logs I had brought in. The hungry tongues of flame didn't take as well to the slightly damp wood as they had to the dried-out kindling. I had been so busy with the preparations that I hadn't brought in our wood ration in days.

I trudged back out to the woodpile. The village looked deserted now. I didn't even see any soldiers as I dug down into the heap of logs, trying to find the driest pieces of wood.

I repeated the process several times. As I re-entered the dwelling with the final load, I was surprised by how much warmer the fire had already made the room. Although, it could have been the exertion of bringing in the wood that had made me feel warm, instead of the fire.

With my indoor woodpile complete, I settled down to watch the fire burn. The events of the night took me back to the even-

THE PREPARATIONS

ing the trials had been announced. In some ways, it felt like Midwinter had been just the day before, but it also felt like another lifetime.

Everything had changed. I had broken more rules in the past two months than in the rest of my life combined. It was kind of shocking to realize how much rebellion the trials had brought out of me. Maybe I wasn't fit to be a Clan Leader after all.

Was I turning into someone bad? Surely none of the other potentials had turned into liars and sneaks. Why had I? Before the trials had been announced, I couldn't remember doing anything wrong at all. Well, except for being rude to Myna every once in a while, but she had really brought all that on herself, so I didn't feel too bad about it.

I had spent my entire life being a perfect student and a model member of The Clan. Due to recent events, it seemed I couldn't go a day without telling someone a lie. I needed to stop. If I got caught, the entire web I had spun would unravel and everything would come to light.

My musings were disturbed by a knock on the door. I jerked awake; I hadn't realized how close I had come to nodding off.

I rose and moved quickly to the door. To my surprise, and delight, Cole was standing there instead of the soldiers I had anticipated.

"Hi," he said as I let him in.

"Hi," I echoed, closing the door behind him. He went to the fire and pulled his hands out of his pockets, warming them over the flames. It seemed odd, until I noticed the snow caked to his clothes and realized he must have come from somewhere much farther away than his dwelling.

"Where have you been?" I asked, unable to stifle my curiosity.

Cole took a deep breath and blew on his hands before answering me. "I was with my father."

I waited silently for him to continue. If he had come to my dwelling instead of going to his own, he must have wanted to talk about something.

"Just after I went to bed last night, someone came pounding on our door." Cole stretched his hands over the flames again and continued. "It was one of the representatives from Riverside. He told us that a Broken had been seen, and that the entire village was in an uproar. My father sent the representative to tell the council. He said they were probably still in session despite the late hour."

Cole paused and glanced at me, and then towards Myna's room. "Your mother and a few others must have been discussing something really important last night to keep them from their beds."

Every night, I thought bitterly but only nodded, willing to allow Cole to think that it was an unusual occurrence.

"Anyway, my father headed out to Riverside. He wanted to make sure everything was ok there. He asked me to run to The Barracks and wake Kullin and have him mobilize the soldiers."

"And you're just now getting back?" I asked, sinking down onto one of the cushions from the table. It was close enough to the stove that I could enjoy the warmth on my skin.

Cole turned back to the fire, shaking his head. "No, after I alerted Kullin, I headed to Riverside to make sure my father didn't need anything else.

"And I wanted to see what was going on for myself," Cole admitted. "When I first got there, I was sure something disastrous had occurred. People were charging around everywhere, and there was complete chaos. I thought a Broken was actually in the village attacking people.

"I found my father trying to calm things down. Turns out, there were three people who saw the Broken. They were down on the beach and noticed something move on the far shore. At first, they had thought it was just a bird." Cole's voice dropped, and I leaned forward to hear his next words. "Then the moon came out. The thing stood up, and they saw it was human. The Broken just jumped into the water. That was when they lost sight of it and ran to tell the village leaders."

I hung on Cole's every word, completely enthralled. Myna might have talked about similar events happening in the past, but they hadn't happened in my lifetime.

"Anyway," he continued, "about half an hour later, a squad from the Barracks arrived. Things calmed down considerably after that, and my father was able to get the village sorted out." Cole glanced back over his shoulder at me. All the snow had melted from his clothes and hair.

"My father said that he was going to travel to the rest of the villages and ensure that nothing was amiss. I would have gone with him, but he sent me back to get some sleep."

I nodded, wanting to ask why he had come to my dwelling rather than going to his own. Instead, I decided to revel in the fact that he had.

"Do you think it was really a Broken?" I asked.

"I don't know," Cole shrugged. "It seems unlikely that three different people would all imagine the same thing."

I nodded.

"Hopefully, the creature drowned," I said.

Cole furrowed his brow. "That's a terrible thing to say—"

"What would happen if a Broken came among our people?" I asked sternly.

"I've never really thought about it," admitted Cole.

"If a Broken ever came here, it would be the end of our civilization as we know it," I told him. "Everything would be a disaster."

"I guess," Cole mused. "Hopefully, they were wrong, and it was just a bird or something."

We were both silent for a moment. "Unless it survives the river, we'll never know," I said.

Cole sighed. "I guess that ruins all of our plans."

I looked at Cole questioningly, unsure of what he meant. Normally, I was never the one behind in a conversation, but it was late, and I was tired, and he wasn't making much sense.

"We can't go to the valley tomorrow," Cole explained. "Or today, or—you know what I mean. We'll have to wait."

"You're right," I realized, finally grasping what he was saying. "I bet there will be at least twice as many soldiers stationed there now." I tried to hide my relief, so he wouldn't think me a coward.

Cole nodded his agreement. Our voices had dropped to whispers throughout the course of the conversation. His next words were so soft I barely heard them at all. "Do you think any of the soldiers will go to the other side of the river to make sure there aren't any more?"

I shrugged. "There's no way for us to know what they do."

"Astra will find out since they'll have to go through The North Wind."

I rolled my eyes. "Why are you so obsessed with her?" I snapped. "It's always 'Astra this' and 'Astra that'. Golla can't come with us, but I bet you'd love to have Astra along."

Cole turned his back to the fire and faced me. He squatted down so our eyes were level.

"Come on Myra," he said. "There's something special about her. Can't you feel it? She's so different from everyone else. It's like…" He paused to carefully pick his words. "She actually reminds me a lot of yo—"

I cut him off before he could finish that dreadful thought. "No, that's not true."

We were silent for a moment. Then Cole changed the subject, for which I was infinitely grateful.

"Do you think the reason the rules aren't enforced as strongly at The North Wind is because they know all of the council's secrets?"

THE PREPARATIONS

In my opinion, the new topic could have been a bit further from the old topic, but as long as we weren't talking about Astra anymore, I was satisfied.

"It would be pretty stupid for the council to give The North Wind that much power over them," I asserted. "But it could be possible."

"Maybe it's been like that since the beginning of The Clan," Cole suggested.

I doubted it. If that had been the case, I was sure Litis would have been able to remove Astra from the trials as she had desired.

"Maybe everyone used to know what was going on," I suggested. "Maybe it's only that people have forgotten, and those at The North Wind still know because they see it every day."

"I hadn't thought of that," Cole said. "I guess it wouldn't really bother the council if everyone knew about the soldiers and stuff. It's just something that goes unnoticed."

Even though I was the one who had put the idea in his head, I wasn't sure his theory was correct. My own suspicions ran along darker lines.

Cole sighed softly. "It's late, Myra; I need to get home."

I hated to see him go, but he was right. I couldn't think of any rules we were breaking at the moment, but if someone found us alone together, I was fairly certain our actions, not to mention our discussion, would have been frowned upon.

He headed out, and I turned back to the fire. It was well that I had decided to build it. What if Cole had come and my dwelling had been dark and cold? He would never have understood that, not when I knew his dwelling was always warm and snug. How could I have explained the bitter winter that I lived with all year 'round?

The fire was dying, so I added a log. It wasn't long before there was another knock on my door. Much as I would have loved it to have been Cole, returning to tell me something he'd forgotten earlier, it wasn't him. Instead, I let in a pair of soldiers, who both looked to be in their thirties.

They were very polite as they inspected the dwelling, not that there was much to see. The main room, my room, and Myna's room. It didn't take them long to clear out.

I considered going back to bed, but found myself returning to the fire once more. It would have been a waste to forsake the warmth for my much-colder room.

So, I sat and stared into the flames. When it was nothing more than a glowing bed of embers, and the sky was just beginning to lighten in the east, I headed to my room.

It was nice that I had the day off; otherwise, I would have already been heading out for training or school, instead of crawling back into bed. I thought I was going to have trouble falling asleep, but I was out as soon as my head hit the pillow.

Chapter 17

VALLEY OF DEATH

I slept late the following day. Myna opening and closing the front door was what finally woke me. I didn't stir until I heard her open and close the door to her room as well.

Only then, did I rise and wander out into the main room. It was still slightly warm from the previous evening's fire. I checked, but the ashes were cold, and I didn't see any point in starting it up again.

Instead, I dressed and headed out. I didn't know where I was going, but I didn't want to be in the dwelling anymore.

The sunlight was blinding as I stepped outside. The cloud cover from the night before had vanished, leaving the sky clear and blue. Most of the people I saw were bunched into small groups, talking quietly; at least half of them were from The Barracks.

None of that bothered me. The only thing I noticed that made any lasting impression was that the snow under my feet was almost completely slush. A thaw would be coming soon. The previous evening had been cold, but the sun had brought spring air with it.

My feet took me to Cole's dwelling, but I didn't knock on the door. He was probably still in bed. And if not him, then Core definitely was, provided he had already returned from his trip to all the villages. I did not want to be the one responsible for waking the First Clan Leader after what had probably been the hardest day he'd faced since the last trials.

As I walked away, not really caring where my feet took me, I heard someone call my name. My heart leapt for instant, thinking it was Cole, but it wasn't. It was Jase.

He jogged over to me, splattering melting snow everywhere. Bala was right behind him, carefully dodging the flurries of slush.

I called a greeting to them as they approached.

"Did you hear what happened last night?" Jase asked in a low voice.

"I'm pretty sure the entirety of The Clan heard about it," I replied, not caring how loudly I spoke.

"They saw a Broken. Wish I had been there," Bala muttered wistfully.

"Why do you say that?" I asked, turning on her in surprise.

It was Jase who answered. His eyes lit up as he began talking excitedly. "I would have caught that rat and killed him! I would have swum across the river and chased him. He wouldn't have escaped from me."

Jase was so serious I fought not to laugh. "You were going to swim across the river? No one does that. The current is way too strong, not to mention it was freezing last night. You would have died of hypothermia if you had even dipped your little toe in the water."

Bala and I giggled. Slightly abashed, Jase seemed to reconsider, as if those thoughts hadn't even entered his mind. I sighed inwardly. Maybe I shouldn't be associating so much with him. He was powerful, but did I really want someone that stupid on my team for the trials?

"Besides," I added. "You know you aren't supposed to leave The Land of the Clan."

Jase nodded. "I know. I just really want to help our people. I'm not good at things that take brains, but I wanted to help and that was something I could have done."

I felt a swell of hope for Jase. At least he knew where his talents lay. Maybe he would be alright to have as a teammate after all.

"I'd better go," Bala put in. "My mother is like a hen right now, wanting to keep all her chicks in the nest. I only slipped out to see if there was any news." She walked off, calling over her shoulder, "See you guys for training tomorrow."

"See you tomorrow," I told her.

Jase and I didn't hang around much longer. After I learned that he hadn't seen Cole since the day before, we didn't have anything to talk about. We parted ways, and I headed back toward my dwelling, without any intention of actually reaching my destination. Ever since the trials started, all my free time had been spent getting dragged around by Cole. Now, I finally had a day to myself with nothing to do.

I walked to the outskirts of the village and considered going to Riverside to see if there was anything interesting going on there, but decided against it. I would probably only add to the chaos of the situation, and that would be wrong.

Just then, I caught sight of Rasby and her father, Cliv. I would have kept walking, except Cliv smiled and waved and then started making his way over to me.

I smiled back as best I could, all the while cringing inside. Rasby looked no happier than I felt.

"Myra, how are you?" Cliv asked. "I haven't seen you in such a long time."

"I'm well," I answered. "I've been very busy since the preparations began."

"Yes, I can well imagine," Cliv told me. "I hardly see my own Rasby. In fact, you probably spend more time with her now than her mother and I."

I didn't know quite how to answer. Rasby and I never trained together. One time we had gone to the same village, but it had been a coincidence, and we hadn't spoken. Normally,

Rasby's group went to where they thought the day would be shortest and the work easiest.

In answer to Cliv's statement, all I did was nod. Cliv rushed on, not seeming to notice. "Since Rasby has the day off, she's offered to walk down to The Golden Fields with me. I need to have the village leaders look over some documents. Would you care to join us?"

At Cliv's invitation, Rasby's head snapped up. She had been intently studying the ground, without looking my way even once.

"No," I answered quickly. "I'd better stay here. My mother only just got to bed, and I don't want her wondering where I am if she wakes up. She's bound to be like a mother hen, wanting to keep her chicks close." I adopted Bala's words, because they sounded better than any I could have formed.

"I see," Cliv told me, not without some regret in his eyes. He glanced at Rasby for a moment, and then the two headed off on the road to The Golden Fields.

I watched them walk away, and I knew they were walking out of my life. Not of their own will, but because I had let them.

Some part of me wondered if I could have chosen a different path. I'm sure that was why Cliv had invited me. Rasby wasn't strong-willed. By the time we would have made it to The Golden Fields, she would have been ready to make up, and by the time we would have gotten back, she would have thought of me as a best friend again.

But that couldn't happen, because nothing had changed. I hadn't changed. Even if Rasby had, she was still far from being the kind of person who would compete in the trials.

I clung to my resolve, while Rasby had yet to find hers.

**

Training resumed the following day. Cole and I went to Riverside with Jase. He desperately wanted to check the place out for himself and make sure there were no Broken hanging around.

I found his notion ridiculous, but Cole decided to humor him. So, we went to Riverside and learned how to make fishing line from certain types of plants. Some plants were tough and stringy, others more flexible. It would have been rather a dull day, except Jase jumped at every sound and sprung into an attack position whenever someone passed by. He seemed ready to clobber anything that looked suspicious.

The following day we went to Treescape, again because of Jase. He'd heard a rumor, who knows where, that a Broken had infiltrated the forest of Treescape. While Jase kept an eye out for imaginary attackers, Cole and I learned how to make a lean-to out of fallen branches.

We had just finished putting the last piece in place, when Jase announced that there was a Broken behind the next tree. He would have raised the alarm if Cole hadn't intervened and told him that it was his imagination playing tricks on him.

Jase didn't seem a hundred percent convinced, but he had learned long ago that Cole was much smarter than he was. So, for him, it was a fact that if Cole said he was wrong, then he was wrong and Cole was right.

Once again, I appreciated the fact that Jase knew his weaknesses so well. There were a great many other people I could name who would have done well to grasp that concept.

As we walked back to The Paramount in the early evening, Cole slowed down and began trailing slightly. After a few moments, I dropped back to join him. Jase was too consumed with watching out for imaginary enemies to notice our absence from the group of potentials heading east after training.

I knew what Cole was going to say before he even opened his mouth, and I knew I wouldn't like it. "Are we going to The North Wind on our next free day?" I asked before he could broach the subject.

THE PREPARATIONS

He nodded.

"Fine," I sighed. "But if there is any extra soldier activity, we are not going into the valley."

Cole nodded again. "We can check it out and see what's going on. Plus, we can…" He trailed off when he saw my expression darken.

"I know," I retorted. "You want to talk to Astra. Fine, let's see what she has to say."

Cole smiled, and I wondered if I should always be giving in to him so easily. We caught up with the others and didn't speak of it again.

Two mornings later, I woke with an ill foreboding. After our last expedition to the valley and Larna's punishment, all I could think about was getting caught.

I tried to push the negative feelings down and summon the excitement I had felt on my first trip to the valley. On that morning, I couldn't have been more excited. Try as I might, however, I couldn't find anything positive about what I was going to be doing that day. Except, of course, that I was going to be spending it with Cole. Truthfully, that was the only reason I was going. If it had been just me and Jase or even Golla, I would have called the whole thing off. But for Cole, I would have been willing to walk through every dark place in The Land of the Clan.

We met on the road leading north out of the village. The sun wasn't visible yet, but the sky was streaked with pink and gold. I was the first one there, which only gave my worries time to fester.

I tried to reason with myself that everything had gone well the first time; we had learned valuable information, and no one had caught us. Well, Astra had, but she wasn't anybody important.

It was only after the sun had actually risen part way into the sky that Cole finally appeared. I wondered if he was still catching up on the sleep he had missed.

"Where's Jase?" I asked softly, when he was near enough to hear me.

"I didn't think Jase would be much of an asset today." I found his statement incredibly strange; Jase and Cole were practically inseparable. Taking in my confused expression, Cole continued. "Did you want to spend the whole day hearing about how the Broken could be anywhere around us?"

I had to laugh. After three days, that topic was getting old. "Well, what are we standing around for then?" I tried to sound braver than I felt, but I couldn't stop the bile from rising in the back of my throat.

We talked on the road, but not about anything important. I was pretty sure both of us were worn out with talking about the valley and the Broken sighting. It was nice to simply chat about the unimportant details of our lives.

We trailed off after the first hour, just as the morning mist cleared enough to allow us a first glimpse of The Mountains of the North Wind. All my ill feelings, which had been soothed by Cole's calming presence, welled up inside me all at once.

I stopped walking. Cole turned back to look at me, unsure of why I had faltered. My hands were shaking, and I had to take several deep breaths before I could admit to myself what was wrong.

The real reason I didn't want to go to The Valley of the North Wind came crashing over me in an instant. All the pain from my father's death, which I had buried so many years ago, resurfaced the moment I saw the mountains in the distance.

"Myra?" Cole said questioningly, when a full two minutes had passed and I still hadn't moved.

I forced myself to take another deep breath and look at Cole. He clearly didn't have a clue what was going on inside my head, and I couldn't explain it.

Cole was the one who knew me best, and he didn't know me at all. There were so many things he didn't understand about me. Things I'd never been able to tell anyone. Like how alone I

THE PREPARATIONS

always felt. How Myna had never been a mother to me. How truly broken I was.

Twice, words rose to my lips that would have expressed and exposed my confused and damaged state of being, but I held them in, unwilling to show weakness. It was my own fault that he didn't understand. None of it was because he didn't see or didn't care, but because I wouldn't allow him to know the truth.

Finally, I was able to say something. Not the whole truth, I didn't think I would ever be able to tell anyone that, but enough to explain my current immobility.

"Cole..." I had to lick my lips before continuing. Even then, my words were hesitant and chosen with care. "This is—going to be very hard for me. I've—I really have a hard time thinking about my father. And going into the valley to try to talk to him, it's—well, I don't think it will work, and I have no idea what I'll say if it does."

"He's your father," Cole told me gently. "You don't have to give him a grand speech; just tell him you miss him.

"If my father were dead, I would want him to know how much I loved him and how hard it was to be without him. I'd tell him that I'd never forget all the times we'd spent together and that I was working hard, trying to do the best I could for The Clan."

Cole's words made a lot of sense and seemed so simple compared to the swirling confusion in my head. "That's what I'd want to say to my father if he were gone," Cole added softly.

I nodded and managed to continue walking. But my feet felt heavy, and each step was a struggle. I wanted to turn back and never return, but I also desperately wanted to continue on.

I stopped again, unable to make my feet move forward. The conflict inside of me raged on with no end in sight.

Cole was at my side a moment later. He pulled my quivering body against his strong, solid one in a warm embrace. My heart slowed its rhythm, and the tightness in my chest began to abate.

"It'll be alright," Cole promised.

When he released me, our eyes met for a long moment, and I knew that if I chose to go back he would be disappointed, but he wouldn't hold it against me. I squared my shoulders, hating to be less than what was expected, and took a step forward. Cole's face broke into a huge smile.

He really was the deciding factor. Without him, I would have ended up standing on the snowy path for hours trying to decide what to do. We walked the rest of the distance in silence. Unfortunately, it left me plenty of time to argue with myself about whether I had made the right choice.

As we neared the outskirts of the village, we could see that there were not nearly as many soldiers as I had feared there might be. Cole turned to me, "Do you want to find Astra or head straight for the valley?"

"Let's find Astra," I said quickly, which was sure to have surprised Cole, but the longer I could put off entering the valley, the better.

However, there was a problem. We didn't even know where to start looking for Astra.

"Let's just ask someone where she lives," Cole suggested.

"Are you sure that's a good idea?" I wondered. "It's one thing if we slip in and have a few words with Astra, but if we start asking around, we're sure to be noticed and will probably become the talk of the village." Cole considered for a moment as I continued. "I mean, we're from The Paramount, and our parents are Clan Leaders. Aside from the council members, we're about as conspicuous as it gets."

"You're right," Cole nodded. "Let's take a quick walk through the village and see if we can find her or get a hint of where she might be."

Since I didn't have a better plan, we did as Cole proposed.

THE PREPARATIONS

In The Paramount, everything was grouped close together with the council building in the very middle. The more important a building was, the closer to the center of the village it stood. The places where The Clan's records were stored and where the scribes worked were located next to the council building. Storehouses, which held the food for the inhabitants of The Paramount, were located farther from the middle, and the dwellings formed a circle on the fringe of the village.

Here in The North Wind, it was completely different. The stables and pastures were laid out in a sprawling fashion, with the dwellings located nearly a half mile behind them off to the west, closer to the mountains.

Neither of us had ever been to the dwellings before. I expected we would be stared at, but when we got there, the majority of those we saw were wearing the gold of The Barracks. There were far more of them among the dwellings than had been present around the stables. I felt a hopeful flutter in my chest. Maybe Cole wouldn't want to risk a trip into the valley after all. One glance at Cole and I knew he was considering the risks.

There was no point lingering among the dwellings. It was clear that Astra was either inside or not there, and I wasn't interested in knocking on random doors, trying to track her down.

We headed to the main stable. Most of the horses seemed to have already been taken to where they were needed for the day. I was worried that Astra might have gone on one of those trips and would be spending the day working in a different village.

We had almost finished searching through the largest barn when we found Astra. She was in a stall with a tall, whitish-gold horse. The animal was thin and not as large as some of the others I had seen. Astra was speaking softly to him and brushing his coat. The animal was standing still, quietly munching hay as she cleaned mud from his side.

It was the horse that sensed us first and turned first an ear in our direction and then the rest of his head. Astra followed the beast's gaze. If she was surprised to see us, it didn't show.

"Hi," she said over her shoulder, continuing to work while speaking to us.

Cole stepped right up to the stall and rested his arms on the half door.

"Hey," he said. He really couldn't say much else because there were two men scooping manure a couple of stalls away, and they would have heard every word that was spoken.

After a moment of silence, Astra stopped brushing the horse, which was pretty much clean—you know, for a horse.

"Do you need something?" Astra turned to face us.

Cole nodded.

"I don't suppose this is something we can discuss in public, is it?" she asked more softly.

Cole shook his head.

"Ok, come with me." She slipped out of the stall and led us through the stable, only pausing once to drop off the handful of brushes she had been using on the horse. Afterwards, she led us to a set of stairs.

The wooden steps creaked underfoot as we climbed. The second level was all one long room, filled with bins of grain and bales of hay. The low roof trusses were being used as tack holders. Bridles, saddles, and harnesses of all kinds hung just over our heads.

We came up in the middle of the open space. Astra turned to her left, and we followed. I heard a sound and glanced behind me. At the other end of the loft someone was sleeping against a hay bale. Their soft snoring sounded like the buzzing of flies. I wondered why Astra didn't give the loafer a kick to send them back to work, but she seemed not to notice.

"Watch your step," Astra instructed us, nodding to numerous holes in the floor. At first, I thought they were a result of the building beginning to deteriorate, but then I realized that the holes were intentional so hay and grain could easily be dropped to the floor below.

Once we'd gotten away from the stairs and the sleeper, I saw that there were lots of blankets and other items resting among a mound of loose hay.

Astra plopped down on a hay bale. There were about ten other bales set up in a circle. Cole sat on the one next to Astra's. I slowly sank down beside him. I could feel the hay poking me uncomfortably through my clothes.

"So, what forbidden topic are we broaching today?" Astra asked us. She seemed to be in a good mood. The sarcasm that usually marred her voice was light and playful. Also, she was smiling. I didn't think I'd ever seen her do that before.

Cole seemed a little surprised too.

"We actually wanted to talk about the valley again," he said. "We want to try talking to someone who's dead."

"Getting into the valley right now is next to impossible," Astra told him.

"I was worried about that," Cole admitted. "What did the soldiers do here when they found out about the Broken?" he asked.

Astra shrugged. "I'm not sure. About twenty of them went into the valley that night and more the next day. Only some have come back. I'm not supposed to go there right now."

"Well that makes three of us," I muttered.

"Do we actually have to go in?" Cole asked. He looked really disappointed that our trek had been for nothing. "Doesn't it ever work outside the valley?"

Astra turned her attention back to him, and I hoped she would say 'yes, we can try it right here', but I doubted she would be clever enough to lie to him and end the whole conversation.

"No," she answered. "There has only been one person in my lifetime that has ever claimed to have talked to the dead, and it was inside the valley."

"Who was it?" Cole asked.

"Her name was Viot," Astra told him. "She was very old and not quite herself when she went in. That was probably why they didn't give her a mark when she came out talking about having heard her life mate speaking to her.

"He had been dead almost ten years at the time, but she swore she had heard him speaking to her when she was in the valley."

"Where is this Viot now?" Cole asked.

I jumped suddenly as something brushed my leg. Looking down, I found a small, golden cat rubbing against my calf. Great, not only was I getting stabbed with straw, but I was also going to be covered in cat hair. There were no cats at The Paramount, and I liked it that way.

"Here Feather, come here kitty," Astra called softly. The cat pranced away from me and leapt into Astra's lap, where it promptly curled up into a tight ball.

"Viot is dead," Astra responded to Cole's question. "When they found out where she had been and heard what she had to say, they sent her away from The North Wind to live with her daughter in Riverside. She passed away less than a year later." Astra began rhythmically stroking the purring lump of golden fur in her arms.

"And she didn't say anything more about what happened to her in the valley?" Cole pressed.

"No," Astra sighed. "She was old and not right in the head. It's amazing she didn't hurt herself."

"But the rumors didn't start with her, did they?" Cole asked.

"I don't think so, but she is the only person I've met who has experienced such a thing, and I know plenty of people who have gone into the valley."

Cole nodded. I knew he wasn't pleased, but the more we learned, the more it appeared that the rumors were nothing but rumors.

THE PREPARATIONS

"Why do you keep asking about it?" Astra asked Cole. "Who is it you want to speak with so badly?"

Cole hesitated before responding.

"Myra wants to try to talk to her father."

Astra looked at me with understanding and sympathy in her eyes. I hated when people pitied me. "Myra," she said, smile and sarcasm completely gone, "it's just a rumor. I don't think it actually works."

"Have *you* tried it?" I asked.

She was silent for a moment. "Yes, I tried once." Astra had dropped her gaze.

"And nothing happened?" I asked.

She shook her head, and when she spoke, her voice seemed to be coming from somewhere far away. "No."

"Are you sure you did it right?" Cole wondered, which was probably the stupidest thing he could have said at the moment. In all fairness, he didn't know the pain of losing a parent, or both.

The sarcasm was instantly back in Astra's voice. "There's no 'right way'. Either you hear something or you don't."

"Just because you failed, doesn't mean Myra will," Cole replied, proving my earlier thought to be incorrect; *that* was the stupidest thing he could have said. At least he hadn't said it in a rude or angry way. He'd just said it. I wasn't sure that was a whole lot better, but Astra didn't respond the way I would have.

Instead of addressing Cole, she turned to me. "Do you want to try? Do you really want to?" Astra's eyes were intense, and at that moment, I knew she was hiding something. Just as Cole had left things out of our conversation with Golla, Astra wasn't telling us everything. Hope welled up inside me. Maybe it really was true, and I could talk to my father again.

"If there's even the slightest chance, I'll take it," I told her, surprising even myself.

"Will you help us?" Cole asked.

Astra glanced at him, and then back at me. "Take my advice," she said. "Go home, and don't think about the valley anymore."

"Please," Cole persisted. "The mystery of it is going to drive me crazy."

"Curiosity killed the cat," Astra mused, still holding the sleeping Feather.

"What?" Cole asked. "What cat got killed?"

"Nothing," Astra told him. "It's just an expression. Cats aren't really that easy to kill. They can disappear for a long time, and you can be sure they're gone, but then they turn up again and surprise you."

I waited, hoping Astra would share whatever she hadn't said earlier, but her eyes had fallen to the animal in her lap.

Cole stared at her blankly for a moment before turning to me. "Let's go. There's no point in staying here," he said.

I rose and would have followed him, but I turned back to Astra. If we came again, as I was sure we would, we might as well know where to find her. "Which dwelling do you stay in?" I asked.

Astra didn't look up. "Why?"

"Well," I said grudgingly, "we seem to keep needing to find you, and I'd like to know where to start next time." I was trying to lighten the mood, but my comment held no humor, even for me.

"You don't really seem to have much of a problem with that." Astra raised her green eyes to mine. She waited a moment before giving me an answer. "Here," was all she said.

"I don't understand," I replied, waiting for further information.

"I stay here," she explained.

"Here?" I echoed, glancing around.

There were quite a few odds and ends among the hay. Did she mean that she had no dwelling, but slept in the stable at night?

THE PREPARATIONS

"Yes," Astra told us. "Myself and several others sleep in the loft to keep watch over the horses. You can almost always find me somewhere in this stable."

Cole and I exchanged a glance. He might have pushed further on the subject, but it was clear to us both that Astra didn't want to discuss it.

"Thanks for talking to us," Cole said. "Let's go, Myra."

I followed Cole down from the loft. We walked out of the stable, and I blinked in the bright light of the day. Cole seemed to be in a hurry; I had to almost run to keep up with him. Once we reached the head of the road, a quarter mile from The North Wind, he stopped.

"What are you doing?" I asked.

"I don't know anymore," he said, turning back to me. I could tell from the look in his eyes that he wasn't accepting defeat that easily.

"Cole, we can't," I told him flatly.

"I know, but—"

"No. You heard what Astra said; we aren't going today." I knew it was time to put my foot down. "We are returning to The Paramount and not coming back to The Valley of the North Wind until everything is back to normal."

"Things might not calm down until after the trials," he pointed out. "And what if we don't end up on the same team?"

"Then I'll tell you about it when we get back," I said, turning away. I wasn't going to let him destroy both of us. I was done with all of it.

"Myra, wait!" Cole called, but I didn't even glance back. "Myra, stop!" Something about his voice was different.

I turned and saw that Cole was looking back over his shoulder. Suddenly, he took off running in the direction we had come from.

There was something going on at the eastern end of the village. About two dozen gold-clad figures and half as many gray-clad ones were gathered there. They had just finished crossing the space between The North Wind and the valley.

I raced after Cole. He was rushing straight for the commotion. I had to get him away before we both got caught up in something we shouldn't have been involved with.

My legs pumped the ground as hard as they could, but he was too far ahead of me. There was no way I would catch him before he made it to the group of onlookers, but I didn't slacken my pace.

Cole reached the edge of the crowd moments before I did. To my relief, he didn't press very far into the mass of people. I put a hand on his shoulder, desperate to pull him away. Then I saw the reason everyone was gathered, and I forgot all else.

The crowd parted, and four soldiers advanced into the village.

They carried a body.

I was instantly paralyzed, because I knew who it was. The light green clothes were enough of a giveaway even before I saw Golla's face. My hand dropped from Cole's shoulder.

Her curly, blonde hair was limp and muddy, her face ashen and red with blood. I stood there, staring, unable to process anything. Golla had been in The North Wind? And she was dead? What had happened? I didn't understand.

An old man, one of The North Wind's village leaders, stepped forward to address the crowd. "I am very sorry to say that someone has died in The Valley of the North Wind." There was complete silence as we watched the soldiers bear the body into a nearby building.

A moment later, the village leader continued. "We don't know yet who she is or why she entered the valley, but it is clear that she was killed in a rock slide. Someone saw her go in this morning, and these soldiers were brave enough to follow at the risk of their own lives. I just wish they had been able to reach her in time."

THE PREPARATIONS

The crowd had tripled in size during the village leader's speech. It seemed half The North Wind had been alerted and come to join the assembly. The village leader continued speaking, but I stopped focusing on what he was saying.

It didn't matter. I met Cole's gaze. We knew who she was and why she had been there. I felt sick. It was my fault. If I had just convinced Cole to let Golla come with us, she wouldn't have gone in, or at least not by herself.

Cole reached out, took hold of my arm, and started pulling me away. I was frozen. I couldn't move, couldn't react. As I finally got my feet working enough to stumble after him, I caught sight of Astra. She must have come with the others to see what all the commotion was about.

She knew. I could tell as soon as our eyes met. She knew that I knew. Instead of pursuing us, she watched us retreat in silence.

Once Cole and I were far away from the crowd—half a mile down the southern road—I lost it. My legs went out, and I dropped to my knees in the snow. I almost dragged Cole down with me, but he released my hand and turned to face me. I sat there, gasping. I couldn't catch my breath. There wasn't enough air; I was going to suffocate.

In my panic, I didn't even realize that Cole had crouched beside me or that he was trying to speak to me, until he started yelling.

"Myra!" he shouted. "Snap out of it!"

I took one more breath and could finally feel a tiny trickle of air make its way into my lungs. "It was Golla—"

"Shhh!" Cole hissed. "I know. I'm sorry; I'm so sorry."

"She's dead. We killed her!" I almost screamed.

Cole put his hand over my mouth to keep me from making any more noise.

"No," he said. "It's not your fault. She made her own choice. She knew the risks."

"But if—" I tried again.

"She didn't tell you she was coming here. You didn't know." Cole glanced back the way we had come. "We need to leave. Now."

He dragged me to my feet, and we walked away from the valley. Cole had to physically pull me along for almost a mile. I couldn't help looking back over my shoulder to where I knew the valley lay. My feet felt numb. I stumbled along, not caring that I was walking through slush and mud. What did it matter anymore?

We had come looking for death, and we had found it.

Chapter 18

THE THAW

I didn't remember much of the trip back to The Paramount, just that it was long and I never seemed to be able to catch my breath. Cole kept a tight grip on my hand the entire way.

Just before we reached the outskirts of the village, he released me and whispered in my ear, "Go home, Myra. Don't tell anyone about what happened today or about Golla."

I nodded. It wouldn't be hard; I didn't have anyone to tell.

Staggering away from him, I managed to find my way to my dwelling. Even though the sun was still hours from setting, I went to my room, peeled back the blankets, and crawled into bed. But I couldn't find sleep.

Is it my fault that this happened? I asked myself a thousand times. There was no real answer. Maybe it wasn't all my doing, but I had fed into Golla's imagination, and she had destroyed herself because of it—because of me. The image of her dead body was constantly before my waking eyes.

I didn't stir from my bed the rest of the day. Finally, long after the sun had set, I fell into a deep, dreamless sleep.

There was an instant, somewhere between waking and sleeping, that everything felt peaceful. Then I opened my eyes and saw Golla's pale face once more in my head.

Nothing would ever be right again.

At the sound of the bell, I rose and went to training, not caring which village we visited or what we learned.

THE PREPARATIONS

Cole took me to The Quarry. I think he chose that particular location because it was as far from The North Wind and The Golden Fields as we could get.

As soon as we returned to The Paramount that the afternoon, we heard the news about someone dying in The Valley of the North Wind the day before. Of course, I had to act surprised and shocked, when, in truth, I felt nauseous and heartsick. Someone mentioned Golla's name, and my throat constricted too much for me to speak. No tears came though, for which I was thankful.

Cole walked me to my door. We'd hardly spoken all day, and he didn't speak then, but he did give me a tight embrace before departing. My mind hardly registered his contact, as I tried to suppress the storm of emotions that threatened to drown me.

To my great surprise, Myna was waiting inside of our dwelling.

"Golla is dead," she announced as I walked into the room.

"I heard," I managed to choke out.

"Tomorrow, in the afternoon, there will be a funeral at The Golden Fields. I am speaking, and I expect you will want to attend as well."

I nodded, without meeting her eyes. "I'll go," I whispered, before escaping to my room.

***

The following day, I trained at The Barracks because of its proximity to The Golden Fields. I didn't want to be late to the funeral. The session ended earlier than I had expected, leaving me ample time for the short walk.

"Do you want me to come with you?" Cole asked.

I shook my head. Much as I would have been comforted by his presence, Cole would only have come out of guilt, and I didn't want to burden him with that.

It hadn't been his fault. He hadn't known Golla's character, so he couldn't possibly have seen what actions she might take. I was the one who should have known. I could have stopped her, but I had been too focused on myself. I had turned out to be a sorry excuse for a friend.

The work day had already been suspended by the time I reached the village. Hundreds of people had congregated in the town center. The mood was somber. Golla had been well-known and well-liked. All of The Golden Fields was in deep mourning.

Naturally, people in The Clan died quite frequently, but those were old people or sick people, not the young and strong.

I found Myna in the town center, standing beside the village leaders. She didn't even glance my way as I joined the group.

Funerals were very simple things. Once someone passed on, what more was there to do than dispose of the body?

I forced myself to look at Golla. Her golden hair had been combed out, and the blood had been washed from her face. In warmer seasons, the children would have brought flowers to place around the body of the deceased, but there were no flowers that time of year.

It was sad to think how lovely Golla would have looked, wreathed in colorful petals, their bright hues adorning her blonde hair.

However, the fields would be void of flowers for at least half a month yet. By the time the tender green stocks appeared, it would be far too late.

Golla's undecorated body rested on a simple cart with low sides. Each year, a field was chosen at The Golden Fields. All those who died were buried there. At the conclusion of the funeral, horses would be brought to draw Golla to her final resting place.

Once spring finally came, her body would begin to decompose and provide nutrients for the crops that would grow under the summer sun.

THE PREPARATIONS

Golla had worked those fields and eaten their yields. Now, she was going to be buried in them, giving back to the plants all the life she had taken.

When I was a child, I had thought it was gross to 'eat people' that way. But there was actually something fulfilling about the cycle. We received life from the ground, and one day we returned to it. Despite what Golla had believed, maybe that was all that happened after death.

Once the appointed time had come, one of the village leaders stepped forward to say a few words. He was a short, stocky man, with close-cropped gray hair. His eyes were sharp and keen, but his voice was gentle.

A wide, wooden box had been placed beside the cart to serve as a small stage. The village leader stood on it so all could see him. Mostly, he talked about what a special person Golla had been and how much she would be missed.

I listened at first, but it was nearly too hard to bear. Golla had been full of joy and laughter not three days ago, but the village leader was reducing her to a string of words that poorly attempted to define her.

After the village leader, it was Golla's mother's turn. Her speech was much the same as the first speaker's, but cut up by numerous pauses. I wasn't sure she was ever going to reach the end. The poor woman looked as though she had been crying for two days straight, with no comfort from her sorrows. Her husband was long dead, and her only child was gone too. She must have felt as if the entire world had come to an end.

Was that how Myna would feel if I died? I glanced sideways at her, standing impassively to my left, but I could glean no thoughts from her face.

As soon as Golla's mother finished, Myna stepped forward. I wondered what she was going to say. Clan Leaders rarely spoke at funerals unless they had known the deceased. Sure, I had known Golla for many years, but when did Myna pay any attention to who was and wasn't my friend?

"Today is a hard day, a day of grieving and sadness," Myna began. Her voice held a trace of sorrow, but it wasn't real. Behind her façade, she was as emotionless as always.

"We all regret the loss of someone so young, who still had much to offer to her people. It goes against nature for the young to die before the old and is the worst of tragedies."

Murmurs of agreement rose from the crowd. Golla's mother buried her face in her hands, and those nearest her reached out to comfort and support her.

"We must look on this dark day and learn from it," Myna continued. "We are safe here, in The Land of the Clan, but only because of our laws and the order they create."

More murmurs, more agreement.

"If we can abide by the rules of our forefathers, we will be safe. Tragedies like this," Myna gestured at Golla's still form, "will not have to arise."

"Go now, and remember Golla. She was a lovely girl. Try to think of the happy times you shared with her, but also remember her as a lesson."

With that, Myna stepped down. The funeral was over.

Two men from The North Wind led a pair of brown horses to the wagon and began hitching them to it. I heard a cry of grief escape Golla's mother.

Myna didn't glance back. She was already heading for The Paramount. Her duty was finished; she had no reason to stay.

I followed her. The idea of watching Golla being lowered into a deep hole and covered in black soil was too much.

We were silent for the first twenty minutes. I was painfully aware that if there was going to be any conversation I would have to initiate it, but I never knew where to start.

Part of me had thought that Myna might be warmer to me on the walk home, since she had just seen another woman lose her only child. I should have known better.

Underfoot, the snow was wet and soft. That seemed as good an excuse as any to say something.

"There'll be a thaw soon," was all I could come up with.

Myna nodded without looking at me, and I feared she wouldn't even bother to make a verbal reply. Instead, she surprised me with three full sentences.

"Yes, the council believes it will come in the next couple of days. It's late this year. The growing season will be shorter than usual, but it will be alright."

"You mean there isn't going to be enough food?" I wondered.

Myna shook her head. "There won't be as much food, but there will be enough." Her words were soft and had a ring of finality.

"Do you think it will be as cold next winter?" I asked. The weather seemed to be the only thing we really had to talk about, so why not milk the subject to exhaustion?

"I don't know," Myna answered.

That was it. That was all I was going to get unless I started a fight or said something that I shouldn't.

"Why do you think Golla was in The Valley of the North Wind?" The question popped out before it had even fully entered my mind.

Myna faltered slightly, but continued on without looking back at me. "I don't know," she said again.

"Do you think it had something to do with the Broken?" I asked. Goodness, lots of words were escaping me without permission that afternoon. I was going to have to work harder on controlling myself.

"I don't know," Myna replied once more, making me want to scream.

"What do you know?" I pressed.

Myna sighed, as if she had been hoping to escape conversation with me but felt obligated since I was asking such inappropriate questions. She was probably sorry that we had been the only ones from The Paramount in attendance at the funeral. If there had been other people walking back with us, she would not have been forced to endure my company.

"Golla was always very impertinent and disobedient," Myna stated. "I often worried when the two of you played together that she was not the best influence. Now you can see why."

It was funny almost. Golla, influence me badly? Wasn't I the one who had shared the rumor that had led her to death? Wasn't it my fault? My bad influence?

"She clearly had a lack of respect for the laws of The Clan. Her death is on her own head," Myna continued coldly. "Honestly, it was better that she died in the valley. Otherwise, she would have been disgraced for breaking the rules of our people. Only her death saved her from a great deal of shame. Personally, I think the shame should have been applied anyway, but it was not my choice."

"Is that why you came to her funeral?" I asked fiercely. What she was saying might have been true; Golla had broken the rules, but it had cost her everything. Was that truly not enough?

Myna's sudden attack on Golla made my eyes sting. I knew the only reason she had said those things was to punish me.

She hadn't intended to share her opinion with anyone, but I had asked questions. Myna didn't like questions, because she didn't like giving answers. Her response had been to lash out at me in the cruelest way she possibly could, to hurt me so I wouldn't speak to her again.

Fine. She wanted silence that much, she could have it. Without waiting to see if she would respond, I took off running. The Paramount was only another mile away, but I wasn't going to The Paramount.

I turned my feet to the right and ran to the amphitheater. I wanted to be alone.

Thankfully, it was empty.

Only as I slowed from a run, did I realize I was literally shaking from anger. I slowly walked to the front of the amphitheater and sank down onto the stone seat directly in front of the ash-filled fire pit.

I remained there for quite a while, trying to stop the shaking of my limbs. I wished the sun would hurry up and set. All I wanted was to reach the end of that ugly day so I could return to my room and sleep.

I longed for the darkness of unconsciousness. It would block out my senses so I could forget—even if just for a little while. Golla's death would always be my fault. I would spend the rest of my life with that knowledge, never able to escape it.

Suddenly, I was aware of a sound. It had been there all along, but I hadn't thought anything of it until that moment. At first, I couldn't place it, although I'd most definitely heard it many times before. Then I knew. It was the drip of melting snow and the trickle of small streams of water running downhill. The thaw had finally arrived.

The world was ready to wake up and start its cycle of life again.

It must have been warmer than I had thought, warmer than it had been in a long time. I couldn't tell though, because even as the ice that encased the world began to melt, I couldn't feel any difference in the temperature.

Would I always be too cold for anything beautiful to grow in my life?

Chapter 19

JUSTICE

Pain exploded in my hand as a wooden staff slapped across my knuckles. My only reaction was to involuntarily drop my own staff. I felt the pain, but it wasn't bad enough for me to cry out.

"Myra!" Cole exclaimed. "Are you ok? I'm so sorry."

"It's fine," I muttered as I bent to retrieve the fallen staff so we could continue sparring.

It had been eight days since Golla's funeral. In that short amount of time, the land had become unrecognizable. Every field and patch of ground had transformed from stark white to lush green.

There were still some watery patches of snow, but they grew smaller and smaller every day. Before too much longer, all the slush would vanish completely until the following winter.

Training had grown more intense with the thaw. Cole, Motik, and I had spent the morning at The Making, learning seven different sewing stitches. The lesson had ended just after lunch, and we had transitioned to the Barracks, where we were participating in a late afternoon sparring session. Jase had joined us after spending the first part of his day with Bala at Treescape.

The Barracks's session wasn't invitation only, anyone could come, but the instructors went much faster than they did during morning training. They had made it clear that it was our responsibility to keep up.

THE PREPARATIONS

Jase, Cole, Motik, and I had come every afternoon for the past four training days. Bala and Ashlo joined us sometimes too, but not that night.

Ever since the extra training sessions had begun at The Barracks, we'd chosen to skip their morning sessions, preferring to just attend the faster-paced classes. So far, we hadn't had too much trouble keeping up with the more intense training.

Jase was the only one with a complaint. He was disappointed that they weren't teaching us to fight with swords or knives, or anything other than sticks. Cole had pointed out to him that once the trials began, we were unlikely to have anything but sticks—and possibly stones—to defend ourselves with. Jase had taken his words to heart and had let the subject drop.

I could have told him the same thing, but recently I hadn't felt much like talking. I was pretty sure my silence was starting to bother Cole. Every once in a while, I'd catch him looking at me like I was made of ice, about to break or melt or something.

"Are you sure you're ok?" Cole asked, lowering his staff.

"I'm fine," I told him again. He didn't appear convinced, so I took a quick swipe at him and almost caught the side of his arm, but he managed to bring his own staff up to intercept the blow.

He struck back, and I blocked him easily. We began running through the series of moves the instructor had shown us earlier.

By the time we were finished, the light from outside was almost gone. The sun had set, and twilight was quickly turning to night. The circular arena was lit by numerous wall lamps that lined the large room.

Three days prior, I had stopped wearing my heavy cloak. It was hanging in the clothing niche at the back of my room, hopefully, unneeded until the following winter. In the arena, with the heat of the small fires and the press of so many other bodies, I had even taken off my jacket and was wearing only a lightweight shirt. Its rich crimson color was my favorite of the tones of The Paramount. Nearly all of the other potentials were also attired in their summer clothing. Sparring was hot work.

The first half hour had been spent watching as the instructors performed complex moves with each other. After we had observed them, we had been given the opportunity to practice the new moves on our own. The cycle had been repeated several times.

Now, with the training session almost over for the night, we were given free time to spar as we saw fit. Cole and I began stalking around each other and looking for an opening to get in a quick blow. Each of us was careful not to injure the other.

I always felt bad for Jase's opponents, since he hit with the force of a charging bull. It was nice to have a consistent partner in Cole, someone who was just good enough to challenge me, without him winning every time.

After twenty more minutes had elapsed, the instructors called an end to the session. I put my staff back in the bin where it belonged and retrieved my jacket from where I had discarded it earlier in the evening.

There was a mass exodus as the swarm of potentials headed out of the village. I fell into step with Cole and Jase. Motik had departed a little before the session had ended, so it was just the three of us.

Remaining silent, I trailed behind as Jase and Cole chatted and laughed. I didn't hear anything worth laughing at. Once we reached The Paramount, Jase left us to head to his dwelling.

I turned toward mine, but Cole caught my arm. I glanced at him, unsure of what he was doing.

"How long are you going to stay angry with me?" Cole asked.

I blinked in confusion. I wasn't angry with Cole. If anything, he should have been angry with me. Carefully, I took in his expression; he did seem agitated, but not necessarily angry.

"I'm not angry with you," I told him.

"Come on, Myra," Cole protested, his hand leaving my arm. "You haven't said two words to me since Golla died. I know you blame me—"

"No." I shook my head. "Why would I blame you?" It had been my fault after all.

"Because you wanted to take her along, and I wouldn't let you. If we had all gone together, it wouldn't have happened."

I swallowed hard, trying to steady my voice. "You didn't know Golla. She was always too impulsive and rebellious."

I sounded like Myna.

"You couldn't have known how stubborn she was or how far she would go, so it can't be your fault. I certainly don't blame you," I told him.

It was true. I didn't know a single person who would have acted as Golla had given the same situation.

"Really?" Cole asked. He seemed surprised.

"I'm the one who's to blame," I added softly. "She was my friend, and I suspected what she would do, even if I didn't know."

"Myra," Cole groaned. "I should have known you'd blame yourself. If anyone is not responsible, it's you. You didn't even want to go to the valley in the first place, did you?"

"No," I admitted.

"Plus, you wanted to tell Golla everything, and I wouldn't let you. You were trying to be a good friend to us both and got caught in the middle. It's not your fault."

I sighed, and Cole seemed to realize that he hadn't convinced me in the least.

"Ok, think about it a different way. Even if it was your fault, what can you do now but move on? The trials are coming up. You need to focus on the future, not fret about the past. Can't you just..." He paused, considering. "Can't you just let her rest? There's nothing more we can do."

JUSTICE

"You're right," I told him. "But I watch it over and over in my head. I am constantly trying to find new ways to save her—ways I could have changed what happened."

"We can't change the past. We can only try to make the future better. That's how our people live as a whole and how we should live individually."

I glanced at Cole. The way he spoke was so noble. He was truly meant to be a Clan Leader.

"Thanks," I whispered.

"Cole, Myra, is everything alright?"

I turned to see Core walking toward us. Cole took an involuntary step back as his father approached. I hadn't realized how close we'd been standing. A light blush touched my cheeks.

Core laughed softly at our embarrassment. "I'm sorry," he said. "I didn't mean to disturb your conversation."

"It's alright," Cole replied. "We were just discussing Golla's passing."

Sorrow crossed Core's face. "Aw, yes, a most tragic occurrence. While I didn't know Golla well, everyone spoke highly of her. She was a natural leader. If her death had not come in such an untimely fashion, I know she would have offered many years of valuable service to The Clan."

I couldn't speak, but only nodded at Core's gentle words.

Core glanced at his son. "Cole, your brothers and sister are coming for dinner, but if you are a little late, it's not a problem."

With that, the First Clan Leader gave me a kind smile and departed.

Cole turned back to me.

"Are you alright?" he asked.

I nodded, still unable to form words.

"Do you want to talk about it?"

I shook my head.

Cole sighed. "Isn't there anything I can do to help?"

"No," I managed. "You should go to dinner."

I forced myself to meet his gaze, trying to show him that I really was alright.

After a moment, Cole turned and headed for his dwelling. "I'll see you tomorrow," he called over his shoulder.

***

The training continued, day after day. Grief and guilt from Golla's death faded to the background, but it was still there. Over the course of the following eleven days, spring came into full bloom. The last of the snow melted, and grass grew long and wispy.

In the mornings, the chirping of birds filled the clean-smelling air. I hadn't been prepared for each village to change so much, but once the last of the cold weather passed, they all sprung to life.

At The Farm, the bleating of lambs and the high-pitched mews of calves filled the air. In The Golden Fields, they plowed the rich soil of the land and planted thousands of seeds. Boats appeared on the lake by Riverside. Soon, we would have fresh fish again.

They stopped cutting as much wood at Treescape, and instead, began putting small saplings in the ground. The young trees had been grown with care indoors for several years and were to replace the old trees, which had been used for firewood that year.

Everywhere, people were busy again. Winter was when we had the most time off. It worked out well because the days were so short and light was limited. As the hours of daylight increased each day, so did the hours of work.

Soon, all the villages took after The Barracks and began to offer training sessions in the afternoons and evenings. I couldn't ever remember being so tired. However, I refused to miss a moment of training. Cole was almost never far from my side, and we planned our days carefully to ensure we made it to as many sessions as possible.

Even with all the activity going on around me, I still felt empty inside. Cold too. I was training hard and, on the outside, appeared as dedicated as before to preparing for the trials. But inside, my mind couldn't seem to find any resolution.

I continued in that state for longer than I'd like to admit. It wasn't until almost a whole month after Golla's death that an event occurred, which brought me out of the uncertain place my mind had wandered to.

Cole, Jase, Ashlo, and I were doing our morning training at The Golden Fields. We were learning which plants were good to eat and what they looked like. Cole was better at identifying them while they were still in the ground than I was, but Ashlo was even better than both of us. One glance at a leaf and she seemed to be able to tell everything there was to know about the specimen.

We were out in one of the large fields, which had been planted as soon as the ground had been soft enough to be plowed. There were about a hundred potentials wandering about, carefully trying not to step on any of the tender, green shoots.

Our instructors had told us that the plants we were looking at had been growing inside for several months and had been transplanted as soon as winter had broken. Just like in Treescape, the plants were protected and started out in a controlled environment. Not all the plants at The Golden Fields were grown that way; there were far too many. Most were sown in the ground as seeds.

Jase and Cole had just started an argument about whether the plant in front of us was a carrot or a radish. Ashlo wouldn't tell them who was right and kept laughing whenever they asked her what she thought.

Of course, we couldn't dig up the roots to check, so until the instructor had a moment to settle the dispute, the boys were left to argue.

The normal me would have jumped in, probably on Cole's side, even though I didn't really know what kind of plant it was. I always liked to be on Cole's side, and anyway, he had a better chance of being right, in my opinion.

"The leaves are too scraggily for it to be a radish," Jase said.

"But there's red on the bottom of the leaves," Cole pointed out. "It has to be a radish."

"It's way too tall," Jase fired back. Ashlo had wandered off and was chatting with a couple of her other friends from The Making. I'd seen her with them before and wondered if they might end up on the same team.

"I'm still sure it's a carrot," Jase persisted. My mind shifted away from the boys and their quarrel. I tried to look attentive and focus on what was being said, but I just didn't care. What did it matter anyway? During the trials, we would have just yanked the dumb thing out of the ground. Although, there was always the chance that even once it was out there would still be no consensus.

My eyes drifted from the fields and focused on the distant road, which led to The Paramount. I had no desire to go there; The Paramount had nothing for me.

Suddenly, I blinked. Someone was coming. There was a rider racing straight toward the village.

"But—"

"Look!" I called, cutting Cole off.

Instantly, both of the boys, and all those near us, turned to see what my hand was pointing to. The rider had reached the fields on the outskirts of the village. Turning his horse down the path, which would lead him to us, he slowed slightly. It was a man in the gray of The North Wind. The horse was large and brown; its flanks were covered in sweat, and the beast was breathing hard.

JUSTICE

The rider pulled the animal to a stop on the edge of the field. We were not the only ones to notice. Although the potentials had scattered a bit to look at the different kinds of plants, it took less than a minute for them to cluster around the horse and rider.

The man appeared grim, and he held the twitching horse with an iron fist. There was an unhappy look in his eyes. He only addressed us once everyone was within hearing distance.

"The Clan Leaders have requested that all potentials assemble at The Quarry by midday," he announced.

I felt the other children's eyes turn my way, wondering if I knew what was going on since I was a Clan Leader's daughter. I couldn't help glancing at Cole; maybe his father had told him something. However, he seemed just as confused as I felt. Whatever our parents wanted, we had no prior knowledge of it.

Without another word, the man from The North Wind spun his horse on its haunches and left as speedily as he had come.

Our instructor glanced up at the sky. It was a gloomy, cloudy morning, which made it hard to get an exact reading on the time of day.

"Well," he said, after considering for a moment. "I guess this session is over. I'm not sure what is going on at The Quarry, but I don't want anyone to be late on my account.

"As far as I know, there will still be an afternoon and an evening session..." He trailed off uncertainly.

Something very unusual must have been going on. I hadn't expected the potentials to be convened together until the teams were announced, but that was still several months away.

Cole, Jase, Ashlo, and I were among the first to leave. It could have been a test of some sort. After the first week, the number of elders observing us had diminished; however, I was certain we were always being watched.

Another reason for our hasty departure was that at least three of us had the strong sense of punctuality that came with growing up in The Paramount. I didn't include Jase in that number, since he was about as timely as he was intelligent.

Traveling was much easier with the snow gone. Before long, the weather would grow uncomfortably hot, but that day it was perfect. There was a cool breeze coming from the south, and the cloud cover began to lessen, allowing the sun to peek through and warm us with soft light.

Unfortunately, The Golden Fields was just about as far from The Quarry as you could get, so we had a long walk ahead of us.

"What do you think is going on?" Jase asked. He glanced between Cole and me, assuming that at least one of us would know something.

I shook my head. "No clue," I told him.

Cole just shrugged.

"Are they going to pick teams?" Jase asked.

"It's way too early for that," Ashlo piped up.

"Maybe not," Jase said.

"It's not likely," Cole said, supporting Ashlo's opinion. "The instructors didn't even know this was going to happen. It has to be something else. Something unexpected."

"Like what?" I wondered. My nerves were getting the best of me. I knew I hadn't been at my best lately and desperately didn't want that to affect which team I ended up on, if they put me on a team at all. That thought horrified me, but not as much as I knew it should have.

"I don't know," Cole said, shaking his head.

The conversation turned to planning our training for the afternoon and evening, if any more sessions were even held that day. There was also some more speculation about what would be waiting for us once we reached The Quarry.

When I was nine, I'd spent nearly a whole month in The Quarry. Myna had been there on council business, and it had just kept getting stretched out. I would have been very lonely and bored, but I'd happened to make a friend on my first day. His name was Hlan of the Quarry.

He was a little younger than me; although, I wasn't sure exactly by how much. He had been small for his age, and I'd towered over him, but he'd taught me a new game. It was played with little stones that moved on small squares and tried to reach the opposite side of the board. Once they made it, they became special pieces and were used to eliminate the other player's pieces. His father had told me it was called 'Checkers'.

We had played about twenty games each afternoon during the duration of my stay. Myna had been busy at the stone pits, investigating a problem concerning the grade of stone being cut and sent out to repair the roads in Riverside.

Hlan and I had ended up meeting the first morning, and he had taught me how to play the game. The first time, he had won. The second time, I had. That was when it had become war. After school each day, the two of us had met and furiously battled every free moment.

Soon, we had started keeping score. In the end, he had won two hundred and eighty-seven times, and I had won two hundred and eighty-six times. We'd been in the middle of a game—which I had been winning—when Myna had appeared, had announced that her work was finished, and had dragged me away.

I'd screamed half of the way back to The Paramount that I had been about to beat him and needed to finish, but Myna had refused to acknowledge my complaint.

Although it had happened a long time ago, I could still remember the injustice of being pulled away at the very cusp of victory.

When Cole, myself, and the others arrived at The Quarry, the place was already packed. The village had a larger town center than most others, but it seemed to be completely full. The space was circular and lined with stone buildings where masonry was done. Most of buildings were two stories tall, and I could see people looking out of the large, second floor windows. In the middle of the town center stood a bell, similar to our own, and a well.

THE PREPARATIONS

From the looks of things, most of the crowd was made up of potentials. I saw the colors of all nine villages represented on children around my own age. There were also some adults from The Quarry wearing royal blue, but the vast amount of potentials dwarfed their number easily ten to one.

I didn't think we were going to able to get through, and we couldn't see anything that was going on from the rear of the crowd. All that was visible from my vantage point was the town bell, which rose high over the heads of those gathered below.

We tried to squeeze through, but the press of human bodies was too dense. I glanced at Jase's bulk and knew he was never going to get to the front.

"Let's split up," I suggested.

Cole nodded. "We can meet back up after."

I left them to their own devises and began to slip through the crowd on my own. I was thin, and it was much easier for me to maneuver than for the boys.

When I caught sight of the square, I froze. Myna was there. A moment later, I continued my progress. We hadn't spoken since Golla's death, and I hadn't forgotten the things she'd said after.

Unfortunately, the path of least resistance led straight toward her. Much as I did not want to be anywhere close to Myna, I did want to know what was going on and what was going to happen, so I allowed myself to move forward, each step bringing me closer to her.

When I was about ten feet from Myna, she turned and looked at me. There was no warmth in her eyes or her voice as she addressed me. "Myra, it is good you have come."

Those nearby parted for me so I was forced to go all the way to her. "What's going on?" I asked.

"You will see," was the only answer she gave before turning back to the scene in the middle of the town center.

Even with the size of the gathered multitude, a small open space was present in the town center around the bell. Myna and

I were standing on the very cusp of the onlookers. Two more steps forward and I would have been away from the press of the crowd.

What I saw in the opening confused me slightly. Core was there, and on either side of him was a woman wearing royal blue. His back was to me, facing the two women of The Quarry. The younger-looking woman, on Core's right, was kneeling on the ground, sobbing into her hands. Such a public display of emotion was shocking. Something was very wrong.

I examined the woman on the other side of Core. She was turned so I couldn't see very much of her face, but she was older and I was pretty sure she was crying as well. She was not sobbing like the woman on the ground, but there seemed to be tears silently coursing down her cheeks.

The second woman did not stand alone. A pair of small children, far too young to be training for the trials, stood with her. They were huddled so close that they almost vanished into the long pants she was wearing.

"What happened?" I breathed.

"Pay attention," Myna almost snapped at me. "You'll see soon enough."

I sighed, but refrained from asking anything else.

It wasn't quite sun high yet, and more potentials were still arriving from their training in other villages.

There was a small commotion on the edge of the town center as a boy, maybe fifteen years old, shoved his way roughly through the crowd. I couldn't make out what he was saying at first.

"That's my mother!" I heard him scream, as he broke through the last clump of people and stumbled into the center. Then he limped toward the woman with the two other children.

At first, I wondered if he had hurt himself pushing through the crowd, but as he came closer, I saw that his right foot was twisted at an awkward angle. I remembered him then. I had seen him several times before, but I couldn't recall his name, not that I was sure I had ever known it.

The only thing I knew about him was that he had been born with a deformed foot. I'd pitied him for a while, but he'd never let it slow him down, and that was admirable.

His mother wrapped her arms around the boy and said something to him softly. There was too much noise to hear what words she spoke, but I wished I could have. A moment later, the boy's eyes filled with horror, and he staggered a few steps away from his mother. Shock was written all over his face. He shook his head slightly, backing away from the woman.

I didn't know what he would have done next, but, at that moment, it was sun high.

Core stepped forward and rung the great bell twice. Silence was almost instantaneous. Every eye was fastened on Core.

"Greetings," he said, using the same word he greeted us with at Midwinter and Midsummer. "Thank you all for coming. I know this summons is unusual, but myself and the rest of the council thought it would be good if you all were present."

He walked as he spoke. His feet carried him around the open space in the town center so that he could address us all and not just one part of the crowd.

"As far as I know, a situation like this has never occurred during the preparations before. Some of you will be the next Clan Leaders, and we wanted you to witness the difficult duty that will be performed here today."

When Core said 'difficult duty', the boy with the twisted foot let out a small, strangled cry. He instantly covered his mouth, as if the sound had been involuntary.

Core must have heard, but he didn't turn or acknowledge the sound in any way. "Early this morning, a man was murdered."

Then I knew. I knew why we were there; I knew what we were going to see. There was only one punishment for murder: exile. All that was left was to determine the guilty party.

I glanced at the two women in the center of the crowd with Core. I doubted either of them was the killer. No, more likely it was their life mates who were involved. Watching the young woman sobbing on the ground and the mother standing tall, holding her children close, I wondered which one had lost a life mate to death and which one was about to lose their life mate to exile.

Both were horrible things to endure. Was it better to bear the grief of a sudden loss? Or the shame of a life mate who had betrayed The Clan itself? A life mate couldn't be held responsible for something their partner had done, but they still had to live with the consequences of justice. I couldn't imagine the horror of thinking that you knew someone so well, only for them to be unmasked as a villain.

I knew that I'd rather have my life mate die than be exiled. Death would bring grief, but a pure grief, not poisoned by treachery. After the time of mourning had elapsed, a person would be free to move on with their life, chose a new life mate if they wanted, and leave their sorrow in the past.

However, if your life mate was exiled, there was no time of mourning. You were expected to forget them immediately. What was more, you could never take on a new life mate because it would be unknown whether or not your first was still living. Their shadow would plague you for the rest of your life.

Still, if you really loved someone, would you rather have them dead? Or just gone? Not that surviving outside The Clan was easy, but there had to be a way.

I tried to imagine how I would feel if my father had been exiled instead of having died, but it was impossible. My father had been kind and gentle; there was nothing in him that could have ever been capable of murder.

"Judgment has been passed."

My attention snapped back to the present as Core finished whatever he had been saying. I mentally reprimanded myself for letting my mind wander. My mental discipline had been sorely lacking of late.

Core looked toward one of the stone buildings off to my left. I glanced that direction and saw the crowd parting as a man, wearing the blue color of The Quarry, walked slowly toward the open space. He was flanked on either side by a soldier from The Barracks. A third followed the procession for good measure.

The man in blue stopped when he was a few feet from Core. He didn't look like a killer. Rather, he looked timid and frightened.

The man took a deep breath and spoke, addressing Core in a voice barely loud enough for everyone to hear.

"Your honor," the man said, licking his lips nervously, "I must beg your forgiveness. I have told you all that was done. Kirst's death was an accident. We were trying to improve the pulley system when the rope slipped and—"

Core held up a hand to stop the man. "We heard your account, but the village healer could tell from the wounds in Kirst's neck that you lied. His report concludes that nothing except an intentional blow with a knife could have made the wound."

"There was no knife," the accused argued.

Core closed his eyes and took a cloth-wrapped object from his pocket. He unfolded it and revealed a knife covered in dried blood to all gathered there. A gasp went up from the crowd.

The man's eyes widened. "Please," he begged. "This is impossible. I would never. I—I mean I didn't. It—It was an accident!

"Punish me another way. Do anything else to me, but do not exile me. Give me two marks, and I assure that you will never have reason to give me a third. I know the work we were doing was not authorized, we were breaking the laws, and it was wrong, but I did not murder Kirst! Please do not send me away!"

There was fear and desperation in the man's voice. The woman who had been on the ground crying, rose then. She looked at the man savagely.

"You murderer!" she screamed. "You knew Kirst always looked up to you! How could you do something like this to him? Now you will get what you deserve!"

The man faced her, and he did look sorry. "I promise you, Deama, it was an accident. If there was anything I could do to change what happened, I would."

Deama's face twisted in anger, but Core intervened before she could speak again.

"We will suffer your lies no longer. The past cannot be undone, just as the laws of our people cannot be undone."

Deama burst into a fresh round of tears as Core continued. "You, Geal of The Quarry, are banished from The Land of the Clan, by the order of the Clan Leaders and the will of the council."

"No," the man, Geal, said softly. And then his voice rose to a scream. "No, don't! You can't! No! It was an accident." He made a move to step towards Core, but the two soldiers from The Barracks seized his arms, holding him in place.

"Please, no!" Geal shouted. He was struggling slightly with the soldiers. Core turned his back on the scene.

When Geal saw that Core would no longer listen to his pleas, he turned and looked at the woman with the children.

"Sadra, I am so sorry," he said. The soldiers began to pull Geal away from her and out of the town center, but he fought them.

"Come with me," he called. "We can survive together. I will take care of you, all of you."

Sadra regarded her life mate with cold eyes. "You think I would endanger the lives of my children for you?" she spat. "After what you have done, how long before you'd turn on us?"

Pain crossed the man's face. "I would never hurt any of you! Genal," he said, turning to his son with the twisted foot. "Come with me," he begged.

The soldiers almost had him completely out of the town center, and others were pressing through the crowd to help them.

Genal looked uncertain for a moment, and then Sadra called to him. "Don't listen to him, Genal," she said, holding out a hand to her son. "He's not your father anymore."

Genal swallowed, and then nodded and limped to his mother's side. He took her hand and turned away from the man that had been his father.

"No," Geal shrieked. "Don't abandon me! I don't want to die alone."

Then he was gone. The crowd closed behind him, and we never saw him again.

After a moment of complete silence, Core spoke. "You have all seen justice here today. Remember what you have witnessed. Hard as it sometimes is, we must always have justice."

Everyone was silent. Few of us had seen anyone exiled before. They were always public ceremonies, but usually children were in school when they took place. The memory of the begging man would remain with me for a very long time.

Was it possible it really had been an accident? I shook that thought from my head. He'd put on a convincing show, but with the knife and what the healer had reported, there had been too much evidence.

"We are The Clan," Core said, starting the words that each of us had learned long ago on our first day of school. A few simple lines, but powerful because we had just lived them out. "We were created to be order when all else was chaos. We have lived in peace as our fathers have taught us. We show justice to all without hesitation. We will continue as we have been: the only perfect society."

JUSTICE

As his recitation came to a close, I found my resolve. Order and peace. That was why I had trained so hard.

Justice. The reason I had always been determined to become a Clan Leader.

Golla and Geal had not followed the rules, and they had paid the price. That was how it was; that was how it must always be.

I let all my questions about life and death slip away. Death happened, but it didn't matter; life mattered. Order, peace, and justice mattered. I would focus on them and forget all else.

I would be a Clan Leader, the best Clan Leader that had ever been.

Chapter 20

Life Mate

After Geal's exile, my vigor and enthusiasm for training awoke once more. I felt like a new person, completely rededicated to the ideals of my people.

The spring days began to fly by. It seemed that every waking hour I was training. As the days lengthened, the other potentials and I stayed out as long as there was light in the sky.

On our off days, Cole and I would go to other villages, usually The Barracks, and ask if there was anyone who could give us additional instruction. I wasn't sure if what we were doing was allowed, but we didn't hide it and no one told us to stop.

Sometimes we would get a lesson, sometimes not. On the occasions when no one would teach us anything, we would watch the soldiers drill and try to learn from observing.

Others, like Bala, took after our example. Soon, we were not the only ones training on our free days. However, I took pride in the fact that Cole and I had been the first. I hoped the elders were paying attention. If they had been disappointed in me during the days following Golla's death, I was certain I was more than making up for it.

Still, as hard as I was working, it seemed that time raced by far too quickly. There was still a great deal I had not yet mastered.

Swimming in the lake at Riverside was something I struggled with. I could usually stay afloat, but the water was very intimidating. It made me especially nervous when I couldn't see whether the water was shallow enough to stand in or so deep you might dive down and never reach the bottom.

Much as I practiced, I wasn't anywhere close to as skilled as the potentials from Riverside. They could glide through the water as easily as if they were on land. Each of them knew multiple strokes and would often swim wholly beneath the water's surface.

Sometimes, they would disappear for several minutes and then reappear in a completely different place. It was difficult for me, who hated putting my head under the water, to even attempt to learn the different strokes.

Jase struggled far more than I did, almost drowning himself a couple of times. He panicked too easily and always tried to use nothing but strength to keep himself upright. I took small consolation in the fact that he avoided the water even more than I did.

At The Farm, we learned how to butcher animals and how to tell what parts of them were good to eat and what parts to throw away. With winter passed, we were also shown how to tan hides in the sun.

The instructor told us that after the hides had been cured, they were sent to The Making so they could be turned into whatever was needed.

I thought of the warm, rabbit skin blanket that was my shield against the bitter cold during the long winter nights. How strange it was to think of it lying in pieces, waiting for the heat of the sun to cure the skin beneath the fur.

There were a lot of skins to be cured. The pelt of every animal that had been slaughtered during the winter had been carefully stored until the thaw. There was a rush among the inhabitants of The Farm to get them all tanned before they went sour. A few had already turned, and the stench of them was truly vile.

Lessons at The Quarry and Treescape remained much the same as they had before the snows had melted. We continued to learn about constructing shelters, making fires, whittling, and sculpting.

I don't know what went on at The North Wind. I had refused to go back ever since my last visit had ended so badly. Cole went a few times. I didn't bother trying to keep him away, but I never asked him about it and he never spoke of what went on there. His visits were few and far between, so I surmised that it couldn't have been too interesting.

I didn't worry about him going into the valley. Maybe he wasn't as brave as Golla, or maybe he just didn't have the motivation she'd had. Either way, I knew he would never venture inside alone.

The Making taught the same things it always had, much like Treescape and The Quarry. However, since it was the one village where almost all the work was done inside, that wasn't too much of a surprise. The Barracks was the same too—more combat training—although, it continued to grow steadily more advanced.

I felt that physical fitness was going to be very important for survival, so I tried to visit at least once a day. The other potentials must have thought along the same lines, because it was the most popular of the villages by far.

It worried me that many of the male potentials who, at the beginning of the preparations, I had counted as weaklings, were well-muscled and looking almost like grown men. Jase was still one of the largest, but even some of the smaller boys could beat him with tactics he failed to grasp. They were gaining strength and confidence, which would make it hard for me to compete physically with them as a female. I would have to rely on my wits and superior intellect.

After The Barracks, it was The Golden Fields where Cole and I spent the most amount of time. I was determined to learn to identify all the edible plants that we might find outside The Land of the Clan. There were hundreds of vegetables, fruits, nuts, roots, and even some barks that could be ingested, so it was quite a challenge, but I liked a challenge.

THE PREPARATIONS

I didn't know what the land outside our borders looked like, but if there was food out there, I wanted to be able to find it. Even Jase took the lessons from The Golden Fields very seriously; I doubted that he'd ever want to skip a meal, trials or not.

***

With little more than forty days before Midsummer, still ten days until the choosing, I found out that a woman of The Paramount, named Kels, would be taking a life mate. I didn't know Kels that well. She was petite and slender, with long, dark brown hair and a heart-shaped face.

Beautiful, she certainly was, but boring too. She was the silent type, who always seemed far older than her years and had never had much personality.

We'd been in school together for a while. In the time we'd spent together, I couldn't recall her speaking to anyone except when the instructors had made her. She was older than me and had missed the trials by two years, not that I imagined she was very disappointed about it.

I didn't think I had ever met the man she was going to bind herself to. He was from Riverside and would be coming to live with her in The Paramount.

I had only been to a handful of life mate ceremonies, which was much fewer than most people. Because the ceremonies were only held in the village where the couple would be living, and The Paramount was so small, we generally only had one or two a year.

I'm not sure why I decided to attend theirs. Perhaps it was because such ceremonies were so rare, or maybe because I had always been fascinated by the idea of two people promising to spend the rest of their lives together.

When I told Cole, Jase, Bala, and Ashlo that I was skipping out on afternoon training for the ceremony, the boys were shocked.

Bala actually told them off for me. "It's not like you didn't bail on us two days ago to take a nap, Jase," Bala started in on them. "And Cole, you're always skipping evening classes now and then to spend time with your family," she pointed out.

After a moment of consideration, Ashlo added, "I don't think Myra's ever skipped before."

No one could contradict her statement.

"I just didn't think you knew Kels that well," Cole said, looking rather abashed.

"I don't," I told him. "But this might be the last life mate ceremony I get to see where I don't have to play a part." They all stared at me in shock for a moment. "You know," I added, realizing what they thought I had meant, "as a Clan Leader."

Cole laughed softly and grinned back at me. "You're so sure of yourself," he muttered.

Giving him an impish smile, I turned my steps toward The Paramount. I heard Jase and Bala laughing about something as they walked away, heading for The Golden Fields. My cheeks burned a little, and I hoped they weren't talking about me.

We had been practicing tree climbing at Treescape all morning, and my pale maroon tank top was sticky with sweat and coated with bark and dirt. I would need to clean up before the ceremony.

As I walked through The Paramount, I could see that things were already being prepared. Long pieces of fabric had been hung in the town center, where the ceremony would take place, as well as along the path to the dwelling the council had assigned the new couple. The fabric was tan, for Riverside, and maroon, for The Paramount.

Idly, I wondered if each village had its own set of colored fabrics, or if it traveled from village to village whenever there was to be a ceremony. It seemed likely that there was only one set, since we had few celebrations among our people. Aside from Midsummer, Midwinter, and the life mate ceremony, births were the only other event communally recognized.

THE PREPARATIONS

Birthdays were also remembered, but privately by the immediate family only. Myna probably didn't remember her own birthday, let alone mine.

I was fine with that. Until now, I had dreaded them, knowing each year took me further from the trials. Not anymore.

Once I reached my dwelling, I grabbed our bucket and hurried to the closest well. Much as I disliked the cold of winter, it was nice to have snow readily available instead of having to bother with retrieving water.

I clipped my bucket to the end of the rope and let it fall down the long shaft of the well. I began turning the handle to bring it back up. In school, we had learned that getting water from wells had once been hard work. But our wells had pulley systems on them, so retrieving the water was as easy as lifting a feather.

With my bucket of water secured, I returned to my dwelling and gave myself a quick wash before pulling on a fresh, bright red shirt. I took a moment to comb out my hair before tying it back into a high ponytail.

Feeling refreshed, I hurried to the town center. I was a little early, but a crowd started gathering soon after. Most of those in attendance were from The Paramount or Riverside, although there were a fair number from other places as well. It appeared that the couple had lots of friends.

Before long, the village representatives and the elders came out of the council building. They formed a small cluster near the door. About fifteen minutes later, the couple emerged from the council building. Kels glanced at the assembly with a shy smile; the man beside her was grinning from ear to ear.

I had learned his name was Hugh of Riverside. He was tall and black-haired but thin and unusually pale for someone who fished and worked on boats all day.

I saw Kels take a deep breath and flash a happy smile at Hugh. He took her hand, and they turned back to face the building they had just left.

The Clan Leaders and the village leaders of Riverside emerged then. Kels and Hugh had probably been in the council building for hours while all the particular rules for life mates had been explained to them.

Myna was the only Clan Leader missing. She hated life mate ceremonies, and I had never seen her at one.

The ceremony was simple enough. First, Hugh told Kels why he wanted her for a life mate and promised to always be loyal to her, to protect her, and to uphold all The Clan's laws regarding life mates.

Next, it was Kels turn. I couldn't really hear what she said since she spoke too softly, but I imagined it was more of the same.

Once they were done speaking, a village leader from Riverside said a few words about Hugh, and an elder from The Paramount did the same for Kels.

Then, each of the three present Clan Leaders spoke briefly. Joel, the Fourth Clan Leader, talked about the joy of living life with someone by your side—not that he would know since he had never taken a life mate. Falow, the Third Clan Leader, encouraged the couple to abide by all the rules laid down for life mates. He explained that each had been set in place to help foster good relationships. Falow had no life mate either.

Finally, Core spoke on the importance of love. Core's speech was the only one really worth hearing. Once he was finished, he reached forward and put a hand on Hugh's shoulder and nodded. Hugh leaned forward and kissed Kels.

Kissing was something inappropriate if not done with one's life mate. Even then, it was not normally performed in public, except at life mate ceremonies. Hugh's lips seemed stiff at first, but a moment later, when they met Kels, they softened. I watched, fascinated.

I had never before been close enough or interested enough to see the details of the kiss. It had always struck me as a vulgar and disgusting idea, but their kiss didn't seem to be.

When they separated a moment later, neither Kels nor Hugh seemed displeased by it. The crowd around me roared with joy.

The crowd cheered for a few more minutes while Kels and Hugh stood and waved to us. Their closest family and friends lined up to give them hugs or pats on the back. Then, we paraded the two down the maroon- and tan-lined streets to their new dwelling, and it was over.

I glanced at the sun. I had just enough time to make it to the evening training session at The Barracks. Cole and Jase had planned to attend the session. If I hurried, I could still meet up with them.

I started heading in that direction but ended up at the amphitheater instead. I was tired, exhausted really, and sore too. Training was taking a toll on my body, but the real reason my feet had carried me to the amphitheater instead of The Barracks was my sudden need for solitude.

The Barracks would be full of soldiers and potentials. It would be a hot, moving mass of people. Voices would be shouting. The sound of wooden staffs striking each other would resound throughout the village.

At the amphitheater, it was silent. The night air was still. A peaceful sunset was only an hour away. I sank slowly down onto one of the stone seats at the top of the hill. It was pleasantly cool and far from the stage, giving me an excellent view of the surrounding area.

No one else was there that night. Everyone was training in different villages or in their dwellings with their families. All except me. Sometimes I resented the solitude I was often forced to endure, but that evening, it was a relief.

I turned my head at a noise. Two potentials were coming down the road nearby. I sighed; more would soon follow. I really didn't want anyone to see me sitting there alone.

Silently, I rose and started walking in the opposite direction, away from The Paramount, towards The Barracks but at an angle to pass it to the north. I wasn't going anywhere specific, just trying to put some distance between myself and the rest of The Clan.

I tried to push down the guilty feeling I was having for skipping training. I wondered if anyone besides Cole had noticed my absence. Probably not. It seemed that most of the council had attended the life mate ceremony. Surely, they couldn't have been watching everything all the time. Although, if they were, they would have witnessed that I had never before skipped a training session.

I hoped they thought I was worthy.

Teams would be chosen in less than twenty days. The realization brought me up short. Where had all the time gone? It seemed like only the day before I had been at The Barracks getting my first lesson in hand-to-hand combat. Soon, I would be placed with the team I might spend the rest of my life with. Some of them would probably die. I had to prepare myself mentally for that.

If the team were made up of six people exactly like me, there would have been a good chance of not losing a single member. But I couldn't trust that everyone on my team would be as well prepared as I was. Much as I wanted to be part of the first winning team to return with all six members, it was quite unlikely.

I knew many of the other potentials were still lacking in skills and discipline. I would make up for their shortcomings to the best of my ability, but I had to be ready to lose them.

To protect myself, I would need to keep my distance. I could probably manage not to get too attached if my teammates were strangers. However, I was sure to know at least one or two of them. Those were the ones it would be hardest to lose, the friends I had known all my life.

How did anyone deal with it? Golla's death had hit me so hard. How would I handle losing a teammate? Maybe a couple of them?

THE PREPARATIONS

I stopped walking suddenly. I had reached the banks of the river that surrounded The Land of the Clan. It was quiet there; the river was flowing with no rocks to disturb the surface. Just from looking at the smooth water, it would have been impossible to imagine the danger beneath.

I hadn't realized I'd come so far. Wandering off wasn't against the rules, as long as there was nowhere you were supposed to be, but I wasn't exactly sure how late it was. The sun was already setting behind me though.

I turned away from the wide, fast-flowing river, ready to head back to The Paramount, when I saw something move. I had only glimpsed it out of the corner of my eye, on the far bank, about a dozen yards away.

Glancing back, I stared wide-eyed across the river, wondering if it had been my imagination. Then I saw the creature. For a split-second I thought it was a Broken, but an instant later, I realized that it wasn't human.

The animal had the shape of a dog, like the ones they used at The Farm to herd the sheep and cattle. Only, the dog on the far side of the river was huge, at least three times the normal size. It was covered in glossy, black fur and its ears stood straight up on its head.

I was frozen, not really in fear but in shock. I had never seen anything living outside our borders. I hadn't even known if life was possible long-term outside The Land of the Clan. Clearly, it was, since the creature before me was alive and well.

The animal turned its long, pointed snout towards me. Its eyes were bright, and I could see a flash of green in them, even from thirty feet away. After a moment, it raised its head straight up so its mouth was pointed to the sky and did something I had never known a dog to do.

It let out a long, low cry. Not a bark but a single, unbroken call. Once the creature ran out of breath, it paused and listened. I listened as well and heard another call, much like the first. The beast turned away from me then and trotted toward the sound.

I left too, adrenalin pumping through my body. I couldn't believe what I had just seen. I couldn't tell anyone either; they would never believe me. Nothing was supposed to be alive out there except trees and birds and a handful of Broken.

Monsters weren't supposed to exist, but they did.

Chapter 21

BEFORE

It wasn't until the day before the choosing that I really started to think about how quickly the trials were approaching.

Cole and Jase were with me at The Making. Jase hadn't visited the place in months. Even he must have been starting to get worn out from the fast-paced training and been eager for a break. That was the only explanation I had for why he'd chosen to spend a quiet morning weaving with us.

I'd just finished my second basket, which had been better than the first, when it struck me suddenly that it was the last day I might spend with Cole and Jase.

The following morning, at first light, all the potentials would assemble at the amphitheater, and the council would choose the teams of contenders. After that, I would do most of my training with my team.

I tried to comfort myself with the thought that I would have at least one friend with me. The council wouldn't put me on a team with no one I knew, would they?

I did come from one of the smallest villages, and I had segregated myself considerably, choosing to focus on my own skills rather than socializing with other potentials. If I ended up by myself on a team, without anyone but strangers, it would probably be my own fault.

The following day I would know. The following day. For a moment, I almost couldn't bear to wait. I felt my heart rate accelerate and my breath begin to quicken. I couldn't wait that long; I wanted to know now.

Then Jase interrupted my sudden panic.

THE PREPARATIONS

"How does this look?" he asked, holding up what was supposed to be a basket. It wasn't the first day we had made baskets. Over the past five months, we had been taught dozens of different designs and weaving techniques.

The ones we had been working on that day were supposed to be quick and easy, designed to hold fruits and vegetables such as apples or carrots.

Jase's basket had such large holes in it, I would have been surprised if it could have held watermelons. It was, however, the best basket he'd ever made. Before I had the chance to point that out, an instructor appeared to review his mistakes.

I never minded being the one to burst Jase's bubble, but I had noticed that Cole didn't like it. He was surprisingly protective. Looking at Jase, it was not apparent that he would ever need protection, but in a way, he really did. During the preparations, he had done little to work on his weaknesses. Instead, he had chosen to develop his strengths.

All his fruit was in one basket, so to speak. If there was a hole in it, he would lose everything. For Jase, there was only one answer to every problem, and I was fairly confident it would not be enough when the trials began.

Not that he wouldn't be an asset. I could certainly make use of him if he were on my team, but he would never be much of a leader.

If the council knew what they were doing, Jase would probably be placed on a team under several strong and intelligent contenders. He would be subject to their orders and wouldn't question them. Beyond The Land of the Clan, he would certainly give his team a great advantage, if managed properly.

Even the monster I had seen after the life mate ceremony would think twice before attacking something as large as Jase.

I hadn't told anyone about the creature. Cole was the only person I would have confided in because I knew beyond a shadow of a doubt he would have believed me. But every time I tried, I always found the words stuck in my throat. It was a secret I would have to carry alone.

I turned my attention back to my weaving and spent almost two hours trying to make a basket that was perfectly square. The instructor had told us it was the hardest shape to achieve.

In the end, it wasn't perfect, but it was pretty close and very functional. Cole had stuck to the traditional shape and had finished three and a half well-made baskets when the lesson came to a close.

I enjoyed watching him work. It was rather soothing to see his strong fingers twist the softened twigs and vines with more skill than most.

On his left, Jase managed to scrape by with one basket that would be able to hold fruit, but they would have had to have been large fruit.

We headed out among the stream of other potentials. The Making wasn't too popular, but there were at least fifty kids there.

"The Barracks?" Cole asked as we headed to the road that led south.

"Yes, please," said Jase, flexing his fingers. "I can't take all that weaving stuff, just give me something to hit."

I had to laugh. It was as if my prior thoughts had just come out of Jase's own mouth. Cole smiled softly at my laughter but gave me a questioning look.

"Sounds good," I told him.

Recently, The Barracks had started training us with real weapons. They were only for the students who had mastered the wooden staves and the hand-to-hand combat. All three of us had been among that group from the first.

There were three kinds of weapons: swords, bows, and long knives. I would have liked to have focused on mastering them one by one, but we were required to spend an equal amount of time with each.

THE PREPARATIONS

Since the beginning of the preparations, my arms had been constantly covered in bruises, and with the new training, I had some cuts to add to the mix. None of mine were too bad though.

Three days earlier, I had seen a boy take a grievous blow to the leg. The healers had been called to come and carry him out. There had been blood everywhere, and training had been moved out of the arena to a nearby field for the remainder of the day.

The bow practice took place in that field already. I wasn't very good with the bow. My instructor had told me that I lacked patience.

I was better with the knife. We had learned lots of tricks for twisting our opponent's weapon out of their hand and disarming them. I was quick—my lack of patience, I supposed—and almost always got a hold of my opponent's knife before they could get mine.

It was the sword, however, that I felt most comfortable with. The ones we used were lighter than those carried by the soldiers. I preferred them, because they allowed for more distance between your opponent and yourself. Knife fighting was up close and personal, but with a sword you were rarely within reaching distance.

When we arrived at The Barracks, they split us up. I was sent out to join the group doing archery. Cole was sent to knife fighting and Jase to sword practice. I missed the days when we had been able to choose our own partners.

The archery instructor for the day was Julin. He was a thin man, with a shock of black hair on top of his very large, round head. He had been the instructor that had called me impatient.

I silently resolved that he would regret those words, and took the bow and quiver he offered.

"It's not quite time to start yet, so hold off on taking any shots, and we'll see if anyone else shows," Julin told us.

I was about to protest that it was their own fault if they missed something, but I swallowed the words. *Patience*, I told myself as I walked down the long line of other potentials waiting to begin.

The Barracks had continued to be the most popular spot for training. There were well over a hundred potentials waiting to start shooting at the line of targets about fifty feet away.

Once we were given permission to begin—a full seven minutes after the appointed time—the practice continued for about an hour. After the duration of shooting, I switched to inside the arena for sword and knife fighting, and then ended up back outside to work on archery again. I didn't exactly make Julin eat his words, but I did perform much better than usual and much better than most of the others.

Cole, Jase, and I voted to spend the rest of the day at The Barracks. At the conclusion of the afternoon session, the weapons were put away and we went back to hand-to-hand combat. Bala showed up and got paired up with me.

Motik came too. He got put with Jase. It didn't seem like a fair match up considering the fact that Jase was twice Motik's size, but Motik was fast and athletic. He could almost always manage to keep out of Jase's reach.

After having spent the previous five months practicing nearly every day, I was confident in my own abilities. Bala didn't have the well-developed skill I did. I knocked her to the ground three times in a row. Frustrated, she threw dirt in my face and tried to strike me while I was blinded.

Before I could react, an instructor came over and gave Bala a tongue-lashing so harsh that when she apologized, all I said was, "Don't worry about it."

"Tomorrow's the big day," Bala said, as the sun began to set and we headed for The Paramount, leaving The Barracks behind.

"No," I amended softly, "it's *a* big day. *The* big day won't come for another month." Bala looked at me like she wasn't sure if I was only arguing because of the dirty trick she had pulled.

THE PREPARATIONS

"I am much more nervous about tomorrow than about all the days that follow," Cole interjected, breaking the tension smoothly.

"Tomorrow, we find out if we will be a part of the trials at all and who we'll be working with, possibly forever," Bala put in.

"You're both right, I guess," I conceded. "But, surely, we'll all be chosen."

Cole smiled, but it didn't touch his eyes. "It's not enough to be chosen sometimes," he said. "It's all about who you're chosen with."

We let the subject drop and instead talked about unimportant, idle things for the rest of our walk. It was a pleasant journey in the cool night air.

When we got to the place where we usually went our separate ways, Cole paused.

"Goodnight, Jase, Motik, Bala," he said, before turning to me. "Can I talk to you for a minute, Myra?" he asked.

I was surprised, but nodded. "Sure. See you guys tomorrow," I called after Jase's and Motik's retreating figures. Jase turned and waved before hurrying away, to a good meal, most likely.

Bala smirked at me for a long moment over her shoulder before heading off in the direction of her dwelling. I hoped she was actually going there and not planning on skulking around, trying to hear what we said.

Cole started walking forward again, not toward his dwelling or mine, but just forward, more slowly than we had walked before. I fell into step beside him easily. The sun was already fully gone; the sky wasn't even pink anymore, just a deep blue color that would shortly turn black.

Cole was silent for such a long time I began to wonder if he would speak at all. Finally, he broke the silence.

"Tomorrow…" He paused to lick his lips. "Whatever happens tomorrow, Myra, I—I don't want it to—change things between us."

My stomach clenched suddenly. That was not what I had expected him to say on the eve of the choosing. My mind had been churning most of the day, imagining all the possible outcomes for the morrow and the days beyond. I had pushed away all else to focus solely on the events close at hand.

"The choosing, the trials, whatever happens," Cole continued, "even if we don't end up on the same team, even if we both lose, I want us to always be friends. I want to see you every day; I want to be able to talk to you."

It was my turn to lick my lips. I wanted to promise him that nothing would ever change between us, but that wasn't quite true. No matter what happened the following day, nothing would ever be the same again. Much as I longed to be Cole's friend, and even more than his friend, was it fair to make a promise I knew would be broken when the sun rose?

Cole didn't seem to notice my mind racing a million miles a minute as he went on. "I trust you and want to know that you trust me too."

Slowly, he raised his blue eyes to meet my gray ones. Everything I had just told myself vanished from my mind, and I finally understood what he meant, what he was asking.

"No matter what happens," I whispered. "No matter who wins and who loses, nothing will change between us."

Cole smiled, a real smile, which made his face twenty times more beautiful than before. It was brief, but conveyed the true happiness my words had given him.

"Even if we don't end up on the same team," Cole pressed, "even if I'm not there to watch out for you, you have to come back. Ok?"

I wanted to laugh. "I will come back. I promise."

"Me too," Cole said.

THE PREPARATIONS

There was a moment of silence, and I felt sure that the joy in his eyes was mirrored in my own. "Even if I was to win, it would mean nothing to me if you weren't here when I got back," Cole told me. "I would feel so lost without you."

"You'll never have to feel lost again," I told him. "I'm coming back, and so are you. One of us is bound to win, and if we are both on the same team, we'll win for sure."

"You're right," he said, smiling. "No one will stand a chance if the two of us are together."

I loved the way he said 'the two of us' and 'together'.

It wasn't until later, after we had gone our separate ways, that my heart stopped beating like the hooves of a charging horse. After eating a quick dinner, I knew I was still too wound up to sleep, so I went to the well and fetched a couple buckets of water. I got enough for a bath, a real bath.

The cold water felt good. My skin was still flushed. From the fight training and the long walk, I tried to tell myself, but I was sure that wasn't true.

As I replayed our conversation in my mind, I realized that Cole hadn't said anything about being life mates. However, that would have been too hasty and inappropriate. I was only sixteen, too young to take a life mate. Cole wasn't of age either, but he was older. He would have to wait for me, but after what he had just said, I felt certain he would.

Our tub was a large, oval-shaped piece of stone, with a flat bottom. It was tucked into a niche at the back of the main room sectioned off with a sliding door. There was a hole in the bottom of the tub that had to be stopped up with another piece of stone.

Once I had finished washing my body and long hair, I pulled up the stone. The water would drain out behind the dwelling.

I climbed from the tub and put on my sleeping clothes, a pair of deep maroon shorts and a simple, light red shirt.

Myna was, of course, not there. In all fairness, I was pretty sure that the entire council would be in session until morning.

BEFORE

They had many decisions to make, and it would probably take them all night. I didn't care; Myna didn't matter anymore.

Even if the thought of the choosing scared me a bit, I let the words Cole had spoken comfort me. No matter what happened, he and I would always be friends and maybe—well, that would come later; there was no point dwelling on it now.

Blowing out the lamp, I climbed into my bed. Excitement or apprehension—I'm not sure which—kept me awake for a very long time.

Chapter 22

THE CHOOSING

I woke before dawn, already so tense I wasn't sure how I had been asleep a moment before. My eyes weren't even fully open as I jumped from my bed. During the night, the blanket had gotten twisted around my left ankle, and I ended up head first on the floor.

Thankfully, no one had been present to witness my clumsiness. Taking a few deep breaths, I tried to calm my racing heart, but to no avail. I pulled on a pair of burgundy pants that ended mid-calf and a red shirt with a v-shaped neckline, and then I whipped my hair up into its customary ponytail.

I stepped into my summer shoes, without bothering to untie the laces, and practically ran out of my room. Without chewing, I swallowed a few bits of food, not even tasting what I ate. The morsels were washed down with several gulps of water.

My hands were literally shaking as I opened the door. Stepping out into the pre-dawn light, it was all I could do to not immediately take off running for the amphitheater.

I knew I would be early, very early. So, I forced myself to walk. There was little to no movement in the village around me. I would probably be the first person to arrive, but I was ok with that.

As I crested the small rise to reach the top of the amphitheater, I stopped dead in my tracks to stare in shock. All my life, it had been the same round half-rings of stone forming row after row of seats, all leading down to the fifty-foot-long stage where the land finally leveled off from the hill.

THE PREPARATIONS

The rock semicircles were the same, but the stage was nowhere to be seen. There was nothing in front of the seats save the wide, open field beyond, which stretched out for miles and miles.

My wits came back to me a moment later. Of course; all the potentials would never have fit on the stage. There were so many of us the stage must have been moved so we could stand in the field.

I hurried down the hillside and took a seat towards the front. I was the first one there but not by much. People trickled in, mostly from The Paramount and The Barracks at first, but then they started coming in greater numbers from all over.

I saw Cole when he arrived, but he didn't notice me and sat with his family. Both his brothers and his sister were present. The only missing family member was Core.

All of a sudden, I wished I hadn't come so early. It would have been nice to sit with Cole and his family. A part of me considered slipping out and coming back down as if I was just arriving, but I would hate to look foolish if anyone noticed my farce. Instead, I resolved to sit where I was, alone.

When the sun was about fifteen minutes from rising, the amphitheater was only half filled. It wasn't until the sun had practically cleared the horizon that everyone seemed to have arrived. The council was nowhere to be seen. I'd expected them to be among the first.

How ironic it would be if they were late, I thought with wry humor. Perhaps being up all night had made them drowsy and they'd fallen asleep in the council building. Long had I suspected that Myna slept there sometimes, but it seemed unlikely that the entire council would have all nodded off at once.

Another few minutes passed, and I glanced around. The place was full, very full. In fact, we almost didn't fit. They'd have to make it bigger soon. A family from Treescape had come to sit beside me. They looked like a fairly young couple with two girls. One of them was clearly not of age to be a potential, but the other might have been just old enough.

I heard a hush fall over the crowd from near the top of the amphitheater. Turning to look along with those seated near me, I saw that the council had, at last, arrived. They were walking, two by two, descending on the path through the center of the rings.

Core and Myna came first, followed by the rest. They marched slowly down the hill, their footfalls the only audible sound. When the procession reached the bottom, the elders stepped to the right and the representatives stepped to the left, leaving only the Clan Leaders in the center. As one, the group turned to face us.

Falow, the Third Clan Leader, was the one to address the crowd. I had never paid much attention to him. He rarely spoke at events where the whole of The Clan was assembled, acting instead as more of a silent supporter for Myna and Core.

"Greetings to The Clan," he called.

"Greetings," we chorused back to him, just as we had to Core exactly five months earlier.

"Today," he announced, "we will be choosing the contenders and teams from among all the potentials who have been in training since Midwinter."

An excited murmur went up from the potentials in the assembly.

"First," Falow continued. "I would like to say a few things about the trials."

I perked up my ears, hoping to hear some information that would assist me in leading my team to victory.

"Please keep in mind that it is a great honor to participate in the trials. If, however, you are not chosen, do not feel discouraged. It simply means that the council believed you better suited to a different path."

His words seemed shallow to me. He was softening the blow for those not chosen by trying to make them feel important.

"Also, as the time of the trials draws near, I ask everyone to remember that it is forbidden for those who took place in the last trials to speak about their experiences. Anyone caught divulging information about the trials will be dealt with most harshly."

Silence met his stern words. I thought briefly of Larna. I glanced around but couldn't spot her. When I turned my attention to the front again, I saw that Core had replaced Falow.

"Greetings," he called.

"Greetings," the assembly murmured once more.

"Please take what Falow has said to heart," Core told us. "In a moment, we will begin calling all the potentials forward. But first, I have something to say as well." He glanced at Myna for a very brief moment. "It has been the decision of the council that this year there will be one hundred and seventy-five teams instead of one hundred and twenty-five."

A great stir passed among the crowd.

"The reason we have added an extra fifty teams is because the council has witnessed so many gifted and talented potentials that we simply couldn't limit the number of teams to only one hundred and twenty-five. Please forgive us while we break with tradition, but this generation of youth is truly exceptional and it would be an outrage to not allow them to participate."

The murmuring died down. Several other potentials sitting close to me were looking very pleased with themselves, as if Core's words had been directed at them alone. I didn't think he was talking about me at all. I was a sure choice, even if there had only been ten teams.

"I would now like to ask Clem, an elder of the council for the past four years, to read the list of potentials." Core gestured to a hunched man, wearing the red of The Paramount. "When you are called, please come forward. Once all the potentials have been assembled, we will begin assigning contenders to their teams."

Clem stepped forward. He was at least sixty-five, with strands of white hair, where he had hair at all. His skin was very pink, and the color only got brighter as he began addressing the crowd. Over his right shoulder, he was carrying numerous scrolls in a satchel. He reached in and chose one seemingly at random.

Hands shaking slightly, Clem opened it and held the parchment close to his face. "Of The Quarry!" he announced. At least his voice was loud and powerful, unlike his hands and eyesight. After clearing his throat, he began reading off a list of names.

Children started streaming toward the front of the stage, all of them in the royal blue of The Quarry. It appeared he was calling them from youngest to oldest. The representatives from The Quarry intercepted the children and started lining them up. They formed about six rows of potentials, oldest in back. They weren't facing us, but had been directed to stand in the field, profile to the seats, on the left side of the amphitheater.

Once Clem finished with The Quarry, he chose another scroll. It was the one for The Making. Quickly, he began to read the names. Those he called were lined up on the far side of The Quarry's potentials.

Village after village followed. I stopped paying attention to the drone of his voice halfway through Treescape. All I wanted was for him to hurry up and pull out the scroll for my village. It was chosen third from last.

Even though I was one of the older potentials in The Paramount, I paid close attention. Each name he read, I knew well. It was almost painful to watch Rasby leave her parents and take her place in the field. I fervently hoped she wasn't chosen for a team.

Ashlo's name was called, and then Motik's, and, shortly after, mine. I rose and marched forward, walking the short distance to the front of the amphitheater. I had to walk down the long line of children before reaching the place where The Paramount's potentials were lining up. We were a good distance from those seated in the amphitheater.

Bala followed practically on my heels. Before we had found our places, I heard them call Cole's name. Close after him, Jase was called as well.

It didn't take long for all the potentials from The Paramount to finish lining up. There really weren't that many of us, especially compared to some of the other villages. Soon, the potentials from the final two villages had been called as well. We stood together, stretching far away from the amphitheater where the morning had begun.

To my left and right, children stirred and whispered to each other. I was still; even my breaths felt non-existent. Only my eyes moved, following the group of council members who were slowly trudging away from the amphitheater to stand across from us.

Each moment seemed to last forever. Core stepped forward to speak for the council. His voice was loud and easy to hear, even considering the distance that separated us.

"The teams will now be announced," he declared. "We shall begin by calling all the team leaders, and then the second leaders, and so on until each team has been filled.

"Once we have called your name, please step across the divide and stand with your team. There will be one hundred and seventy-five teams, with six members each. A total of one thousand and fifty names will be called. If yours is not among them, please return to your seat.

"To aid you on your quest, each team will be supplied with a few weapons. The first team leaders will each receive a sword." Core glanced to his left, where the amphitheater lay, and nodded to a man wearing the gold of The Barracks. He looked familiar, but I couldn't say that I knew his name.

THE CHOOSING

The man waved his hand, and a unit of men and women, all dressed in gold, came forward carrying numerous wooden crates. I hadn't even noticed either the soldiers or the large crates.

They were deposited out in a line opposite us. A council member went to where each had been placed in the grass.

"The second leaders will receive a bow and the third leaders, a knife. The rest of the members will be given wooden staves." As he named each weapon, a council member somewhere along the line held one up. They were identical to the weapons we had been practicing with for the past month.

There was a moment of complete silence as another one of the council members stepped forward. He didn't address us, but merely handed Core a scroll. My stomach was doing flips as he unfurled it and began to call off names.

"Galns of The Barracks," was the first he called. A large, dark-haired boy stepped forward smiling. He marched proudly across the field to where a council member, an elderly woman named Leka of The Paramount, stood. She handed him a sword, which he took eagerly before turning back to face us.

The names continued to come off the list. Once called, each potential stepped forward and claimed a sword, and then stood ready to be given a team.

Core was about halfway through the names of team leaders. I kept hoping he would call my name next. I wanted one of those swords; they were shiny and represented power. If I held one, my entire team would respect me.

"Cole of The Paramount," Core called. He paused for a fraction of a second and looked straight at his son. It took him a moment to find his place when he once again looked down at his scroll.

Slight disappointment gripped me; my mind was split. I had hoped to be a first team leader, but wouldn't it be worth being second leader if Cole was first? I chewed that over for a moment while several more names were called.

THE PREPARATIONS

It didn't take me long to decide that I'd rather be Cole's second leader than have a team of my own. Several minutes later, Core came to the last name on the list.

"Reefa of The Making," he called. The girl who stepped forward was tall and gangly. She seemed to lack the confidence most of the first leaders possessed. Instead of looking pleased, she seemed nervous as she crossed the field and was given the last sword.

The girl staggered, hardly able to bear its weight. I pitied anyone who ended up on her team.

"These are the first team leaders selected by the council," Core announced. They had been lined up in the order they had been called. The first called was the farthest to my right, closest to the amphitheater. I had almost forgotten that we were being watched. It seemed as if nothing else existed except the field and those filling it.

"Now we will announce the second team leaders. They will be called in the same order as the first team leaders," Core explained, before launching into another round of names.

I examined those chosen to lead teams. Most of them were older than me, but a few looked about my age. There was only one who appeared to be under fifteen. She was a small, brown-haired girl—the skinniest person I had ever seen—wearing the light green color of The Golden Fields.

As the first of the second leaders were called, I realized my heart was thundering in my chest. Every time Core took a breath I hoped he would not call my name.

Generally speaking, the first team leaders greeted the second leaders warmly. Bala practically skipped across the field to stand beside a large boy from The Quarry when she was called to be his second leader. I supposed it was very uncommon to pair a first and second leader together that didn't know each other, since their relationship was the most important.

My hands were clenched into fists, nails biting my palms. *You have to be calm*, I told myself. *Be calm*. I forced my eyes to stare straight ahead, ears straining to hear.

Then it was time. Core opened his mouth to declare who Cole's second leader would be. I was ready to step forward, ready to cross the field and take the bow that was meant for me.

"Astra of The North Wind," Core declared.

I felt the blood drain from my face. It was all I could do to keep my knees locked and body upright as I saw Astra, wearing gray for once, walk to Cole. She took the bow that was offered to her and smiled at Cole, and he smiled back.

If my entire life hadn't been so full of disappointment and misery, I knew I never would have been able to bear the agony.

Astra had taken my place. My future, all of my hopes and dreams, had been ripped away suddenly and given to her.

Quickly, I glanced down the line of team leaders. *Please call my name*, I thought desperately. I didn't care whose team I ended up on, even the girl from The Making's, just so long as I was a second leader. I couldn't bear the thought of Astra being considered better than me.

More and more names were read, none of them mine. *I will not cry*, I promised myself, fighting to control my stinging eyes. Somehow, I managed to blink the tears away just as the last second leader was called.

"Toruc of Riverside," Core announced, and a blond, shaggy-haired young man crossed and took the last of the bows.

Chapter 23

TEAMMATES

Everything had gone all wrong. It was all spoiled. As Core began reading the names of the third team leaders, I found myself hoping that I would wake up in my bed and start the day anew.

Maybe I was just caught in some horrible dream brought on by anxiety. But I never dreamed.

I still stared straight ahead, even though I wasn't excited anymore. My muscles ached from being clenched so tightly, but I remained as rigid as ever. I refused to show any emotion, certain I looked just like Myna. When they neared Cole's team again, I couldn't seem to breath. I had a horrible feeling that I knew what was coming.

"Myra of The Paramount," Core read my name. He even had the audacity to sound pleased about it.

It took a full three seconds before I could actually force my body to react. My limbs seemed to have become frozen solid. Somehow, I found myself moving forward, walking across the field, and accepting the knife that was pressed into my hand, before being greeted by Cole.

The warmth of his blue eyes was the only thing that helped to thaw me. He grasped my hand tightly and smiled with so much joy that I started to feel a little better.

"I'm so happy," I heard him whisper, before turning back to see who was being placed on the other teams.

Just then, Astra caught my eye. She was smiling too, but it was not a warm smile of welcome like Cole's. I was sure that the

THE PREPARATIONS

twist in her lips was a suppression of laughter. Suddenly, I felt horrid again. I vaguely remembered the night Core had seen Cole, Jase, and me coming back to The Paramount. We had told him that we had gone to see Astra. He must have thought we were friends and that he was doing us a favor.

I ripped my eyes from her, focusing my attention on the names being called. So far, almost no one I knew had been placed on a team. The Paramount was so small; places like The Golden Fields and Treescape had at least ten times the number of potentials we did. Ashlo was made third leader of a team, which already had two girls.

Only after Core started calling fourth team members, did I start to hear more names that I knew. Motik was placed on a team made up completely of potentials from The Golden Fields. Judging by his reaction, he didn't know any of them.

One of the two sisters, Tirea, the older one, was assigned to a team a couple down from us. I could see her sister clinging to her hand as they parted.

When the time came for us to receive our fourth teammate, I hoped it would be Jase. If the three of us were together, old habits would form, and Astra would very likely go unheard.

"Joss of Riverside," Core announced. For just a moment, I had been tricked into thinking it was Jase; the two names were so similar.

The boy who crossed to join us was at least two years younger than me. He was a bit on the scrawny side, but he appeared to be filled with the vigor of youth. He had dark hair, shaved very close to his head. Giving us a sunny smile and a nod, he took the staff that was handed to him and stood beside Cole.

It took me a moment to realize I had seen him before. He was the boy from Riverside who'd sprained his ankle saving a cat. I had to admit, I thought he would be an excellent teammate. Even when injured, his spirits hadn't been dampened for a second.

Larna was called to Ashlo's team.

Genal, the crippled boy whose father had been exiled a short time ago, was called. It took him twice as long to cross the field as everyone else.

When they got around to fifth team members, Jase was put on the team with Bala. She was grinning ear to ear. Bala wouldn't have looked more pleased if she had been able to handpick her team. Why couldn't that have been me?

Flant ended up being put on Motik's team as fifth leader.

When our turn came around again, Core called out, "Kisa of The Golden Fields."

Our fifth team member was a little, golden-haired, blue-eyed girl. She couldn't have been more than thirteen. I was discouraged when I saw her size, but she came over to us with a bright smile on her face.

It was all for the boy, Joss, I realized a moment later. The first thing she did was throw her small arms around him. He had to remind her to get her staff.

Instantly, I pegged her as the first one to die. Not that I planned on letting anyone die, but since I was only third leader, I wasn't sure I'd be able to do anything to protect my team.

Cole will still listen to you, I had to tell myself, gritting my teeth as Astra welcomed Kisa with a smile much friendlier than the one she had given me.

Finally, Core started reading off the sixth, and final, members of each team. Some of the potentials looked discouraged, others hopeful. Rasby certainly seemed pleased that she hadn't been called yet.

Tiera was also put on Bala and Jase's team. Bala didn't look half so pleased with her as she had been with Jase. I saw Tirea burst into tears as her sister walked to a different team than she had been assigned to.

Our final member was announced as 'Rollan of Treescape'. Like our fourth team member, Joss, he looked about fourteen. In spite of his age, he was broad, not exactly fat, but every part of his body was thick—his arms, his legs, his neck. He was only a little shorter than me and looked strong; that would be good.

"This is my cousin," Joss told us softly. "Our fathers are brothers."

The pair looked nothing alike, even if you didn't count Joss's small stature and slender build.

Rollan's hair was a lighter shade of brown and several inches longer. It framed a strong, square-jawed face. In contrast, Joss's face was round and boyish, with large eyes.

So, this is it, I thought. *My team. It could have been much worse.*

At least they hadn't given me Larna. Although, if I had had the choice of trading Astra for Larna, I would have been sorely tempted.

The names ceased to be called a moment later. I glanced back at the potentials who had not been chosen. Most were young, and only a few, a very few, appeared disappointed. The rest seemed relieved, several of them racing back to where their parents waited on the stone seats.

Rasby was among them. It was a huge weight off my mind to know that she hadn't been chosen. She belonged in The Land of the Clan, and everyone knew it.

The rest of us remained where we were, in tight little knots of six.

Core rolled up the great scroll of names and handed it back to the council member he had gotten it from. I expected him to address us, but it was Myna who stepped forward to speak. She did not look at me once.

"You are all contenders now," she told us. Her voice was softer than Core's; I was sure those in the amphitheater wouldn't be able to hear her. "Starting tomorrow, training will continue for another month, and then each team member must qualify. After that, the trials will begin.

"I recommend listening to your first and second leaders. They will be in charge once the trials begin, and it will be in your best interest for you to start working within the chain of command now."

Her words were like a cold slap in the face to me. "Training is completely up to you and your team leaders. Sessions will be held every day after this, from sun up to sun down. No one will be watching you except your own teammates. Do not disappoint them.

"Remember, you are the future, and some of you will be the next Clan Leaders." Cheers broke out at her words, but not from my lips. Everyone else may have been pleased with the outcome, but I wasn't.

I glanced over to the amphitheater. Falow was addressing those in the seats, the ones who would never take part in the trials, the unimportant ones. He was unimportant too. And I was just like him.

Third. Third leader. I was better than that, and everyone knew it. Why had I been treated so unfairly? It had to be Myna's doing; she'd always tried to make my life as miserable as possible. I glowered at her as she stood in front of us, giving the same speech she had given the first day of training about not wasting time.

Even my anger didn't draw her gaze. She was ignoring me or oblivious to me.

Then she finished, and it was over. The ceremony was done. My team was set. Together, we would live or die. I meant to live and more than that, I meant to win.

The amphitheater began to empty. Some of the parents waited for their children who were contenders, but the children didn't go. They were too busy talking with their new teammates.

My team was standing in a tight circle, surrounded by many other circles. Joss, Kisa, and Rollan were all looking expectantly at Cole. I'm sure he was completely overwhelmed because he seemed to be a little unsure of what to say.

THE PREPARATIONS

I was about jump in and save him by suggesting we get to know each other a little, but Astra literally took the words right out of my mouth.

"Maybe we should all introduce ourselves," she suggested. "Start with your name, to make sure everyone's got it, and then tell us what you're good at."

I wished I had spoken up first, but I was too late. "I'll begin," I said instead.

All their eyes fell on me. "I'm Myra of The Paramount," I started. "I've been spending most of my time training at The Barracks. I've also spent a considerable amount of time at The Golden Fields, Treescape, Riverside, and The Making."

The others nodded.

"She's really good with a wooden staff," Cole chimed in. "I've got the bruises to prove it." I smiled graciously at his praise, but I couldn't help it from being rather forced. It was more for show than anything else.

"You want to go next?" Astra asked Cole, who nodded.

"I'm Cole from The Paramount." He paused as if not sure what else to say.

In the silence, Kisa leaned over to Joss and I heard her whisper, "It's great to have two people from The Paramount on our team. They'll know exactly what to do all the time."

She had a soft, gentle voice, and even though I didn't think anyone else had heard her, I was encouraged. Astra was only from The North Wind; I was from The Paramount.

"I like sword-fighting, fist-fighting, and any type of combat," Cole said, finally finding his voice. "I promise to do my very best to lead this team to victory. I am truly honored to have each and every one of you here with me."

His words broke the tension a little, and everyone else seemed to relax a bit, except for Astra. There had been no sign that she'd been at all tense in the first place.

After Cole, Astra spoke up. "I'm Astra of The North Wind," she announced. "I'm very good at horseback riding."

You don't say, I thought wryly.

"I've also done my fair share of combat training, foraging, and basket making."

She stopped speaking and glanced at Rollan on her left. Instantly, he started talking. "I'm Rollan of Treescape. I'm not very skilled at fighting." His voice was deep but halting, any more so and he would have had a stutter.

"I like knocking trees down and cutting them up." Just from looking at the boy, I would have pegged him for manual labor. However, the more he spoke, the more I realized it would have to be simple manual labor, one instruction at a time.

"I can swim and..." He trailed off, like he couldn't think of anything else to say.

"He can whittle almost anything," Joss jumped in to support his cousin. "And he's really strong too."

After a moment, he continued. "I'm Joss of Riverside, by the way. I was born half fish and love the water. I also enjoy climbing trees and exploring."

I smiled in satisfaction, liking Joss more and more.

Kisa glanced around, and then piped up. "I'm Kisa of The Golden Fields. I'm—well, I'm good at cooking," she said. "I know all the herbs and spices and stuff."

Nice as it would have been to finally have someone to cook for me, I doubted we would be worried about the seasonings on our food once the trials began.

Cole frowned slightly. "I don't remember learning anything like that at The Golden Fields," he said. "Is it something you learned in school?"

Kisa shook her head and blushed slightly. "No, I learned it because I was an apprentice healer."

I quietly took a new opinion of the girl. Maybe she was going to be useful after all.

"That's great," I said, enthusiastic at last. It seemed that our team was actually pretty well-rounded. Cole and I were good at combat, Kisa could cook and treat injuries, we had some muscle

THE PREPARATIONS

in the form of Rollan to do the heavy lifting, Joss would be able to feed us if we were close to a lake or river, and Astra could replace Kisa as the first to die. I smiled to myself. We might end up being the perfect team after all.

"What's the plan for training?" Joss asked, looking at Cole.

Cole was ready with an answer and didn't need Astra to help him. "We'll train together every day. Everyone should either be on time or early.

"We'll start off at The Barracks tomorrow, first thing in the morning. Bring your weapons," Cole said. "I want to see what skill level everyone is at."

"I would suggest that we carry our weapons with us everywhere," I added, trying to think ahead. "We should get used to having them, so when the trials begin they are natural extensions of our bodies and not hindrances."

The others nodded.

"Easy for you to say," Cole teased. With a smile, he held up his sword to compare it with my small knife. My blade was only a third of the length of his.

There were a few laughs. After that, no one seemed to know quite what to say. Some of the other teams were breaking up; a few had started walking off together, as if they were going to start training right then and there.

"Take the rest of the day easy. Tomorrow the real work starts. Please don't be late," Cole stressed. "And come ready to show me everything you've got. After The Barracks, we may head over to The Making or something. So be ready to do some walking."

"You mean visit two different villages in the same day?" Kisa asked, her eyes going wide.

Cole nodded. "Most likely."

From the surprised look on her face, I would have been willing to bet that she hadn't done nearly as much training as Cole and I had. Glancing at the others, I wondered how much they had done.

When we split up, Rollan headed west, while Joss and Kisa went south. Astra walked with Cole and I toward The Paramount. I wished that she'd just go away.

"I think our team is going to be great," Cole announced, as the three of us climbed the slope to The Paramount.

"Yes," I replied, at the exact moment Astra said, "Indeed."

Neither of us said anything else, each of us walking on an opposite side of Cole. He didn't appear to sense the tension between us.

"I'll need you both to help me a lot," Cole went on. "I want to do some team building exercises outside of the regular training. I don't know what we need to do for qualifying, but I want everyone to be prepared."

"Sounds like a good idea," Astra agreed. We had reached the path that led north, and she, finally, took leave of us.

"We did it! We're on the same team!" Cole exclaimed as soon as Astra was gone. A joyful laugh actually escaped his lips as our eyes met. I felt a blush rise to my cheeks, until the next words came out of his mouth. "You, me, and Astra; it couldn't be more perfect."

Easy for you to say, I thought.

"We will win," I promised him. He seemed slightly deflated at my lack of enthusiasm, but it was all I could do not to tell him what I really thought of Astra.

He didn't hang around long, either because of my sour mood or because he was eager to see his family, I didn't know.

What I did know was that there wasn't anything waiting at my dwelling for me. It had been so long since I had had a day without training of some kind that I wasn't sure what to do with myself.

Maybe I should just sleep, I thought. I certainly felt tired enough to go back to bed, even though it wasn't even midday yet.

I reached my dwelling and went inside. It was as deserted as usual. I lay down on my bed and tried to sleep, but all I could think about was Astra's smile when I had been made third leader.

Chapter 24

SKILL LEVEL

The day after the teams were announced was no better that the day of the choosing itself.

On my way out of The Paramount, I noticed several contenders, Flant and Larna among them, standing in the town center, waiting for roll to be taken. Didn't they understand? That was over. The council had seen all it wanted to of us and had passed its judgment.

I considered waiting for Cole but decided against it since I didn't really feel like talking.

I made it to The Barracks just as the sun was rising. No one else was in sight; I smiled smugly at being the first to arrive.

Soon, I saw Cole walking towards me. "So, you are here," he said.

"Yes," I nodded.

He looked confused. "I waited for you in the town center," he told me. There was a question in the statement.

"They're done taking roll," was the only answer I gave him.

He blinked a couple of times but didn't say anything. Instantly, I regretted the terrible way I'd been treating him since the choosing. My apology was on my lips, but I choked it back because we were no longer alone. A handful of other contenders came cutting across the land from the south. Joss was among them. The others passed on, but Joss, completely full of energy, came bounding over to us. I forced myself to smile at him, even though his presence made it impossible for me to say anything to Cole.

"Hey," Cole greeted the younger boy.

"Hi," Joss shot back. "Anyone else here yet?" He glanced around.

I shook my head.

"I'm sure they'll be here soon," Cole added. "It's nearly sun up."

"Rollan might be a little late," Joss warned us. "He's got—well, he's not so good in the mornings."

"Who is?" Cole asked lightly.

A tense under current in Joss's voice tipped me off that he was leaving something out.

"What about Kisa?" Cole wondered.

"She's usually good about being on time," Joss answered. "Every once in a while, she's late because she's helping her mother and loses track of time."

"Rollan is your cousin," I recalled. "But how do you know Kisa?"

"She used to live in the dwelling next to mine," Joss answered. "Her family transferred to The Golden Fields last year."

"Why?" Cole asked. It was unusual for families to transfer. Once you had taken a life mate and started having children, you normally stayed there at least until the children were grown. The council didn't like letting young families transfer. They felt it was detrimental to the children's education.

"Kisa's mother is a healer," Joss told us by way of explanation.

I nodded in understanding. Healers had to go where they were sent.

"It was really hard on Kisa. There was a whole gang of us who used to play together after school. She still comes over on most of her days off. We go swimming and stuff."

Just as Joss finished, Astra appeared, wearing her customary black attire once more.

"Morning," she said.

SKILL LEVEL

I didn't acknowledge her at all. The boys didn't seem to notice my silence as the other two greeted her, but Astra did. Her eyes met mine for a fraction of a second before I looked away. Her gaze wasn't hostile, just curious.

We didn't have to wait long before Kisa joined us. I was glad to see she was still excited and enthusiastic. Half of me had expected her to be all weepy and scared with the trials about to become a reality. However, all she seemed able to talk about was how happy she was to be on a team with each of us. I guessed the gravity of the situation hadn't hit her yet. When it did, I was certain her reaction would not be so pleasant.

Rollan was late, as predicted. Cole didn't say anything about it. I would have, but Cole's merciful nature, mixed with the fact that Rollan wasn't all that late, kept him silent. It was also the first day of team training. I hoped that if it happened again, Cole wouldn't be as forgiving.

The Barracks was so crowded I wasn't sure we would be able to find a practice space as we entered the arena. It seemed that nearly every team leader had been thinking along the same lines as Cole. There were a lot of younger contenders present, who, from the way they handled their wooden staves, clearly hadn't practiced with the weapons much over the past five months.

Our group found a small patch of open space on the far side of the arena. When Cole paired us up, I expected that he would want to be my partner, since that was how we had always practiced. Instead, he took Rollan and paired me with Astra.

There wasn't much room, so we had to take turns sparring. Astra and I went first, while the others watched. Since we couldn't very well spar with my knife and her bow, we ditched them in favor of a pair of wooden staves borrowed from a nearby bin.

I didn't think Astra had put in nearly as much training time as I had. Confidently, I gripped the wooden staff tighter and gave it a few warm up swings. Just before we began, Astra re-

THE PREPARATIONS

moved the lightweight jacket she had been wearing, leaving only a black tank top. I hadn't brought my jacket and was wearing a dark red tunic.

The first time our staves met with a sharp crack, I could sense that I was better than her. However, what Astra lacked in technique and practice, she made up for in speed. As many times as I struck out at her, she dodged.

Frustrating as it was being unable to hit her, I kept her on the retreat, and she only managed to strike at me twice. Both attempts I easily knocked away. After about fifteen minutes Cole called us to stop. We were covered in sweat and breathing hard.

Astra's pale cheeks were flushed, and her loose hair was ruffled from the exertion. I didn't know how she could stand to have it flowing freely around her head all the time.

Astra and I both stepped out of the way as Cole directed Joss and Kisa to take our places. As I watched the two begin, I realized that I felt much better. If nothing else, I knew that there was at least one thing I was better at than Astra.

Joss was quick and had some skill with the stave, but Kisa had almost none. Joss seemed to hit her every time he moved. Not that he hit her hard, each of his blows looked so gentle I doubted they would have cracked an egg.

After less than a minute Cole had seen enough.

"I'm sorry," Kisa said, head hanging low.

"It's ok, Kisa," Joss assured her. "You'll get better."

"That's right," Cole added. "Plus, not everyone can be good at everything. I'm certain there are lots of other areas where you can help us in the trials."

Kisa brightened a little. "I'll try harder," she promised.

Cole and Rollan were next. It looked more like a fight between a snake and a bull than between to two young men. Rollan wasn't very quick, but he was immensely powerful; I could see how hard each of his blows were when they fell on Cole's weapon.

SKILL LEVEL

After one particularly hard blow, Cole removed one hand from his staff and shook it a couple times. The boys went on sparring almost as long as Astra and I had. They were none too gentle with each other. I wasn't surprised to see bruises starting to form on both of them by the time Cole called a halt.

Next, he pitted me against Joss. Joss was better than I had first thought. He must have been going really easy on Kisa. However, my longer limbs and extra inches in height gave me all the advantages I needed against him. He almost hit me once when I couldn't get my staff up in time. I had to leap to my right to avoid the blow. Other than that, he didn't even get close. I was able to land a number of blows on him, but I tried to be gentle.

Astra and Rollan were next. Unlike Cole, Astra didn't stay in one place as she blocked Rollan's blows. Instead, she moved easily in circles around him, dodging and occasionally lashing out herself. It was very one-sided. It didn't take long before Rollan had dropped any technique he might have been attempting and just started swinging at her in frustration as hard as he could. It might have gotten out of hand, but Cole called a stopped to it before anyone got hurt.

Cole and Kisa replaced them. The little girl glanced up at Cole nervously. He was nearly twice as big as Joss and, I think, she was more than a little afraid of what he might do.

Her fears were greatly misguided. Cole didn't take even one swing at her. He let Kisa do all the attacking and simply blocked her blows.

"All right," he said, after a few minutes. "I think I have a pretty good idea where everyone stands. We'll stay here until sun high and practice. I'll train with Rollan. Astra, you train with Joss, and Myra, you can work with Kisa."

I saw what he was doing. He had paired the weak fighters with the strong. But still, did he have to give me the worst of the lot?

Turning to Kisa, I saw that she was watching me with big, eager eyes, like I was an instructor or something. Never having had a real younger sibling, I wasn't quite sure how to begin. Even when I had still been friends with Rasby, I rarely taught her anything. She wasn't sharp, so most of the time it was easier just to do everything for her.

"You have a lot of strength," I heard Cole tell Rollan. "You just need to know how to direct it."

Encouraging. That was a good approach.

"Umm...your grip is good," I told Kisa. "What you need to work on is committing. When you swing the staff, you have to know exactly where you want it to go."

Kisa nodded.

I held my own staff out to the side. "Try to hit it in the exact middle as hard as you can," I instructed her. Kisa swung, but the blow was very light.

"Harder," I ordered. "Don't be afraid to step into it."

She took my advice and stepped forward, but her stance was all wrong. I quickly corrected her, and she tried again.

Kisa was very bright and picked up on things quickly. After half an hour, she was hitting much harder and with better accuracy. She paid close attention when I demonstrated the different stances and forms and was already improving.

A couple of times, an instructor paused to watch us. They never intervened. I wondered if they would have corrected me if I had done something wrong, or if we were completely on our own.

Around sun high, we left the arena to have lunch. All I'd brought was a few strips of meat and some dried fruit. Kisa produced an entire apple pie and told us that her mother had baked it for her to share with us. The pastry was soft and flaky on the outside, and the fruit within was perfectly sweetened. Altogether, it was completely delicious.

"This is so good!" I exclaimed after my first mouthful.

"The best I've ever had," Astra echoed my praise.

SKILL LEVEL

The others murmured their approval as well, but not as loudly.

"Thanks," Kisa said shyly. "She'll be so happy to hear you liked it. She was really worried about me becoming a contender, but when I tell her how nice everyone is, I'm sure she'll feel better."

"Do you have siblings? Are any of them contenders?" Cole asked.

"I have a sister who is two years younger than me. She's not old enough to be a contender. I also have a baby brother who was just born this past fall," Kisa told us.

"How about you, Joss?" Cole turned to the boy sitting next to Kisa.

He licked the pie from his lips before answering. "I have a big brother and two little sisters," he said. "My brother is third leader on another team. Only one of my sisters was old enough to be a potential, but just by a few months. She didn't get chosen to be a contender. It was just as well; I think she's too young to leave home." It was funny to hear Joss call anyone young.

"You have it so easy," Rollan said to Joss. "You've only got one big brother."

"How many do you have?" I asked.

Joss laughed lightly and clapped Rollan on the shoulder. "My cousin here is from a brood of boys. He has five brothers."

"Wow!" Cole exclaimed. "I thought I had it rough. Are they all older than you?"

"Almost," Rollan answered mournfully. "There is one who's younger, but the rest are all older."

"Out of all my cousins, Rollan is the only one I can actually stand," Joss told us, giving Rollan a sympathetic glance.

"That's awful," Cole chuckled.

Rollan nodded.

"Did they end up becoming contenders?" I wondered.

"All but the oldest and the youngest," replied Rollan.

THE PREPARATIONS

"I have a couple older brothers too," Cole told him. "They can be a little annoying sometimes, but it's my sister who rules the roost since she's the oldest."

"I know," Rollan said.

Cole gave him a confused look. "You know?"

"Of course," Joss piped up. "You and Myra are the Clan Leaders' children. Everyone knows about you."

I blinked, never having considered the fact that others would know anything about me just because my mother was the Second Clan Leader. Maybe, since I had grown up with it and never known any differently, I hadn't notice. I had certainly never felt like I had received special attention.

"What do you know about me?" I asked.

"I know you're sixteen and an only child. You always liked coming to Riverside when you were young because you could collect pebbles while your mother did business."

I stared at him. "Where did you hear that?"

Joss shrugged. "It's just something I was told by this one old woman, Viot."

I heard Astra draw in a sharp breath. My mouth opened but nothing came out. Where had I heard that name before?

"She's dead now," Joss continued. "But once she told me that she had seen you staring out at the waters of the lake at sunset. She said…" Joss paused, as if to ensure that his wording was completely correct. "She said that 'the water was calling you home'."

Everyone was silent for a moment.

"Viot was kind of crazy, so I don't know what it meant, but I always remembered it," Joss said by way of explanation.

"I see," was all I could think to say.

Kisa sensed that it was time to change the subject. Unfortunately, the change was definitely for the worse.

"What about you Astra?" she asked. "You haven't told us about your family. Do you have any siblings?"

There was a moment of silence. Cole and I exchanged an awkward glance.

"No," Astra said. "I don't have any siblings." There was another, longer pause. "I don't have any family."

"That's too bad," Kisa said in a small voice. She seemed to know she had asked the wrong question.

"What are we going to do now?" I jumped in.

"I was thinking of heading to The Making," Cole sounded thoughtful. "But it's such a nice day, maybe we should go to The Quarry instead."

I nodded. The sun was out, but the temperature was very pleasant. Soon, the days would grow hot, and training outdoors would be a lot less fun. Might as well save the indoor lessons until then.

We left for The Quarry shortly thereafter. On the way, Kisa dropped back to talk softly with Astra.

"I'm really sorry for what I said," Kisa apologized.

"It's fine," Astra told her. "It's all I know. I just don't really like to talk about it."

Kisa looked at the ground. "Sorry—" she started again, but Astra stopped her midsentence.

"It's not your fault. You had no way to know. Please don't let it bother you; I try not to let it bother me."

Astra's voice had a light note to it, but I could sense the tension underneath her words. It appeared too subtle for Kisa to pick up on though, because she smiled brightly and said, "Great! I'm so happy to be on your team!"

That makes ones of us, I thought sourly with an inward sigh. During our training and when we had been discussing our families over lunch, I'd been able to put aside most of my resentment. All the bitterness was back now. *If only Astra wasn't on my team, and then everything would be perfect.*

Chapter 25

TEAM WORK

Functioning as a team was very different from functioning as an individual. Nearly all I did was teach the younger members of my team the skills I had already learned. After the first couple days, I could say without question that Cole and I had put in the most time training. We were experts at almost everything.

Shortly thereafter, Cole decided that our team should train together every day. I wasn't particularly thrilled with the idea. Cole and I would have trained together regardless, and I missed having one on one time with him.

Now, all we had were the mornings when we walked to training from The Paramount together and when we returned in the evenings. Even then, we weren't always left in peace, as our teammates often accompanied us much of the way, heading to their own villages.

To keep things interesting, Cole tried to find challenges for us to face that would help us develop our teamwork. One day at Treescape, he asked the instructors if we could try to fell a tree by ourselves. I was pretty sure the request amused them, but they gave their consent readily enough.

It took us nearly all day to do it, and we wouldn't have gotten very far without Rollan. Being from Treescape, he had seen lots of trees felled and possessed a fairly good grasp of the concept.

First, Joss shimmied up the tree with several ropes. He secured them to different branches before dropping them down to

THE PREPARATIONS

those of us on the ground. We took the ropes and tied them to several nearby trees.

Rollan said that using the ropes would ensure the tree fell where we wanted, so no one would get accidentally crushed. He was also the one to mark exactly where on the trunk it would be best to start using the axe.

We all took turns with the axe. Kisa's turn consisted of exactly two swings, neither of which left any visible marks on the trunk.

Joss went next. Only the fact that Kisa had preceded him made it look like the damage he caused was significant. He had climbed the tree in a matter of seconds, but it would have taken him days to chop it down. Seeming to realize his own inadequacy, he handed the tool off after less than five minutes.

Cole and Rollan did most of the work. Even though Cole hadn't spent too much time chopping wood during earlier training sessions, his muscular arms made good use of the axe.

Astra and I had no trouble with the axe, but we lacked the strength of the larger two boys.

All in all, we made good progress and had the tree on the ground before midday. The afternoon was spent cutting the wood into pieces small enough for a team of horses to haul away. At least we didn't have to manage the horses ourselves; although, I was sure we could have left that to Astra.

"There are still several villages we haven't visited yet as a team," Astra pointed out that evening, just before we left Treescape. Rollan had already gone to his dwelling, and Joss and Kisa were nearly out of sight on the road to the south.

"Would it not be wise to visit each of them?" she asked. I recalled that she had used the same strategy when the preparations had begun.

"Some of the villages teach useless lessons," I said, shaking my head.

Astra glanced my way, and I could see that she had correctly guessed my comment was aimed at The North Wind.

TEAM WORK

"Might be a good way to find everyone's hidden talents," she put in, undeterred. "Everyone knew Rollan would be handy with an axe, but I wouldn't have learned that he could make a fire out of anything, even the dampest wood, if we hadn't been here in Treescape two days ago while it was raining."

"It's not a bad idea," Cole told us, before I could argue with her. "We should give it a go. Maybe tomorrow we'll try a new village instead of The Barracks after lunch."

I swallowed my protests until after Astra had started down the road that led to The North Wind. Only once Cole and I were alone did I finally voice my opinion. "You know she just wants to see us all on horseback so she can have a good laugh," I told him.

Cole chuckled. "That would be pretty funny."

I sighed; I hadn't been making a joke.

"Can you imagine Rollan on a horse?" Cole asked.

I couldn't help but crack a grin at that image.

Cole implemented Astra's suggestion the following day. We went to Riverside instead of The Barracks, and we did learn something new. More than half our team were amazing swimmers. Joss and Kisa had both grown up on the shores of the lake, so it was no surprise that they were as agile in the water as they were on land. Rollan, it turned out, spent nearly all of his free time in Riverside with his cousin, trying to avoid his brothers, so he'd had a lot of practice too.

What shocked me most was that Astra could swim nearly as well as Joss, Kisa, and Rollan. When Joss asked her where she had learned, she just smiled at him and said, "I have a private lake." No one knew quite what to make of that since The North Wind had no lakes.

I still wasn't so sure of the water, but Joss gave me some tips, which actually helped a lot. For the first time in a while I felt like a student instead of an instructor.

As we continued our circuit of the villages, I found that Joss was pretty much a jack-of-all-trades. He could climb anything,

THE PREPARATIONS

build anything, and would eat anything. He had really impressed me at The Making, when, instead of making a basket from the reeds and sticks we'd been given, he had woven a wall, stating that it would be a good start to a shelter.

With the trials beginning in the middle of summer, I doubted we would need shelter, but we didn't know how long we would be gone. It was one of those facts that wasn't discussed. For all I knew, it could be years. That was a scary thought. I could do anything for a couple weeks or months, but I wasn't sure how we would survive winter on our own.

Kisa proved to have a vast knowledge of herbs, even more than most contenders from The Golden Fields. It was quite impressive, especially considering that she hadn't lived there all that long. She did confess to us that her mother had been teaching her for years, even before she became an apprentice healer. Once she'd been selected, she'd advanced quickly and sometimes would even help her mother treat patients.

With the three lower-ranked team members going up in my estimation, I started feeling like we had a real advantage. I observed several other teams training, and a lot of them had at least one member who was completely useless.

Eventually, we did make it to The North Wind. Cole had saved it for last. I didn't think he liked the village any more than I did. However, he must have felt that some hardship would help us bond, because one day he dragged us all up north for training.

Astra met us there.

When she brought us into the training ring, the instructors only glanced at her. No one came over to help us out; they left everything to Astra.

I had to hand it to her, she was amazing with horses. It took only fifteen minutes for us to get three horses brushed and saddled. I was happy that we would be taking turns; the less time I spent riding the better.

Astra claimed a fourth horse for herself. Not even bothering with a saddle, she leapt onto its back.

Her lesson was a lot more useful than the other I had endured at The North Wind. She showed us how to get up and down quickly and told us what to do if the horse started to buck or rear.

"Why are we learning this?" Rollan complained. "None of these horses are going to do anything like that."

"No," Astra replied. "But I seriously doubt you'll find any horses half so well trained as these while we're competing in the trials. Plus, if a horse gets startled, even the best trained animal could do something unexpected."

"I guess." Rollan didn't look convinced.

He was unable to mount without standing on a block no matter how hard he tried. I could see the frustration growing on his face as Astra constantly told him to loosen his reins.

Kisa was the only one who loved riding. She was good at it too. Astra said she had the best balance out of all of us, but I was fairly confident that that was because she was so light and short.

We ended up spending most of the day at The North Wind. I hoped it was Cole's way of making sure we spent an adequate amount of time there without having to go back.

The sun was dipping toward the west as we prepared to leave. Astra accompanied us to the outskirts of the village. The people of The North Wind were beginning to return from their work. They came riding in from all directions, most leading other horses behind the ones they rode.

One of the animals whinnied sharply as it approached us. A young man on a large, bay mare was leading it. The horse that had whinnied was pale gold. He was either the same horse Astra had been brushing the day Golla had died, or was one with exactly the same color fur.

I recognized the young man as well; I'd seen him on my first day of training at The North Wind. He was wearing all black again, and he was steering his horses straight toward us. There were two others on a line behind the golden horse; both of them were a deep reddish-brown.

"Astra," the man called.

She had already turned at the sound of the whinny. "Hi, Gann," she said in greeting. Then gestured to us. "This is my team for the trials."

"Hi," Gann said to us, bringing the horses to a stop a short distance away.

The only other time I had seen Gann was from a distance. Now, I could make out his features; they were strong and well-defined. His ash blond hair was straight but not very long. He had clear blue eyes, several shades lighter than Cole's. It was hard to tell with him mounted on a horse, but I was fairly confident that he was pretty tall.

"Do you have more training today or are you free to give Rickie a little exercise?" Gann asked Astra.

Astra smiled at the large, golden horse. "We're done for today," she told Gann. Stepping forward, she knelt beside Rickie and lifted one of his forelegs. "Looks like he's almost ready for new shoes," she observed, running her hand over the metal horseshoe on the bottom of his foot.

"Should be fine for another half month," Gann replied. "I'll put Luka and Dutch up." He started his horse walking again, leading the small herd toward the main barn. Rickie kept looking back and even nickered over his shoulder at Astra.

"I'll be right there," she called. I wasn't sure if she was talking to Gann or to the horse.

"Tomorrow, let's meet at The Golden Fields," Cole said. Astra turned her attention back to us and nodded. Cole had only been looking at Astra as he spoke. There was something in his gaze I wasn't certain I liked. An uncomfortable twinge found its way into the pit of my stomach.

"Sounds good," Astra replied. "You'll be the teacher tomorrow, Kisa."

Kisa grinned. "Great!"

We set off as Astra hurried away to the main barn. Rollan headed for Treescape toward the west, but the rest of us took the same path as far as The Paramount.

"Why do they wear black?" Kisa asked, as soon as we were on the southern road.

I shrugged. "No clue."

Cole shook his head when she glanced his way.

"Why don't you ask Astra?" Joss suggested.

"No," Kisa said. "It might be a rude question."

"Then she would just tell you she didn't want to talk about it," Joss pointed out. "I don't get the feeling Astra is very easy to offend. Maybe I'll ask her."

"Don't!" Kisa all but shouted. "Astra's really more likely to tell you something because she wants to, not because you ask her."

I hadn't thought of it like that before, but Kisa was right. When Astra wanted you to know something, she'd be sure to tell you.

"But it's not just her," Joss argued. "That guy was wearing black too, and I've seen a couple others who did it as well. There has to be a reason."

"They mistakenly washed their clothes with ink?" I joked.

No one laughed.

"How many more days of training do we have?" Joss asked a moment later.

"Nineteen," Cole and I answered at the same time. The gift of coming from The Paramount: you always know the numbers.

"That's all?" Kisa asked. She seemed nervous. I fervently hoped that she wasn't about to get homesick.

"We'll be ready," Joss promised her. "Everything's going to be great." Kisa nodded, but didn't look completely certain. They left us when we reached The Paramount.

"What are we going to do tomorrow after The Golden Fields?" I asked Cole.

He sighed. "I don't know." Defeat was thick in his voice.

THE PREPARATIONS

I was startled. He had sounded perfectly normal not two minutes earlier when we had bid Joss and Kisa goodnight. "What's the matter?" I asked.

"I don't have a clue what I'm doing, Myra," he told me. "I don't know why they made me a team leader; you would have been a much better choice. I'm just making things up as I go along. I don't really have a plan. How can I? All I know is that in less than a month we have to go through qualifying. Then, the day after that, the trials begin, but I can't even start to guess what qualifying will be like, much less the actual trials."

"No one knows," I told him. "You're doing a wonderful job. Everyone is getting along, and we all work together really well. For right now, that's all that matters. No one could expect more from you, so just relax. You aren't alone in this. If you need help or someone to talk to, I'm here."

"You're right," he said, sounding more like himself. "I just—they are all depending on me. Their lives might be at stake. If anything happened to one of them, I don't know what I'd do."

"Cole, you're a leader; you can do this. But only if you stop worrying about the 'what ifs' and do the best you can. You're not our parent, and we aren't helpless kids anymore, except maybe Kisa."

Cole smiled slightly. "She's not as helpless as you think, and if anyone gets injured, we'll be glad to have her."

I smiled back. "Joss can build us shelters, and Rollan can make the fire. You and I can just sit back and relax."

"And leave the thinking to Astra? I like it," he laughed. I wasn't so pleased with the part about Astra, but it was good that his spirits seemed to have been lifted.

"You're a leader," I told Cole again. "But I'll always be here to help you."

"Thanks." Cole's deep blue eyes were serious again. "I'm never going to stop needing your support. I know I wouldn't be able to face any of this without you."

"You'll never have to," I promised.

Chapter 26

INTERNAL DISPUTE

The Golden Fields was beautiful that time of year. Plants of every shade of green grew in rows across hundreds of acres. Most of them were flowering in the early summer air. My favorites by far were the cherry trees, with clouds of pink and white petals clinging to thin branches I couldn't imagine a lovelier sight.

Cole and I walked together that day from The Paramount. Every morning seemed earlier than the one before it, and none of the contenders were getting much rest. I'd heard that two or three of the younger ones had collapsed during training due to exhaustion.

"Maybe we should cut our session short today," Cole suggested when I relayed the incidents to him. We were approaching the edge of the first wheat fields and only had another half mile to go. Villagers from The Golden Fields had gotten an early start working among the crops, doing whatever it was they did to make the plants grow strong and healthy.

"They need to learn to cope," I told him.

"Yes," Cole agreed, "but wearing everyone out right before qualifying isn't going to help us make it through. It will be better if everyone is well-rested."

I shook my head. "They're too soft," I insisted. "Training long days will build up their endurance. They should have been doing it all along. Then, they wouldn't be feeling so fatigued right now."

"They aren't as old as we are. How far do you think we'll get if one of them collapses the first day of the trials?" Cole asked.

I shrugged. There was no easy solution.

"Maybe we should talk it over with Astra," he suggested.

If I hadn't been absolutely certain Cole would never have said anything knowingly hurtful, I would have sworn he had just taken a stab at me. He probably didn't realize the effect his words would had. Every time he spoke of consulting Astra, it tore at my heart. He may have been doing it unintentionally, but to me, it was just another reminder that she was standing between us.

"Whatever," I muttered, hastening forward, fuming to myself. I knew it wasn't quite fair to act that way. Cole probably didn't realize that he had upset me, but I couldn't help myself.

If Cole really cared more about her opinion than he did about mine, then that was fine. They could do what they wanted. I would train on my own if necessary. I meant to be victorious, whatever it took.

"Myra," Cole hurried after me, confusion in his blue eyes. "I'm not saying we take a whole day off, but maybe just a half day or an evening here and there. Everyone needs to rest sometimes. That's why our society is set up with rest days. We all need to relax once in a while. Surely, a few shorter days would only help us in the long run."

We both knew that by 'us' he meant Kisa. Cole and I were strong from our training throughout the preparations. Rollan was built for endurance. One day, I imagined he would end up nearly as big as Jase. Astra was strong too. She had spent her whole life working the stables, and you could see it in the hard muscles that lined her limbs. Joss wasn't even close to as powerful as his cousin, but he had that wiry, almost unending vigor, which boys his age were nearly always gifted with.

Kisa was the only one to worry about. As Cole had said, she was young and hadn't done nearly enough training on her own.

Unprepared as she was, she pressed doggedly on, always behind but never giving up or whining. That was the best part about her: she never complained. I had seen contenders much older than her making a fuss and griping about a lot less than what we were putting her through.

She's leader material, I thought. *We all are.*

"Fine," I agreed. Although, I knew keeping Astra out of it was my main reason for going along with Cole's idea. "We'll take a few half days, but I would suggest that we spend the first part of those days doing something strenuous, like sparring."

"That's excellent!" Cole beamed, clearly thrilled to have reached a compromise. I actually felt my anger dissipate a little. It was so hard to stay upset with him when he was smiling at me like that.

The day was already getting hot by the time our entire team had arrived. Rollan was last, as usual. Perhaps, we needed a training day at The Paramount. Even though Cole had said that we would visit every village as a team, we had chosen to skip The Paramount.

It had just seemed so pointless. Both Cole and I knew pretty much everything there was to learn about time management, scheduling, list keeping, etc. We had also spoken to a few contenders who had trained there with their teams. They had all said the same thing: 'don't bother; we aren't going back'.

Nice as it would have been to watch Rollan get a lecture on punctuality, we, ironically, didn't have the time.

"Kisa, today you get to teach us everything you know," Cole told the little girl.

She looked pleased and slightly embarrassed to be singled out. "Let's start with the edible roots," she suggested. "They're the hardest because you can't see the food part of them, and a lot of their leaves just look like leaves."

We spent the better part of the morning identifying the different plants Kisa pointed out to us. After roots, we moved into an orchard and began looking at the different trees.

THE PREPARATIONS

We were a little over halfway through all the plants when Kisa singled Rollan out and asked, "Do you know what kind of tree that is?"

"No." Rollan sounded bored and slightly sullen. It was an easy question; there were already small oranges growing on splayed branches. They hadn't taken on their fiery coloring yet, but it was still pretty easy to see what they were.

"It's an orange tree," Kisa told him, unaffected by his mood. "How about that one?" She pointed to a nearby plum tree.

"I don't care," Rollan said. Everyone looked at him, startled. "This is stupid. If the fruit is ripe, it'll be obvious what it is and won't matter if we know what kind of tree it is based on the leaves."

"That's not true," Kisa protested. "There are lots of plants with poisonous fruit that look similar to real fruit. We need to be able to tell the difference!"

"Well, show me a tree with poisonous fruit, and then I'll know not to eat it," Rollan said flatly.

"We don't grow poisonous plants here; that would be stupid," Kisa announced.

"Let's finish this another time," Cole interjected before Rollan could snap anything back at Kisa.

"We cou—" I started, but Astra cut me off, either because she didn't hear me or because she didn't care what I had to say.

"All the leaves do start to blend together after a while," she sympathized. "We should come back later to learn the rest, and we can review some of the harder plants as well."

Neither Rollan nor Kisa looked thrilled, but they didn't say anything.

After taking a break and having some lunch, Cole suggested we go to The Barracks, which I thought was a good choice. I didn't know if fighting would be part of either qualifying or the trials, but being in excellent physical shape couldn't hurt.

Astra and I were paired together. I didn't mind so much because it meant I occasionally got to land a blow on her with my staff. She got me too every once in a while, but not nearly as often. I was careful to check my blows, somewhat.

We switched partners every twenty minutes. I preferred Cole, but that was because we had been sparring together for so long that we knew each other's rhythms; we could almost move as one. We hardly ever landed a blow as we circled each other, demonstrating our excellent skill and technique.

An hour later, I was sparring with Joss when I suddenly heard a shriek from Kisa behind me. I turned and saw her cradling her hand to her chest. One of her fingernails was split, and blood was running down her hand.

Joss dropped his staff and was at her side in a moment. He wrapped an arm around her protectively and began to examine the wound.

Kisa gazed up at her opponent, which was Rollan. "Why did you hit me so hard?" she asked, fighting tears.

"Because that's the third time you haven't blocked the same thrust!" Rollan said in exasperation.

Kisa looked even more upset. "I tried, but—"

"Tried nothing! You don't even have the basics of this!"

"Ok, enough!" I said stepping forward to put myself between the two. Kisa was crying now, whether from the pain or from Rollan's harsh words I didn't know, but she'd buried her face in Joss's chest. I could see her small shoulders quivering as Joss rubbed her back soothingly.

"She's not as big or as strong as you are," Cole said, coming to stand by my side, facing Rollan. "You shouldn't hurt her, especially not on purpose."

"I'm only trying to make her better," Rollan growled.

"Well, that's no way to do it," Cole told him grimly. "She won't learn anything if her hand is injured."

Joss hadn't been paying attention to anyone but Kisa. "Let's go find your mother and get this taken care of," he said softly.

Kisa nodded and let Joss lead her away from the rest of us. Her big, blue eyes still full of tears.

"Don't worry about coming back afterwards," Cole called after the pair. "Tomorrow we'll meet at The Golden Fields." Joss glanced back over his shoulder and nodded to show that he'd heard.

"If we're done, then I'm out of here," Rollan announced, throwing down his wooden staff. It was a borrowed one, since he hadn't bothered to bring his own.

"Not so fast," Cole told him. "We need to have a talk."

"Let's take this outside," Astra suggested mildly. There were quite a few other contenders staring at us. Bala was among them since her team, including Jase, was training close by. I didn't care for the amused smile she wore as she observed the conflict within our team.

Emotional outbursts were a rare thing among The Clan. If anyone had seen two children at play and a fight had broken out, the proper punishment would have been implemented and no one would have thought anything of it. However, as contenders, we were considered to be almost adults, no matter our real age.

The four of us crossed the loose dirt of the arena and emerged into the evening light. It was later than I had thought. We'd trained right up to the normal time for dinner.

Rollan, who was in the lead, swung around to face the rest of us as soon as we were through the door.

"What do you want me to say?" he snapped at Cole. "That I'm sorry? I've known Kisa a long time, and she's too soft!"

"Calm down," Cole began.

"I am calm!" Rollan interrupted. "This is all her fault! I don't care what you think!"

Cole looked shocked. I was a little surprised myself. I had heard rumors that outside The Paramount discipline wasn't always properly enforced, leading to ill-mannered children, but I hadn't really seen the proof until now.

"Why won't you listen to what I'm trying to say?" Cole asked. "I'm the team leader." To his credit, Cole was remaining remarkably calm. I wasn't though; I was ready to go to the council and demand a replacement for Rollan.

"It doesn't matter who you are!" Rollan yelled. "You aren't the boss of me."

Cole had no answer for that.

"You're being rude and childish," Astra told Rollan. It was exactly what I would have said, but my voice would probably have been considerably louder.

"I didn't do anything wrong!" Rollan shouted defensively. He jabbed a finger at a welt on Astra's arm that had been my doing. "Everyone else was hitting their partners."

"That was an accident," Astra told him.

Well, sort of, I thought. I had meant to hit Astra, but she had jumped the opposite direction I had been expecting, and my stick had struck her harder than I'd intended. As soon as I'd done it, I'd stopped and apologized.

"I can take a hit," Astra added. "Kisa can't. She's half your size—"

"I know that!" Rollan snarled, interrupting again. An angry red color rose into his cheeks as he yelled.

Suddenly, I figured out what was wrong. I understood exactly where Rollan was coming from and why he was so upset.

Cole raised his hand to rub his forehead, as though he was getting a headache. Rollan sprang back a few paces, causing all three of us to stare at him. The defiant look on his face darkened under our gaze.

I turned to Astra and Cole. "Why don't you two head out?" I suggested. "I'll talk with Rollan."

All three of them looked at me like I was crazy. I met and held Cole's gaze. After a moment, he nodded, trusting that I knew what I was doing.

"Let's go Astra," he said. Astra glanced at us both questioningly, but followed Cole without a word.

Rollan stood there, looking slightly confused but still very defensive.

THE PREPARATIONS

"Let's take a walk," I suggested.

Without waiting to see if he would follow, I struck out to the west, not on the path to The Paramount, but on an angle to avoid it and pick up the road to Treescape on the other side. A moment later, I heard Rollan shuffling after me.

Perfect, I thought.

After we had been silently walking for about twenty-five minutes, he broke the silence. "Why are you walking me home?" he asked.

I didn't answer his question, opting instead to go with a different approach.

"Do you know what village I come from?"

"The Paramount," he said flatly.

"Yes, and do you know who my mother is?" I asked him.

I could hear the scorn in his voice as he answered. "Of course I do. She's the Second Leader of our people, Myna of The Paramount."

"Indeed," I said and was silent a moment longer. "And what do you think those two things say about me?"

My pace had slowed when we had begun conversing, and Rollan had finally caught up to me. We were walking side-by-side then, instead of him trailing me as he had for most of our journey. He thought about my question for a while, and then I saw him shrug out of the corner of my eye. "I don't know."

"Alright, well, what do you think everyone else would think those two things say about me?" I tried again, hoping he would see what I was getting at.

He took some time to think before answering. "That you were born to be a leader," he muttered.

"Yes," I answered softly. "It always did seem that way to me."

"But you are leading," Rollan said.

I smiled without joy. It was nice for him to say so. "Do you know where Astra is from and who her parents are?" I asked him.

He was silent for almost a full minute. "Are you saying you think you should be second leader instead of Astra?" he guessed suspiciously.

"You're missing the point," I told him.

"What is the point?" he asked, still sounding exasperated, but not so much as when he had talked back to Cole.

"Astra doesn't have the same leadership credentials I do. She's from a village where leadership isn't really prized or nurtured. She doesn't have a Clan Leader for a parent to set her an example, but—but they chose her over me because she has other gifts."

I had finally figured some things out. They had only become clear to me when I had understood what Rollan had been feeling and had looked at the situation from an outsider's perspective.

It was the first time I had actually stopped to consider why the council had chosen Astra over me. There was some logic behind it. Cole and I had too much in common. We both thought in the same way. If one of us couldn't figure something out, then the other one wouldn't be able to either.

Astra was unique, her thought process completely different from ours. Listening to her, our team might be able to avoid a disaster that neither Cole nor I could even fathom. That was why she had been put above me, so that we would hear things from a different perspective.

They didn't think I wasn't good enough; they thought I was too good. They knew that if Cole and I were made first and second leaders, we would lead the team between the two of us, without giving much heed to any other opinion. To a certain extent, we still did. I remembered the discussion from the morning. We had made a team decision without talking to anyone else.

"I give up. What you are trying to say?" Rollan asked me. We had reached the far side of The Paramount and were on the road to Treescape. There wasn't another person in sight.

I smiled to myself; I had him exactly where I wanted him. He was finally ready to listen. "I'm saying you're just as good as Kisa," I announced. "I know you're upset because you feel like having a little girl above you is stupid, but there are reasons for it, and it has nothing to do with you not being good enough."

His mouth dropped open. "How did you know—"

I cut him off. "I felt the same way for a while, until I realized that the council didn't rank us by how skilled we are. They built teams for survival."

I refrained from mentioning just how recently I'd come to that epiphany.

"Everyone told me it was because I was so worthless," he started again. "And then, she's so good for nothing. What does that make me? I mean, I know I'm not very smart or—"

"Who said anything of the sort?" I interrupted him. "Your teammates?" I shook my head. "No one thinks you're worthless. And Kisa has her own talents. Personally, I am counting on her to do all the cooking for us. If she can make anything as good as her mother's pie, I'll let her continue once we get back."

Rollan actually laughed, but he grew serious again a second later. "You, Cole, and Astra really don't wish I wasn't on your team?"

"No," I said. "In fact, we're really happy we got you. You round out the team perfectly. Remember when we felled that tree by ourselves? Without you, there's no way that would have ever happened.

"Where did you get the idea that we didn't want you?"

Rollan shrugged. "I—I don't remember a time when I was ever really good at something. Now, I have to constantly prove that I am worth being a member at all."

"That's not true," I told him. "Stop thinking that way. Start thinking about how you can help your team prepare for what's coming. Kisa is the most inexperienced of us all. We should be helping her get better, not discouraging her."

"Ok," Rollan said. "I'll try."

We walked in silence for a little while, until we got fairly close to Treescape. There was still one more thing I wanted to ask, and I didn't want to do it where other people could hear, so I stopped and looked straight at Rollan.

"Why did you mouth off to Cole like that?" I asked. Rollan seemed taken aback by my direct question. "You knew you shouldn't have been so rough with Kisa, but you still played it off like Cole was the bad guy."

Rollan looked down. "I don't know. I guess that's how I deal with my brothers when they get upset. They usually just smack me around, but sometimes, if I argue enough, they'll get bored and leave me alone."

"You thought Cole was going to hit you?" I asked.

Still looking at the ground, Rollan nodded.

"Cole will never do that," I promised Rollan. "I can't imagine him ever hurting anyone."

"If you say so," Rollan replied. "But I don't know how he survived his brothers with that attitude. Mine respect me more when I hit back."

"Why does your mother allow you guys to fight so much?" I asked, shocked by the idea of so much physical violence. I had figured his brothers roughed him up sometimes, but it sounded a lot worse than I had imagined.

"She's busy with—stuff," he said, still not looking at me.

"I guess it would be rather difficult to raise that many boys."

"Yeah, I'm pretty sure she wanted girls," Rollan told me.

"Looks like no one got what they wanted," I sighed. Rollan smiled slightly.

He started walking in the direction of his dwelling, but I couldn't let the conversation end on a down note.

"Rollan," I called after him, and he turned back to look at me. "We're here for you now. If you need us, you only have to ask."

THE PREPARATIONS

"Thanks, Myra," he all but whispered. "No matter what the council thinks, you're the smartest person on our team."

I smiled, and then laughed. Maybe he was right, but they thought that Astra was better equipped to help us survive.

As I walked back to The Paramount, I began to think over the advice I had given Rollan. I would need to start implementing it in my own life. It would be hard, but I was always prepared for a challenge.

Chapter 27

THE CLIFFS

When Cole and I reached The Golden Fields the following day, Rollan was waiting for us, along with Kisa. The two appeared to have made up. Kisa was chattering incessantly, and Rollan was patiently listening to her.

When they saw us, Kisa stopped talking. Rollan got up from where he had been perched on the low stone fence that bordered the field we had spent the previous day in. There was a short, awkward pause, and then Rollan approached us. In his hand, was the wooden staff that had been given to him on the day the council had assigned teams.

"I'm sorry for my behavior yesterday," Rollan apologized.

"Don't worry about it," Cole replied in surprise. "Everyone gets frustrated once in a while."

Rollan nodded and turned back to Kisa, who began actively describing some of the poisonous plants carefully grown by the healers for medicinal purposes. She'd never been permitted to see them, but her mother had told her about a few.

Cole turned to look at me in amazement and mouthed, "What did you say to him?"

I smiled and shrugged. Leaning close to his ear, I whispered, "He just needed someone to talk to."

"I tried to talk to him," Cole said quietly.

"Yeah, but it was three against one, and I'm pretty sure he felt outnumbered. Plus, I don't think he responds too well to guys because his brothers push him around sometimes."

"But I didn't mean to—"

"What are you two whispering about?" Astra asked, interrupting Cole. She had approached from behind us, and I hadn't noticed her until she spoke. Much as I was willing to overlook the fact that she had been made second leader instead of me, that didn't mean I was going to have to start liking her. At least that morning I felt like I maybe hated her a little less.

"Nothing," Cole said a little too loudly, making us seem guiltier than we really were.

"Sure," Astra almost laughed, giving him a wink.

We were saved from further interrogation, because, at that moment, Joss came running up.

"Alright, Kisa, let's pick up where we left off," Cole announced.

Under Kisa's supervision we finished the plants, and then had a review of some of the more important ones. We finished just before lunchtime. The weather was a lot warmer than it had been the day before.

"What are we doing this afternoon?" I asked Cole. It was the first really hot day of the year, and I could feel sweat running down my back.

"The Making?" Kisa suggested. It was a good thought. We could sit in the shade and relax while still being productive.

"What about Riverside instead?" Joss piped up. "We could go swimming. The water will feel great today!"

"That's perfect!" Cole said enthusiastically.

My lips pursed at the idea. I was only slightly more comfortable in the water than I was on the back of a horse. Normally, I could keep my head above the surface, but the thought of underwater currents was never far from my mind. Especially, since I'd been told repeatedly during the preparations that even the best swimmers were helpless in the strong undertow of the river.

However, everyone else seemed thrilled with the idea of swimming, so we struck out for the short walk between The Golden Fields and Riverside.

THE CLIFFS

At Kisa's suggestion, we didn't follow the road between the two villages but instead followed the shoreline. I had never walked that path before, and it was actually rather pretty. The water murmured as it passed us, flowing the opposite way we traveled.

The grass that grew there was long and golden-green. Its stalks and leaves tickled my legs as I passed through the denser patches. The land started to climb under our feet and, when Riverside was almost in sight, we came to the cliffs.

For the first time, I realized that there were places in The Land of the Clan that I had never been to. If I had seen those cliffs before, I would have remembered them.

They weren't that high, maybe twenty-five feet above the water. Astra walked right up to the edge and looked down. I wasn't scared of heights particularly, but I exercised more caution as I approached.

Cole had stepped up beside Astra. Joss and Rollan were looking too, but they hadn't gotten quite as close to the edge.

Kisa was standing a good ten feet back. "Don't go up there!" she called. "It's dangerous!"

Everyone ignored her.

When I looked down, I saw the smooth surface of the lake directly beneath us. About twenty feet to my right there was a natural staircase, leading down to a small spur of rock. The cliffs stretched out over part of the bay. The water below was almost perfectly calm, but I could hear small waves lapping against the base of the cliff below.

"I never knew this was here," Cole said. "It's really amazing."

Joss shrugged. "It's just a cliff."

"Yeah, but look how high up we are," Cole pointed out.

"It's not that high," I commented, remembering the climb we had taken in The Valley of the North Wind. That journey seemed like it had taken place in a different lifetime.

THE PREPARATIONS

"What's the water like down there?" Astra wondered aloud, ignoring our conversation. Her eyes were studying the glittering surface below.

"It's part of the lake," Joss said. "Some of us swam over here once. There's a place to climb out and do some fishing under the cliff."

"Is the water deep?" she asked.

"Yeah, I'd say it's at least fifteen feet."

Astra nodded, not lifting her eyes. "Any rocks down there?"

"It's a cliff; it's made of rocks," Rollan cut in.

"No, I meant in the water. It looks pretty clear, and I don't see any."

Joss came to stand beside Astra and glanced down where she was looking. "I don't remember any," he told her.

"Perfect." There was an excited light in Astra's eyes.

"Wait," I said, finally figuring out what she was getting at. "You are not thinking of jumping, are you?"

She gave me a smile so full of mischief she could have been six years old. "The real question is, why aren't the rest of you?"

I was speechless. "Because it's a really bad idea," Cole declared.

"It's dangerous," Kisa called again. She was still five feet back. Her eyes were huge as she watched those of us standing on the brink of the cliff.

"Life is dangerous," Astra said. "Getting up in the morning is dangerous; riding a horse is dangerous; the trials are going to be dangerous."

I couldn't argue with that.

"It's still a *really* bad idea," Cole repeated.

"Why?" asked Astra.

"You could get hurt," said Cole.

"I'm not afraid," Astra told us. "It's just water down there."

"Well—" Cole started

"Please don't!" begged Kisa.

"It's all right, Kisa. I'm going to be fine," Astra promised.

"Are you sure?" Joss asked.

"Only one way to find out," said Astra softly, and then she jumped.

With her hair streaming out behind her and her hands raised over her head, she plummeted toward the blue lake. Her feet hit the water, and she vanished from sight. The clear surface below clouded with ripples and air bubbles.

I heard a choking sob from Kisa, who had come to stand beside me on the rocky edge. The rest of us held our breath, waiting.

A moment later, Astra's head and shoulders emerged from the water. She let out a long gasp, sucking in air.

No one moved on top of the cliff. Astra tilted her head back and looked up at us.

"Come on down," she called.

I didn't really think anyone else would jump, but I was proven wrong a moment later by Joss.

"Might as well," he said to no one in particular before taking a running start and hurling himself from the cliff top.

Kisa screamed as Joss's head disappeared underwater, but he was back up a moment later. "It's not that bad," he announced. "Come on, Rollan!" he called.

Rollan looked doubtful. Cole met my eyes. He was serious at first, but then his lips broke into a smile, and I knew he was going to jump. Until that moment, I hadn't even considered jumping myself; it had not crossed my mind once.

But as Cole joined those in the water, I knew I would have to steel myself and prove that I was not afraid.

I took a small step closer to the edge of the cliff. It was a long way down. Part of me really wanted to jump. The water looked refreshing, and the day was hot. Plus, I wasn't that bad of a swimmer. I readied myself for the jump.

But my feet wouldn't do it. I couldn't make them let go of the cliff. *Some of us must have stronger survival instincts than others,* I mused to myself.

THE PREPARATIONS

"Are you going to jump?" Kisa asked.

"Yes," I told her.

She looked at me miserably. Rollan was preparing to jump too. "I don't want to be up here alone," she told us.

There was my way out. I could help Kisa find a way down to join the rest, and I wouldn't have to jump. But I wanted to. I wanted to be like Astra and Joss and Cole, who were willing to forget for a moment that they were mortal.

"See if you can a find a way down, and then you can swim with us," I directed Kisa.

She nodded unhappily and started to scramble down the cliff toward the water. I turned to Rollan. "Going to do it?" I asked.

He nodded. "You?"

"I think so." I stepped back up to the edge of the cliff, but again, my feet would not leave the ground. "Rollan," I said.

"Yes?"

"Can you do me a favor?"

He came over to me. "Sure, what do you need?"

I lowered my voice. There wasn't anyone else on the cliff, but sound had a funny way of carrying among the rocks. "Can you give me a push?" I asked.

He looked surprised by my request. "Are you sure?"

I nodded. "Don't tell anyone, but I can't seem to get my feet off the ground."

He laughed softly. "It'll be our secret," he said.

I turned and faced the water. My heart was beating faster than it ever had before. The anticipation was worse than trying to jump. After about two seconds I was ready to tell Rollan that I had changed my mind, when suddenly I felt his hand on my shoulder, and then there was no more ground beneath me.

I had the presence of mind to keep my feet pointed down as I fell. I had never felt an adrenalin rush as powerful as I did at that moment. It seemed to take forever and no longer than a heartbeat. A scream of pure exhilaration left my lips as I fell.

THE CLIFFS

I was still screaming when I hit the water. It closed over my head. There was one brief moment where I panicked, but before it could take hold of me completely, I pushed it away. Before jumping, I had known I would hit the water and had already told myself what to do. *Hold your breath and swim up.*

I did exactly that, but it felt like ages before I broke the surface and was able to take a mouthful of air. The others crowded around me then, whooping in excitement.

A moment later, I spotted Kisa. She had climbed more than half way down the cliff and was on another, smaller ledge. After a brief pause she jumped the remaining ten feet into the water.

That just left Rollan. I looked back up at the cliff, feeling very grateful that I had not been the last one left up top. It took him longer than the rest of us. We must have spent twenty minutes calling up encouragements before he finally braced himself and jumped.

It was a wonderful day. Several times we climbed the cliffs and jumped again. I didn't need to be pushed anymore, which made the experience even better.

However, every time my head went under the water, I still had to fight the panic, but it got easier as the day went on. It felt like I had learned more about swimming in one afternoon than on all my training days combined.

Before, I had been nervous about getting in the water and had hated putting my head under. All that had changed in the span of only four hours. I began to love the weightless feeling of floating and the soft way the water received me every time I leapt into it.

We even got Kisa to jump from the top. She had only been able to do it by holding Joss's hand on one side and Cole's hand on the other. Astra had counted down for them, and I was fairly certain she had been more pulled than willingly escorted, but afterwards, in the water, she had been so pleased with herself that no one had mentioned it.

THE PREPARATIONS

I can't say how much that day actually counted for training, but it was the first time we had all felt like friends.

"Maybe we should have fun together more often," I said to Cole as we walked back to The Paramount.

Astra and Rollan were with us. "I agree," Cole said. "Today was one of the best I've ever had."

"Certainly the best since the trials were announced," Rollan put in.

I nodded in agreement. It was nice to be able to put away all our worries and just act like children again for a little while.

"I bet no other team has ever trained like that before," Rollan added.

"I bet you're right," Astra agreed. "Although, I would find it hard to believe we were the first people to have jumped from those cliffs."

"Really?" Cole asked.

"Come on," Astra said. "I'm sure they have seen their fair share of jumpers. Not that anyone would talk about it because then, I'm sure, the council would make a rule against it."

"You're probably right," Cole mused. He looked worried, like he was wondering if we shouldn't have jumped just because the council might not have liked it.

"It is their job to keep us safe," I pointed out.

"Why?" asked Astra. "I knew the risks when I jumped. Why should they be able to say, 'no, you can't do that'?"

"We owe it to our people to be useful members of this society," I told her.

"Learn that in school, did you?" Astra wondered scornfully.

"Yes, I did," I announced. "That's where I learned a lot of stuff, instead of in some smelly, old stable."

The moment it was out of my mouth, I wished I hadn't said it. Making personal jibes at a member of my team was probably not a good idea. Especially, when she was the second leader, and I was the third.

But Astra surprised me by laughing. "Fair enough," she conceded. I got the feeling she didn't really agree, but she was in too good of a mood to argue.

Rollan and Astra left us once we reached The Paramount. As we said goodbye, I realized I was actually sorry to see Astra go. Even if we had bickered a little, that was ok. We had made up afterwards.

Maybe that's how real relationships were supposed to be: fighting and then becoming friends again. Cole and I fought sometimes, but I had always liked Cole so I hadn't thought it counted.

Myna and I were different. We fought plenty but never made up. Was it too late to start? Perhaps we could salvage what was left of our relationship after all.

Chapter 28

A TEAM

E verything was better after our day at the cliffs. I actually looked forward to getting up and meeting my team each morning, instead of seeing it as a duty to be endured.

A shift had been made. We stopped worrying so much about training and started enjoying ourselves. There were no more fights—a few disagreements, maybe—but nothing major. Even Astra didn't frustrate me as much as usual.

A couple days later, something woke me before it was even light outside. I lay still for a moment, wondering what had disturbed my rest. Then I heard someone moving in the main room. Why had Myna been out so late? The teams were chosen. What could the council possibly be doing at such an hour?

After a few minutes of tossing and turning, I gave up. Slowly, I got out of bed and walked to the door. I hadn't seen Myna in days, maybe she would actually be willing to talk to me. Still wearing nothing but the tank top and shorts I slept in, I opened my door just in time to see Myna vanish into her own room.

I sighed inwardly. Instead of knocking, I went to the main door and glanced outside. It was just before daybreak. Most of the stars still dotted the navy-blue sky above. Dressing was an easy thing. It was probably going to be hot again that day, so I pulled on a sleeveless, light red tunic and a pair of dark red shorts that cut off just above my knees.

Try as I might, I couldn't loiter around the dwelling very long. I hated how cold and isolated it always felt. Nothing good had ever happened to me there. Almost all the pleasant memories of my early years were in other people's dwellings with other people's families.

I threw a handful of nuts, some meat, and a piece of dried fruit together for my lunch. Without bothering to eat more than a chunk of cheese, I headed out, leaving my dwelling wrapped in shadows.

The Paramount was still sleeping for the most part. The sky was streaked with indigo and pink. I headed over to Cole's dwelling to see if they had lit their lamps. All was dark when I arrived.

Standing in front of his dwelling seemed awkward to me, so I headed to our normal spot, the town center. No one else was there; even the council building was still and silent.

I leaned against one of the posts holding up the village bell and waited.

We had only nine days of training left before qualifying. *Am I prepared?* I asked myself.

My thoughts drifted back over all the days of training that had passed and even to before that, when I had sat in school and daydreamed about having a place in the trials. All those days, bored in class, I'd wished to be right where I was now. I'd always felt so ready, but with the qualifier so close, I didn't feel ready at all.

I couldn't put my finger on the reason, but something was standing in my way. It was as if there was some unfinished business I had to attend to before I would be free to start the trials.

Is it Myna? I wondered.

I will talk to her. I'll find time and we'll talk, really talk. If I can get along with Astra, I can probably get along with Myna too.

I glanced at the sky; the sun was starting to rise. I was growing chilly from standing still so long. It had seemed foolish for me to bring a jacket. I might want it for the first half hour, but after that, it would simply be another object for me to lug around the rest of the day, along with my lunch pack and knife.

We were going to spend the morning training at Treescape, so I started walking toward the western edge of the village. It was still early, but if I traveled slowly, Cole could catch up. I always beat him to our meeting spot. When he saw I wasn't waiting, he would know that I had already headed out. It wouldn't be the first time I'd left before him and he'd caught me on the road.

After I'd covered a quarter mile, I gave up walking slowly. My shoes were drenched in dew, and my feet felt cold. I picked up a steady jog, trying to get my blood flowing.

The land was always the most beautiful at that early hour. The long shadows stretched out before me as I headed west, and I could feel the sun at my back. Soon, it would be uncomfortably hot on my skin, but for now, it was just a light caress with only the smallest hint of warmth. A thin layer of mist was rising from the ground, and dew sparkled on every leaf and blade of grass.

A few other contenders passed me on the road. I also saw numerous horses and riders. Those from The North Wind were already on the move. I was pretty certain Astra typically got up early and helped with the morning chores at the stable before joining us.

I wondered if Astra had ever considered asking for a transfer once she reached the appropriate age. Truth be told, she was far too good for that place. Although, she did seem to like it well enough, so maybe not. However, once she got older, her feelings might change.

As I reached Treescape, it was just starting to stir. Contenders wearing forest green clothing were trickling out on the roads to the other villages.

I went to wait at the crossroads where all the paths merged into one. To my surprise, Astra was there already.

"You're early," she said when she saw me.

"Look who's talking," I fired back. She was almost never early.

THE PREPARATIONS

"Yeah, well, I ended up bringing a couple horses over this morning, and I figured it was stupid to walk halfway back to The North Wind and then turn around."

"Makes sense," I replied.

Just then, Ashlo and Larna's team passed us, heading toward the training area.

"Should we wait for everyone else or go see if Rollan's around?" Astra wondered as the six contenders, all of them girls, passed us.

"Let's go get Rollan," I suggested. He had pointed out his dwelling to us on our last visit, and I was pretty sure I remembered where it was.

As we approached what we thought was his dwelling, the door swung open and six boys came tumbling through it. They were Rollan and his brothers. A woman's harsh voice emanated from the dwelling they'd left, splitting the morning air.

"Get out!" she shouted. "And don't come back until there's no more day left. I've had enough with your bickering, and I'm sick and tired of your—" The door slammed then, and I never found out whatever it was that she was sick and tired of.

Rollan didn't see Astra and me right away, and his brothers didn't pay us any attention. They were all big. The oldest two were pushing six-foot, and the next pair weren't far behind. Rollan was going to have some catching up to do. He was a good head and shoulders shorter than they were. Even the last one, the youngest, was almost as tall as Rollan.

As we approached, one of the biggest brothers gave Rollan a hard shove. He stumbled a few steps and ended up on his knees. The other boys laughed. "Hey stupid," the brother yelled. "Too weak to fight back?"

I glanced at Astra and saw my fury reflected in her eyes. As one, we marched forward purposefully.

Rollan had regained his feet just in time to get shoved back down by another brother. "Stay there, last leader," that one spat at him. "You shouldn't bother with training this morning. You're worthless to your team anyway."

"He is not!" I practically screamed. Astra and I were right in front of the group now. The brothers turned to look at us.

Rollan, forgotten by his brothers for a moment, managed to get up. His eyes were wary.

His fear made my blood boil. Even with five of the largest boys I had ever met staring down at me in cruel amusement, I didn't feel afraid. After all those hours of combat training, I was almost hoping they would start something.

It was a stupid thought. Sure, I probably knew more tactics than all of them put together, but at some point, size and brute strength cancel out skill. However, in the heat of the moment, all I felt was exhilaration, like I was jumping off that cliff again. My voice was calm and steady.

"Rollan is immensely important to us, and we will thank you not to lay another hand on him," I told them.

The biggest boy, a man really, too old to be a contender, laughed. "Well, if it isn't a little wench from The Paramount," he chortled.

I choked down my outrage. 'Wench' was one of the most derogatory words in our culture. The fact that he used it so easily proved him to be nothing but a vile coward.

"Come to quote us some rules?" the next largest boy asked me. He was by far the ugliest. His face was covered in acne and lumpy, red boils.

"She probably will," Astra said, standing on my left. She sounded utterly untroubled by the five hulking boys before us. "But, if I was you, I'd listen to her. Especially, since all she has to do is ask her mother nicely and all of you will be given a mark or two."

I cringed inwardly; I had no such power. Myna didn't care who I thought deserved marks. The brothers exchanged nervous glances. "Not if she doesn't make it back in one piece," the oldest boy hissed.

Suddenly, I laughed. Those boys were nothing but bullies. I doubted they were brave enough to lay a finger on us after what Astra had said. And if they thought idle threats were going to work, then they were stupider than I imagined.

Astra chuckled too but not as loudly. "I have faced down stallions twice the size of all of you put together. Do you really think I am going to be frightened by your childish attempt at intimidation?"

The brothers looked even more uncertain. I supposed they were used to getting whatever they wanted. Having two girls stand up to them must have been something entirely new.

All five seemed to be slowly trying to work out exactly how far they wanted to go. The oldest one seemed ready to walk away. Two of the smaller ones appeared ready to charge, but neither of them were brave enough to be the first to act. The youngest was leering at us, and the ugly one just looked confused.

Everything was still undecided when Cole, Joss, and Kisa joined us.

"Hey guys, we've been looking all over for you," Cole called.

Joss took in the scene at once. He was probably used to his cousins' unruly behavior. He instantly went to Rollan's side and brought him to stand beside the rest of us. Kisa seemed to sense the tension in the air. Cole remained the only one oblivious to what was about to explode right in front of him.

"You all must be Rollan's brothers," Cole said, holding his hand out to the oldest. "I'm Cole."

The brother looked at Cole's hand and then at the rest of our team. I could see him trying not to use his fingers as he counted up the numbers for and against. Finally, he must have figured out that excluding Kisa, who wouldn't have been useful at all in a fight, we had the same number he did.

He turned and stalked away from us, leaving Cole's hand still extended. The other boys followed him wordlessly until just our team was left.

"That was odd," Cole said, lowering his hand.

I let out a sigh of relief. Rollan wouldn't meet anyone's eyes. He turned and walked away towards the training area. The rest of us followed at a slight distance. Cole kept glancing around, still trying to figure out what he had missed.

Astra was looking after Rollan. She seemed just as frustrated as I was with the situation. However, there was nothing we could say or do to make life better for our friend.

Even though she didn't know exactly what had happened, Kisa ran to catch up with Rollan. I was worried she would say something foolish, but all she did was take his hand. He accepted hers easily enough. Joss walked up on the other side of his cousin and put an arm around Rollan's shoulders. The trio led us to where we would be training for the morning.

After a few hours, Rollan was almost back to his usual self. Towards the end of the day I heard him ask Joss quietly if he thought it would be all right for him to stay the night in Riverside. I never really found out what kind of backlash Rollan received for our actions.

Chapter 29

MISSING

A few days after our incident with Rollan's brothers, Cole and I headed to The Barracks for our morning training. Kisa was the first to meet us there. Joss and Rollan arrived, one right after the other, a short time later. Rollan was pretty much always on time anymore.

We stood around joking while waiting for Astra. She was normally one of the last to arrive and had been sporadically late in the past, but never by more than twenty minutes.

As the sun cleared the horizon, Cole decided we would start training without her. We found a place in the arena close to Bala and Jase's team and began practicing. It seemed like I saw the pair more at The Barracks than I did at The Paramount anymore. Their first team leader must have really been having them focus on combat.

Since we couldn't pair off with an uneven number, I ended up working with Kisa, while Cole took on both Joss and Rollan.

Astra finally showed up about an hour and a half later.

"You ok?" Cole asked, halting practice when he caught sight of her.

"Fine," Astra answered quickly.

"Did you over sleep?" Joss asked lightly.

"Nope," Astra told him, seizing the nearest wooden stave and looking around like she was ready to hit something.

Astra always trained seriously, but that day was different. When she sparred against me, her staff struck mine so hard the vibrations stung my hands. I was glad she only seemed interested in aiming for my weapon and not my body.

The only person she eased up on was Kisa.

Cole didn't say anything about her odd behavior, and I followed his lead. The day drug on, and we moved to The Making at Astra's suggestion. When we got there, she seemed antsy and stood up to move around every fifteen minutes or so.

Normally, our group was one of the last to leave, but that afternoon, the minute one of the other teams called it quits for the day, Astra rose.

"See you tomorrow," she threw over her shoulder, heading for the door.

"Wait," Cole said, scrambling to follow her, but she didn't stop. "We'll be at The Barracks again in the morning," he called at her retreating figure before sitting back down with the rest of us.

I glanced at where Astra had been working. The sewing project she'd spent all afternoon on was still unfinished.

The rest of us lingered for at least another hour before ending early for the day.

"Do you know what's going with Astra?" Cole asked me as we headed to The Paramount. The five of us were all going in the same direction, but Joss, Kisa, and Rollan had pulled ahead. They were engaged in their own conversation, so they hadn't heard Cole's question.

I shook my head. "How would I know?" I wondered.

Cole shrugged. "You two are a lot alike. I thought you might know if something was wrong."

"Alike?" I all but laughed. "How do mean?"

"You just seem to have a connection," he said. "Like with what happened to Rollan. If you two hadn't been so in sync, things could have gotten really ugly, really fast."

I had filled Cole in on the situation with Rollan when we had walked home together the evening after the incident. Once he'd known everything, he'd been worried that Rollan might face some sort of revenge for what we had done. I had agreed, but hadn't thought there was any way for us to help. Cole had suggested we go to the council and make sure that Rollan was protected until the trials started. It had been all I could do to keep him from storming the council building.

In the end, he had decided to talk to his father privately about the situation. I don't know what Core had said to him, because that had been the last I had heard of the matter.

"Astra and I are nothing alike," I told Cole flatly.

Cole didn't answer, but I could see laughter in his eyes. It was infuriating.

"I'm sure Astra will be fine by morning," I said, eagerly changing the subject. She and I had been getting along pretty well those days, but I didn't like Cole comparing us. I was Myra, and she was Astra.

When we reached The Paramount, the others each went their own way. Once it was just the two of us, Cole turned to me again. "I think our progress has been very good. Hopefully, we are completely ready for qualifying and then for the trials."

I nodded at his assessment. "We are a fairly well-balanced team."

"I couldn't agree more with that," Cole replied.

"Kisa is a weak link," I admitted. "I'm worried about how she'll handle the trials."

Cole frowned. "What do you mean?"

"She's very young," I reminded him, "and bound to be homesick."

"We'll have to help her get through that," Cole said. "You're not worried about how she'll do during qualifying?"

I shook my head. "She's pretty bright. Even if her nerves get to her, we only need four people to make it through. You, myself, and Astra shouldn't have any problems. So, as long as one of the others makes it through, our team will still pass."

"We don't even know what we have to do to qualify, and you're already certain we'll pass."

I nodded. "Of course."

Cole laughed. "Your confidence in our team is inspiring."

I smiled but didn't tell him it wasn't really confidence. More than anything else, it was that I needed what I said to be true. We had to complete qualifying, just as I had to win the trials.

We parted ways, and I went to my dwelling. Half of me was hoping I might find Myna there, but the other half was hoping not to.

When I opened the door, I found the place empty. To my surprise, I was disappointed and was forced to admit that I had more than just half hoped.

Instead of remaining inside, my feet carried me to the amphitheater. I sat for a while, watching the sun sink behind The Paramount.

I tried not to think about anything, allowing my mind to clear. The evening was warm and pleasant. Crickets and cicadas were in the long grass all around. The sound of their chirping had a calming effect. For nearly an hour, I did nothing but sit and listen. Only once twilight was settling on the land, did I rise and head back to The Paramount.

Astra was late again the following day. I knew Cole was displeased, but he didn't say anything. All morning Astra's mind was elsewhere. She didn't initiate conversation with anyone, and none of us could get more than one or two words out of her.

"Can we go to Riverside and go swimming?" Kisa asked when we were having our midday meal.

"That would be great," Joss put in, his mouth stuffed with food.

"Well..." Cole considered.

"If we are going to waste time messing around, I would like to be excused," Astra announced. It was the first time she'd spoken in hours. Everyone turned to stare at her. That one sentence was more than she had said all day.

"Why?" Cole asked.

Astra didn't answer. Her lunch was set out before her, untouched.

"Myra," Cole said. I turned to look at him. "Why don't you take everyone to The Quarry? I think it might be best to spend the afternoon practicing crafting arrow heads."

I nodded and glanced at Joss, Rollan, and Kisa. They had mostly finished their food. "Let's go," I told them, quickly wrapping up the remains of my lunch.

I knew Cole was going to talk to Astra, but I doubted he'd get very far.

The four of us had gone less than a mile when Astra and Cole caught up. I glanced at Cole as he fell into step beside me; he just shook his head. Astra trailed behind us the entire way.

Making arrowheads was tedious and not much fun, but everyone pitched in with a will, even Astra. She seemed to find something satisfying in grinding the two rocks together until one was razor sharp.

Astra didn't abandon us early that day, even when other teams started to leave. Instead, she kept on doggedly until Cole decided we were done for the day.

"Tomorrow, we'll have a half day," he announced. "In the morning, we can start at The Golden Fields and then call it quits after lunch. The day after, we'll do more practicing at The Barracks."

"Great!" said Joss.

Kisa and Rollan looked pleased as well. Astra stared straight ahead, like she hadn't heard. The moment Cole finished speaking, she turned on her heel and was gone.

Once we started our journey to The Paramount, I asked, "So, what did Astra say?"

"She told me she didn't want to talk about it," Cole replied. "I don't understand. If something's wrong, I'd like to help, but she won't let me."

THE PREPARATIONS

I sighed. How could I explain to him that there were some problems no one could help you with, and you just needed to work them out on your own?

At least Astra wasn't late in the morning. However, she looked like she hadn't slept at all the night before.

"Are you ok?" Kisa asked softly, while the rest of us were waiting for Joss and Rollan.

"Yes," Astra replied. She didn't speak the rest of the morning. Kisa, who was quizzing us on the different plants and trees, never addressed any questions directly to her.

As soon as we all sat down to have our lunch, Astra headed out. No one called after her.

Cole and I were silent for much of our journey back to The Paramount. The sun was directly overhead, and it was very hot. I would have been happy to go to my dwelling and seek shade and, possibly, a nap; however, once we reached the village, Cole suddenly seemed ready for a conversation.

"Can we talk?" he asked.

I nodded. He headed over to the woodpile and sat down with his back against it, just as he had the day we had discussed returning to The Valley of the North Wind.

"Do you feel ready?" he wondered.

I plopped down on a small log facing him. "What do you mean?" I asked.

"The trials are starting so soon, and I don't feel ready. I thought I would, but I don't. Do you think the team likes me? Do you think they trust me?" The uncertainty in Cole's voice was almost tangible.

I sighed inwardly. Cole was an intelligent and able person, but he needed so much reassurance sometimes. I didn't know why he worried about what other people thought. As far as I knew, there wasn't a single person who had ever disliked him.

"Cole," I began seriously, "you need to stop stressing." He looked at me with surprise. "We all want to trust you, but you don't trust yourself. You don't know exactly what will happen;

none of us do. What you need to do is believe that no matter what we face, we will find a way to overcome it."

It took a moment for him to digest what I had said. "You're right," Cole sighed. "There are only four more days to train. That's it; that's all we have."

"It doesn't matter," I told him. "We could have four hundred more days and you'd still be second-guessing yourself. Why?"

Cole looked down at his hands, which were resting in his lap. "I just—I mean, I never expected to be in the trials." He glanced up, and I could see traces of panic in his eyes. "Of course, I always knew it was a possibility, but I never really gave it a moment's thought."

Well, that makes one of us.

"Then they announced the preparations, and I was excited, but terrified at the same time. You know?"

I nodded, even though I didn't understand at all.

"I want to do this," he said. "I want to lead and be good at it." He paused and shook his head miserably. "You said Kisa was the weak link, the only one who's likely to get homesick, but you're wrong. I'm already horribly homesick. I can't imagine walking through The Valley of the North Wind in a couple days, knowing I might never return."

I couldn't believe what I was hearing. Well, actually I could. Cole had never known loneliness or fear. He'd never had to hope that by proving himself to be the very best, he might be able to win the love and respect of a parent. His whole life he'd been happy and accepted. Why would anyone ever want to leave that?

"Cole, we are going to come back," I assured him. "All of us."

There was desperation in his blue eyes. He really wanted to believe me, but he feared the worst.

THE PREPARATIONS

"I understand the stress is getting to you, but really, you need to get it together. We are all counting on you, and if you lead us, we will succeed."

He laughed a little. "Thanks for not adding any more pressure."

"That's not what I meant," I retorted. "Come on, this really isn't a big deal. It's going to be just like what we do every day. Meet with our team and learn new things."

Cole nodded. "You're right. I wish they had made you team leader," he murmured.

I smiled. *If only.*

"Well, they didn't," I replied. "So, you're just going to have to start trusting yourself and stop doubting your abilities. It's not helpful to anyone."

"I'll try," Cole promised.

"Good," I said. "Now, what are we going to do about Astra?"

Cole shrugged. "No clue. She won't talk about what's wrong. Maybe she's feeling the same way I am."

I shook my head. Astra didn't really have any reason to be nervous. She didn't have a family to try to impress. The entirety of The Clan wasn't watching her like it was watching Cole and me. Plus, it seemed that most of her village really didn't even want her to participate.

"It could be that guy," I proposed.

"No," Cole replied quickly, too quickly.

"What makes you think it isn't?" I wondered.

"It just seems unlikely."

"Ok, well what do *you* think is wrong?"

"I already told you," he said. "Nerves." I shook my head as he continued. "Tomorrow, if she's still upset, we'll have to make her talk about it."

As if, I thought.

***

His plan was foiled the following day because Astra didn't show up at all. We spent the morning at The Golden Fields. No one said anything about Astra's absence. We continued training until a little after lunch, in the hopes that she might join us, but she never appeared. By early afternoon, we gave up.

"Let's go swimming," Joss suggested to Kisa and Rollan, when Cole announced we were done for the day.

"Yeah!" Kisa exclaimed. "That would be fun!"

Rollan nodded eagerly. I was sure he would be happy to do anything that kept him away from his dwelling. We had that much in common.

"Cole, Myra, you guys should come too," Joss told us.

I couldn't help smiling. It was nice to have friends, friends who didn't want anything from you but the pleasure of your company.

"I'm in," I told him. Cole agreed to join as well.

We didn't go back to the cliffs, but we did have a nice afternoon splashing around the lake.

Core happened to be in Riverside; Cole and I ran into him as we were heading back to The Paramount. I felt slightly self-conscious walking along beside the First Clan Leader, my hair dripping wet and my soaked clothing clinging to my skin.

Core asked a lot of questions about how our training was going and what we thought of our teammates. Cole did nearly all the talking. He gave his father a detailed account of our activities, but I noticed he didn't mention anything about Astra's recent absence.

Eventually, the conversation turned to Cole's brothers and other topics I wasn't really interested in. It wasn't until near the end of the conversation that I began to pay attention again.

I wasn't sure how they got on the subject, but Core said, "I'm really going to miss you when you leave in a few days."

"Don't worry about me; I'll be fine," Cole promised. "I've got Myra to look after me."

Both of them smiled, and I blushed.

"I am thankful for that," Core said, looking in my direction. "Make sure you keep him well fed or he'll get whiney."

"Good to know," I laughed.

"It'll be strange after the contenders leave," Core mused, almost to himself. "The Paramount is going to seem so empty." It was true; nearly every child of The Paramount had been placed on a team. Rasby and a few of the youngest children would be the only ones left behind.

It was almost dark when I entered my dwelling. We had stayed at Riverside with our teammates a long time.

To my surprise, Myna was there. Her door was closed, but I could tell from the light coming through the crack at the bottom that she had a candle burning. I approached quietly and lifted my hand to knock, wondering if she would admit to missing me, as Cole's father had to him.

Probably not, I told myself. After a short consideration, my courage deserted me, and I lowered my hand.

Not tonight, I thought, *but soon.*

Chapter 30

FINDING

Our team met up at The Barracks the following day as planned. Because there were only three days left to train, Cole wanted everyone in top physical shape.

I kept expecting Astra to arrive at any moment, but she didn't.

"This is ridiculous," Rollan muttered to Joss as we had to break into uneven groups for sparring. Joss just shrugged, like he hadn't given it much thought.

Cole pursed his lips but didn't say anything. Honestly, I found sparring two on one a great way to practice. It was a challenge for me to ward off two attackers. I also got the experience of working with a partner against a single foe.

After we'd been training for a couple hours, Cole pulled me aside. "Don't hate me, Myra," he began, "but I need you to go find Astra."

My mouth dropped open. "What?"

"I can't go. She didn't want to talk to me last time, and I can't imagine that has changed," he explained.

"What makes you think I can do any better?" I asked.

Cole gave me a long, steady look. "Because you understand how people think. You did an amazing job with Rollan, and I know you can do the same with Astra."

I sighed. He was going back to that 'we had a connection thing', and I didn't want to hear it.

"How am I supposed to find her?" I wondered.

"Head north, I imagine," Cole told me with an impish grin.

"You—" I started.

"Please, Myra," Cole said, completely serious. "Please do this, for me."

How could I say no to that? I nodded. "Alright."

"Thanks," he said, before heading back to the others.

I spent the rest of the morning walking to The North Wind. I actually jogged quite a bit of it. The huge fields were filled with golden grass and flowers of nearly every color. The trees, growing in small clumps, were clothed in young leaves.

The path was deserted, as was most of The North Wind once I reached the village. Not a single team was training there that day.

I headed into the main stable where Cole and I had found Astra before. The place was nearly deserted. I didn't see Astra or find any clue of where she might have been.

Moving on, I entered another stable. That one seemed to be filled with mares and their foals. It was much smaller and didn't take me very long to search, but I still found nothing useful.

I tried another, and, as I walked by the first couple of stalls, I passed a figure in black.

Disappointment filled me as I realized it was only Astra's friend, Gann, and not Astra herself. However, I decided that he might be useful, since he could probably tell me where Astra was and why she had been playing hooky from training.

A plan formed suddenly in my mind. Even if Gann didn't want to tell me anything, I'd have to coax the truth out of him. Astra was going to be ten times harder to crack, so her friend would be a good warm up.

I approached Gann from behind. He was filling a row of wooden buckets with feed and didn't notice me until I was standing right next to the one he was about to fill.

He started a little when he saw me. "Oh, it's you," he said, looking slightly relieved. He dumped the scoop of grain into the bucket, and then turned back to the feed box to get another.

"Yes," I replied, and then waited. From his reaction to my presence, I had a feeling he knew exactly why I was there, and I was willing to let him do the talking.

It took several minutes for him to start, but I knew how to be patient, whatever the archery instructor had said. Gann was nearly finished with the row of buckets by the time he finally spoke again.

"She's not here," he told me, and then paused, as if hoping I would just walk away.

I didn't.

He filled the last bucket, dropped the scoop into the feed box, closed the lid, and turned to face me.

"Astra didn't go to training yesterday because she was treating a sick horse," Gann explained.

I should have figured. Nothing mattered more to her than her horses. "Is that why she's been in such a bad mood for the past three days?" I asked.

Gann nodded.

"Is the horse still sick?" I pressed.

"No," Gann said softly. "He died last night."

Great, Astra was going to be even more of a head case, and qualifying was in three days.

"Horses must die all the time," I pointed out. "Why is Astra so upset about this one?"

Gann was quiet for a long moment. "It was Rickie," he told me.

"Oh." I didn't know what else to say. I wasn't very good at telling one horse from another, but I sort of remembered seeing a golden horse that had gone by that name.

"Was he special to Astra?" I inquired.

"He was the first horse she trained on her own," Gann replied.

I was silent as I considered what the best plan of action would be.

THE PREPARATIONS

"If she's not here and she's not at The Barracks with the rest of our team, then, where is she?" I wondered.

Gann didn't answer. Completely ignoring direct questions must have been a special skill learned by those of The North Wind.

"Is she in the valley?" I guessed.

Gann gave me a shocked look. "What?" he gasped.

"Is she in The Valley of the North Wind?" I repeated slowly, so he could keep up.

Gann didn't answer, but I was pretty sure my suspicions were correct. I turned and began to march out of the stable. Gann caught me by one of my shoulders and pulled me to a halt.

"Where are you going?" he hissed at me, glancing around to see if anyone else was paying attention to our conversation.

"I'm going to find Astra," I told him evenly.

"You can't go into the valley after her; you aren't allowed," he whispered to me.

I smiled. "So, she *is* in the valley."

Gann was speechless, again. It seemed to be a common ailment for the poor fellow. I twisted out of his grasp and started to walk away. Not too quickly though; I wasn't quite done with Gann yet.

"Wait," he called after me.

Suppressing a smile, I turned to face him. "Yes?"

He nodded over his shoulder to a less-peopled part of the building. I sighed, wishing he had chosen somewhere outside to talk. I hated the stable's filthy odor, which was sure to cling to my clothes and hair for days.

Gann led me to an empty hallway and ducked into a stall. At least there wasn't a horse in it; I had no desire to be in a confined space with something large enough to squish me.

Once we were inside, I waited for Gann to speak. He kept glancing around, nervously. I tried to be patient, but I'd really had enough of all Astra's secrets, her absences, and the whole wretched, stinking village.

"Well?" I asked, looking at him expectantly.

"How much do you know?" Gann spoke softly, but with urgency.

I wanted to roll my eyes and scream. *Here we go again,* I thought. *Are all these people crazy?*

"All I know is that the trials are starting in a few days, and Astra is off sulking in The Valley of the North Wind about some horse that died—"

"Was killed," Gann interrupted.

I stopped short in confusion. "What?"

"I guess you deserve an explanation," he conceded.

Finally, I thought. *Maybe something around here will actually start making sense.*

"There were people who were very displeased when Astra started training for the trials," Gann started.

I instantly thought of Litis, yelling outside the council building almost six months ago, when she had been told that Astra was to continue training.

"It was even worse when she was actually put on a team," Gann continued. "Then, several days ago, Rickie began to act sick. Astra stayed with him as much as she could, and, for a while, he was getting better. But then she had two long days of training, and when she got back on the second day, he started to get worse."

Gann glanced around again, and then leaned in close to whisper in my ear, "We think someone poisoned him."

I was surprised to hear that. It seemed so dark. I had always gotten the impression from Astra that the people who lived in The North Wind were a tight knit group who would never betray each other. Clearly, they had some fairly ugly disagreements.

"Astra has been with him day and night since, but it was too late. He died just before dawn, and Astra took off right after."

"To the valley?"

THE PREPARATIONS

Gann nodded. "Most likely." He paused and continued in a softer voice. "There is a secret cave there that she goes to sometimes."

"A cave?" I asked. "How can I find it?"

"I don't think you should," Gann told me. "It's very dangerous—"

"Astra seems to have managed," I retorted. "I bet you didn't try to stop her."

Gann smiled; he was actually kind of cute when he smiled. "Astra will do what Astra will do. She really doesn't care what anyone else thinks."

"Well, I'm the same way," I insisted, cringing inwardly at admitting to a similarity between Astra and myself.

"Astra's been there many times," Gann said. "You..." He trailed off, unsure of my experience.

I had trusted Gann so far, but I didn't feel like incriminating myself by admitting that I had entered the valley before. I folded my arms across my chest instead.

"Then what do you suggest?" I demanded.

"She won't stay in there forever," Gann promised. "She'll be back before dark, I'm sure."

His words didn't convince me. "Just tell me how to find the cave," I ordered. He sighed, clearly wondering whether to help me or not. "I'm going either way," I told him. "It'll be a lot easier if you tell me where it is."

That decided him. "Right," he muttered. "Here's the valley entrance." He held up his right hand in front of him. "Where the path splits for the first time, take the left path." He stretched his left arm forward.

I nodded, remembering that the right path lead to nothing but dead ends anyway. "When you come to the third turn-off on the left, take it. The cave is at the end. You'll have to look up to see it."

"Great, thanks," I said, ready to leave.

"Astra's very upset," Gann told me almost guiltily. "Try to help her."

I nodded and left the stall.

"Please be careful," he called after me.

A few minutes later, I was out of the stable, in the fresh air, and trying to decide if I was really going to enter The Valley of the North Wind alone.

No one was anywhere in sight by the time I reached the trailhead. I glanced around, unsure of myself. It had been so easy to act brave in front of Gann. He was such an idiot. It had been easy to make him believe that I knew everything about The Valley of The North Wind.

Either that or he thought Astra and I were good friends and I would be able to help her. If he knew the real relationship between the two of us, he probably wouldn't have been so helpful. Truth be told, in the last few weeks, we had been getting along really well. We weren't friends exactly, but we didn't seem to be adversaries either. I had a bad feeling though that if I did or said the wrong thing now, we would be enemies forever.

If only Cole had come instead of me. Not that he would have ever been able to get Gann to tell him anything. Gann clearly had strong feelings for Astra and, probably, was already a little jealous of Cole for being assigned to her team. I couldn't imagine he would hand Cole directions on how to find Astra in a secret cave. Since Gann seemed to know Astra so well, I was a little surprised he hadn't gone after her himself. But maybe he couldn't get away since he was an adult instead of a contender.

Still, I was probably the very worst person to try to talk to Astra. If Cole hadn't been so far away, I would have considered just telling him where she was and making him talk some sense into her. But, I was already there, and he was at The Barracks.

I sighed and took a step forward into the valley. Even though it was a warm day, I could feel the cold chill emanating from the rocks that surrounded me as soon as I entered. Shud-

THE PREPARATIONS

dering, I thought of what Astra had said about the dead being able to talk in the valley.

It certainly felt like the kind of place where someone could be watching you. I tried not to think about the skull I was sure I had seen on my last visit.

Calm down, I told myself, very thankful that I still had tons of daylight and knew where I was going. Wandering around the valley at night would be enough to frighten anyone. I supposed that was what must have happened to Golla. Her mother had said she hadn't returned the night before her body was found.

I wondered if she was present—her spirit at least. I knew her was buried at The Golden Fields, but the rest of her, the part that was freed when her body had died, surely that had gone somewhere. Would she be mad at me? Did she hate me? If not for what I had told her, she would still be alive.

Trying not to think about Golla or anything else, I hurried forward. Every sound still made me jump, and my heart thundered in my chest. The wind began to pick up, and I quickened my steps. By the time I made it to the first split, I was practically running. Without pausing, I turned to the left and started looking for turn-offs.

As the path grew wider, I saw the first one. I was sprinting now. Not the smartest decision, but I couldn't help it. Rocks kept coming loose for no reason, and the clattering they made as they fell from the cliffs and crags above was unnerving. Plus, if there was going to be a landslide, I'd rather it be behind me and not on top of me.

Finally, I reached the third turn-off. I slowed down and caught my breath before taking it. I didn't want Astra to know how nervous I had been. When I could again breathe without gasping, I marched forward. The turn-off was not long, and soon, I found the end of the path. Towering stonewalls were before me, making it impossible to keep going.

I did not see a cave. I looked up and all around as I came to a halt.

"Astra," I called softly, in case my voice was shaky. It wasn't too bad, so I called again, stronger. "Astra? Are you here?"

There was no answer. I was still looking for the cave, turning in circles in case I had missed it. I called again, as loud as I could. "Astra!"

My voice echoed off the rocks, and a few stones began to fall from above.

A voice behind me made me jump. "Shhhh! You'll cause a rockslide."

Chapter 31

THE CAVE

It was Astra. She was standing on a ledge about ten feet above my head.

"What are you doing here?" she asked sharply, but in a low tone.

Having a leisurely walk, was the retort that rose to my lips, but I bit the words back. "Looking for you," I told her instead.

"How did you know I'd be here?" Astra was calmer than I had expected, but she was clearly not pleased to see me. That wasn't a big surprise.

"Your boyfriend told me," I informed her.

Astra made a face and sighed, "Of course he did. What do you want?"

"To talk," I stated.

Astra stared at me for a long moment. I was pretty sure she was trying to decide if there was a way to get rid of me without talking. Considering the great lengths I had just gone through to find her, there was nothing she could have done that would have made me leave without speaking my mind. She must have recognized my determination because after a moment of deliberation, she said, "Come." Then she turned and disappeared from view.

I scrambled up the rocks as best I could and, finally, caught sight of the cave. If I hadn't known it was there, there was no way I would have ever found it. I could have searched The Valley of the North Wind for a year, and I still never would have suspected what was behind the stones right in front of me.

THE PREPARATIONS

I crouched to enter the mouth of the cave. When I straightened on the other side, my jaw dropped. The entrance was low and narrow, so I had expected the cave to be small and dark. It was neither. The walls rose at least sixty feet above my head. There was a large, jagged hole in the roof, and sunlight was streaming down onto a pool of water.

The liquid was crystal clear, and I could see the bed of stones underneath, which was the most breathtaking thing of all. The stones were brilliant in color, some dark green, others pale red. I saw blues and purples also—too many colors to count. They sparkled beneath the water, throwing rainbow-colored flecks of light across the dark gray walls of the cave.

"This is amazing," I breathed.

"I know," Astra said, retreating to a corner where a number of large rocks formed natural seats. She plopped down on one and stared out at the pool without seeming to see anything.

"This is it, isn't it?" I asked. "The place where you're supposed to be able to talk to the dead."

"Yes, it's one of them." Astra's voice was even. "Supposedly, this is a place where the dead still speak."

"That old woman you told us about, did you find her here?" I pressed.

Astra shook her head. "No, I found her—somewhere else."

I closed my eyes and listened. The wind outside was just a hushed whisper, and there was the gentle murmur of trickling water from somewhere near the back of the cave, but I didn't hear any voices.

"It doesn't work, Myra," Astra warned me. "It's just a legend. The dead are gone."

"Gone where?" I asked, opening my eyes.

Astra shrugged. "I don't know. Far from here I guess. This valley—it's nothing special. What would possibly bring them here?"

"This place is beautiful," I said, moving my hand in a gesture that encompassed the entire cave.

THE CAVE

Astra gave a hard, little laugh. "There are many beautiful places, but they are just that: fair to the eye. There is nothing more."

I sighed; she was being difficult. However, I did believe that she was right. I didn't feel anything special there. Even in the valley itself, where the wind moaned through the canyons and the rocks moved even though no one touched them, I hadn't felt anything.

It was hard, but I managed to tear my eyes from the beauty of the water. I walked over and joined Astra on the rocks.

"I know why you're here," Astra admitted. "I'm sorry I missed training. I just needed some time."

"We're out of time, Astra."

She didn't answer verbally; instead, she let out a long sigh.

"Look," I began, "I know how hard it is to lose someone. He was the first horse you worked with, so he was special to you."

Astra shook her head, making her long, auburn hair fall across her face, hiding half of it from me. "He wasn't the first horse."

I furrowed my brow. "Gann said he was."

"Rickie wasn't the first horse I was given to train," Astra said softly. Her voice had a raw edge to it, and I didn't know what to say.

She was quiet for so long I didn't think she would go on, but she did. "There was another—a bright, spirited animal. He was so beautiful; the pick of the two-year-olds. So, of course, they gave him to me."

Astra's voice was bitter. "The prodigy." She paused. "Not that I didn't want him; we all did. I was the youngest. Most of the others were at least eighteen, and I hadn't even turned fifteen yet. But they gave him to me anyway."

Astra still wasn't looking at me. Her eyes were focused on the other side of the cave, as if she could see her memories written there.

"I have often wondered since that day if things would have ended differently had it fallen to another to train him." She shook her head slowly. "We can't change the past or see the path untaken."

I had never heard anyone speak about wanting to change the past, at least, not with an air of seriousness. I certainly had no desire for things to be different. I was very happy with how I had lived my life. Some unpleasant things had occurred—my father's death and Golla's, not being a first team leader, having a stranger for a mother—but those were all things I had come to recognize as out of my control. All the actions of my life had combined to make me who I was.

"They helped us, naturally." Astra's voice broke into my musing. "We had lots of instruction. I did everything right. My colt was just as good as the rest of them. Better even. Everything was smooth sailing. I spent every waking hour thinking about him, even when I couldn't be with him.

"It all seemed perfect, too perfect. Just like a dream." Astra closed her eyes as she continued. "It was the big day, when we all got to actually ride the horses we were training for the first time. We had put in six months of groundwork, but no one was supposed to have gotten on their horse yet.

"We went one at a time. The first trainer, a boy of seventeen, had this pretty little filly. He got on her and rode right off. It was flawless, like he had been riding her all along. Everyone was so pleased, so happy for him. I remember wishing that my first ride would go like that.

"The next boy, a little older, had some trouble. He got up, but his colt started bucking. The boy kept his cool and leaned back; he pulled the horse's head up, and it stopped. After a few more minutes, he got it under control. I thought, 'even if that happens, it will be ok. Every horse is different.'

"And so they went, most having only a few minor issues. Then it was my turn."

Astra opened her eyes, and they were full of unshed tears. "I got my horse into position and mounted him. He started bucking, but I told myself it was ok. I leaned back and tried to get his head up, tried to get him under control, but I couldn't.

"I told you, he was the pick of the foals. He was big and strong, and as hard as I pulled the reins, he wouldn't stop wrenching them out of my hands. He wouldn't stop bucking and rearing. I had never been thrown from a horse before, and I don't even remember hitting the ground.

"Once I was off, it still took him a while to calm down. I was horrified, but I kept it all in check. The instructors told me that it was ok to take things at my own pace. After all the others had gone and there were only a few people around, I tried to mount him again. The result was the same.

"Everyone was a little concerned. His actions were surprising. They decided to give us both more time to work together.

"I spent the next three months doing groundwork with him, but something was changing. He was growing bold and arrogant, defiant even. I tried to work past it, but I couldn't."

Astra's voice was a million miles away, reliving again the struggle she had endured. "They said he was ill-tempered at first, but it was more than that. I knew it, too. I knew it before any of them did. He wasn't right; there was something wrong with him."

She let out a long, painful sigh. "I tried to ride him again. I didn't do it when anyone was around. I hoped it would be different with just the two of us, but it wasn't. I had to jump off him, just as he threw himself to the ground, trying to crush me."

Astra shook her head slightly as she stared out across the water. "I knew that night what was going to happen. Every day he grew stronger and more dangerous. We all feared he would hurt someone or himself. He was a stallion, and sometimes they are ill-natured, but not like him. He was volatile and aggressive; so, the decision was made. He needed to be put down."

The cave was silent for a long moment, and I half wondered if she'd reached the end of her account. However, I had a feeling there was more.

"I loved him so much. I wanted to save him, but—" Astra cut off suddenly with a sharp glance in my direction. She opened her mouth twice to continue, but closed it again each time.

"I poisoned him," Astra finally whispered. "I took him out to the field where we bury the horses. I put the poison in his food. I was the only one able to get close to him, so it was just the two of us. He trusted me, and I betrayed him. He died that night. I stayed with him until the end and then spent all night burying him."

Taking a deep breath, Astra continued. "It was the worst day of my life, until today.

"That horse—he was my greatest failure, but I loved him as I would my own child, and he broke my heart.

"A few months later, I was given Rickie to train, but I was afraid. I was afraid of getting hurt and afraid of failing again.

"It is hard for people who haven't spent much time around horses to understand, but sometimes, you find a certain horse you trust implicitly. No matter what they do, you aren't afraid because you know it will be alright. If Rickie hadn't been that horse to me, I might have stopped training altogether.

"It took me a long time, and until the day I got on him and was able to ride without a problem, I hadn't trusted him. After that, I let Rickie into my heart, and he started healing it.

"I've trained a few other horses since then, but none of them are to me what Rickie was. He fixed me after I was broken. He was the success that followed my failure. And he was a smart, well-mannered horse to boot.

"And now he's gone, and one of the people I have known all my life is to blame," Astra said harshly.

"How do you know?" I asked. "He might have just gotten sick."

THE CAVE

Astra shot me a look that questioned my intelligence. "I know what happens when a horse is poisoned. That's how we put down most of the horses."

"But you said that your first horse died the same day you poisoned him; Rickie was sick for a long time," I argued.

"They must not have given him enough the first time, so they came back to finish the job."

"Astra," I sighed, "you're being unreasonable. Why would anyone want to poison Rickie?" She didn't answer and I continued. "Gann said that some people were mad at you, but—"

"Is there anything Gann didn't tell you?" Astra snapped.

I ignored her question. "If someone was mad that you were leaving, you'd think they'd have wanted to keep Rickie alive so you'd try harder to come back."

"I know," Astra said. "It doesn't make any sense to me, but it happened."

Fine, I thought. *Ignore logic. The people from your village are good at that.* Aloud I said, "I'm sorry. I'm sorry for your loss, but there is really only one thing to do: keep going forward and hope it doesn't catch up with you."

"Is that how you deal with your grief?" Astra asked me.

I shrugged. "It's worked so far, and right now there are more important things for us to be doing."

I rose and, much as I wished I could have stayed there and enjoyed the beauty all around me, headed toward the entrance to the cave.

"I'm going to The Barracks," I said over my shoulder. "We'll be training there the rest of the day. I don't know where we'll be training tomorrow. You'll have to track us down if you feel like joining."

I turned back to look once more at the cave and jumped to find Astra right beside me. "I'll come," she muttered.

"Good," I said. Inside I was greatly relieved, surprised too. I had never expected I would be able to get Astra to do anything. Maybe Cole was right about me being able to read people.

THE PREPARATIONS

I honestly hadn't had to do that much, just listen to Astra talk for half an hour or so. Maybe she had been ready to head back anyway. I bet she'd spent the morning crying. People always felt better after they'd cried.

Together we headed out of the secret cave. *I'll come back*, I thought. *After the trials, I'll come back and see it again.*

As we walked through the valley, I turned to Astra with a last question. "What was his name?"

Astra glanced at me. She knew whom I was speaking of. "Todd."

Chapter 32

Last Ride

Astra and I made it out of The Valley of the North Wind without getting caught. To her, it might not have been a big deal, but my knees felt weak as we approached the exit. I doubted Astra was really allowed to go traipsing through the valley when she wasn't on official business. However, I had a feeling that had never stopped her.

Once we were a good hundred yards from the valley entrance, I began to breathe easier. "Do you want to go straight to the Barracks or do you need to stop by The North Wind first?" I asked, wondering if Astra had eaten anything in the past twenty-four hours.

"Let's just go," she decided.

"Are you sure?" I pressed. "Your boyfriend was awfully worried about you."

Astra made a sound between a snort and a laugh. "Guess I deserved that," she muttered.

I wished she would have protested more; then I would have known she liked him back. As it was, I couldn't tell how she felt about him, or anyone really. All her emotions were so well-concealed most of the time.

In the cave, she had shared something from her past that she probably hadn't ever talked to anyone about before. However, I had a feeling that such divulgence had been a one-time thing, and our relationship had returned to its normal—well, I wasn't really sure what kind of relationship we had.

THE PREPARATIONS

The road was very long, and the sun was hot above us. We made excellent time though and arrived in the early afternoon.

"Good, you're here." Cole beamed when he caught sight of us. He didn't sound surprised at all. He had figured all along that I would get Astra to come, ignoring the impossibility of the task.

"We are," Astra replied. She didn't say one word about her prior absence, and no one asked, although Joss seemed like he might.

Everyone jumped back into sparring, Although, the others were pretty worn out with combat training. Not that walking to and from The Valley of the North Wind wasn't good exercise either.

We finished up our day at The Farm, where we spent the afternoon chasing young goats. I supposed that since we had no idea what kind of food sources we would find out there, we might as well learn as many ways as possible to obtain sustenance.

"You know," Astra said as we prepared to begin. "I could just shoot the goat and save everyone the exertion."

"Too bad you forgot your bow," Joss pointed out cheekily.

Cole chuckled. "And where would the fun be in that?" he asked.

Astra smiled at them, but it was forced.

Catching goats proved to be harder than we had originally thought. Well, catching the little ones was anyway. The older ones paid no attention to us and let us walk right up to them. Only the little kids ran, so that was what we ended up chasing. They were fast, and it ended up being great team building, if nothing else.

We finally learned to spread out around the chosen goat and close in slowly, trying to make a net with our bodies. Often as not, the kid would bolt before we were close enough together for anyone to grab it. Even when we were tighter in, the goats were quick and only half the time were any of us fast enough to stop one from escaping.

Kisa never was. I think that might have had something to do with the fact that she was afraid of them. A shadow of doubt crossed over my heart. She wasn't going to be good for anything. She was the smallest, the weakest. Yes, she knew about treating injuries, but she was the one most likely to get them in the first place.

Our team would have been stronger if she hadn't been on it. Someone was always having to watch out for her. It would be much worse when the trials actually started.

However, she was a team member, and we couldn't leave her behind. Even if she did get homesick and try to go back, I would drag her away myself.

Training ended, and everyone headed to their own village. Cole had announced that we would have a short day at The Barracks the following morning. He and I headed to The Paramount. Astra joined us as well, since she could go straight from there to The North Wind.

We made small talk most of the way. Astra didn't chime in much, unless she was directly asked something.

Finally, Cole turned to her and asked, "Are you going to be at training tomorrow?"

She met his gaze evenly and nodded. "I'll be there. There is nothing to keep me in The North Wind anymore."

Cole nodded, even though he didn't know what she meant. After Astra left, I told him what had been happening the past couple of days and how she thought someone had poisoned Rickie.

"That's horrible," he said. "No wonder she was a no show. Was she at the stable?"

I shook my head.

"How did you find her?"

THE PREPARATIONS

"Her friend Gann told me she was in The Valley of the North Wind." I spoke softly, since we were almost inside The Paramount.

Cole stopped walking. "You went into The Valley of the North Wind?" he gasped.

"Yes," I replied. "Astra was in a cave there."

"A cave?"

I nodded. For some reason, I didn't want to tell Cole about the beautiful cave, with its azure pool and rainbow-colored rocks. I also didn't want to tell him what Astra had confided to me about the first horse she had tried to train.

It had been too deep, too personal for me to relate. Astra would probably never tell another living person, and neither would I.

I didn't get much sleep that night. I mostly just tossed and turned, trying to get comfortable without success. I thought some about what Astra had told me, but mostly, I thought about the trials. It was unlikely that I would get much sleep until they began, and after they started, who knew? We could be facing anything.

Ironically, even after all the time I had spent daydreaming about the trials, I had never really considered what the world would be like outside The Land of the Clan. Was it very big? Bigger than what was here?

According to the Telling we heard each Midwinter and Midsummer, it was a barren wasteland, or at least had been hundreds and hundreds of years ago. There had to be a way to survive. Lots of teams did it every cycle. Of course, some contenders died, but most had to make it back.

Before I had met my team, it had been easier to imagine losing some of them. I couldn't feel quite the same way anymore, since I saw them as living, breathing people, rather than imaginary placeholders. I wanted to protect them and keep them safe, but I knew I might not have the ability to do so. Hopefully, they had all learned enough skills to keep themselves alive.

Kisa was the weak link, I had said it a thousand times. Rollan was as well, to a certain extent. He was strong, but he lacked in overall skills. I couldn't see any of the others dying. Cole and I had trained too hard. Joss seemed like the kind of person who could recover from anything and escape anything. Then there was Astra; I was pretty sure nothing could kill Astra.

A small voice inside whispered, *No one has to die. If you convince your team to give up, everyone can stay here, safe and sound.*

Every time the trials came around, two or three teams just didn't go. Nothing happened to them; there was no rule against it. They simply decided they didn't want to compete and went back to their normal lives. It was the safe choice.

However, I knew if I did that, I would never forgive myself.

There was always the option of remaining in The Land of the Clan, becoming an adult, and then getting assigned a job in The Paramount. Eventually, I would certainly be chosen as a village leader. After that, I might be asked to return to The Paramount to spend the remainder of my life as a council member. But even if all of that happened, it still would not be enough for me.

No matter how great a task I was given, I would spend the rest of my life wishing that I had taken the chance to become a Clan Leader.

The other reason I would never give up was Myna. Right now, she didn't look at me, didn't see me. I had learned to live with that. But, if I was to quit or fail in the trials, she would look at me then. Not with sympathy or even pity, but with disdain and accusation. 'You could have been something great,' her eyes would scream at me every day, even if her lips didn't form the words. 'You could have had everything. You could have been like me.'

That would have been the worst thing in the world, because even though I wasn't sure if I had a drop of love for Myna in my body, I desperately wanted her approval. If I could ever be good enough for her, then I felt like I would be perfect. All I needed

THE PREPARATIONS

was to know that Myna was proud of me, and then nothing else would matter, because I would have already achieved the hardest thing in the world.

Midsummer was only three days away, and dawn came early, as it normally did that time of year, Midsummer being three days away. It didn't feel early to me; it felt late. As I slipped on my clothes, I wondered if I had actually slept at all. My heavy eyelids said no, but there were a few moments in the wee hours of the morning that were fuzzy.

Cole met me at the road to The Barracks. He seemed to be in a good mood, eager to train. We didn't talk much; what more was there to say? We had spent the last six months constantly together. I knew him better than I had ever known anyone before in my life.

The day at The Barracks went smoothly. Astra was not only there, but she was on time for once.

We trained until about sun high when Cole said we were done for the day. "Anybody up for some swimming?" Joss asked. Riverside wasn't far, and I knew how much Joss loved the water.

"I'm in," Rollan said at the same time Kisa cried, "Sure!"

"What if I took you guys for a horseback ride instead?" Astra asked. Everyone was silent for a moment. I almost declared that I would rather swim until the trials began than spend one second on a horse, but I managed to hold my tongue.

"It wouldn't be like training," Astra promised. "It'll be fun."

She and I had radically different interpretations of the word 'fun', especially since she liked to jump off cliffs and ride wild broncos. I was hoping that Joss would press the swimming issue; I would be very, very happy to support him.

"That actually sounds great," Cole announced.

Traitor, I thought. He disliked horses as much I did.

The rest of the team consented too, without much protest. After Cole and the others agreed, I had no choice but to go along, of course. We were a team.

So that was how I found myself trekking to The North Wind for a second time in as many days.

I fell into step with Cole. We were in the front, and when he happened to look my way, I mouthed to him, "Why?"

Cole's eyes were amused. He leaned towards me ever so slightly. "Because Astra hardly ever asks for anything, and I want her to feel like she's part of this team."

I sighed and whispered back, "Did you have to pick such a dreadful way to do it?"

Cole laughed, and I saw Astra watching us out of the corner of her eye. I expected a jibe, but she didn't have one for us. Maybe Cole was right about making her feel like she was part of the team.

Everyone had spent enough time at The North Wind to know how to catch and saddle their own horse. Rollan couldn't remember some of the knots, and Kisa couldn't lift the saddle high enough to place it properly on her horse's back. Astra helped the two of them, while the rest of us took care of our own animals.

We led our horses around the side of the stable. Instead of ushering us into a small arena or round pen, Astra guided us into a large field. I was slightly uncomfortable, but didn't want to mention it.

Astra helped everyone get up. Cole and Joss could do it on their own, but I needed a little assistance, as did Rollan. Kisa needed a lot since she was too short to even reach the dangling stirrups.

Once we had all mounted, I expected Astra to go get a horse for herself. Instead, she walked through the field on foot, giving us tips and the occasional correction.

"Aren't you going to ride, too?" Kisa asked.

Astra shook her head. "No, not today."

Kisa looked confused. I would have been confused too if I hadn't known about Rickie. I wasn't exactly sure why, but I assumed the two things were connected.

THE PREPARATIONS

Astra was right about one thing: it was a lot more fun to ride in the field than it had been in the arena.

"Not many people come here to train," I observed.

"A good thing too," Astra replied. "We don't have the manpower to spare many instructors and horses. Plus, horsemanship is a craft that takes years to master."

Ignoring Astra's superior tone, I said as mildly as I could, "Well, if qualifying or the trials require any sort of horsemanship, at least we will have all been on a horse."

No one bothered to respond. A moment later, Kisa asked a question, because she didn't understand that you don't have to fill every silence with words. "What do you think the trials will be like?" she asked.

"We can't talk about that," I said quickly, resisting the impulse to look around and see if we'd been overheard.

"Why not?" Joss asked. "I think we're allowed to guess, just not talk to anyone who's been in the trials before."

I opened my mouth to reply, but Cole spoke first. "Still, we probably shouldn't worry about it too much. Let's just take it one day at a time. Tomorrow is our last day of training. After that we have to qualify, and then, well, we won't have to guess anymore."

That was the end of the conversation. We talked about other things, most of them trivial.

Astra encouraged us to get our horses into a trot and a canter, if we felt comfortable. Cole and I were the first to try, since Astra advised us to not all go at once, lest we cause a stampede. She held the reins of Kisa's horse, which made Kisa feel better, while Cole and I took our turn.

I had trotted before, and I remembered that it had been extremely uncomfortable. I didn't know if it was the horse that was better or if it was because we were in the field, but the trot wasn't half so bad as I recalled. I finally had the nerve to go into a canter after watching Cole's horse outdistancing mine. The canter was easier; it wasn't as jarring, and when I moved with

LAST RIDE

the horse's motion, it was actually pretty smooth. I knew I would feel sore in the morning, but right then, for just that one moment, I understood why Astra loved riding. There was something incredible and exhilarating in the speed.

We finally stopped and turned the horses back. Joss and Rollan went next. Kisa said she was too afraid to try, but she looked as if she really wanted to.

"Do you want to ride double with me?" Joss asked her.

Kisa's blue eyes lit up with delight.

"I'm not sure that's a good idea," Astra said softly. "If Kisa starts to slip, I don't think you weigh enough to keep her in the saddle."

Joss looked down, slightly deflated.

"It's ok," Kisa told him. "Thanks for offering."

"What about me?" Cole asked. "Could she ride double with me?"

Astra nodded. "If you're careful."

Kisa clapped her hands in delight.

Astra helped transfer her to Cole's horse. He was a dark brown creature, with a black mane and tail. Kisa sat in front, and Cole put his arms around her while still holding the reins.

"Don't let me fall," the little girl pleaded.

"Never," Cole promised, and then they were off. Kisa gave a small cry when they went into the canter. A moment later, they were back; Kisa was all smiles.

She got back on her own horse, and we returned to The North Wind, training completed for the day.

Except Astra, we all headed south together. Rollan turned off a bit before The Paramount, but Kisa and Joss were with us the whole way.

"I'm really nervous about the trials," Kisa admitted when it was just the four of us.

"Why?" Joss asked. "They're going to be great! No parents, no rules; we'll have so much fun."

If that was what Joss anticipated, he was in for a rude awakening. The trials were not meant to be taken lightly. They helped decide the future of The Clan and were serious business.

"It'll be alright," Cole promised Kisa. "You'll have us, and we'll look after you."

His words seemed to comfort Kisa, but she still wore a worried frown.

Chapter 33

TRAINING'S END

I didn't expect to sleep at all that night, but I did, really well actually. I woke up feeling refreshed. Normally, I am a morning person, but when I opened my eyes, I felt like I could do anything. *Too bad the trials don't start until the day after tomorrow*, I thought.

My nerves wouldn't let me wait for Cole at The Paramount. Our plan was to meet at The Golden Fields, so I set out along the road as the sun began to peek over the eastern horizon.

Cole seemed to be really worried about us feeding ourselves, so we were scheduled to review edible plants again. He'd promised that if we did well, we could spend the rest of the day relaxing at Riverside, since we had gone to The North Wind instead the day before.

The cool water would be incredibly pleasant during the hottest part of the day. It wasn't that warm now; a fresh, summer breeze was coming from the west, bringing with it the scent of growing things.

The southern path to The Golden Fields was a gray line surrounded by flowers. The birds were chirping in the trees. It was a perfect morning.

I expected to be the first to arrive, but Astra was already there when I got to our usual meeting spot on the edge of the fruit tree fields. Something was different about her. She looked healthier, the bags under her eyes were gone, and her face had more color than usual.

She nodded in greeting when she saw me.

THE PREPARATIONS

"Morning," I said. "Did you bring over a horse earlier?"

"No," Astra told me. "I'm not helping in the stables anymore."

My mouth fell open. "But—" I started.

Astra held up a hand. "I told them I just couldn't handle it with the trials starting in a couple days and all. I actually got a decent night's sleep for the first time since I can remember last night."

"But," I started again, and she didn't stop me, "you love working with the horses."

"I do," she replied. "But that part of my life is over, maybe forever, maybe just for a while. I don't know. What I do know is that it's time to focus on what's ahead of me, not behind me."

Astra's words made sense, but I knew there was another reason. Whether those at The North Wind understood it or not, she was punishing them for Rickie's death. She would probably never know who had poisoned him—if anyone really had—but her message to that person was loud and clear: you hurt me and mine, and I won't give you what you want.

Just then, Kisa appeared, walking up from the cluster of dwellings around the town center. The Golden Fields was the largest of the villages, and it seemed the entire population poured out behind her. Most of the adults split up and went to the various fields and orchards. The contenders headed out along the north and west roads.

Kisa smiled at us, but it seemed forced.

"Hi," she said.

"Hey," I greeted her.

Astra nodded.

The others joined us shortly.

"Let's do this quick," Joss announced as he came trotting up, fighting the crowd of contenders who were still exiting The Golden Fields. "It's going to be hot, and we're wasting swimming time."

I wondered offhand if Joss really was part fish as he'd claimed when we'd first met. "Only if we get everything right the first time," I reminded him.

Joss let out an exaggerated sigh. "If we don't know it by now, we probably aren't going to get it. And what's so important about being able to tell an apple tree from a peach tree?" he asked. "Plus, we'll have Kisa with us, and she can name everything with her eyes closed."

I could see how, for a high-energy guy like Joss, spending days in the fields looking at the same plants over and over again would be really boring. However, he would think differently when he wasn't getting a food ration delivered to his dwelling every day. Boys' thinking always changed when they were hungry.

For the most part, we did get everything right on the first try. Cole misidentified an onion sprout as a leak, and Rollan thought the leaf from a pear tree was a leaf from a plum tree, but those were the only mistakes.

Joss whooped with delight and took off running for Riverside. Rollan trailed after, with Kisa right behind him.

"I worry that they will not enjoy the trials as much as they think," Cole said to Astra and me.

"I don't think they understand exactly how hard survival is going to be," Astra replied, echoing my earlier thoughts.

"Joss is convinced that it'll be fun," I added.

"They're in for a shock," Cole agreed.

"I think we all are," I told him. The other two looked at me in confusion. "Come on," I continued. "Whatever we are expecting, no matter how hard we imagine it's going to be, I bet it'll be at least ten times worse."

Astra looked to be in thoughtful agreement, but not Cole.

"We've trained; we know what we're doing," he said.

I nodded. "Yes, but after training every day, we go back to a warm fire and a hot meal." Well, he did at least. Astra and I had

THE PREPARATIONS

a few bites of whatever was lying around, and then wrapped up in blankets to keep from freezing to death during the winter.

"She's right." I was surprised that Astra was backing me up. "There is no way to prepare for the unknown, and that is the hardest part of what we will face once the trials begin."

Cole nodded. "We'll have to keep up a good face for the others," he said. "If we can make them think everything is fine, then they'll keep trying. The minute we get discouraged, it's all over."

"I agree," I said. In a lot of ways, the three of us were the adults of the team. I was a little less than two years older than Joss and Rollan, but their lack of maturity made the gap seem much larger.

We caught up with the rest of our team before they made it to Riverside. We found them waiting for us close to the village entrance, panting and out of breath.

The afternoon of swimming was fun, but we ended it early. Cole wanted everyone to have plenty of time to rest, so we would be fresh for the following day.

We left Riverside around the middle of the afternoon. It was only Cole, Astra, and I on the road north.

"Kisa's not doing well already," Astra observed. The little girl had seemed more fragile than usual all day.

At one point, Joss and Rollan had each grabbed one of her legs underwater and had pulled her under. She'd come up spluttering, but also crying. They had apologized, but it had taken her a long time to calm down.

"At least she's aware of how homesick she'll be," I pointed out. "If Joss or Rollan are homesick, it'll completely surprise them, and who knows how they'll handle it."

"I don't think Rollan will feel very homesick," Astra replied quietly.

Recalling the way his brothers had treated him, I couldn't help silently agreeing.

TRAINING'S END

"Joss seems like the kind of person who can deal with it," Cole added. "Even if he's homesick, I think he'll be fine."

"It's good that they have all known each other a long time," said Astra. "That will help; it'll be like they have a little piece of home with them."

"I'm pretty sure the council builds teams that way on purpose," Cole told her. "They give everyone at least one friend."

Astra shrugged. "Not me. I hardly knew any of you."

Cole and I exchanged a guilty look, but neither of us wanted to fess up about the night we had told Core that Astra was our friend.

"Well," said Cole, "they couldn't put everyone from The North Wind on the same team."

Astra let the topic drop. She left us at the turn-off to The Paramount and continued north alone.

"See you tomorrow at qualifying," Cole called after her.

"Let's take a walk," I suggested, not that I was really interested in walking. In the past six months, we had walked across The Land of the Clan nearly every day. It was the dread of my empty dwelling that had prompted my suggestion. It would get dark late, and I really didn't have anything to do for the next couple hours while the sun was still high overhead.

I didn't want to be alone. Not then.

"Sure," Cole agreed, even though I was sure his family was waiting for him.

We walked east, not following a path, just heading toward where the sun rose every morning. We were also heading toward the place I had seen the large creature on the far side of the river.

"Do you want to talk?" Cole asked after about fifteen minutes of silence. He took my hand in his. It felt nice. Even in the heat of summer my skin always seemed cold to me. His hand was warm and gentle.

Yes, I wanted to yell, longing to confess to him all my fears and doubts that I would soon come face to face with. But I couldn't, my lips were frozen. I felt tears brimming in my eyes; I couldn't remember the last time I had cried.

My vision was still blurry after I tried to blink them away. Not trusting my voice, all I did was shrug.

"I've been thinking," Cole mused, "about what I would have done if the trials hadn't been announced. I'm not really sure a life of book-keeping is what I would have wanted."

I stiffened, was Cole really saying that he would have left The Paramount? Didn't he understand that it was a great privilege to be there? That those of The Paramount were considered the most important of The Clan? That he would have made a great village leader?

"Where would you have gone?" I asked.

Cole shrugged. "I don't know. That was always the problem. There seem to be so many mundane tasks out there. I don't know that I'd ever be content just doing one thing for the rest of my life."

"That's why The Paramount is the best," I told Cole. "You may start out with a boring job, but you can move up. Some of the scribes travel, so you wouldn't have to be cooped up all the time. If you became a village leader or a council memb—"

"I know," Cole replied, cutting me off. "But I'd never love it. I always kind of thought everyone just endured their work every day. You know, they got it over with so they could go home and be with their family. But that thought changed after meeting the members of our team. Joss loves the water and boats and fishing. Kisa wants to be just like her mom and help people. Then there's Astra. She's about my age but already does a full day's work on top of everything else. They knew what future they wanted, but not me. I never knew. And now the trials are here." He trailed off, and then turned to me. "Are you afraid?"

"No," I said firmly. It was a knee-jerk reaction. I hadn't really let myself think about the question.

"I'm not anymore," said Cole. "I know I'll have you with me, and that's enough. If we don't get farther than the other side of The Valley of the North Wind, it's enough. Even if it means I'm stuck in a mundane task for the rest of my life, so long as you're with me, I won't complain."

His words made my heart begin to race, but they also disappointed me. Would he really be content to fall so far short of the goal? Did he lack the ambition to do all that was necessary for us to win?

I might have been enough for him, but he was not enough for me. Not yet. I had to win first, had to prove myself worthy of leading The Clan. Then we could be together, not before. I realized I might have to distance myself from him, since I was clearly a distraction that we couldn't afford.

I was sure he hoped I would respond to his words in the same way, but I couldn't. Instead, I slipped my hand out of his and turned to him. "We have to win, Cole," I told him. "We have to win."

"Ok," he said, unable to hide the hurt in his eyes.

I suddenly regretted asking him to walk with me. "Let's go back," I suggested. "Our families will be waiting dinner for us." It was only half a lie; his family would be waiting.

I wondered if Cole knew about Myna and me, if he had picked up enough to understand that she wouldn't be there. Cole wasn't the most observant person in the world, but how hard could it be to see that I was so very much alone?

Impossible, a voice whispered in my head. *How is he supposed to get through the impenetrable walls you have put up?*

He could, I argued stubbornly with the voice.

He just tried, it hissed back, *and you shut him out.*

"See you in the morning," was all Cole said to me as we each went our separate ways.

There was no point in not going to my dwelling now. Maybe I didn't want to be alone, but I seemed unable to escape it. Inside my fortress, I was always alone. Cole had come closer than anyone else to gaining admittance, but in the end, I couldn't let even him in. At least, not yet. I couldn't allow myself that kind of weakness right now.

One day, I promised. *One day you'll both be happy.*

I didn't really believe it.

Happiness is an illusion. It takes so long to find, but can be lost in the blink of an eye. Once it has faded, you are left with two options. Try to reclaim it or forget about it. No matter what you choose, you will fail.

Chapter 34

THE QUALIFIER

Of course, the instant I was alone in my dwelling, I started to fret. I had spent so much time worrying about how I was going to do in the trials, I hadn't thought much about qualifying. All along, it had seemed like just one more step in the process that would come and pass without incident. Now, it was staring me in the face, and I didn't have a clue what the following day would bring.

The only good thing was that worrying about qualifying almost completely distracted me from my conversation with Cole. I didn't want him to settle for just me when we could have so much more.

Although my mind wouldn't stop running, all the physical activity of the past couple of days caught up to me, and I passed a peaceful night. In fact, I slept until the ringing of the village bell woke me. I was normally out the door before it even sounded. Panic gripped me as I hurried to dress and find something to eat.

When I arrived at the town center, I found that I wasn't the only one who had slept in. Cole was there but almost no one else.

"Sleep well?" I asked, coming to stand by him.

"Yeah," he answered. "You?"

I nodded.

It was a good twenty minutes before roll was called. No one talked much while we waited. It felt too weird to interact with the other contenders.

Bala, Jase, Motik, Ashlo, Larna, Flant, and all the rest we were rivals now; even those who I had counted as friends not two months ago seemed disconnected from me.

Although Cole and I didn't talk much, I found it very comforting to have him by my side. He and Jase did exchange a few pleasantries before Jase went to stand by Bala and Tiera, his teammates.

After roll was called, we were directed to go to the amphitheater, where we would wait with the rest of the contenders for the qualifier to get underway.

We were obviously the first group to arrive. Instead of sitting together as a village, we spread ourselves out among the stone seats. As the contenders from the different villages trickled in, each would split off to sit with their own teammates.

Kisa was the first to arrive, followed by Rollan. When I saw him, I leapt to my feet in surprise. He had a nasty black eye, which was swollen half shut.

"Who did that to you?" I asked.

"No one," he said, with a sharp glance at Kisa. "I'll tell you later."

I resumed my seat, biting my tongue against all the things I wanted to say. It wasn't hard for me to figure out where the black eye had come from. However, the crowded amphitheatre really wasn't the place for an emotional outburst, and I didn't want to upset Kisa.

Rollan sank down next to me on the stone seat and didn't talk to anyone. Kisa kept shooting him little worried glances. Joss joined us shortly after. He and Rollan exchanged a long look, and then he turned to Kisa and began chatting with her about her family. I was sure he was trying to distract her.

Astra, and the rest of the group from The North Wind, were the last ones to arrive.

Almost before they had taken their seats, one of the elders began giving us instructions.

THE QUALIFIER

"The qualifications will commence as follows," he began. I liked his all-business attitude. "Groups of contenders will be called. They will assemble here." The man gestured to the front of the amphitheater, where he was standing.

"The groups will then be taken to The Paramount where the qualifier will be held. After the group has finished, each individual is to return to their own village. On no account is any contender who has completed the qualifier to return to the amphitheater or linger in The Paramount. There will be no training today. Please remain in your own villages.

"Each team only needs four members to successfully complete the qualifier for the entire team to pass. Results will be read in each town center later this afternoon."

That was all the information we were given. An elder stepped forward then and started reading the first list of names. She appeared to be calling the contenders from youngest to oldest. After calling the first thirty names, she directed them to follow another council member. The group left, and she began calling more names. She repeated the process eight times. Kisa was called to the fifth group, but the rest of us were not.

Once the elder had finished calling the first set of names, I turned to Rollan. "What happened?" I asked him.

"One of my brothers hit me," Rollan said. He still didn't want to meet anyone's eyes.

"Why?" Cole asked.

Rollan shrugged. "It happens from time to time."

"Only to you," Joss muttered under his breath. "It's not right." He seemed completely disgusted.

"This has happened before?" Astra asked.

Rollan nodded. "Sometimes."

"What do your parents do?" I pressed.

"They intervene, when they see it," Rollan told us. "But my brothers tend to know when they aren't going to be around."

"Rollan—" Cole started, but was cut off.

THE PREPARATIONS

"Don't worry about it," Rollan insisted. "After tomorrow it won't matter anymore, right?"

"That's not the point," I heard Astra say softly.

"It's fine, really," Rollan stated. "My parents will both be home tonight, so nothing more is going to happen." He really seemed to want to drop the conversation, so, for better or worse, we let him.

Less than an hour later, another eight groups were called. Both Rollan and Joss headed out with them.

It took longer for the rest of us to hear our names. Finally, around midday, it was my turn. I smiled at both Cole and Astra.

"Have fun," I told them before walking to the front of the amphitheater.

I didn't really know anyone in my group of contenders. I had seen a few of them during training, but I'd never spoken to any of them.

Silently, we followed a council member to The Paramount town center, where my day had begun. It appeared that eight different buildings were being used. My group waited outside one of them. The other groups weren't far behind us and lined up by the other buildings. It took another ten minutes before we were allowed inside.

The building I entered was one of the places where the scribes normally worked. It was the place where they made copies of the schoolbooks that were falling apart and could no longer be used.

Each of us was told to take a seat at one of the desks. Then we were handed a stack of papers face down.

A test? I thought.

I couldn't believe it. A written test was the very last thing I had been expecting.

The elder in charge told us to turn our papers over. I did so, and began reading the first question. The entire thing was written in the high language, which didn't bother me in the least. I just hoped it hadn't fouled up any of my younger teammates.

THE QUALIFIER

The test took me less than half an hour to complete. It was a lot of mathematics, some science, and a few questions about the geography of The Land of the Clan. The entire thing seemed pointless to me.

We had been given forty-five minutes, so I doubled-checked my answers; they were all correct. Finally, the elder announced that time was up and took our tests from us.

I saw the next groups lined up to go in as I emerged from the building. I steered clear of them. I didn't want anyone to think I was trying to cheat, even though Astra and Cole were nowhere in sight.

I had to take a roundabout route, but I soon made it back to my dwelling. All that was left was to wait. I hated waiting. Before long, I had second-guessed every answer I'd given on my test.

It was the longest afternoon of my life, but finally the bell rang, calling us all to gather once more. I raced to the town center. Cole was my only teammate who would be present. He joined me a moment later, and we stood side-by-side with baited breath.

The business-like elder from earlier was the one who stepped forward to address us now.

"Sixteen teams have been eliminated," he announced.

I wished he would simply give us the names of the first team leaders for the teams that had been eliminated. Instead, he started at the beginning, reading each first team leader's name, and then told us how many members had passed for that team.

My knees felt like water by the time he got to our team and called out, "Cole of The Paramount. Five passes and one fail."

A smile spread across my face. I looked at Cole; he was grinning ear to ear. We had made it. We were going to be in the trials.

He hugged me, and it was all I could do not to cheer.

After our brief moment of exaltation, we had to listen respectfully while the rest of the team's results were read out. I don't think a single team with a member from The Paramount was eliminated because no one seemed disappointed when the contenders were dismissed.

Briefly, I wondered who on our team had failed, probably Kisa. Although, Rollan had had plenty of things on his mind to distract him that morning. I decided it didn't matter; I wouldn't even bother bringing it up. Our team had qualified, and that was the important thing.

Cole and I parted a short time later. There were rules about the night before the trials. At dark, everyone was required to be in their own dwellings. It was supposed to be a night for the contenders to say goodbye to their families. I wasn't quite sure how that was going to work out for me, but rules were rules, so maybe Myna would actually turn up.

CHAPTER 35

MYNA

I entered my unlit dwelling. Outside, the sun was hot enough that I had been sweating while listening to the results of the qualifier. Inside, it was so cold I was surprised I couldn't see my own breath

I didn't bother to build a fire; it wouldn't make the room any warmer. Instead, I lit a candle. Not for the heat, just for the light. I took a few bites of food from the bins that were stacked up everywhere.

In the past, I had always been the one who had tidied up and thrown out the trash. However, ever since training had begun, I hadn't been as good about keeping the place clean. In the last month, I'd given up altogether.

The main room was filthy. The subtle layer of dust, which normally graced every surface, had been replaced by an almost black coat of grime. The table overflowed with boxes of food that no one was ever going to eat.

It was as if no one lived there. In a way, no one did. Myna lived in the council building, except for the few hours she slumbered each night, and I spent as little time in the place as possible.

Long ago, I had learned that my dwelling was not a home. It was walls and shelter, but a home was different. I had seen it at Rasby's dwelling and Cole's, but never in my own.

I considered cleaning up while waiting for Myna, but I rejected the idea.

I was leaving.

THE PREPARATIONS

If Myna wanted the dwelling clean, she could do it herself. Instead, I leaned on the one corner of the table that was still vacant. I wiped the grime off first and faced the door.

There were still several hours of daylight left, but I didn't have anything else to do. Eventually, I moved to one of the dusty pillows on the floor.

The sun started going down. I watched the shadows grow longer as the light came slanting in through a crack in the shuttered window. The candle burned itself out, and I lit another.

I didn't do anything else, I just waited. Finally, the sun disappeared, and it was still just me and the candlelight, in that cold, dirty room.

I had almost given up hope, figuring that Myna would actually sleep in the council building that night, when the door opened and she walked in.

I didn't rise, but I lifted my eyes from the candle to the door. I'm not sure what I had thought she was going to do, but she disappointed all my hopes. Without even glancing in my direction, she walked into her room and closed the door.

That was it. She didn't want to talk to me. She wanted the last night we had together to be just like all the others.

But I didn't.

She had her walls, and I had mine. I wasn't asking her to let me in, just to pretend like she cared for fifteen minutes, maybe half an hour. Didn't she owe me that much at least?

I stood, and, taking the candle with me, walked to Myna's door. How many times had I stood there and not knocked? A hundred? A Thousand?

I raised my hand and knocked on the wooden door. There was no answer, so I knocked again and Myna opened the door.

"What do you want?" she asked in a dead voice.

"To talk," I said, not letting any emotion into my words. Myna did not like emotion.

"About what?"

"I want to know—about my father," I told her as loudly and clearly as I could. She recoiled from me then and tried to close the door, but I caught it. I was taller than her now. How had I not noticed? Stronger too. She sat all day in council meetings while I had been training for the last six months. She couldn't shut the door while I held it.

After a moment, she gave up.

"Fine," she consented.

It wasn't an invitation, but I came in anyway and she didn't protest. I sat down on her bed just to show her how comfortable I was.

"What do you want to know about him, Myra?" I didn't like the way her lips twisted my name into something ugly.

"What was he like?" I asked. I remembered him as warm and loving, but surely, he had been more.

"Tall, blond, fair-skinned." Myna rattled off the list as if she were describing an animal.

"No, what was his—soul like?"

"His soul?" Myna spoke the word as if it were an insult. It was an unusual term, hardly ever used. It referred to the part of the person that was not physical. Some people doubted the existence of such a thing.

"Was he smart? Or funny?" I asked.

Myna shook her head and didn't speak for a long time. When she did, her voice was different, as if she was speaking from the past. "Your father's name was Rilk. Before he came here, he was Rilk of The Making. He was a fool, almost like a child in the way he viewed the world. He was the sort of person who believed everything would work out in the end."

"Oh," I said. It was far more than I had expected to get from her. There was so much to process. He had come from The Making? I never would have guessed. I was ok at building stuff, just like I was ok at swimming. That didn't mean I enjoyed it or excelled at it.

"Do I look like him?" I wondered. "Am I anything like him?" I couldn't remember his face anymore. It used to bother me, but I had told myself that it was his body I was forgetting, and my father was more than flesh.

"No," Myna answered quickly. "You are nothing like him. I made sure that you weren't like him at all. You are like me. A survivor, and you will survive."

That stung. I was nothing like my father. Not even one piece of him had survived in me. To hear that when people saw me, they saw Myna and Myna alone, was almost like losing him all over again.

"How did he die?"

They had never told me. I had been six years old when it had happened. Everyone probably assumed Myna would tell me when I got older, but she never had. I couldn't remember her ever speaking of him. Even on the nights, long ago, when I had called his name in despair, all she had ever done was tell me to be quiet and go to sleep before closing her door.

"How did he die?" I asked again. She wasn't going to answer; I could tell by the way she was pressing her lips together.

"Mother," I had trouble making the word form on my lips, "I'm leaving tomorrow. I might never come back, and I want to know." Something about my words stirred her.

"He killed himself," she said spitefully.

I gasped. Suicide was the most disgraceful way to die. It meant you were too cowardly to go on living. Was she lying? No, I didn't think she was. I wouldn't put it past her, but Myna preferred to use the truth to hurt me.

"Are you happy you know?" she asked me.

I shook my head. "Why?" I asked.

"I can't tell you."

That was when I got angry, really angry. I felt the heat rise in my face. "He was my father, and I have a right to know!" I all but screamed at her. "I'm an adult now. I have been since he died. There's nothing I can't take. You have to tell me."

Myna's chest rose and fell quickly. If I hadn't known her incapable, I would have suspected that she was getting angry too.

"He found out certain things that upset him too much to go on living."

"What things?"

"Things I am not going to tell you, because even he should not have found them out." Was Myna afraid that I would kill myself too? No, she wasn't worried about that, because I wasn't like him.

We were both silent for a moment. "Did he compete in the trials, too?" I asked softly.

"You know I can't answer that," Myna told me.

"Yes, you can," I retorted. "You don't have to tell me anything except 'yes' or 'no'. Did he compete in the trials?"

Myna sighed and gave in. "Yes. Is there anything else you would like to know?" she asked. Throughout our entire conversation, she hadn't moved from her place by the door.

There was one more thing I wanted to know.

"Were you in love with him?"

Myna's answer would tell me whether she had once been a loving person. Perhaps it had only been through pain and loss that she had become the cold creature I perceived. I could understand, even sympathize a little, if losing her life mate had hurt her so deeply that she had become unable to feel anything anymore. I could almost forgive that.

"No," she answered me. "I was not in love with him."

Of course not. She had been born a heartless person, and without a heart, how could she love anything?

I stood up and saw relief in her eyes. Relief that I was leaving. Maybe the months during the trials would be the best of her life. She wouldn't have to close her door every night, because there wouldn't be anyone to shut out anymore. I bet she would shut it anyway. Whether symbolically or out of habit, her door would always be closed.

I was almost out of the room, but I turned back.

THE PREPARATIONS

"Do you love me?" I asked. I tried to meet her gaze, but she wouldn't look at me. She had never looked at me, never seen me, never wanted to.

I wouldn't repeat the question, so I waited. It felt like a lifetime before she answered.

"Yes."

I couldn't believe it. She loved me, and she treated me like a stranger. How had she treated my father whom she never loved?

"I—I—" I didn't know what to say.

She raised her hand to stop my words. "Go to bed, Myra. The trials start tomorrow, and you need your rest." If her voice hadn't been so dead, I might have actually believed that she cared for my well-being. Instead, it just came out like a ploy to remove me from her space.

I turned to my room.

"Goodbye," I whispered, without looking back at her.

I had my hand on the door knob to my own room when I heard her say, "Things will be very different when you come back."

I thought I'd imagined it and paused for a moment. Then turned to look at her, but all I saw was the door closing.

It felt like I didn't have a mother anymore. I had said 'goodbye' not 'goodnight'. Things might be different for her when I got back from the trials but not for me.

The burden I had carried for so long was lifted. I didn't want or need anything from her. In a few years, I would be old enough to get a dwelling of my own, and nothing would stop me.

I was as much an orphan as Astra. My father had been dead ten years and my mother—had I ever even had one?

As sleep claimed me, I closed my eyes and for one brief moment I was able to see my father. I didn't know if it was an image my mind had stored as a child or if it was something my brain had put together from Myna's description. Either way, it comforted me.

MYNA

What did Myna know? She rarely spent time with me. How could she tell that I didn't have any of my father in me?

Chapter 36

BEGINNING

I woke before dawn, adrenalin shooting through every part of my body as I remembered what day it was.

The trials begin today, I thought. *I have waited my whole life for this.*

I was shaking so hard it took me twice as long as usual to put on my clothes and lace up my boots. I should have packed the night before, but I had been too concerned with Myna.

There wasn't much to take with me. We were only allowed one backpack each, for clothes, and a canteen for water. That was it. Everything else we needed had to be found once we were through The Valley of the North Wind.

I had never really used my canteen, so it was practically brand new. The only people who normally used them were those who did strenuous, outdoor labor.

I packed quickly after deciding to wear a pair of knee-length shorts and a short-sleeved shirt with my boots for the day. In my pack, I placed a pair of pants, another pair of shorts, and several other shirts. I also had a pair of long, thick winter pants and a warm shirt to match. The only other item I was able to shove into my backpack was my winter cloak.

It would be a pain lugging the winter clothes around for the rest of the summer, but when the cold weather came, they could mean the difference between life and death.

Myna was already gone when I got to the main room. I didn't feel hungry at all, but, considering the fact that we would only be given enough food for a couple of days when we left The

THE PREPARATIONS

Land of the Clan, I tried to cram down as much as I possibly could. All I managed to eat was an apple, a handful of grain, and several strips of dried meat.

Still, I left the dwelling feeling sick and bloated. I went to the well by the town center. It was crowded. Even though the sun wasn't up yet, all of the contenders were there filling their canteens. I even saw a few from other villages who had decided to fill theirs in The Paramount instead of carrying them full from their own villages.

I turned and went to the second well, located by the community woodpile. There were a few people there, but not half so many. I waited my turn, and then pulled up a bucket of water. I filled my canteen and took a long drink. Not that I could get much water into my stomach with the huge breakfast that was already there. Once I was done drinking, I topped off my canteen again. The line had grown longer behind me, and I quickly got out of the way to allow the next contender access.

More and more contenders kept streaming into The Paramount. Everyone had packs on, making the space seem even smaller.

Astra was the first member of my team that I saw; her black clothing was easy to pick out among the other colors of cloth.

"Hey," she said, appearing to be in a good mood.

I nodded to her. "Let's find everyone else," I suggested.

We struggled against the crowd and managed to make it to Cole's dwelling. The sun was just coming up, and I could see lights on inside. I knocked on the door and Cole's mother, Wren, opened it.

I could see that she had been crying, but her face lit up when she saw me. "Hi, Myra," she greeted me. "If you're looking for Cole, he's already gone."

"Ok, thanks," I said.

"Be careful out there, sweetheart." Wren stepped forward and gave me a long, warm hug before going back inside. I was very much in danger of crying myself after that.

BEGINNING

Astra and I headed to the town center.

"Astra! Myra!" someone yelled behind us.

We turned back and saw Joss pushing his way through the crowd.

"This is crazy," he yelled to be heard over the noise.

Astra actually laughed. "Especially since this is supposed to be the one place where everything is always in perfect order."

I gave Astra a scowl, but I wasn't really offended, and she knew it.

"Try to stay together," I called as we continued to the town center. It was so jammed with contenders that we could hardly even see the council building.

Rollan found us there a few minutes later. Like Astra, he seemed unusually cheerful. I guess the morning of the trials was very telling when it came to who was going to be homesick.

"Does anyone need water still?" I asked.

"Already got mine," Astra said.

"I got mine before I left Treescape," answered Rollan.

Joss held up a full canteen.

I wondered where Kisa could be; there were already plenty of contenders from The Golden Fields rushing around and getting water at the wells.

I stood on my tiptoes, trying to see over the crowd. Although, Kisa was so short I doubted I would be able to spot her. I also kept an eye out for Cole, but I couldn't locate either of the two.

A hush started to fall over the contenders in the town center, and those outside followed suit. I strained my eyes and saw that the door to the council building had been opened. Core was there.

He spoke loudly, and we could just hear what he was saying. "Welcome, contenders. The trials begin today!" There were deafening cheers.

Once the crowd had grown silent again, it took several minutes, he continued. "We will begin calling the teams into the

THE PREPARATIONS

council building ten at time to examine their packs. Each will be called by their first team leader's name. We will begin with Galns of The Barracks."

Teams started moving through the crowd to enter the council building. It only took about five minutes or so for each group. Once finished with the inspection, they were ushered out and moved to a field beyond the edge of The Paramount. Slowly, but surely, the village began to empty.

I still hadn't spotted Cole or Kisa when they called for our team. The other contenders made way for us as we entered the building.

Just as we reached the door, I saw Cole walking through the crowd, leading a crying Kisa by the hand. He smiled at me. I nodded back at him, worried that Kisa had already lost her focus.

It had been a long time since I'd been inside the council building. The solitary room was circular, aside from the short entranceway. There were cushions on the floor, forming a ring around a short, wooden platform. I could easily imagine Myna standing atop it, looking down on the other council members as she gave speeches about efficiency and punctuality.

Other than that, there were no other furnishings at all. The entire council was there, minus a few of the representatives who were waiting with the contenders outside The Paramount.

We each handed our packs to a council member for examination. They looked through what we were taking and gave each of us a small sack of food while Core spoke.

Had he cried for his son too? I couldn't tell. He handed Cole and each of the other first team leaders a rolled-up piece of parchment.

"Don't open it," he instructed. "Don't open it until you get through of The Valley of the North Wind."

He addressed all of us then. "This scroll contains the instructions for the trials." I felt my heart beat quicken. "Follow them, be the first ones to complete the task, and you will be Clan

BEGINNING

Leaders. This cannot happen unless you have at least three living members when you return to The Land of the Clan.

"All or any of you may return at any time before completing the task, but that will constitute failure, and your time as a team will be over. You must win together or not at all. At the time of your return, you will not discuss the trials with anyone ever again, even each other. Do you have any questions?"

We were silent. Everything made sense to me. Follow the instructions, don't come back until we've completed the task, and don't talk about it once we do get back.

I thought we were done, but then Core spoke again. "After you have gotten through The Valley of the North Wind, you don't have to follow any of the rules you have grown up with until your return. Go now and prepare your minds for the greatest challenge you will ever face."

Let's do this, I thought.

I was dying to open the paper Cole had been given. He held it securely as we left the council building.

One of the village representatives escorted us to where the other contenders were waiting. It was a huge, grassy field, about half a mile north of The Paramount. It was covered with flowers. Teams were sitting or standing close together, not really interacting much with each other. I didn't think I'd be able to sit down even if I had wanted to. Instead, I ended up pacing back and forth in the grass.

Cole knelt and began rearranging his backpack.

Astra dropped her bag and calmly stood, looking off into the distance.

Joss and Rollan flopped down on the grass and began chattering away. Kisa sank down, close to where I was pacing, and hunched herself up into a miserable, little ball.

After about five minutes, she broke down and started sobbing.

THE PREPARATIONS

"It's ok, Kisa," I said, patting her on the head and trying to be comforting. I had not had a good role model in that department, so I wasn't quite sure how to help.

Astra did better; she settled down on the grass beside Kisa and pulled the little girl over next to her so they could talk quietly.

"I'm sorry," Kisa cried. "I just—I don't want to leave my family!"

"It's ok," said Astra.

"I don't want to be so weak!" Kisa sobbed. "I want to be strong like you and Myra! I want to be brave and do amazing things like the rest of you, but I can't. I'm not as good as you are."

"That's not true, Kisa, and there's nothing weak about crying," Astra told her. "It's ok to be homesick. It's ok to cry and show what you feel. As long as you walk into the valley with us that's all the courage we can ask of you. No one here thinks you're weak."

Well, I kind of did, but I thought it prudent not to mention that.

"This is going to be fun," Joss told Kisa, just as he had the other day. However, he sounded a little unsure, which probably wasn't the most comforting thing for Kisa.

She just nodded and, after a few more sobs, got her tears under control. She wiped her eyes and nose on one of her sleeves, and then gave a long sigh. She remained seated with her head resting on Astra's shoulder.

The little girl looked exhausted. I couldn't help wondering what the scene had looked like at her dwelling the previous evening. It was sure to have been very different from what had taken place in mine.

There were a few other people, not contenders, who had come simply to say goodbye. Most of them appeared to be the mothers of the younger children. A few were crying, but the

BEGINNING

wiser ones remained strong for their children and encouraged them.

I looked over and saw Rasby bidding farewell to Tirea. They were both crying, Rasby crying the harder of the two as she clung to Tirea's neck. For a moment, I wished she'd come and say goodbye to me too. But the thought of having her hold onto to me and sob uncontrollable in front of my whole team was not pleasant, so I turned away and hoped that in her weakened emotional state she wouldn't approach me.

She didn't.

Instead, Rasby moved on to Tiera as soon as her team arrived in the field several minutes later.

"I told my mother not to come." Kisa was watching a woman hold her crying son across the field from us. "Now I wish I hadn't," she said miserably.

"It'll be alright," Cole assured her. "We'll just take a quick trip out, follow this paper," Cole brandished the scroll in his hand, "and return after we win."

"We'll be back in no time," Astra promised.

"And we'll never have this chance again," Rollan added.

What he said was the truth; we would never again leave The Land of the Clan. After the trials, we would spend the rest of our lives on the peninsula. We should take advantage of our opportunity and make the very most of it.

I was glad we had only one person on the verge of tears. There were a couple teams where at least half the members were crying.

I saw one girl, from The Farm, who was as old as I was screaming like a three-year-old. Some people just weren't cut out to make it through the trials.

The sun was a third of the way up the sky when the last teams joined us on the field. They were followed by the council. Myna was with them, but aside from noticing that she was there and breathing, I didn't pay any attention to her.

Some of the council started walking north, and we followed them. I think the ones who stayed behind were those who were too old and crippled to make the trip quickly. It was at least a two-hour walk.

At first, everyone was silent, but that didn't last long. The group of council members who didn't come with us, along with the mothers and friends of the contenders, grew smaller and smaller behind us.

A few of the younger children started screaming after the first mile. One tried to run back, but a large, male member of his team picked him up and carried him forward. The child struggled and fought for another mile, and then went limp and let the older boy lug him along like a sack of potatoes. Much as I felt for the small child, I would have been completely willing to do the same to any of my team members small enough for me to carry—which pretty much meant Kisa.

I was impressed that she didn't look back once, although a few silent tears did run down her face. That was fine, as long as she kept moving her feet to the north.

We finally arrived at the entrance to the valley. A couple of the council members produced a scarlet cord at least fifty yards long. They stretched it out parallel to the valley opening and had us line up along it.

I was itching to make a run for it the moment they let us go, but I heard Astra hissing, "If everyone rushes headlong into the valley, there is no telling what kind of landslides they will cause. We need to go slow and steady. It's the only safe way."

Cole and I nodded. We already had the advantage of knowing the way through. Not that it was really cheating since we had ended up with Astra, and she knew the valley better than anyone.

Core raised his hands for silence. There was so much excitement and emotion in the air that it took a while for the contenders to quiet down. I could almost hear the beating of

BEGINNING

each individual heart, hundreds of them, pounding together. Ready. Waiting.

"This is where the trials begin," Core announced. "This is where the trials have begun throughout the entire history of The Clan.

"Through The Valley of the North Wind our ancestors came, long ago, into this place that the darkness had left untouched. Here they made a new life, free of that which stalked them for so long.

"Our people have become strong and united. Here, in this golden land we thrive. Elsewhere, we would perish. You honor that memory and our traditions with your participation.

"The last six months have been nothing compared to what you will now face. The trials were not meant for the weak, only for the strong. Each of you have proven yourselves, and we, The Clan, rely upon you. You are our future. Just as we," he indicated the council standing beside him, "and all those who have gone before you, are your past."

He stopped speaking. The only sound was the moan of the wind as it came whistling out of the valley behind him.

"Remember," Core said, "do not open your scrolls until you have made it through The Valley of the North Wind and out into the lands beyond."

I licked my lips, ready to leave everything behind in the face of this new adventure. Things would never be the same again. When I returned, I would be a new and better person; someone who could lead The Clan and leave behind a great and powerful legacy.

ABOUT THE AUTHOR

Danielle N. McDonough spent her childhood being inspired by books. The stories she read, paired with her imagination, allowed her to experience hundreds of adventures to different places and times. Every new book took her to a new world.

As a young adult, Danielle continued in her love of art and fantasy and graduated from Full Sail University with a degree in film. After spending several years working on television and movie sets, she decided to step away from the film industry and pursue her passion for storytelling by writing her debut novel, *The Preparations*.

It was in Colorado, on a mission trip with her church, that Danielle had a dream which inspired *The Legacy* series. It took her four years to complete the series, but the journey has been the greatest adventure of her life.